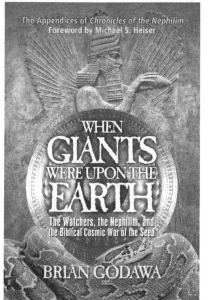

# Praise for Brian Godawa's novel *Noah Primeval*

"I've read the entire Harry Potter series three times, a bunch of Star Wars novels, Lord of the Rings and Narnia. I read a ton. And I LOVE Chronicles of the Nephilim!"

– Sam Jenkins, Junior high school, son of filmmaker Dallas Jenkins

This is the origin of sorcery and vampire tales. *Noah Primeval* will keep you on the edge of your seat with its primal struggle of good and evil. Supernatural fiction, fantasy, and Biblical speculation all as **a cinematic novel. It reads like a blockbuster movie!"**

– Ralph Winter, Producer (*X-Men, Planet of the Apes*)


**"A great, spiritual fantasy full of thought and imagination.** *Noah Primeval* is a provocative look at what could have been the life and times of Noah. The cinema-like action and suspense will keep you turning pages until you are finished, while the themes and concepts will remain long after you're done."

– Bill Myers - Bestselling Author, *The God Hater*


"Anyone who has read the *Lord of the Rings* trilogy has silently mused about how fantastic it would be if it were all real—a place on earth that transcended our own mundane reality, a time when the unseen world was tangible. Noah Primeval made me stop wishing and start believing. Brian Godawa re-imagines the supernatural storyline of the Biblical Noah blended with Mesopotamian epics. The result is **a stirring tale of gods and men that confronts us with biblical reality through mythical fantasy. Noah Primeval is what Tolkien called "sanctifying myth" that we need in our own place and time."**

– Michael S. Heiser, Ph.D. Hebrew and Semitic Languages
Academic Editor, Logos Bible Software

**"Imaginative yet well-researched.** As Biblical scholar, I have a great appreciation for imagination in religious storytelling of the past. I was enthralled with Godawa's grasp of the Mesopotamian world and enchanted with his modern adaptation of antiquity into an entertaining action fantasy. Such a fictional adaptation may be a big problem from some religious believers with strict views of the Bible, but in my book, Godawa brings to the surface the drama of the original story. **He gives to us the Noah of the Bible in a fresh and provocative way."**

– Peter Enns, PhD. Near Eastern Languages and Civilizations
Author *Inspiration and Incarnation*

"When it comes to supernatural fiction, all the publishing industry seems to think about these days are vampires. Then, fortunately for us, along comes Brian Godawa to shake things up and remind us all where good and evil really come from. *Noah Primeval* **is the kind of story that will make you think, and allow you to see the world in a different way**." "Brian Godawa's imagination is incredible. When he writes, he conjures up worlds that make you re-think what's possible. *Noah Primeval* is a fascinating new take on an ancient story that makes the word 'epic' seem far too small. **Pick up the book, but don't expect to put it down until you're finished.**"

– Phil Cooke, filmmaker, media consultant,
author, *Jolt! Get the Jump on a World that's Constantly Changing*


"**Noah Primeval represents the new generation in novel writing. It's compact, concise, and fast paced. Intelligent yet entertaining.** Godawa brings a screenwriter's sensibilities to the material that will draw in a postmodern audience that prefers books that read like movies."

– Jack Hafer, Chair, Cinema and Media Arts, Biola University;
Producer, *To End All Wars*


"Here is **a disturbingly powerful novel** that "sings the Lord's song in a strange land" at the same time it sings a strange song in the Lord's land. Godawa captures the spiritual and theological truth behind the biblical story of Noah with **an action packed fantasy adventure that reminded me of C. S. Lewis' Narnia, or the graphic novel *Watchmen*.** If you are religious or not, believe the Bible or not, know the story of Noah or not, but you have an imagination, you will love this novel."

– Leonard Sweet, best-selling author, professor (Drew University,
George Fox University), and chief contributor to sermons.com


"We assume we are familiar with the "old stories" of the Bible, but Godawa colors in the details, without violating the letter or the spirit of the text. His admirable storytelling will lead readers to return to the Genesis text and read it with fresh eyes, our imagination having been baptized through the experience of reading the *Chronicles of the Nephilim*."

– Rankin Wilbourne, Pastor, Pacific Crossroads Church (PCA), CA

# Noah Primeval

*Chronicles of the Nephilim*
*Book One*

By Brian Godawa

NOAH PRIMEVAL
5th Edition

Warrior Poet Publishing
www.warriorpoetpublishing.com

ISBN: 9798710405727 (Hardcover)
ISBN: 978-0-615-55078-7 (Paperback)

Scripture quotations taken from *The Holy Bible: English Standard Version.*
Wheaton: Standard Bible Society, 2001.

Dedicated to
my Emzara,
my Muse,
my Kimberly.
Song 2:1-2


and to
Michael S. Heiser,
whose scholarship has opened my eyes
like Elisha's servant.
2 Kings 6:1

# ACKNOWLEDGMENTS

Special thanks always goes to my wonderful wife Kimberly, without whose support, I would not be writing much of anything, including this novel. Another special thanks to Neil Uchitel for all our rambling discussions all those years ago about fallen angels, vampires and the Nephilim. Thanks to my editor, Don Enevoldsen for his friendship and fellowship in the passionate and weary struggle of the life of writing. And to John Kleinpeter for his excellent proofreading. And to Sarah Beach for her excellent editing of this fourth edition, that made it so much better. Most importantly, I thank Yahweh Elohim, my Creator, for his inspiration of imagination within his poetry, stories, and creation.

Inspired By True Events.

# PREFACE

The story you are about to read is the result of Biblical and historical research about Noah's flood and the ancient Near Eastern (ANE) context of the book of Genesis. While I engage in significant creative license and speculation, all of it is rooted in an affirmation of what I believe is the theological and spiritual intent of the Bible. For those who are leery of such a "novel" approach, let them consider that the traditional Sunday school image of Noah as a little old white-bearded farmer building the ark alone with his sons is itself a speculative cultural bias. The Bible actually says very little about Noah. We don't know what he did for a living before the Flood or even where he lived. How do we know whether he was just a simple farmer or a tribal warrior? Genesis 9:2 says Noah "*began* to be a man of the soil" *after* the Flood, not before it. If the world *before* the flood was full of wickedness and violence, then would not a righteous man fight such wickedness as Joshua or David would? Noah would not have been that different from Abraham, who farmed, did business and led his family and servants in war against kings.

We know very little about primeval history, but we do learn from archeological evidence that humanity was clearly tribal during the early ages when this story takes place. Yet, nothing is written about Noah's tribe in the Bible. It would be modern individualistic prejudice to assume that Noah was a loner when everyone in that Biblical context was communal. Noah surely had a tribe.

There is really no agreement as to the actual time and location of the event of the Flood. Some say it was global, some say it was in upper Mesopotamia, some say lower Mesopotamia, some say the Black Sea, some say the earth was so changed by the flood that we would not know where it happened. Since Genesis has some references that seem to match Early Bronze Age Mesopotamian contexts I have gone with that basic interpretation.

The Bible also says Noah built the ark. Are we to believe that Noah built it all by himself? It doesn't say. With his sons' help? It doesn't say. But that very same book *does say* earlier that Cain "built a city" (some scholars believe it was Cain's son Enoch) Are we to assume that he built an entire city by himself? Ridiculous. Cain or Enoch presided as a leader over the building of a city by a group of people, just as Noah probably did with his ark.

One of the only things Genesis says about Noah's actual character is that he was "a righteous man, blameless in his generation. Noah walked with God" (Gen. 6:9). The New Testament clarifies this meaning by noting Noah as an "heir" and "herald" of righteousness by faith (Heb. 11:7; 2Pet. 2:5). The popular interpretation of this notion of "righteousness" is to understand Noah as a virtually sinless man too holy for his time, and always communing with God in perfect obedience. But is this really Biblical? Would Noah have never sinned? Never had an argument with God? Never had to repent? As a matter of fact, the term "righteous" in the Old and New Testaments was not a mere description of a person who did good deeds and avoided bad deeds. Righteousness was a Hebrew legal concept that meant, "right standing before God" as in a court of law. It carried the picture of two positions in a lawsuit, one "not in the right," and the other, "in the right" or "righteous" before God. It was primarily a relational term. Not only that, but in both Testaments, the righteous man is the man who is said to "live by faith," not by perfect good deeds (Hab. 2:4; Rom. 1:17). So righteousness does not mean "moral perfection" but "being in the right with God because of faith."

What's more, being a man of faith doesn't mean a life of perfect consistency either. Look at David, the "man after God's own heart" (Acts 13:22), yet he was a murderer and adulterer and more than once avoided obeying God's will. But that doesn't stop him from being declared as "doing all God's will" by the apostle Paul. Or consider Abraham, the father of the Faith, who along with Sarah believed that God would provide them with a son (Heb. 11:8-11). Yet, that Biblically honored faith was *not* perfect, as they both laughed in derision at God's promise at first (Gen. 17:17; 18:12). Later, Abraham argued with God over his scorched earth policy at Sodom (Gen. 18). Moses was famous for his testy debates with God (Ex. 4; Num. 14:11-24). King David's Psalms were sometimes complaints to his Maker (Psa. 13; Psa. 69). The very name *Israel* means "to struggle with God."

All the heroes in the Hebrews Hall of Faith (Heb. 11) had sinful moments, lapses of obedience and even periods of running from God's call or struggling with their Creator. It would not be heresy to suggest that Noah may have had his own journey with God that began in fear and ended in faith. In fact, to say otherwise is to present a life inconsistent with the reality of every human being in history. To say one is a righteous person of faith is to say that the completed picture of his life is one of finishing the race set before him, not of having a perfect run without injuries or failures.

Some scholars have even noted that the phrase "blameless in his generation" is an unusual one, reserved for unblemished sacrifices in the temple. This physical purity takes on new meaning when understood in the genetic context of the verses before it that speak of "Sons of God" or *bene ha elohim* leaving their proper abode in heaven and violating the separation of angelic and human flesh (Gen. 6:1-4; Jude 5-7). Within church history, there is a venerable tradition of interpreting this strangest of Bible passages as referring to

3

supernatural beings from God's heavenly host who mate with humans resulting in the giant offspring called *Nephilim*. Other equally respectable theologians argue that these Sons of God were either humans from the "righteous" bloodline of Seth or a symbolic reference to human kings or judges of some kind. I have weighed in on the supernatural interpretation and have provided appendices at the end of the book that give the Biblical theological foundation for this interpretation.

This novel seeks to remain true to the sparse facts presented in Genesis (with admittedly significant embellishments) interwoven with theological images and metaphors come to life. Where I engage in flights of fancy, such as a journey into Sheol, I seek to use figurative imagery from the Bible, such as "a bed of maggots and worms" (Isa. 14:11) and "the appetite of Sheol" (Isa. 5:14) and bring them to life by literalizing them into the flesh-eating living-dead animated by maggots and worms.

Another player that shows up in the story is Leviathan. While I have provided another appendix explaining the theological motif of Leviathan as a metaphor in the Bible for chaos and disorder, I have embodied the sea dragon in this story for the purpose of incarnating that chaos as well. I have also literalized the Mesopotamian cosmology of a three-tiered universe with a solid vault in the heavens, and a flat disc earth supported on the pillars of the underworld, the realm of the dead. This appears to be the model assumed by the Biblical writers in many locations (Phil. 2:10; Job 22:14; 37:18; Psa. 104:5; 148:4; Isa. 40:22), so I thought it would be fascinating to tell that story within that worldview unknown to most modern westerners. The purpose of the Bible is not to support scientific theories or models of the universe, but to tell *the story of God* through ancient writers. Those writers were people of their times just as we are.

I have also woven together Sumerian and other Mesopotamian mythology in with the Biblical story, but with this caveat: Like C.S. Lewis, I believe the primary purpose of mythology is to embody the worldview and values of a culture. But all myths carry slivers of the truth and reflect some distorted vision of what really happened. Sumer's Noah was Ziusudra, Babylon's Noah was Utnapishtim, and Akkad's was Atrahasis. The Bible's Noah is my standard. So my goal was to incorporate real examples of ANE history and myth in subjection to that standard in such a way that we see their "true origin." Thus my speculation that the gods of the ancient world may have been real beings (namely fallen "Sons of God") with supernatural powers. The Bible itself makes this suggestion in several places (Deut. 32:17; Psa. 106:34), and it also talks of the Sons of God as "gods" or supernatural beings from God's divine council (Psa. 82:1; 58:1; Ezek. 28:2). See the appendix at the back for my defense of this interpretation from the Bible.

Lastly, I have permitted myself to use extra-Biblical Jewish literature from the Second Temple period as additional reference material for my story. The most significant is the book of *1 Enoch*, a document famous for its detailed amplification of the Genesis 6:1-4 passage about supernatural Sons of God mating with human women and birthing giants, as well as leading humanity astray with occultic knowledge. I use these ancient Jewish sources not because I consider them completely factual or on par with the Bible, but simply in an attempt to incarnate the soul of the ancient Hebrew imagination in conversation with the text of Scripture rather than imposing my own modern western one upon the text. I am within the tradition of the Church on this since authors of the New Testament as well as early Church Fathers and other orthodox theologians in church history respected some of these ancient manuscripts as well.

Many of these texts from the Second Temple Period, such as *Jubilees*, *Testaments of the Twelve Patriarchs* or *The Life of Adam and Eve*, and others found in the Pseudepigrapha, were creative extrapolations of the Biblical text. These were not intended to deceive or overturn the Bible, but rather to retell Biblical stories with theological amplification and creative speculation while remaining true to their interpretation of the Scriptures.

In short, I am not writing Scripture. I am not even saying that I believe this is how the story *might have* actually happened. I am simply engaging in a time-honored tradition of the ancient Hebrew culture: I am retelling a Biblical story in a new way to underscore the theological truths within it. The Biblical theology that this story is founded upon is provided in several appendixes at the back of the book for those who are interested in going deeper.

The beauty of fiction is that we can make assumptions regarding uncertain theological and historical information without having to prove them one way or another. The story requires only that we establish continuity within the made up world, and accepting those assumptions for the sake of the story does not imply theological agreement. So, sit back and let your imagination explore the contours of this re-imagined journey of one of the most celebrated religious heroes across all times and cultures.

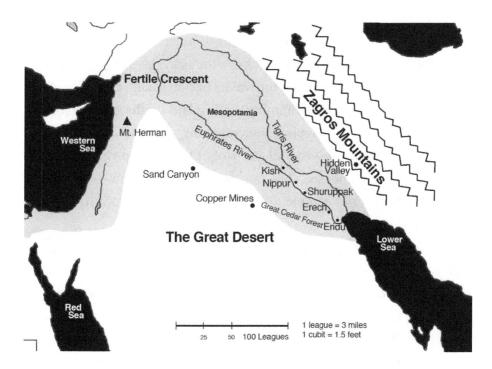

# PROLOGUE

Methuselah squinted through half opened eyes. Enoch traveled beside him as they descended onto crystalline blue waves, the eternal sea. Above him, the deep black sky, painted with a pulsating wave of ethereal color, stretched endlessly into the distance. Methuselah knew where they were — in the waters above the heavens. Before him, a lone ancient temple rested upon the waters like an island, crafted from white marble with gold trimming and inlaid with innumerable precious jewels; jasper, sapphire, emerald, onyx, and others. Around this temple hovered a myriad of the Holy Ones, like phantasms of starlight that he could see, but not quite see. He knew what the structure was — the temple of Elohim, and it was terrifyingly wondrous.

Methuselah sighed with disappointment. Another vision. He was approaching his eight hundred and fiftieth year of life and these visions wearied his old soul. His father, Enoch, hounded him like a ghost in his dreams. Enoch was known for being a righteous man who walked with Elohim, and Elohim spoke with him in visions. When he was young, Methuselah would often complain about his father's "head in the clouds," until he learned the frightening truth that Elohim's holiness was unbearable to sinful human nature. It made him more sympathetic to the effect it had on Enoch.

Elohim had taken Enoch up to heaven alive before he could experience the dismal universal experience that is death. No aching joints, no wavering eye sight, no difficulty in peeing as the years would wind him down to the grave.

From all this Enoch was spared.

*It's not fair*, thought Methuselah. *But alas, Elohim is the creator of all things, and surely has the right to do as he pleases, no matter how strange or incomprehensible those actions may be to us mortals made of clay and nephesh, God's own breath.* Methuselah took the lesson hard. One day soon, this heavenly temple will be his permanent home. But not today. He resigned himself and took in the fearful symmetry of a terrifying yet wondrous cosmos through which Enoch escorted him on the wings of the wind.

Despite his sense of helplessness, Methuselah considered that maybe these visions were worth the irritation, after all. Who else is allowed to see such awesome marvels before their time? Maybe Elohim may yet take him, as he did Enoch.

Out of a myriad of stars some fell from the sky and plunged into the waters below. Pulled beneath the waters, Methuselah watched their descent. The murky depths deadened their shining.

A shiver went through Methuselah's spine as he continued descending into the deep. Then he saw the reason for his chill. The spiny armored back of a long serpentine creature swerved just below him, and disappeared into the darkness. Gigantic, the creature measured maybe three hundred cubits long, a shadowy impression of its full fearful presence in the murky blackness. This was Leviathan, the seven-headed sea dragon of chaos, and the guardian of the deep. Few had ever seen it, fewer still had lived to tell about it. The only thing more terrifying than Leviathan was its mother, Rahab.

Methuselah and Enoch landed on the bottom of the heavenly ocean and began to move through a solid crystalline floor, known to his people as *raqia*, the firmament of heaven. Below this raqia the heavens and the earth were enveloped by the firmament like a vaulted dome. Embedded in the vault of heaven glittered the stars, planets, and the greater and lesser lights that rose upon the ends of the earth in the east and set upon the gates of the west.

As Methuselah and Enoch watched, the luminaries passed through the clouds and approached the earth, a flat disc surrounded by the waters, under which were the pillars of the earth, and below that, Sheol, the underworld. Two hundred of them landed in succession on Mount Hermon in Bashan in the northwest and he knew he was watching many years of the past moving before his eyes. The shining ones spread out across the earth from that cosmic mountain to reign as gods over mankind. These were the *Bene ha Elohim*, the Sons of God.

"Weep for mankind, Methuselah," said Enoch. "For every intent of the thought of his heart is only evil continually. And behold, the Lord will come with ten thousands of his holy ones to execute judgment on all, and to destroy the wicked. But I saw a vision of a Chosen Seed who will bring an end to the reign of the gods and bring rest from the curse of the land. Elohim promised in the Garden that the seed of the Woman, Havah, she who is also known as Eve, would be at war with the seed of the Serpent, Nachash. But through this chosen seedline will come an anointed King who will crush the head of the Nachash, the seed of the Serpent and their abominations in the land."

Hundreds of leagues southeast from Mount Hermon, directly below Methuselah's feet, sat Mesopotamia, the center of the earth, the land between the rivers Tigris and Euphrates. The rivers produced a fertile crescent that rose from the Lower Sea in the south up to Ebla and Amurru in the north, bounded on the west by the vast Great Desert, and on the east by the Zagros Mountains.

Methuselah descended to the southern part of Mesopotamia near the Lower Sea into the fertile land of Shinar, now called Sumer. He was being taken home to the great cedar forest, where his nomadic tribe's camp was hidden from the city-states that bordered the rivers. He felt the vision fading to its end.

"I am not the Chosen Seed," complained Methuselah, "so why do you keep troubling me with these visions?"

"Because," replied Enoch, "the Chosen Seed is not listening. But you have his ear."

Methuselah knew who the Chosen Seed was. And he was going to tan his hide.

# CHAPTER 1

Noah ben Lamech dashed through the sparse brush surrounding the mighty cedars, easily twisting his spear to avoid tangling low hanging branches. Five of his tribesmen trailed behind him, clad in animal skins, carrying spears, bows, and maces.

Lemuel, Noah's protégé, ran fast, nocking his arrow and aiming the flint tip at the prey. The target was a pazuzu, a black monster with a double set of bat-like wings, talons for feet, and a ghastly looking doggish face. The arrow, loosed too quickly, buried into the tree inches from the pazuzu's head. The vile creature let loose a shriek that pierced the human's ears, and fluttered with increased frenzy.

A second pazuzu panicked and almost ran into the first one. They both flitted erratically around the thick trees, seeking shelter from their pursuers' missiles. Unable to find an opening through the heavy canopy of foliage overhead to reach the sky and freedom, they split apart to escape their predators.

Noah gestured to his men to split as well, three on one. Lemuel and Shafat veered into Noah's footsteps after the first pazuzu. The other three turned after the second one.

*They are enemy spies,* Noah thought, *scouts for the city gods, gathering information on the last of the human tribes evading the conquering will of their Lords. We may have started the day hunting for food, but these things are no food for us. We must destroy them.*

Until now, Noah had managed to avoid detection by staying nomadic and hiding in the forest with his people. His family had originally settled the city of Shuruppak in the midst of the southern plain generations ago.

His father Lamech was the priest-king of the city-state and Noah had inherited the position as a young man. But when the pantheon of gods extended their dominion throughout the land of Shinar, Noah's clan left the city because of their dedication to Elohim. They became nomads and roamed the forests, deserts, and mountains.

Noah's tribe had traversed all these territories and had found the forests to be the most inhabitable. But as his people grew in number, presently a few hundred, with children and herd, it was becoming more difficult to pick up quickly and move. If one of these damnable creatures got away and reported to the gods, Noah's community would be in jeopardy. They would run to the mountains where the city gods refused to follow. The desert was bone dry, scorching and brutal for child mortality, and mountain life was not much less miserable to raise a family like the ancient cave dwellers who died out long ago. There were not many of the human tribes left, and Noah was determined to remain one of them.

His desperate need fueled him. Noah's spirit surged. His team spread out and surrounded their pazuzu. Hindered by the closeness of the trees and underbrush, the creature's wings slowed its progress, and the pursuit steadily gained ground. The pazuzu twisted and turned in confusion. With the desperation of a cornered animal, the quarry looked for an opening to strike back at the hunters.

Lemuel glanced away to check his position. He nearly ran headlong into a cedar tree.

The pazuzu pounced in that instant. It took its eyes off Noah for one moment to swoop down.

That was all Noah needed. He drew back and released his spear with the power of an arm accustomed to strenuous labor. The wooden shaft flew straight into the breast of the creature with such force that it impaled the pazuzu's body and pinned it into a tree. It screeched its last shriek and died, black blood oozing down the rough bark of the cedar.

Noah, Lemuel and young Shafat approached the beast. Their long hair, and beards flowed over their animal skins. Noah knew that it gave city dwellers the impression of uncivilized brutishness. But they would be wrong. His nomadic people were highly cultured, and their earthiness was a deliberate expression of their refusal to worship the city gods. His were the people of the Creator Elohim and they were proud to be separate from the rest of humanity who had rejected Elohim's kingship and descended into the worship of the gods of the land. Noah felt that the nomadic tribes could rightly be called the last of humanity.

Noah was over five hundred years old and in his prime as the leader of his people. This was middle age in a community where many lived as long as nine hundred years. As Lemuel was Noah's apprentice, so young twenty-year old Shafat was Lemuel's. They were as close as brothers in their community. They did everything together and protected one another.

"Stand back!" Lemuel snapped to Shafat. "These things are treacherous. They will feign death just to bring one of us with them to the grave. If its talons get hold of you, we will have to cut your arm off to loose you."

Its death throes were genuine. The pazuzu's legs twitched and the last of its air gurgled from its lungs.

"It stinks like excrement," blurted Shafat, with his hand over his nose in disgust.

"It is an abomination," said Lemuel. He reached up and jerked the spear out of the monster, letting it drop to the forest floor in a heap. He handed the spear to Noah.

"It is getting worse, Noah. There will soon be nowhere to hide. We cannot run forever."

Noah ignored the point. He prodded the creature with the tip of his spear, exposing a brand of the god's name in cuneiform on the twitching leg. "This is a scout of Anu."

"We killed a scout of the god Anu?" exclaimed Shafat.

"Quiet your fear," Noah said. "We bow to no god."

"No god but Elohim," Lemuel amended.

Noah shot an irritated glance at Lemuel, then caught himself and nodded reluctantly, "No god but Elohim."

This was a sensitive issue for Noah. He was not always on speaking terms with Elohim, who seemed to be quite distant, only conferring with crazy men like his grandfather Enoch and leaving so much to the *mal'akim* angels to do his bidding.

Noah had served Elohim through the years. He remained pure in his generation. He walked upright and kept separate from the pollution of the city gods who came from heaven and sought to mix their blood with humanity. Noah's tribe and the other human tribes of nomads refused to worship these pretenders to the throne of Elohim, and refused to participate in their corrupting sorceries.

But this was not enough for Noah. Though he knew Elohim was Lord of creation, he sometimes felt that there was little difference between the servitude Elohim expected and the servitude that the city gods demanded of their subjects. A god was a god after all, and in either case man was a servant.

Noah did not like being a servant. He yearned for freedom. *Why can we not be left alone to live our lives? Why must we fight evil all the time?* In a wicked generation, evil never sleeps. And Noah was growing weary from eternal vigilance. He preferred to hide away from it all and just enjoy his family, his beautiful wife, and his own concerns. He wanted to work the land and enjoy the fruit of his labors and be left alone. He had enough on his back to survive in this difficult world and to build his own community based on his own beliefs. If

Brian Godawa

evil was left to run its course, it would destroy its own servants anyway, so why not let it? They deserved it. Why did Noah and his companions have to fight Elohim's battles for him?

The sound of breaking twigs interrupted his thoughts. The three turned toward the sound, tensed and ready.

Tobias and the other two warriors came through the brush. Noah instinctively glanced at their spears, hoping for a sign of pazuzu blood. There was none.

Tobias looked uncertain. "I think we got it. We reached the forest's edge and it broke out to the clearing. But we struck it twice. It managed to stay in the air, but I do not believe it could make it back the distance to the city with two flints in its flesh."

Noah pondered a moment. "We had best have an elder's meeting tonight and make a decision whether to move on."

Shafat let out a sigh of disappointment. Noah slapped him on the back of the head and gave him a warning glance. Without a word, Noah stomped off toward the camp.

Lemuel wondered just how long they could keep going like this. He had followed Noah's lead for many years and had always trusted him. Noah would do no wrong to any man. He was the patriarch of their tribe, a warrior who knew the land well and would not compromise with wickedness. But he could also be impatient and insensitive with those who lacked his resolve. Some men needed understanding and encouragement in the ways of the Lord. Zeal for righteousness did not mean one should give up compassion. Lemuel shook his head sadly as he walked.

But then again, Noah did listen to Lemuel. His passion meant he might be quick to anger, but he was also quick to repent. Lemuel had never known a better man in all his days. He repressed another sigh and tramped after his leader.

# CHAPTER 2

Far away in the skies over Mesopotamia, the wounded pazuzu flapped its double wings struggling to navigate the air streams that helped it remain aloft on its journey to the city. The two arrows burned its muscles with searing pain, one in its left thigh and the other in its right calf. It had lost much blood. Its wings felt heavy. It labored on, knowing if it landed to rest, it would never make it back into the air.

The desert landscape gave way to the unmistakable marks of civilization as the pazuzu reached the outskirts of the city. Erech encompassed over one hundred hectares of land. Below the creature's labored flight stretched the agricultural fields and farms watered by canals from the bordering Euphrates River. Since their very lives were interwoven with the river, the residents became expert canal builders. Levees and dikes brought water to their crops in the outlying areas within the city multiple man-made canals and aqueducts criss-crossed the various residential divisions, channeling lavish amounts of water for everything from cooking to cleaning to waste disposal. In between those channeled sections were the adobe and sun-dried brick homes. The Sumerian citizens went about their daily business, unaware of the flying presence high above.

In the center of this metropolis that boasted a populace of close to ten thousand, a raised hillock overlooked the city and its outlying farming villages. On the elevation rose the temple called *Eanu*. It was dedicated to the patron deity of the city, Anu, the father god of heaven. It consisted of a huge platform mound seventy-five cubits high, built from mud brick and limestone at the bottom. At the top of the platform terrace, raised another twenty cubits high, sat the White Temple, the holy place of the gods. Its intense whiteness, the result of gypsum plaster, created a shining glow in the hot sun.

Next to this temple complex stood a smaller temple district called *Eanna* for Inanna, the goddess of sex and war, and consort of Anu. Eanu dwarfed the Eanna temple. The compound of the goddess had a different design, reflecting the lesser divine status of the female deity. The Eanna district harbored cult prostitution and other deviant whims of the goddess.

Erech was one of the largest and most advanced cities of the alluvial plain. It was originally settled by Unuk ben Cain, son of Cain, who also built Eridu, the oldest city named after Unuk's son, Irad. The original human inhabitants had arrived from the Zagros mountains to establish the first urban civilization on the plains. Those inhabitants formed a slave force that would help them achieve their urban paradise.

Each city was independent, ruled over by a god. Every year at the New Year Festival the pantheon of city gods would meet in assembly in Erech and deliberate their divine decrees for the upcoming year. Anu arranged his pantheon after Elohim's divine council of heavenly host. It pleased Anu to mock the Most High with his own hierarchy of power.

The gods had no desire to burden themselves with the petty worries of human administrations, so they each chose a priest-king to rule in his stead through a governorship. Scribes referred to the arrival of the gods and their rule as the time "when kingship descended from heaven." But ever since then, the princes of the cities vied for prominence amongst themselves as the gods also sought distinction. The hierarchy was unstable. Bureaucracy always courted ambition and rivalry.

The White Temple on the top of Eanu was the highest point in the city. The large platform structure imitated a holy mountain, a connection between heaven and earth. The people called the artificial mountain a ziggurat. Its four corners pointed to the four corners of the earth. The long straight limestone stairway that ascended from the base to the White Temple at top inspired the name Stairway to the Heavens by the people. The gods assembled in the White Temple for their deliberations and liturgy. Only the priest-king and his servants could enter it

The priest-king of Erech, Lugalanu, stood in the temple performing sacred duties when the wounded pazuzu crashed onto the floor.

Lugalanu hurried his pace through the long dark underground tunnel connecting the ziggurat and the palace in the Eanna district. With practiced effort he balanced his sacrificial bowl in the flickering torchlight without spilling the blood offering for Anu and his consort Inanna. They always wanted blood. It was the food of the gods and they were ravenous.

Lugalanu's father, the previous priest-king of Erech, had died not long before, leaving his son as the new ruler of the city, called the Big Boss. Lugalanu's name meant "leader of Anu," and his name reflected his job. His responsibilities included not merely the overseeing of ceremonial and priestly activities but the civil governing of the city and the military defense of the outlying area. This combined religious and civic responsibility sometimes wore him out. He had even pleaded with the father god Anu to divide the duties between two leaders, one civil and one religious, but Anu told him it was not yet to be. Concentrated power was always more efficient at getting things accomplished, and Anu had a lot to accomplish with his priest-king.

The positive result of such multiple responsibilities was a certain breadth of wisdom. And wisdom made Lugalanu a good ruler. He had studied some of the dark secrets of the gods, and he was trained in the art of leadership and war. He pitied his people and sought their good, even if they did not understand that good, and the gods richly rewarded him. He had everything he wanted in this world of power and privilege — except a wife. Oh, he had concubines plenty. His nights were filled with selfish gratification of every desire, both natural and unnatural. What he longed for was to be known, to make a true connection with another human being, to have a queen who would rule by his side. But how could the supreme human ruler of the city ever find a woman he could trust amidst this crowd of sycophants, manipulators, and usurpers?

Such thoughts fluttered through his mind as Lugalanu passed into the palace area. His royal robes flowed behind him as he whisked over mosaic floors and engraved walls of brick. Palace guards stiffened to attention at the sight of him.

He was pure royalty, a youthful three hundred years old, muscular, and handsome with his regal oblong cranium. All the servants of the gods and their entourage practiced head binding. It expressed devotion to the deities. Infants were taken early and their skulls bound with straps until they protruded like an extended egg. As the infant's skull matured and hardened, it maintained its oblong shape permanently.

Lugalanu was completely hairless, like all royal servants. Not a hair on their heads, not an eyebrow or a single nose hair was allowed. It was a sign of perfection to transcend humanity by freeing oneself from the most mammalian of physical traits, hair. It made one look more like the sleek hairless gods he worshipped.

Lugalanu marched through the outer court of the palace, striding past lines of bird-men soldiers. These chimeras with bodies of men and heads of hawks and falcons stood at perfect attention, motionless as statues. Their stoic rigidity masked the savage brutality of fierce warriors, created by the sorceries of the gods to build an army for conquest. But the bird-men were a mere trifle compared to the apex of the gods' creativity: the creatures which Lugalanu now approached at the doorway of the inner court.

The gigantic doors loomed over Lugalanu's head. They were ten cubits tall, two and half times the size of the largest man, made of the mightiest cedar and inlaid with gold. Guarding either side of the gateway were two immense Nephilim.

These Nephilim were giant warriors eight to nine cubits tall, nearly as tall as the inner court doors, demigods created by the mating of the divine Sons of God with the human daughters of men. They were the personal royal guard of deity. Their bodies were covered in occultic tattoos used in magic. They had an extra digit on their hands and feet for a total of twelve fingers and twelve toes. No one on earth had seen anything like their armor, coverings made of a light metallic alloy unknown to man. The Nephilim were also called the Seed of Nachash, titans of war that could not easily be defeated by man born of woman. From the perspective of the gods, they were a strategic achievement of intermingling the human and the divine. From the perspective of Elohim, they were an evil corruption of creation. They struck terror into the hearts of everyone who saw them, including Lugalanu. Though they seemed to defer to his authority, he could never quite bring himself to look them in the eye. He stared blankly at the floor ahead of him and continued his purposeful march.

Lugalanu passed the giants into the inner court, the doors closing behind him like a barrier of magic. He paused to take a deep breath before looking up. This moment always astonished him. The most beautiful atrium ever conceived by the mind of deity lay before him. The vast space measured seventy cubits long and forty cubits high, a man-made paradise. It hosted a mixture of architecture sculpted by the most trained of slave craftsmen, and flora cultivated by the most practiced of horticulturalists. As Lugalanu proceeded down the path toward the throne room, a flurry of doves flew out of the foliage around him past the brick columns into the vaulted ceiling above, a heaven on earth. Gemstones glittered everywhere, embedded in the marble: lapis lazuli, sapphire, beryl, topaz, and amethyst. His own adjacent courtroom as priest-king, though full of its own luxuries, looked like a poor imitation of this chamber.

The smell of exotic incense burning on braziers filled his nostrils, as Lugalanu approached the throne room. He saw the shimmering curtains to the throne room were pulled back to display the forms of Anu and Inanna seated on gem-laden thrones. Two large crossbred sphinx-like creatures that the gods called *aladlammu*, guarded the pair. One had the body of a bull, the other of a lion, and both the bearded heads of a human being. They were born of the gods' magical warping of creation. The stone sculptures outside the palace depicted this pair of living breathing monstrosities. The sight of them sent a shudder through Lugalanu. Their penetrating eyes followed his every move with sentinel alertness.

Anu and Inanna silently watched Lugalanu pour out his libation of blood into crystal chalices on the altar. Lugalanu then genuflected and waited for their command.

The gods lounged resplendent in their royal finery. When standing, they towered well over five and a third cubits, much more than Lugalanu's own four cubits. Their eyes shimmered with blue lapis lazuli reptilian irises. Their tongues split lizard-like. Despite their androgynous appearance, Inanna dressed the part of a goddess. They had elongated heads, which the head-binding of their servants sought to mimic. Anu and Inanna would tolerate nothing less than human attendants molded into their likeness. They both wore the horned headdress of deity common throughout the region. Both wore royal robes created from the feathers of vultures.

Inanna cultivated a flamboyance that set her apart from Anu. She wore heavy makeup and pierced her body all over with rings, studs, and spikes. Her nose, eyebrows, and other body parts hosted these symbols of the forced pain that she pleasured in. She also gloried in outrageous outfits as a display of her ironic status as goddess of sex and war. This day, she was more restrained with her red leather and chains.

The skin of the gods appeared smooth, but Lugalanu knew that close up fine subtle serpentine scales that sparkled in the light covered them, producing a visible aura of constant radiant luminescence. Many described this radiance in terms of beryl, crystal or shining bronze. When their passions flared for good or bad, their shining would increase in brilliance, giving the impression of flashes of lightning. Because of this, they were called Shining Ones.

Lugalanu could always count on Anu to have a certain detached playfulness about him, as if he enjoyed being deity and played up the formalities of royalty with a sardonic loftiness. Inanna, on the other hand, was unpredictable and dangerous. She had a violent temper because everyone always seemed to be in the way of her accomplishing her plans. She would instantly kill servants who made mistakes in her presence. She might smite even those who gave her gaudy appearance a strange look. Lugalanu sought to ingratiate himself to them at every opportunity.

"My priest-king, Lugalanu, lord of the city, how dost thou fare?" pronounced Anu with a touch of playful overstatement in his voice.

"Well, my lord Anu, king of gods," Lugalanu responded, promptly followed by a nod to Inanna. "Queen of heaven, my worship."

"Up, up. What do you want?" blurted Inanna.

Lugalanu straightened up quickly and replied, "I have intelligence from one of our pazuzu scouts of a human tribe of nomads in the great cedar forest."

"Well, go slay them," she snorted.

Anu stepped in. "We want loyal, willing subjects, not rebels of insurrection, Inanna."

They argued about this frequently. Anu knew that Inanna wanted to eliminate all the remaining human tribes who worshipped Elohim. But he thought they would accomplish their purposes more effectively if they concentrated on defiling the human bloodline as a way to thwart Elohim's plans for a kingly seed.

It frustrated Inanna to no end that she had to submit to Anu's kingship. Ever since her colossal failure in the war of the titans, called the Titanomachy, she had been demoted from co-regent with him to his consort so he could keep an eye on her. She had massive scars on her back to remind her of the consequences of insubordination. She reined herself in with calculated self-interest.

Lugalanu curried the Queen's favor, "My lord, I humbly defer to her highness. Every rogue human tribe is a possible fulfillment of the revelation."

Anu bristled with annoyance. "The Revelation," he snorted, conveying the impression to the human that he did not believe it. But he did believe it. He sickened of the dread that seized everyone when this revelation business was brought up. Fear was healthy; dread was self-destructive.

"Ah yes, the Revelation," Inanna shot back. "A 'Chosen Seed' who will end the rule of the gods. Are you not concerned, lord? *We* are among those gods who rule. And you are the head of the pantheon, the high and mighty one." She matched Anu's annoyance with sarcasm. "Unless you think you have nothing to lose."

She knew how he would respond. For the hundredth time, he said, "If they worship us, then we have no concern, and are free to use them as slave labor for *our* kingdom."

The gods of the pantheon kept hidden from Lugalanu and most humans their real identities and goals. Anu's real name was Semjaza, and Inanna's, Azazel. These divinities were not gods like Elohim. They were in fact the Sons of God who rebelled from Elohim's divine council that surrounded his very throne.

Elohim himself sat on the high throne, the Creator and Lord of all. Though mortal eyes could not see him, he was visible in his vice-regent, the Son of Man, The Angel of the Lord, who mediated and led God's heavenly host. The members of the host were the Sons of God, or *Bene Elohim,* ten thousand times ten thousand of his Holy Ones who deliberated with the Almighty and would carry forth his judgments — except those who had fallen.

Two hundred of them had rebelled and fallen. They were called "Watchers." By masquerading as gods of the land, they sought to usurp the throne of Elohim and draw human worship away from the Creator. To further enslave the sons of men in idolatry, they had revealed unholy secrets of sorceries, fornications, and war. Enoch had pronounced judgment upon them in faraway days, but the manifestation of that judgment had not yet fallen upon the Watchers. The fullness of their iniquity was not yet complete.

Elohim had created mankind as his representative image on earth, to rule in his likeness. If the fallen Sons of God could transform the image of God into *their* image, their revenge would be almost complete. By mixing the human line of descent with their own, they could stop the bloodline of the promised King from bringing forth its fruit, and thereby win the war of the Seed of Nachash with the Seed of Havah.

Anu had a mellower side that Inanna lacked. He preferred to keep humans alive to serve him rather than destroy them. It was all a matter of perspective. He believed wisdom dictated that his own interests be portrayed as compassion to the humans. Perhaps they would even one day love him instead of fear him. Was this not what it was like to be Elohim?

Lugalanu interrupted Anu's thoughts. "These nomads killed our scouts. They are ruthless savages."

Anu responded, "I too would kill those ugly little beasts if they were sniffing around my residence."

Inanna snorted with disapproval but refused to keep fighting. She would choose her battles. This was not one of them.

"Meet with the tribal leaders and allow them every opportunity to submit," Anu decreed.

Inanna's ire went up. "And if they do not?"

"Then enforce the will of the gods." He was not about to appear weak. His patience only went so far.

Lugalanu bowed low and backed away from their presence. He wondered if he had kept a proper balance of flattery for Inanna without disrespect for Anu's supremacy.

When the human was gone, Inanna grinned with delight to herself. Her vampiric fangs glistened red as she guzzled the blood offering with satisfaction. Perhaps she had not lost this battle after all.

# CHAPTER 3

Noah, Lemuel and the others trudged into the camp after their pazuzu hunt. Noah hoped that the evening feast would distract the tribe's attention from the somber faces of the hunting party. The news would not go over well with the community. They had been discovered, and while they could not be sure that the pazuzu escaped to deliver the information, they had to consider it a strong possibility. They would have to discuss it with the elders tonight. Even if the pazuzu did not make it back to the city, its disappearance would eventually bring more scouts to the area.

The camp nestled in the thick cover of the great cedar forest. Ancient trees blocked much of the light, but they also blocked the view of hostile airborne eyes. Old fallen trees provided dry wood to minimize smoke. Tents and other shelters spread over the large encampment with plenty of camouflage to conceal their presence. The livestock of sheep, goats and donkeys were penned off to the east face as an early warning of arrivals from the river cities. The middle of the camp vibrated with mothers boiling soups over low fires, children playing and giggling, and elders cleaning up loose ends.

These were a happy people who served Elohim. Since they had become nomads, they had seen the wonders of a world so much bigger than they had imagined as city dwellers just a generation ago. Weathering snowstorms in the north, surviving the waterless places of the desert, hunting mountain wildlife. They had been at their current forest location for some time now and had become familiar with all its rhythms and cycles, integrating themselves into it all with a confident caretaker's dominion. They could think like deer, hide like foxes, hunt like bears and fight like lions.

Noah nodded silently to his companions and turned toward his personal encampment. Though he was the tribe's patriarch, his tents were no more than appropriate for a family of his size: one goatskin tent for his wife Emzara and himself, one to the side for his children, and one on the other side for his parents, Lamech and Betenos. They lived with his grandfather, Methuselah. Noah detested the arrogance of royalty and sought to lead by example and merit rather than through power and station. He would not live with special privileges. He would not ask sacrifice of his people that he would not himself also give.

Noah went first to check on his parents. He loved his father and mother deeply. They had raised him with a stern but steady love. Though they were well over six hundred and sixty years old – Noah lost count – they had been mighty in the dark past as giant killers with his great-grandfather Enoch. They spoke little of those days. They did not want the clan to lose vigilance in thinking they had special warriors in their midst. They were human after all, and not invincible. But they taught Noah how to fight and how to be a leader.

Lamech had built the city of Shuruppak after the Titanomachy had almost destroyed their world. But when followers of Ninlil, the consort goddess of Enlil, overran Shuruppak with their worship of the goddess, Lamech walked away from his royal station to become a humble nomad. He chose to worship Elohim as he saw fit, removed from the influence of the wicked masses upon his descendants. He often told Noah that Elohim had special plans for Noah. Not many years before, Lamech had lost his right arm in a battle, and chose to retire and hand over leadership of the tribe to Noah as the new Patriarch.

When Noah stuck his head in the tent, all he saw was grandfather Methuselah snoring away in his afternoon nap. Lamech and Betenos must have gone for one of their many walks in the woods, reminiscing about their past, a time of adventure and danger that they hoped they would never have to face again.

Noah moved on to his children's tent, a sense of anticipation rising in him. These were his true achievements: his two sons, Shem, age five, and Japheth, age four. He took his responsibility to Elohim's command to be fruitful and multiply very seriously. He took everything seriously, too seriously. And these two little gems were just the antidote he needed to bring him back down to earth and enjoy life a little more. "Stop once in a while and smell the crocuses," Emzara often told him. Had he ever even bothered to smell a crocus flower before? He would make sure to do so next chance he got. But this was the immediate pleasure. "Where are my little pups?" he called out as a warning. With a sudden burst of movement, he yanked back the tent flap and jumped inside.

Instead of the expected giggles of two young boys, a laconic, "Baaah" greeted him. No one was there, only a pet lamb tied up in the middle of the tent. His sons called the lamb Lemuel, naming their favorite pet after their favorite of father's friends. Noah used it as a joke to tease Lemuel, calling him "my little lamb." That often ended in a wrestling match of some kind, with Lemuel usually winning because Noah was laughing too much. At least that's the way Noah told it.

Noah looked all round outside the tent. No sign of the boys.

He called out, "Shem? Japheth?"

No response. A single "Bah" punctuated the silence. Noah back glanced at the lamb, as though he expected an explanation from the creature. He looked around the tent again. It was a mess, with everything strewn around like a pack of dogs had been set loose. Was this demolition the work of a couple of rowdy boys playing their hearts out? Or was something wrong? Suddenly, his eyes tightened and he became concerned.

"Shem? Japheth? My sons, where are you?"

He looked frantically around the room. That is, he pretended to. Because he knew exactly what would happen next. Two miniature predators jumped out from hiding and pounced on their victim with wooden axe and mace.

"Aha! We got you! We tricked you!" yelled Shem in his triumphant warrior-lord voice. He and his younger brother hailed blows upon their prey. Noah cowered and protected himself while carefully allowing them easy access with their weapons.

"Ah! You distracted me with a sacrifice! You clever little warriors!"

"A sacrificial lamb!" shouted Shem.

Japheth could not stop giggling. Noah's free hand had reached out to tickle him with targeted precision. Japheth always fell victim to tickling. He dropped his mace and completely lost control.

Shem, however, continued to rain blows on Noah. Shem was a chip off the old limestone. He had his father's determination. Noah knew that one day he was going to have his hands full with a young man who was a reflection of himself, stubbornness and all.

"You are an abomination!" screamed Shem, absorbed in his righteous slaughter.

Noah abruptly stopped tickling and sat up, sternly. "Where did you learn that word?" he asked.

A wave of fear rushed over Shem. He did not know what was wrong. It horrified him to displease his father. "Jared's father Lemuel uses it."

Noah knew that it was not a guilty attempt to shift blame, but rather a genuine appeal to justice, something Shem did far too often. The boy was right. Lemuel did use it all the time as a curse word. That bothered Noah. He could not force Lemuel to stop, but he could do something about his own son.

"Stop using it. It is an adult word, not for children."

"I am sorry, father," Shem said meekly.

Noah's eyes looked deep into Shem's. The boy stared back, praying now for mercy.

Noah softened. His eyes brightened and a big toothy grin appeared. "No harm done, my son."

He grabbed them both in a big hug, refusing to let go, crushing them tighter and tighter.

"Uh oh," he said, "giant sloth hug!"

The boys giggled and squirmed, trying to escape their father's embrace. Japheth shrieked with pleasure, the childish shriek that pierces one's eardrums, especially when done right next to the father's ears.

Noah grunted and released the boys, fingering his ear to rub out the pain. "Japheth, remember to use that voice if a wild animal ever attacks you. It may never attack another human again."

Japheth grinned impishly.

Noah added, "Speaking of wild animals, where is that she-wolf of a mother of yours?"

He looked up and saw Emzara standing in the tent entrance smiling. Backlit by the bright sun rays upon her red dye linen dress, she was a goddess to him—every bit a tribal queen, and every inch a magnificent vision of Elohim's creative capacity. Her long, dark, auburn hair caught a breeze and shifted. The sight sent shivers down Noah's spine. The linen tightly wound around her voluptuous form beckoned to him, drawing him into a trance. Noah was under her spell, body and soul.

He kept his eyes locked on her as he spoke. "Boys, stay in the tent for a while. I have to consult privately with your mother."

Emzara gave an ever-so-slight grin and walked away, leaving the little boys to play and the bigger boy to stumble after her. Unaware of how parents played, Shem and Japheth fell back into battle with each other.

Emzara had known Noah all her life. They both had spouses that had died. For many years, Noah had avoided grieving as he poured his heart and soul into care for the clan. He had avoided Emzara as well. The mere sight of her doubled the pain of losing both his wife and his closest confidant, Aramel, Emzara's dead husband.

But one day, Emzara had confronted Noah, exhibiting the independent strength he would later become intimately familiar with. She refused to leave Noah's presence until he discussed with her their mutual pain, in an attempt to overcome it. In that encounter, Noah suddenly saw Emzara as he had never seen her before. They were soon married. They were later than usual in starting a new family, but it was never too late for the blessings of Elohim.

Noah's favorite blessing from Elohim was the intimacy he shared with his wife. Their oneness was a God-honoring expression of their earthy spirituality. In a way, adoration of his wife's splendor calmed the troubles he had with Elohim. As he caressed her, he knew God was good. As their lips met, he knew he was known, thoroughly known, and yet still loved. To have this most excellent and brave woman of strength willingly give herself to him humbled him. He felt honored and strengthened by it. His pet name for her was Naamah, which meant "lovely."

"You wore my favorite dress we got from that caravan from the land of the Nile," he said.

She held up her copper covered wrist, smiling "And the bracelets." The benefit of a nomad life was its connection with exotic trade.

"Now, let us take them all off," he snickered.

Emzara's mood changed suddenly.

"What troubles you?" he asked.

"The clan is in turmoil," she said. "We are weary of living like a pack of wild dogs, always on the run."

"It is the price we pay for our freedom from the gods."

Emzara sighed. Lately, he had been speaking more of freedom than of Elohim.

But before she could bring that up, he changed the subject. "We found more pazuzu in the forest. It seems that evil follows us like a jackal."

"When will it end?"

"When the gods stop demanding obedience to their proud rule."

"Thus saith a proud man," she reproved.

"And this is bad?"

Emzara was the most submissive of women. She knew Elohim created woman out of man's side to be his *ezer*, a helper beside him. But sometimes that meant speaking the truth that was hard for one's beloved to hear.

"My love, pride leads to a fall. It is faith that leads to freedom."

Noah knew she was right. She was his wisest counselor. But his stubbornness rose up. *What does she know of leading a tribe?* he asked himself, avoiding the truth.

She continued, relentlessly loving. "Do you think I have not also suffered? We both lost everything once. Must you try to be so alone?"

He pulled away, though he did not want to admit it. Irritation replaced his romance. "You are a woman of faith. It is no secret my devotion to Elohim has waned as his interest in me has waned. But I am still devoted to righteousness."

She held his head in her hands and stared into his eyes. He had the greatest integrity of any man that she had ever seen, even if that integrity sometimes got in the way of the Creator who gave it to him. "I am with child, my Utnapishtim," she whispered.

Noah's eyes flashed from shock to joy. The news took his breath away. Utnapishtim was her pet name for him. It meant "he who found life." She thought it was quite appropriate for Noah's earthy gusto.

"My Naamah," he said and hugged her desperately. He kissed her passionately. Apart from Emzara's presence, a child was the one thing that melted Noah's warrior heart. Children were arrows for warriors and he wanted a quiver full. Because they started their family late, he would not have as many offspring as others, but to him that just meant that each one of his own would be cherished that much more.

"Husband, you are not a god. But sometimes I think you want to be one with your self-reliance and aloofness."

"Wife, you could not handle a god. You can barely handle me."

She jumped into his arms, wrapping her legs tightly around him, knocking him off balance. But he caught her. They laughed, and melted together before their Maker.

Noah choked awake, disoriented, underwater. He fought toward the surface in search of air, and broke through gasping.

An endless sea stretched around him, nothing but water to the farthest horizon. He turned about and saw a beautiful white temple resting on the waters before him. He swam to the edifice and pulled himself out of the water, dripping wet. He climbed the steps up into the temple and cautiously stepped into the inner courtyard, onto a pavement of sapphire stone.

Dizziness swept over him. The inside of the temple did not match the outward size he had seen. On the outside, it stood about forty cubits wide by seventy cubits long. Inside, it seemed as if he had walked through a portal into another world. In that other world ranged the flaming messengers of Elohim's heavenly host. Their brightness hurt his eyes. They did not speak. They just watched Noah in silence—a myriad of them.

Noah stood still, his feet riveted to the sapphire floor. The presence of the Shining Ones intimidated him. He could not move. Then his eyes caught sight of a marble pedestal set out in the open by itself, with a large clay tablet resting on it.

With trepidation, he approached the pedestal and looked upon the tablet. The crowded triangular markings of cuneiform covered it, the writing system used in the Land Between the Rivers. Only the scribes and the upper classes of city palaces were taught cuneiform. But Noah could read it because his father had been a city ruler and his great grandfather Enoch had been an *apkallu* wisdom sage, so they passed down knowledge of this important new means of communication. Even Methuselah, who tended to be antisocial, had taken it upon himself to stay learned in such matters.

Noah studied the tablet. At the center was a drawing of a large rectangular box structure similar to the barges he had seen on the shipping docks of Shuruppak when he was younger. But this was different. The dimensions next to the box made it larger than any barge he had ever seen. It looked more like a warehouse. He studied it curiously.

A sound behind him made him turn, expecting to see an angel.

But it was no angel. It was the god Anu. The being jumped at him with a *hiss* of viper fangs!

Noah sat up abruptly, shaking off the dream. Beads of perspiration gathered on his forehead. He reached for Emzara for support. She was gone.

Outside, the shadows grew long. It was getting late. Time for the feast and assembly.

He took a couple of deep breaths to settle his thoughts, then got dressed quickly. He stopped one moment to smell the sweet savor of memory in the red linen dress lying on his bedding. The scent of crocus filled his nostrils. He smiled and left the tent.

Outside, he found the clan already celebrating around the fire with music and dance. Families were enjoying one another and cooking their meals. Some gestured for him to join them. But Noah had something to take care of first.

In the children's tent, Lamech and Betenos were enjoying their grandchildren before the assembly meeting started. Lamech loved telling Shem and Japheth fantastic legends of warriors battling strange monsters with dragon heads and lion bodies, mystical trees guarded by demonesses, and wars of giants and Cherubim. He would tell the boys not to share the legends with others, that they would be their own special tales of adventure, which made them feel very special indeed.

The boys would often wonder why grandmother Betenos would jump in and correct grandfather's fabulous tale as if he did not tell it properly. They had no idea that Lamech's tales were true. Lamech told them what he and Betenos had actually experienced in the past as Karabu giant killers, under cover of a made-up tale. He and Betenos felt that the intensity of their experiences were too traumatic for little children to handle the reality. It was better served through the safety of imagination. They would grow up soon enough to face the wicked world from which Noah was protecting them.

Lamech and Betenos gathered Shem and Japheth into their arms for a moment. Lamech pulled out the leather case that held his special weapon. The boys' eyes went wide with excitement. They had seen it before and knew that grandfather had a nickname for it.

"Rahab," gasped Shem.

"What does Rahab mean?" asked Japheth.

"Rahab is the giant sea dragon of chaos that gave birth to Leviathan, its own sevenfold increase of terror," said Lamech. "This weapon moves like the body of Rahab and bites with ferocity." Shem leaned in to get a closer look at the case. Lamech snapped at Shem's nose with a growl. Shem jerked back with a giggling yelp.

"Tell us the story again about where you got it," the boy blurted out.

Betenos saw Lamech's eyes brighten. He loved to tell his stories. It made him feel significant in his old age. She knew Lamech loved her with all his heart. But she also knew that he was a man, and men need to feel that they are doing something significant or they wither and fade into depression. Lamech was no different. Losing his arm in battle and stepping down as Patriarch had taken its toll on Lamech's sense of worthiness. That he had to hide his achievements behind a fictional façade did not help.

"Well," said Lamech with deliberate exaggeration, "Rahab is a very special weapon, forged in the heavenly volcano of Mount Sahand amidst the stones of fire by the archangel Gabriel himself. It was given to me to watch over." He didn't explain that he was also trained how to use the weapon in the secret angelic order of the Karabu giant killers.

The boys listened in rapt attention, though they had heard the story a hundred times. They stared at the strange leather case with handle sticking out. Inside was a flexible blade made of unearthly alloy, all seven cubits of its length rolled up into the case. They had never seen or heard of anything else like it. It was virtually indestructible. It unrolled and flowed like a whip. No known metal on earth could do that. And this whip would cut giants' heads from bodies and sever villains in two.

"But remember, it is our secret," said Lamech.

"Our secret," the boys repeated in unison.

Betenos smiled warmly. Boys will be boys. And men will be boys.

Lamech continued. "And now, Shem, because you are the firstborn, I have a very special commission for you."

Shem sat speechless, wondering what it could be. Japheth fidgeted, a little jealous.

"I am handing down Rahab to you as an heirloom," said Lamech.

Shem's mouth dropped in shock. No sound came out. His eyes bulged so wide, they hurt.

"I will leave it with you, but you will not withdraw it, and you will not use it until your father lets me teach you how to use it. Do you understand me?"

Shem could only nod his head yes, still staring at the special weapon in its case.

Japheth started crying. He did not get a special weapon like Shem.

Lamech looked at Betenos. She reached behind her to pull out the special bow that she had used to kill giants, mushussu, and human wolves so many years ago.

Lamech held the bow. "Japheth, to you we bequeath your grandmother's special giant killing bow. The same goes for you as for your brother. You will not play with it until your father allows us to teach you how to use it. Do you understand?"

"Yes!" shouted Japheth with joy.

Both boys gave their grandparents hugs and kisses that Lamech and Betenos would treasure for the rest of their lives.


Methuselah's eyes popped open. The tip of a dagger pressed against his throat.

"You are slowing down, Grandfather, getting dull," said Noah. "I respect your wisdom, but what of your strength?"

"You are already dead," Methuselah replied. Noah felt a sharp point prick his belly. He looked to see Methuselah's dagger sticking in his abdomen. "Or at least without *your* manhood."

Noah pulled back, chuckling.

Methuselah sat up. "And I can still handle a battle axe, young buck," he said. "I just need a nap now and then. You will understand in a couple hundred years. If you survive that long." He made no mention of his accuracy with a javelin in his younger years.

Noah loved his grandfather and cherished his advice on everything in life. He also appreciated Methuselah's dry wit. He might be the oldest man alive, but he was also one feisty poet warrior. He never let Noah get lazy in thought or deed, because, as he always said with annoying redundancy, "Elohim's Chosen Seed needs to grow."

Noah sat back with a sigh. "I had a vision."

Methuselah came alert. "The heavenly temple on the waters?"

Noah looked surprised. "How did you know?"

"Because I had the same vision."

"Did you see the building plans?" Noah asked.

"No. Building plans for what?"

"*Tebah*. A large box. Huge. Like a fortress or warehouse." Noah scribbled out in the sand from memory a phrase he had never read before the dream. "What does this mark mean?"

Methuselah said, "Covered in and out with pitch."

"What is pitch?" said Noah.

"Maybe it will be revealed. How large is this box?" Methuselah asked.

"Three hundred cubits long, fifty cubits breadth, thirty cubits high. Several floors."

"Have you told your father?" asked Methuselah.

"Not yet. I think he is with the boys," said Noah.

Methuselah pondered.

Then he spoke with the certainty of a sage. "You must build this box—this warehouse."

"Me? Why?" Noah complained.

"Elohim gave me a similar dream. But he did not show me his plans as he did you."

"Why will not Elohim just speak clearly to me?" complained Noah. "Is that too much to ask? How do I know that he has not gotten our dreams mixed up?"

"Elohim does not make mistakes," said Methuselah. "*You* must build the box."

"It would take the entire tribe years to build such a structure," protested Noah. "It does not make sense."

Methuselah chuckled. "Well, then, we had better get chopping."

Noah drew back annoyed. "It was only a dream!"

"Sometimes that is how Elohim speaks to hard-headed men." Methuselah returned. He thought of himself and how Elohim had hammered his own hard head so many years ago.

Noah rolled his eyes. Methuselah continued, "I remind you of my father Enoch's revelation."

Noah could not keep disdain from his voice. "Oh, you have much reminded me of great-grandfather's delirious revelations."

"I also remind you," said Methuselah, "that Enoch walked with Elohim—and was taken by him, never to die. Is that delirious?"

Noah could not argue with that. As much as he thought his great-grandfather had sounded a little too holy for his taste, he could not deny that he walked with Elohim. He remembered that the Sons of God first came down from heaven in the days of Jared, Enoch's father and Noah's great-great-grandfather. That was when Enoch began having his dream-visions. Enoch had foretold all this. But Noah found it difficult to accept that Elohim would want everyone to be so heavenly minded when there was work to be done on terra firma.

Noah's father Lamech and Methuselah told him very little from the earlier years when Enoch had ascended into heaven before he was born. They would only reveal bits and pieces as he grew up, but never the whole story of their experiences in the Titanomachy.

"I do not know what happened to Enoch. But I do know that I want to live a life in peace, away from this wicked world. If we move, we are left alone and avoid trespass. If we put down roots and build this structure, we become a sitting target for the gods to conquer and rule us."

Methuselah looked straight into Noah's eyes. "Noah, do you really think you can avoid evil?"

"I have no choice. Avoid it or we all die."

Methuselah paused to consider his next move. He was cornering Noah and they both knew it. "Do you really think you can avoid Elohim?"

Noah would not respond.

Methuselah pressed harder. "We must tell the elders of this dream."

"No!" Noah blurted.

"You are the Patriarch. It is your responsibility," said Methuselah.

"As Patriarch, I forbid you to tell the elders."

Methuselah threw up his hands in exasperation. He would not trump authority.

Noah added, "But we will tell them we are moving on the morrow."

# CHAPTER 4

Shafts of morning light broke through the tall timbers of the forest, accompanied by the music of birds welcoming the dawn. Noah woke to the sweet smell of Emzara's hair nestled in his neck and shoulder. Their breathing synchronized as one. She stirred and he could not help but thank Elohim for another day of life with her.

The flap on his tent slapped open. Lemuel stuck his worried face inside, which only an emergency would make him do.

Noah looked at his friend. "Lemuel, we have all day to pack up for the move."

"A royal entourage from Erech is encamped near the brook," whispered Lemuel.

Noah sat up abruptly, waking Emzara. "What? How many? Are they armed?"

"A small delegation," Lemuel said. "Should we muster our forces?"

"No," said Noah. "It must be an ambassador. Go gather the elders. We will ride and see what they want."

The royal encampment was a third of a league distant from Noah's settlement. A large ostentatious tent dominated the center, twenty cubits in diameter, made of embroidered fabric from the Indus valley. A line of bird-men soldiers with spears, maces, and axes guarded the perimeter. The banner of Anu flew high overhead on a golden standard.

Noah, Lemuel, six elders and an escort of a couple of warriors halted briefly at the edge of the brook, still partially concealed in the dense forest. Noah patted the neck of his onager as he looked at the horses of the visitors. He trusted his durable domesticated ass, but he had known of the horses which recently traded all over the Levantine and Mesopotamian plains. They provided stronger mounts and faster travel for flight or fight, either of which might happen in the next few moments.

Noah and his men crossed the brook with caution, leaving the escort of two warriors behind as watch. A truce would automatically be in effect for such a meeting, but it would not hurt to have a reserve. Noah plodded forward, eyes straight ahead, oblivious to the fact that most of his companions, with the exception of Lemuel, did not share his courage in the face of such large numbers of hostile soldiers, truce or not.

As they reached the edge of the royal camp, a priestess greeted them. She had painted eyes, hairless elongated skull, and flesh full of tattoos and body piercings. She walked up to Noah with a seductive gait in a translucent gown.

Noah thought, *This heathen religion is a lascivious one.*

The priestess hissed in a whisper, "If you please, you and your man may follow me. The others may refresh themselves."

She gestured to a lavish banquet table out in the open filled with golden cups of wine and silver platters of wild boar and vegetables.

"Thank you," replied Noah, "but we already ate breakfast. Early risers." He dismounted, followed by Lemuel and his men.

"Well, then," she said, "This way."

Noah and Lemuel followed her through a gauntlet of bird-men and portable bronze pillars leading to the tent entrance. Noah wondered at the kind of conceit that would produce such luxurious waste of resources. The vast number of slaves needed to maintain the excess of royalty and deity astounded Noah. He noticed that Lemuel kept his hand on his belted mace.

As they entered the tent, four human officers greeted them, and then stepped aside, bowing in deference. Behind them sat open chests of gold, silver and precious gems, sparkling in the rays of light that peeked in through the tent entrance. It was a king's ransom. Noah glanced at it briefly. If the display was meant to impress him, it failed miserably.

Behind the treasure, Lugalanu lounged on a miniature throne in his royal vestments, like a miniature version of Anu. He spoke to Noah in a mimicry of Anu's own lofty, light-hearted grandeur.

"Welcome to our humble delegation from the mighty sky god Anu, Lord of heaven and earth, father of the gods. I am his priest-king, Lugalanu."

Noah sniffed. "I know a certain Creator who would beg to differ with those titles. And I am not impressed by pompous exhibition."

"Well, now that I know what you are not, pray tell, who you are?"

"I am Noah ben Lamech, son of Methuselah, son of Enoch, Patriarch of my clan."

Lugalanu's brow rose with interest. "Noah, son of Enoch. I have heard of you. You are most respected among the human tribes."

Noah, dismissed the small talk. "We are nomads and we seek no trouble with the gods of this land."

"I believe you," Lugalanu responded. "The gods, however, are not so easily persuaded." He paused to add gravity to his tone. "Especially when their servants return to Erech grievously wounded by nomad arrows."

Lemuel looked nervously at Noah, then at the officers, his eyes on constant watch.

"Some token of respect might alleviate their concern," Lugalanu continued. "Simple obeisance to prove your peaceful intentions, perhaps."

The priest-king was no match for Noah, who made his own pronouncement. "We will bow the knee to no god…," the pause was noticeable "…but Elohim."

"Indeed?" questioned Lugalanu. "And I suspect you even have trouble doing that." No detail escaped Lugalanu's eagle eye. Years of court intrigue honed his senses to pick up the slightest nuance of body language and tone that betrayed underlying motives and meanings. He could tell instantly that this man before him had a proud sense of self-importance such as he had not encountered in a decade. He decided to throw out some bait. "Every man is ruled by a god. Except perhaps the man who will end the rule of the gods."

Noah ignored the bait. "My people are leaving this forest this very day. We will leave you alone. We beg your indulgence to leave *us* alone."

Lugalanu stared at him for what seemed an eternity. Then matter-of-factly, he said, "I cannot indulge you."

The answer did not please Noah. Lemuel fidgeted uncomfortably.

"But I have a counter offer," Lugalanu continued. "You are influential with the remaining nomadic tribes. You and your people will not be taxed like everyone else. You will not even be forced to join in public worship. I only ask that you bow the knee to the gods in private and not obstruct the rest of the human tribes from submitting to the pantheon." His voice was almost conciliatory. "Then you will be left alone."

Noah stared at him unrelentingly. Lugalanu clearly had no idea whom he was talking to. "I will not bow the knee," said Noah.

Lugalanu let out a deep sigh. Noah clearly had no idea whom *he* was talking to. "Very well, then. Pazuzu!" he barked.

Noah and Lemuel whirled to see one of the black hideous dog-faced creatures at the doorway of the tent.

"Pass the order. Destroy the village."

The pazuzu took off in flight.

"NOOOOO!" Noah screamed as he realized they had been betrayed.

In a flash, he and Lemuel were out of the tent, their maces ready to strike.

They stopped in their tracks. A hideous sight confronted them. The six elders and two warriors from the brook hung limp from pillars by their broken necks. The bird-men had managed to completely surprise their quarry with silent death.

Noah's world spun around him.

Lemuel's screaming voice brought Noah back to reality. He dodged just in time to avoid an axe that almost cleaved him in two. He backed up against Lemuel. Twenty bird-men surrounded them, weapons at the ready. But these mutant creatures had cornered the wrong two fighters. As a battling duet, Noah and Lemuel swung their weapons in a macabre dance of death, taking out soldiers left and right.

Noah downed a soldier behind Lemuel. Lemuel spun and hacked an attacker in Noah's blind spot. Methuselah and Lamech had trained them together most of their lives with the secret art of the lost order of warriors called the Karabu. They were seasoned and unbeatable.

Unbeatable until the net dropped from above.

It enveloped them like a spider's web. They were trapped prey. Their weapons were useless. The soldiers rained blows upon them, pounding them into submission. Noah's raw anger kept him conscious. Lemuel blacked out. When the soldiers stopped, Noah knew they were not going to be killed. He dropped his weapon.

Someone yanked the net away. The prisoner's arms were held back by five soldiers each. Lemuel came to from his black-out.

Lugalanu stepped up to Noah, reveling in his victory.

Noah spit at him. "You piece of filth. I should have known never to negotiate with the wicked."

Lugalanu crowed, "I would expect the nemesis of the gods to be smarter than that." He gestured toward the trees behind Noah with a slight nod of his head. "Your village is no more."

Noah looked up in the sky in that direction. Billowing clouds of black smoke in the distance told him all he needed to know.

Noah broke down into tears struggling in vain to get free. He pleaded, "Please. No."

Lugalanu looked at Noah with feigned surprise. "Again, you beg my indulgence? Well!" He made a dramatic pause. "I must admit, until I found out who you were, I did not anticipate you would be such a valuable treasure. Your friend, however, is not."

A wave of dread washed over Noah. He locked eyes with Lemuel, firmly held in place by the soldiers. Lugalanu nodded to one of them, who reached over and cut Lemuel's throat with a dagger. Lemuel dropped to the ground, dead.

Lugalanu grabbed a mace from one of the soldiers. "Every man is ruled by a god," he declared, and clubbed Noah into unconsciousness.

It was a massacre. Noah's camp fell swiftly, taken completely by surprise. The men tried to gather their arms but a contingent of soldiers and a squad of Nephilim warriors overwhelmed them before they could get organized. It would not have mattered if they had. The tribe had last seen the fearsome giants many years before, but no amount of past experience prepared them for this new terror. The giants' armor was more frightening, their weapons more vicious, their killing more ruthless. If it was even possible, they were *more evil*.

At twice the height of humans, Nephilim could sweep their strange blades like a scythe, cutting through a circle of surrounding enemies. The extra digit on their hands gave them a more powerful grip on their weapons. The extra digit on their feet gave them a wider surface area for balance. The armed strike of a single Naphil shattered both weapon and limb of a human opponent.

At the first alarm of the attack, the tribe scrambled for their weapons and mustered for defense. The women and children hid. The circle of evil titans squeezed the tribal fighters into a cluster, ready for reaping. The captains rallied as best they could, calling out for formation.

Lemuel's protégé, young Shafat, joined the inner ring as the more experienced fighters took the perimeter. Every man faced out toward the circling giants.

For the first time in his life, Shafat was scared, truly scared. Lemuel had taught him well, and Shafat had proven himself single-handedly worthy on more than one occasion with lions and bears. But these were not wild beasts; these were demonic monsters. Vomit rose in his throat and he urinated in his loincloth. It was a natural bodily reaction in the jaws of death. Others around him did so as well. The real test was how you responded now that your body had evacuated the toxins.

He saw the impossibility of victory that was crushing in on him. He saw his fellow soldiers struck down in waves before him. He knew he was going to die. The Nephilim were too strong, too coordinated, and inexhaustible. His heart went weak. He would never see his beloved Shemariah again. They were betrothed. Their marriage was supposed to be celebrated at the next moon. *But it was not to be now*, he thought. He would never look into her true eyes again, never kiss her velvet lips. And he would never have the joy of seeing his sons and daughters grown into families of their own—because he was not going to have sons and daughters. All his hopes and dreams would die with him this day, mere moments from now.

His training kicked in. He pushed his fear aside to focus on the task at hand. True courage seized him, not some fantasy of fearless glory, but the resignation to his duty to face his fears like a man, to act like something he was supposed to be, not like something he felt. He would do his best, and he was best with a bow. He nocked an arrow, raised his bow arm, and found his target, one of the gargantuan monsters hedging them in. He released without hesitation.

The arrow found its mark—in the right eye of the Naphil. The monster lurched back in pain and screamed hideously. The other Nephilim quickly covered their comrade. The wounded one stepped back and painfully ripped the arrow out, pulling its eye with it. It then set its sight on Shafat with revenge and renewed its advance.

Shafat's boyhood friend, Akiva, saw it all and shouted, "Good shot, Shafat! Elohim is with you!"

Elohim *was* with him. He was with all of them, but not in a way that some might expect. Elohim obliged no man life or blessing. He dispensed his purposes as he wished and he did not owe an explanation for his ways. He was the potter and humanity was the clay, as their creation story explained. If Elohim chose to craft some of those vessels for destruction and others for glory, that was his choice. He was accomplishing his purposes for his people. Shafat would trust Elohim to be just and ultimately put the world to rights one day. Elohim only promised victory in the end, not in the entire process. He promised that he would be with them through the fire. This was Shafat's fire of testing, and he shone forth with the glory of refined gold before he fell to the blade of the wounded Naphil. This is the glory of Shafat's victory: no one would live to tell his story, the only warrior of Noah's tribe to seriously wound a Naphil that day, but Elohim knew. And Elohim would not forget Shafat.

The defending warriors were slaughtered to the last man.

Lugalanu's human soldiers went after the women and children. They did not take much concern for the elderly, which was their mistake.

One-armed Lamech and his elderly wife Betenos scrambled to the tent of Shem and Japheth. They pulled the two little boys inside.

Then Lamech and Betenos stepped back out front to protect their grandchildren from the onslaught. Betenos raised her bow. Lamech unfurled his whip-like weapon Rahab. He had lost his right arm years ago, but had worked hard to relearn with his left hand as best he could. His abilities might be sorely diminished, considering he had taken down giants in his youth. But he still had enough strength in him to swing Rahab accurately enough for her snakebite of death to kill plenty of attacking human soldiers. Together, they felled over a dozen of those soldiers before being taken down by a Naphil from behind. A human soldier entered the tent after the boys.

Two warriors dragged Emzara behind her tent. She caught a glimpse of the soldier exiting her boys' tent, wiping his bloody dagger on the tent cloth. Her boys were dead. She screamed in horror and crumbled into weeping. She knew in her heart that Noah must have been ambushed. It was all too coordinated. She prayed to Elohim that her demise would quick, so she could be reunited with her beloved and the cherished fruit of her womb.

One of Emzara's captors snarled, "This one is comely! I want some time with her!"

Before he could even say another word, a javelin pierced him from behind. As he fell to the ground, Emzara saw Methuselah behind him with eyes afire and a maniacal snarl to match.

"Have your time in Sheol, you jackal!" he bellowed.

Methuselah was old and curmudgeonly, but he was no feeble relic. He still had his teeth, and his tactical wisdom made up for his lessened strength. He did not get to be the oldest man on earth without learning a thing or two about battle. In his day, he had been a mighty Karabu warrior, now he was a seasoned veteran.

But he was still no match for the camel that blind-sided him from behind, knocking him into unconsciousness.

# CHAPTER 5

The marketplace of Erech buzzed with celebration. Citizens lined the streets cooking food on grills and drinking too much beer. Men were bare-chested with sheepskin skirts wrapped around their waists. Women wore fabric tunics with embroidered adornments. Everyone stayed out of the street in eager anticipation of the triumphal procession.

In the early days of the cities, when gods and kings conquered an adversary, they commonly paraded the captured leaders, dead or alive, along with the plundered booty, through the city streets in a procession of victory over their enemies. It commanded respect from the populace for their leaders and engaged them in the victory and complete humiliation of the vanquished foes. It was a time of state pride and unity.

The trumpets blew, announcing the arrival of the parade. The people interrupted their banter and play to settle in for the entertainment. Everyone lined the Processional Way, a long wide paved road that ran from one of the main gates all the way through the city and up to the gates of the priest-king's palace.

Lugalanu led the procession in a four-wheel chariot drawn by horses, which had recently replaced his onagers. He felt that the horse was much more powerful and regal. It was stronger, swifter, and far more pliable for domestication. They had only recently been bred and introduced into royalty and military use. Lugalanu liked the authoritative feeling he had riding horses. Glorious in his royal robes, he waved to the masses with a proud arm of power.

A wave of awe rolled through the crowds, keeping pace with him. What helped to breed that awe was the squad of giant Nephilim escorting him through the streets. They marched in complete coordination and created a wake of fear in their path. The ground shuddered beneath their feet. Apart from their sheer height, their tattoos, strange armor and weapons proclaimed them as the demigods they were.

Following the Nephilim, a herald shouted, "Behold, the victory of Anu and his spoils of war! The human tribe who would live as rebels without law and without the gods!"

The cart with Noah tied to a stake, stripped naked and beaten bloody, followed behind the herald. The people jeered and threw rotten vegetables at him. Some of the missiles hit their mark, stinging him and covering his body with a sticky putrid scum.

After Noah, a train of carts carrying the bodies of Lemuel and the other elders of Noah's tribe rolled along. The corpses hung from stakes, surrounded by kindling wood that would be set ablaze when they reached the town square. The people cheered with bloodlust.

The sun settled on the horizon of the cityscape. Inside the royal palace throne room, Anu and Inanna contemplated the dead goat lying on the stone altar before them, its throat freshly cut. They would soon suck it dry of every drop. Inanna worried about getting blood on her elaborate makeup and ornate costume of satin and wild ostrich feathers She set those thoughts aside. The first matter at hand was before them: Noah.

Three armed guards held him, but Noah was in no condition to be a threat. He could not see through his left eye, a black bulge of pus. He had lost a few teeth. So much of his blood had spilled that the court physician had to care for him to make sure he would not die on them.

Lugalanu stood beside the prisoner. He remained judiciously silent.

"So, this is the mighty tent-dweller of the human tribes, Noah ben Lamech, a son of Enoch," mocked Anu. The term "tent-dweller" was a word of scorn to urbanites. It reeked of primitive ignorance.

Noah could barely focus on the deities. He was too dizzy.

Anu continued, "We are familiar with the revelation of Enoch. Are you the Chosen Seed to end the rule of the gods?"

Noah did not respond.

Inanna exploded, "SPEAK, MORTAL! ARE YOU THE CHOSEN SEED?!!"

Noah coughed. He made them wait.

And then he laughed.

The act confused Anu and almost set off Inanna.

When Noah spoke, his voice burned slowly. "All I value is dead. My God, my tribe, my family. You murdered them. And you now have the power to end my life. What power do I have to end anything?"

Noah had given up the fight. Elohim was nowhere in sight. What was the difference between a God who existed and did nothing, and a God who did not exist at all? He resigned himself to obliteration. He truly did not care what happened anymore. "Just execute me and choose another for your foolish prophecy."

"That, my dear captive, is why I will not execute you," countered Anu. Inanna and Lugalanu both looked at Anu with surprise.

"If you are the Chosen Seed, and I kill you, then Elohim will simply raise up a new man to take your place. No, I will do the one thing that can thwart the revelation. I will keep you alive but forgotten. Erased from the history of man." Inanna and Lugalanu listened eagerly for the pay off.

"In the slave mines," Anu finished with a treacherous grin. He nodded to Lugalanu.

"Yes, my Lord and god," said Lugalanu. He gestured for the guards to carry Noah back to the dungeon, to ready him for his transfer.

"Oh, you are diabolically clever," quipped Inanna.

"Thank you," Anu replied. "I must display my superior nature every once in a while."

Anu rose from his throne. He bared his fangs and plunged them into the goat's neck to drink its blood. Inanna pulled off her ostrich feather shawl, so it would not get splashed, and joined him.

# CHAPTER 6

The train of guards pulled cloaks over their mouths to protect their lungs from the sandy wind whipping around them. The desert night made it difficult to see. The five camel-back Sumerian officers led thirty cubits ahead of the twenty bird-men foot soldiers that guarded the cart transporting the shackled Noah. It would take them three days march at this pace to reach the copper slave mines at the edge of the great desert.

A human guard, a fat ugly mug with terrible breath, sat in the cart with Noah. He muttered snidely to Noah, "You will enjoy the mines. The only place more godforsaken is Sheol." He snickered.

Noah held his breath so he would not gag. *Or your mouth*, he thought.

Sheol was the underworld, the place of the dead. Hidden under the pillars of the earth below the Abyss of subterranean waters, it was the place from which no man returned. Many stories had built up around Sheol. A common saying that Noah often heard and recounted himself was, "the jaws of Sheol are never satisfied." It was the farthest one could be from the land of the living. It was where all people, big or small, rich or poor, were forgotten. To say that the slave mines were one notch up from Sheol was not a pleasant proposition.

"HALT!" The Captain of the Guard's voice barely penetrated to the back of the train over the howl of the wind. They could hardly hear him. The convoy stopped abruptly. The bird-men positioned themselves at the ready.

The Captain squinted his eyes in the dusty wind at the silhouette of a hooded man standing in their path about one hundred cubits in front of them. The faint moonlight shimmered through the dust and outlined the lone figure like a phantasm.

The Lieutenant piped up, "Could it be an ambush?"

"Do you see a single place for a war party to hide?" spit the Captain.

The Lieutenant looked around. The desert land lay flat for leagues in all directions in this stretch. They would not reach any rocky areas until tomorrow. Even with poor visibility, there was nowhere for a war party to hide, unless they buried themselves in the sand, waiting to rise up. The Lieutenant considered that possibility.

"Let us dispatch this annoying desert vagrant," commanded the Captain. He led the five camel riders toward the figure.

Noah strained to see what was going on, but the dust and the fat guard both obscured too much of the path ahead.

"What fool would be out here during this contemptible weather?" squawked the guard.

The Captain and his five officers approached the lone man within a few cubits. The stranger wore a loose hooded robe, his face wrapped in shadow.

"You there, drifter!" yelled the Captain. "Stand aside!"

The man stood like a statue, even his robe seeming oblivious to the wind and the command.

The Captain grew irritated. He would not brook insolence from a lone vagabond. "You stand in the path of the army of Anu! Stand aside!"

Still the man did not move. He showed no sign of even hearing the order. *He is either deaf or stupid*, thought the Captain.

The five camel riders circled him, their steeds snorting. The wind whipped up to a new frenzy, as though energized by the unfolding drama.

The Captain gave him one last chance. "What god do you serve?"

The lone man still stared silently from the hooded shadow. The Captain stared back. "Kill him for his disrespect," he finally growled.

The Lieutenant smiled with glee. He had not had the opportunity to kill anyone in a while. He enjoyed the feeling of god-like power that came from extinguishing life. He trotted his camel over to the hooded stranger and raised his axe high to smite him down. He swung his weapon.

The stranger dodged the blow with preternatural timing. He caught the Lieutenant's arm and pulled him from his camel, somehow turning the ax back against its owner and burying it in the soldier's head. So quickly did it happen, it took a moment for the others to realize what they had seen. This gave the stranger time to stand up and slough off his cloak. A paladin warrior in strange leather armor stood revealed. He was muscular, youthful, with sandy hair and a wide jaw line.

The thought cut through the Captain's mind, *What a handsome scoundrel.*

The paladin finally answered the Captain's question. "I am a servant of Elohim, whom you are about to meet."

The men drew their weapons, but could not hold them steady. Their camels reared up out of control, terrified by unseen forces.

The paladin pulled the axe from the dead Lieutenant and flung it through the air. The Captain's mouth opened to shout an order, but the ax embedded in him before a sound could emerge. The stunned, lifeless body dropped from his camel.

The paladin drew double weapons, one in each hand, long huge daggers with a curved hook blade that might be used by a twenty-foot giant. The soldiers had never seen this kind of weapon before. These were in fact sickle swords. This sword had not yet been introduced to humanity. But this warrior was no mere human.

The paladin cut down each of the remaining four officers in four swift moves. Then, with purposeful strides, he closed in on the prisoner convoy.

Noah could hear the pandemonium, but still could see nothing. Dust obscured everything.

The fat guard could not see much either. He belted out, "What is going on?!"

Someone yelped back, "It's a fight! Prepare for battle!"

The bird-men responded with military precision, lining up to receive the intruder. The stranger was almost upon them at a running gait.

The fat guard complained, "It's only one man! What could one man possibly do?"

But it was not one *man*. Unfortunately, none of them knew that.

The paladin hit the first guard and cut him down without losing stride. The next human screamed, "Enemy upon us!" But he was on the ground before he could finish his breath.

The bird-men were another matter altogether. They were in battle mode and they were ready.

They just were not ready for a superhuman warrior to slice through them like animal fat.

The stranger swiftly cut through to the middle of the last of the soldiers, surrounded on every side. They squeezed in for the kill. He held his sickle swords out to the sides. Then with a supernatural strangeness, he began to spin like a human cyclone. The blades became a twirling death trap that cut down every last bird-man in seconds. It was over before anyone knew it had begun.

The paladin looked up at Noah on the cart.

For the first time, Noah could see the source of the commotion. His jaw dropped, and he finally grasped the situation. The stranger was here to rescue him – or kill him.

The fat guard's mind leapt to a keen sense of self-preservation. He drew his dagger and placed it at Noah's throat. "Stop, or the prisoner dies!"

The fat guard had calculated correctly. The stranger was here for rescue.

The paladin did not take his eyes off the fat guard, though he would have liked to because the guard was rather ugly. Slowly, the rescuer set his blades down on the ground.

The fat guard smiled smugly and began to calculate his next move. He relaxed his hold on Noah ever so slightly.

It was just enough. His mind was no match for the stranger's unearthly speed. The paladin grabbed two daggers from his belt, one in each hand, and threw them with perfect timing and accuracy. They hit their marks, one buried in each eye of the fat guard. Anu's servant was dead before he hit the ground.

Noah had been speechless the entire time, in awe of this creature. He could not believe his eyes as the paladin sheathed his strange weapons. Noah had never seen their like before. The rescuer hacked at Noah's shackles.

"Who are you?" Noah asked, his voice quivering from fear. "*What* are you?"

The stranger answered him, "I am Uriel, your guardian."

"My guardian?"

"Yes, your guardian. Elohim sent me to protect you and help you accomplish your calling."

In the chaos of the moment, Noah floundered. "What calling?"

Uriel looked at him impatiently. "Have you forgotten already?"

Indeed, Noah had forgotten.

"The box?" Uriel reminded him. He shook his head, thinking, *This one is just as obstinate as his grandfather.*

Noah's sarcastic tongue returned like a flood tide at the ludicrous suggestion. "Right! The box! How could I forget the ridiculously large box?" he sputtered.

Uriel frowned at his ward. "Sometimes I am vexed why Elohim chooses people like you."

The insult took Noah aback. He paused to reflect. He responded, "On that, you and I agree. Though I would think your attitude is not properly befitting a guardian sent by Elohim."

Uriel rolled his eyes.

Noah caught a camel wandering near him and mounted it. "Well, Uriel, I thank you for your"–what should he call it?–"guardianship. But I have more pressing concerns."

"You do not get off that easily," Uriel said.

Noah whipped his camel and bolted off into the night.

Uriel looked upwards to heaven with frustration. "Lord, why me?" After a moment of thought, he added, "Why *him*?"


Noah rode his camel hard to the cedar forest. Though the attack had happened only days before, he could see smoke still lazily drifting up into the sky from the desolation. He did not want to see the ruin of the encampment, but he knew he had to. He had to face his past head on and let it fuel his thirst for revenge in the future.

As he approached the edge of the camp, the destruction engulfed his senses. His eyes clouded and his throat choked up. Why? Why would Elohim allow this to happen? If there was any thought of him being this Chosen Seed, it was thoroughly put to rest, vanished into the underworld with his family.

Everything had been razed to the ground. The animals all lay slaughtered, or had escaped. The destruction scattered debris everywhere. The only movement came from surviving children, still picking through the wreckage to find anything to eat or to use. Rather than mercifully killing the children, Lugalanu let them survive to be starved or ravaged by wolves and other predators.

But Noah's mind did not stay on the waifs now gathering around him. He barely saw them. He came to the origin of the rising smoke.

He fell off his camel. His hold on reality began to slide away.

The dark vapors rose from the smoldering aftermath of a great bonfire—of the bodies of his kinsmen. Massacre.

Noah stumbled closer to the burning pile. At the edge of the smoldering ruins he saw a burnt linen cloth. A red linen cloth. The dress Emzara had worn when they last saw each other. He pulled it out of the flames. One of Emzara's copper bracelets, blackened by the fire, rolled out. He picked it up with the cloth and wept bitter tears. He murmured to himself the name of his beloved, trying to resurrect her, demanding that Sheol would not allow her to be forgotten.

He looked to heaven and raised his fist in anger. "And you expect me to obey you?"

A child cried out in hunger.

Then it hit Noah. His sons. His sons! He jumped up and ran full tilt for his tents. He arrived at a jumble of goatskin canvas and piles of rubble. He saw a bulge in the tent and ran over, ripping it apart, digging for the truth.

It was the pet lamb, lifeless and spattered with blood.

"Father!"

He thought it was a dream-voice. He looked up.

It was no dream. Shem and Japheth stood a short distance away, shadowed by a bandaged Methuselah watching over them.

Noah cried out for his sons and ran to them. They crashed into each other and fell to the ground in weeping happiness. He kissed them. They held onto him for dear life, a pair of cubs reunited with their parent.

"I thought you were dead!" Noah cried. "I thought you were dead!"

Shem stopped him. The boy pulled away and stood upright. "No, father. We did as you taught us. We distracted the bad men."

"With a sacrifice," added Japheth. They proceeded to tell him the story of their strategy. They opened the back flap to make it appear they had left, and then burrowed into their hiding place. The soldier had followed them into the tent. They had left Lemuel out to distract him, just in case. When the soldier could not find the boys, he killed the lamb. It satisfied his frustration, and he left.

"They were *abonimations*," yelled Japheth, hopelessly mangling the pronunciation.

Shem scolded his little brother, "Japheth, you are not allowed to say..."

Noah interrupted them both. They looked into their father's eyes, expecting a chastisement. But he calmly said to Japheth, "The correct word, my son, is *abominations*."

"Abominations!" Japheth yelled.

Noah gave a sad smile of approval, because it was time for his sons to shed their innocence. They were too young. But he had no choice. It was forced upon them.

The boys noticed the red linen and copper bracelet in Noah's hand. Too late, Noah tried to hide it. They all knew, and none of them could speak. They merely embraced one another and wept again for a loss greater than words.

Young Japheth alone softly whimpered his pain into Noah's breast, "Momma."

Methuselah stepped up to them.

"Father and mother?" asked Noah.

"Gone," said Methuselah. "But they left this earth protecting your little ones."

"Grandfather," said Noah. It was like a plea for salvation.

Methuselah would have none of it. "Fortunately, the soldiers do not suspect the elderly, which is why they did not bother to burn me when they thought me dead. I killed a dozen of the jackals before I was knocked senseless—by a camel no less!"

For the first time since his captivity, Noah laughed heartily. "You are full of surprises, old man." They hugged desperately, an unspoken recognition between them of their great loss.

Suddenly, Noah sensed a presence. He pulled his sons behind him and drew his axe from his belt. Methuselah joined him with a mace. A figure stepped out from the bush.

It was Uriel.

Noah dropped his readiness. Methuselah wondered what the Sheol was going on.

Noah snapped, with a tone of disdain, "How did you get here?"

"I rode a camel," Uriel replied. "What did you expect, I had wings?"

Noah kept trained on Uriel. "I thought I released you."

Uriel laughed. "If only you could. I told you, you do not get off that easily."

"Well, I'll be an onager's uncle," said Methuselah. "Uriel, you old hyena."

Uriel retorted, "Look who's talking, you ancient relic. Sometimes, I think you will outlast me."

Confusion hit Noah "You know him?" he asked his grandfather.

Methuselah embraced Uriel. "Where have you been? It has been so many years since I last saw you, I was beginning to wonder if Elohim was pulling our tails."

Uriel laughed.

Noah said, "I want an explanation right now."

Methuselah said, "This is Uriel, your guardian angel."

"That much, I have gathered," said Noah.

Methuselah continued, "Uriel protected your father before you were born. He was there at your birth."

"I guess you were right, grandfather," said Noah. "I am so hardheaded that Elohim will not bother to speak directly to me. He prefers to use writing on tablets that do not make sense, dreams of old men that do not tell me things, and angels I cannot endure."

"Actually, I am an *arch*angel," Uriel offered.

Noah and Methuselah knew the archangels were the mightiest of Elohim's warriors, on the level of the divine council. But they had never realized just how mighty.

"Well, I guess that explains your ability to kill so expertly, and with such speed and elegance," remarked Noah, mining the moment for further irony. He turned on Methuselah. "Grandfather, you do not tell me enough for an elder."

"Noah, you do not listen enough for a Patriarch," said Methuselah. "Besides, I am old, I forget a lot."

Uriel laughed again. "I guess it runs in the family, does it not?"

The two men could not deny that.

Methuselah knew exactly what all this banter really meant. The time was fast approaching. God had sent this guardian to finalize Noah's calling. The old man did not know how many archangels it would take to bend this stubborn onager's will, but he suspected one was not enough.

They had spent some time putting together a proper shelter for the children. Uriel caught some fowl, and their bellies were full. Methuselah took the fifty children aside, and explained to them that they were going to be taken to a small tribe he knew on the eastern plains near the Tigris. That tribe would then take them to a special hidden valley in the Zagros Mountains to start anew. Methuselah had discovered the valley many years before in his adventures with

Lamech. Noah and Methuselah would meet the children there after the men took care of some business that needed attending.

It was the hardest thing in his life for Noah to do, letting his sons out of his sight after losing them once. It went against every grain of his being. But a deeper grain inside him pushed out everything else.

Revenge.

The children slept and the men sat around the fire strategizing. Methuselah spoke up, "You must not do this, Noah. You would be a fool to assault Anu on his own ground. He is guarded by a host of Nephilim in the center of the city." He knew the Nephilim were offspring of the Watchers, bred as killing machines. They did not die easily. He had taught Noah that much. Methuselah had seen their horrible power when the Watchers first came down from heaven.

Uriel added, "Even an archangel is no match for a horde of Nephilim."

Noah looked at him surprised.

"We are not invincible," explained Uriel.

Noah played with the blackened copper bracelet he had found in the fire. He stretched it wider, as he spoke. "I will fight Anu on *my* ground."

Uriel shook his head, incredulous. "With what army? The entire land worships the gods. The only human tribes of any significance are scattered to the four corners in windy mountains, death dry deserts, and deep forests. And they are not likely to join you in certain death to avenge your personal loss."

Methuselah sighed. He had been right. It would take more than one archangel to rein in this wild donkey.

"Then I will go to the one place where humans have lost all hope in the gods," Noah proposed. The others looked at him, wondering where that would be.

"Where they were taking me," he explained.

"The slave mines? You want to start an uprising in the slave mines?" Methuselah did not bother to hide his shock. Had Noah gone mad with feverish revenge?

Uriel put it into perspective. "How do you plan to assault a garrison of soldiers and guards as one lone man?"

Noah looked at him with an impish grin. "I am not one lone man. I have a guardian angel—pardon me, *arch*angel." He mimicked Uriel's previous accent.

Uriel sighed and sat back with a moan.

Noah finished widening the copper bracelet enough to fit it on his own wrist.

Methuselah found his grandson's plan appealing. "*And* you have the oldest man on earth," he chuckled.

Noah lifted up his wrist brace with a fist. His macabre humor in the face of impossible odds brought the point home, "That triples my odds."

Uriel did not find this funny.

A faint sound started them. The men turned to see Shem and Japheth standing behind them. How much had they heard?

Shem raised Lamech's strange weapon, Rahab, now in its leather case. Japheth carried Betenos' bow. "Grandfather and grandmother told us you would teach us how to use their weapons when it was time," Shem said. "Is it time, father?"

Pride and pity welled up within Noah. "Not yet, Shem, but soon." He had to pause to suppress his emotion. "Carry those with you to the Hidden Valley and when I meet you, it will be time. Now, back to bed."

The two boys trudged back to their tent.

Noah turned back to the others. "We leave in the morning."

# CHAPTER 7

Deep behind the palace walls of the Eanna district harem quarters, twenty women of Noah's tribe tentatively adjusted to unfamiliar surroundings. Some of them had been saved from the attack on the camp to be prepared for the gods. They were scrubbed clean in beautiful pools, and clothed in fine linen and exotic fabrics. But they did not exactly fit in. The expensive garments looked and felt unnatural.

Shazira, a young beauty, made her way over to a fountain to comfort Emzara. Noah's wife sat, softly crying into her reflection in the pool. The lead officer had noticed Emzara before her assailant could hurt her, and had stopped the deed.

"Why are they treating us like royalty?" Shazira asked her.

Emzara looked up at her. The poor girl was too young and naïve to know the evil that was about to extinguish her innocence and dignity. Should Emzara tell her and fill her with additional terror that would only add to her misery? Or should she not tell her, thereby increasing the depth of the young girl's painful suffering when awakened by reality? Either way, she lost.

"They are preparing us," Emzara answered.

"For what, Emzara?" Shazira's doe-like eyes wide, her lashes fluttering "Are we to become servants of Anu?"

"You could say that," said Emzara darkly.

She could not do it. She could not bring herself to be party to the breaking of this sweet girl's spirit earlier than need be. One more hour of purity and innocence was a lifetime to her now.

Shazira might have launched more questions, but Emzara was spared the pain of outright lies by the sound of clacking rods. Someone was arriving. Everyone's attention focused on the doorway.

Lugalanu stood there with his Palace Guards. "Follow me, ladies."

The women stumbled in single file along the dark, cold tunnel connecting palace and ziggurat. They were told to be quiet on their journey and they obeyed. Because of the dark, Emzara stumbled and bumped into one of the guards. He kept her from falling and she returned on her course.

The tunnel soon led up into the ziggurat, up to the very top chamber, the White Temple with its lime-painted walls.

At the top of the climb, guards ushered them into a special room lined with ten stone altars.

Emzara felt sick to her stomach at the sight of them.

The women lined up and whispered amongst themselves.

Lugalanu shushed them with a strong clicking of his tongue.

Emzara stared at the ground, hoping to block the truth of her situation from her own sight. The tongue clicking stopped and a long silence followed. Emzara finally glanced up.

Lugalanu stared at her, unmoving as though in a trance. It made her feel uncomfortable. But rather than shift her eyes away, she locked onto his gaze, defiant and unyielding.

Lugalanu snapped out of his trance and marched down the line of women, proclaiming, "You are blessed to be in this holy chamber. You have been chosen by Anu for sacred marriage."

Shazira gasped. Her fate started to dawn on her. She whispered, "Emzara?"

"SILENCE!" shouted Lugalanu. "You will be respectful in this kingdom. You are no longer wild beasts of the desert. You are now sacred wives of the mighty god Anu, and you will obey him."

Emzara saw Shazira tremble. She was so frail. Emzara knew the poor girl would not survive this atrocity.

Lugalanu continued, "You will have the honor of bearing Nephilim, the seed of the gods."

Emzara held back her horror. From the dawn of time, depraved men had sought to indulge their lusts with imaginative excess. But to be violated by these monstrosities was an evil so deep she could not square it with her faith in Elohim. She had lost her complete family not once, but twice in this life. That was more than most could experience and still maintain a semblance of sanity, let alone faith. But to become host for a parasitic abomination? For what purpose could Elohim allow such suffering? What could he hope to accomplish? Or had the wickedness grown to such an extent that it was out of Elohim's control?

It was too much for Emzara to comprehend. All she could do was cling to her faith in spite of what was happening to her. But she found the handle of her secreted dagger just the same. It was the dagger she had slipped from the guard she bumped into in the tunnel.

Maybe she was created for such a time as this.

Emzara became aware of Lugalanu stealing glances at her, as if he could not keep his eyes off her. Maybe she could slit his throat as well.

His next announcement broke the nervous silence. "And now, kneel before your master the Almighty Anu, and his consort, Inanna, Queen of Heaven."

Most of the women hesitated, unused to such orders.

"KNEEL!" Lugalanu barked.

They dutifully obeyed. Emzara was the last to do so. She stole another glance at Shazira, who sniffled and held back a flood of tears. They locked eyes and Emzara sought to transport her thoughts to the girl, *You can be strong, Shazira. Be strong.*

Shazira straightened up, as if she had heard those thoughts. When Emzara glanced back to the entrance, she saw the towering forms of Anu and Inanna coming her way.

Lugalanu commanded the women to rise and they did. Anu and Inanna strode down the line in their regal attire, taking a moment to inspect each woman. Inanna struck Emzara as brazenly vulgar in her gem-laden glittering outfit and bright pink wig of a mountain of hair. She looked to Emzara as if a man had made himself up as a woman. She looked away from the sight and caught the priest-king still watching her with interest. When she glanced back, Anu and Inanna were examining Shazira. She could hear them in counsel.

Anu muttered something to the frightened Shazira that caused her to tremble.

Inanna appeared jealous of Anu's attention to the females before him. "Do not play with her too hard. Remember their purpose is for breeding."

"Yes, yes, of course," he replied. Then they stepped over to Emzara.

A chill ran through Emzara as she felt the gods' reptilian eyes on her. Anu leaned in and sniffed her. Emzara's blood ran cold. She saw Inanna snarl. Emzara's hand positioned closer to the handle of her secret dagger, considering her chances.

Anu pulled back with a look of surprise. "Lugalanu!" he called.

Lugalanu came running, "Yes, my Lord and god."

"This one is already with child," Anu hissed.

Inanna broke in, impatiently, "Get rid of her, now!" she barked, "and be more circumspect in your choices next time."

"Yes, your highness," Lugalanu groveled. He barked a command and a soldier grabbed Emzara's arm. As he and Lugalanu pulled her away, she could hear Inanna's comment, "Disgusting."

When the three of them were out of earshot, Lugalanu whispered to the soldier, "Place her in my private chamber." Emzara realized her troubles were not yet over.

But she still might slit his throat.

The soldier half pushed, half dragged Emzara through a maze of passages, back to the palace. He finally shoved her through a door and into a chamber. He stayed outside the door, guarding her. Escape was out of the question. She decided to look around to find another way out.

It was a grand regal bedchamber. Large marble columns checkered the room. Exotic tapestries from the Indus valley hung on the walls. They depicted idolatrous art from the East, multicolored deities engaging in unspeakable behaviors.

A large circular bed dominated the center of the room, the extravagant mattress covered with glistening sheets of a fabric she had never seen before. The cloth felt silky smooth to her touch. The decadence repulsed her. Not the wealth itself or the beauty it could buy, but rather the perverse purposes for which such money and beauty were engaged. Elohim created beauty, and mankind turned beauty into an ugly god.

She turned around lost in thought. Lugalanu's silent presence shocked her. He stood watching her from the shadow of a pillar. She stepped back.

"What is your name, nomad?" he asked.

"Emzara, my lord, wife of Noah ben Lamech," she responded respectfully.

He struggled to hide his surprise from her. She had no idea that the man before her just sent her husband to the slave mines to be forgotten by God himself. On the other hand, if that husband was the Chosen Seed, this woman before him was a treasure of inestimable value. At first, Lugalanu's interest in her had been tender, even altruistic. Her mature queen-like beauty and composure entranced him. It was why he could not take his eyes off her in the temple room. It was why his heart had leapt with hope when the gods placed her into his hands. But now, the discovery that she was the very consort of the Chosen Seed himself carried political and historical weight of which he could only dream.

He stepped closer. She cringed.

"Fear not, Emzara," he assured her, "I will not hurt you. You please me."

She could feel his eyes all over her. They were hungry eyes. But they were not the same as the god Anu's. They had a tenderness that surprised her.

"Does this please you?" he gestured around the room. He could see she was shy about it all. "You may speak your mind."

Emzara had nothing to lose. "My lord, how could I have pleasure in the kingdom that killed my husband and family, and destroyed my people?"

*Excellent*, he thought, *she thinks he is dead.* That increased his chances. Of course, his responsibility in killing those most dear to her would certainly decrease his chances with equal weight, if she knew.

"But I saved you," he murmured. It was feeble. But it was only his starting point.

"Perhaps you should not have," she said.

"I am sorry for your loss," he said. "The rule of the gods is not always equitable to their subjects. If you must know, I argued against it. Nevertheless, we subjects must obey the commands of our superiors, even if we disagree with them. Surely, you respect authority."

She replied, "Integrity sometimes requires defying authority." She thought of her dead husband now, and how proud she was to have been his wife. How wrong she had been to think that he was stubborn. She understood now the value of integrity that her own stubborn will had refused to see.

*Yes*, Lugalanu thought, *this is the woman I want more than anything.* He would do anything to have her by his side, but it would only satisfy him if she did so willingly. He knew now he would have to woo her, because force would not maintain her dignity. He accepted this challenge with a heart full of hope. He was a patient man.

"Emzara, I am different from the gods. I will not force myself upon you. I shall make you one of my maidservants. Perhaps in time, you shall change your mind about this kingdom—about me."

Emzara could not believe her good fortune. Her hand moved away from the dagger handle secreted beneath her robes. *Let him think what he wanted.*

# CHAPTER 8

The copper slave mine was a vast circular strip mining operation deep in a canyon on the outer region of the Great Desert. Spiral pathways wound their way downward like a whirlpool in pursuit of copper, the life food of a new age begun by the discovery of bronze. Bronze was an alloy more durable than its copper predecessor, being used in everything from tools and decoration to weapons and armor. It was discovered by mixing tin with copper, which resulted in the harder bronze that would last longer and kill more efficiently in weaponry. For all those reasons, especially the last, gods and kings needed plenty of bronze to build their kingdoms. Extracting copper ore from the ground was laborious work. It required many men to unearth the volume demanded by such rulers. The necessary work force could be met by only one thing: Slaves, and lots of them.

That slaves would come from humankind was ingrained in the thinking of the world from days of old. Uriel hated slavery, and he hated what the Watchers had done to craft a mythology of slavery to support their purposes.

Their first goal was to eradicate Elohim from the minds of men and replace him with their own pantheon. They disseminated myths that supported their hierarchy of the four high gods reigning over the earth. The four were: Anu, father god of the heavens; his vice-regent Enlil, lord of the air, wind, and storm; Enki, god of water and Abyss; and Ninhursag, the earth goddess. Below them were the three that completed the "Seven who Decreed Fate": Nanna the moon god; Utu the sun god; and Inanna, goddess of sex and war. The Sumerians called these and the other gods of the cities *Anunnaki*, which means "gods of royal seed."

Their creation story bothered Uriel the most. In their narrative, the Anunnaki created mankind to be slaves of the gods, and bear the yoke of their labors, to mine their precious elements and build their holy kingdoms. Clay was mixed with the flesh of a god and then spat upon and mankind was birthed. So Elohim's purpose of male and female created in his image to rule over creation was displaced with an opposite narrative, one that carried an irony not lost on Uriel: that at one and the same time, man was more exalted than Elohim made him, and yet that man was created to be a slave of the Anunnaki. In this way, the Watchers built a complete religion of idolatry that opposed Elohim's rule and corrupted the entire human race. The fallen Sons of God could not attack the living God Elohim directly, but they could attack him indirectly by despoiling his heaven-bound image of royal representative into an earth-bound image of debased slave.

Uriel lay on a butte overlooking the mine with Noah and Methuselah. Below them, thousands of slaves lined the spiral pathways with pickaxes and wheelbarrows, endlessly hacking away at veins of copper ore deposits. Dog-soldiers watched over them. The guards were more chimeras of Anu's kingdom, with bodies of men and the vicious heads of wild dogs, wolves, and jackals. Only fifty guards had this duty, because not many were needed. These slaves were broken men, some bearing the weight of a lifetime of sweat and toil, only to die in the dust having been shorn of every ounce of their self-respect. A rigid discipline kept the slaves so busy that any thought of freedom could not gain a foothold in their minds. The slaves worked from morning until night with only enough food to keep them barely alive. Hunger starved any rebellious intentions.

"So, Chosen Seed," asked Uriel dryly, "has the Almighty revealed how to conquer this impossible target?"

"I thought archangels communed directly with Elohim," Noah responded. "Can you not ask him yourself?"

Uriel shook his head. "In heaven, yes. But on earth, we are bound by the limitations of the flesh." Of course, Uriel knew that Elohim could speak to anyone he wanted, whenever he wanted, in whatever way he wanted. And sometimes he did. But his choice of using these vessels would remain a mystery to Uriel.

"Can you die?" asked Noah.

"No. But we are bound in all other ways," Uriel said. "Mal'akim and Archangels eat, sleep, and partake in all bodily endeavors, including pain. But we cannot die like men."

Uriel's limitations seemed greater than his advantages to Noah. "Are you here to help me, or just to irritate me?" Noah jabbed.

"To ensure you build the box," the archangel replied. "I can only wonder at Elohim's disappointment with me now."

Noah smiled. He was beginning to appreciate the archangel's wit.

Methuselah interrupted them, "Stop your bickering, lovebirds. I see our plan. Down there is the pen for the slaves."

They followed Methuselah's pointing finger. At the top of the vast pit was a fenced-in area with gates that housed large sleeping quarters. He pointed at a spot about seventy cubits away from the pen.

"Over there, the guards' quarters. There are not many to contend with." They saw a single earthen structure with a thatched roof.

Uriel said, "You do not need many guards for broken starving slaves."

"Once they taste freedom," Noah offered, "they will die for it."

Methuselah looked at the setting sun. "Slave or free, everyone must sleep."

Noah took the reins. "There is not much time. Let us prepare."

Shortly before midnight Noah's three-man squad made their move. They thanked Elohim it was not a full moon, for the darkness aided their concealment as they descended upon the guardhouse and slave quarters.

Noah and Methuselah slipped up to the guardhouse. Through the window, they could see the majority of the guards sleeping in tight military style rows. They took a couple logs from the woodpile and silently wedged the two doors shut. They found a cart and filled it with brush, pushing it over to one of the windows of the guardhouse.

By the slave pen, a dog-soldier marched the perimeter. He stopped to look up at the moon and suppressed the urge to howl.

The sound of soft footsteps made his ears stiffen.

He jerked around. Nothing but night surrounded him. He was on the back part of the pen, separated from the guard post up front that held his comrades. He sensed something. He drew out his horn and placed it to his snout, ready to blow.

An arrow pierced his throat sending him to the ground choking to death. Uriel trotted quietly past him.

The second sentry paced not far from the first. He saw a figure walking toward him in the darkness. He assumed it was his fellow sentry. He gave a soft yelp of recognition.

The figure yelped back.

The sentry relaxed and thought of relieving himself.

The figure stopped, and aimed a bow at the sentry. It did not register with him what was happening, until the arrow pierced him, dropping him to the ground.

By the guardhouse, Noah finished barring the other windows. Methuselah grabbed a torch from the perimeter and poked its flaming tip into the brush cart. He moved it steadily until the dried twigs sparked into flame. Then he tossed the torch up on the thatched roof.

Four dog-soldier sentries warmed themselves at a fire by the gates of the slave pen. It was nearing the end of their watch and they were all a little tired. The orange and yellow flutter of flame caught the eye of one of the sentries. He looked over to the guardhouse and saw the roof engulfed in flames. He barked in surprise. The others saw the fire. They howled to awaken the rest of the guards. One of the sentries pulled out his horn and sounded it.

Uriel came around the corner of the pen livid with anger. "They were supposed to wait for me," he grumbled. He shook his head and pressed forward silently.

At the guardhouse, the sounding horn surprised Methuselah and Noah. Methuselah turned to his grandson, a puzzled expression clouding his face. "Were we supposed to wait?" he asked.

Inside the guardhouse, the warning of the horn wakened the other dog-soldiers. Coughing from the smoke and the barking of confusion sounded under the crackling of the fire.

Uriel rushed the sentries by the gates of the pen with his drawn swords. He slew three of them before they even knew what had happened. But the fourth was already running toward the guardhouse, continuing to blow his infernal horn.

*For Elohim's sake,* thought Uriel, *he was waking the entire desert!* He threw his sword like a spear at the sentry. It covered the thirty-five cubits and pierced the running sentry. The horn died in a whimper.

Uriel ran for the guardhouse. He passed the downed sentry, drawing his sword from the body without slowing down.

Inside the guardhouse, the dog-soldiers sought in vain to open the doors and windows. But they were locked in. One window remained open. Barking and howling, they clambered out the window single file, only to be speared by Noah. They fell howling into the flames of the burning cart. Methuselah supported Noah with a bow and arrow.

On the far side of the guardhouse, some soldiers managed to break through the other barred window and climb out to freedom, but Uriel arrived to cut them down. He slammed the window shut and re-barred it with the log.

Very quickly, the guards were dead and the guardhouse was a smoldering ruin. The roof collapsed and engulfed the soldiers in an inferno.

Noah, Uriel, and Methuselah walked over to the slave pen.

"You were supposed to wait," Uriel griped to Methuselah.

"My memory is failing," said Methuselah. "Have some compassion for an old man."

"I will not suffer your excuses," said Uriel.

"You certainly took your time dispatching those sentries," countered Methuselah. "Did you stop to pet them?"

Noah interrupted them with a chuckle. "Respect your elder, Methuselah." Uriel as an archangel was a few thousand years older than even Methuselah.

Uriel looked over to see the two of them grinning like griffons. He shook his head, and opened the large gates single-handedly. The three of them walked inside.

The flickering firelight of their torches illuminated a thousand emaciated slaves fearfully wondering their fate. They had not been able to see what was going on outside their pen. They had no idea who these warriors were standing before them.

Methuselah immediately released the ropes that tied the slaves together through metal rings staked to the ground.

Noah stepped forward and spoke like a general. "I am Noah ben Lamech, a son of Enoch. I have freed you from the tyranny of the gods."

Baffled silence met Noah's inspiring proclamation. The slaves did not know how to respond to such a claim. Most thought it a nightmare, others, a mass hallucination. Anything but true liberation.

Eventually, a scrappy slave named Murashu stepped forward and spoke up. "What do you mean, *freed*?"

"You are now free to live by your own choices," said Noah.

Another uncomfortable silence met him.

"We have lived as slaves most of our lives. We do not know how to make *choices*."

"Anu feeds us and gives us work!" yelled another slave.

"We will die on our own," added another. The mass of sleepy slaves began to stir.

Uriel flashed an "I told you so" look to Noah.

"Then join me!" shouted Noah with a strong, sure command. "Join my army to defy the gods and free all men from slavery and idol worship!"

Now Murashu got bold. "We cannot fight trained soldiers. Look at us. We are shades of men."

Another voice shouted from the crowd, "Why should we die for you!" It was more of a statement than a question. The crowd became restless.

Murashu matched Noah's resolve. "We will be punished when the gods see what you have done! Why have you done this to us?"

Murmurs of angry agreement went through the crowd.

Methuselah stopped releasing the ropes. He began to think it might not be such a good idea to release an angry crowd of ingrates from their restraints.

Noah realized a truth about human society: not everyone wanted freedom. When a people willingly or unwillingly become wards of their rulers, they eventually lose their capacity for self-determination. Like helpless children, they actually prefer security in exchange for their freedom. Better the misery they know while being taken care of than the misery they do not know being freely accountable for their own actions. Noah pitied them. They had lost their souls.

Then a big burly man stepped out of the ranks. He had a heavy beard and arms the size of most men's legs. Evidently, he got more to eat than the others. The slaves quieted down.

Uriel stepped closer to Noah in protection.

The man walked right up to Noah, fearlessly ignoring Uriel, and said, "I am Tubal-cain, distant son of Cain."

Methuselah snapped a look at him. The name of Cain did not bring pleasant memories to mind. Cain, the cursed, the man of wrath, had once hunted him and Noah's father Lamech.

Noah's eyes went wide. "Cousin?" Noah had known of his cousins from the line of Cain, son of Adam. They resided in the land of Nod far to the north. But he had not known that they too had become captive to the Watchers.

Tubal-cain glared unblinkingly at Noah. "You say you defy the gods. What of Elohim?"

"I have an archangel of Elohim with me," said Noah, hoping that would say enough.

Uriel mumbled, "Tell everyone, why don't you." It was clearly to his advantage to remain anonymous in his identity and Noah knew that.

Tubal-cain continued to stare down Noah. Then he turned and called behind him, "Brothers!"

Two other men stepped out, and Tubal-cain introduced them as Jabal, a shepherd, and Jubal, a minstrel of music. They were twins with completely opposite personalities.

"You have a nice family," said Uriel, "but not quite an army."

*So, this was the lineage that Cain had deserted for his wolf tribe,* thought Methuselah. *And now, they are our allies. Or at least they appear to be.* Methuselah did not trust them.

Noah and his companions looked around. The slaves were becoming more agitated. Methuselah stepped up to Noah and whispered, "We best leave before they think of using us as ransom."

"Follow me," said Tubal-cain. "I have something you will need."

Tubal-cain led them out of the quarters a short distance away to a cave at the outer ridge of the pit. They entered the cave to see a vast smelting furnace area with a pile of coal, molds, anvils and other metalworking implements. "What is this place?" asked Noah.

"It is called a forge," replied Tubal-cain. "The gods taught me how to mix metals to make them much stronger for better tools... and weapons." He finished the sentence with a punctuated grin. But he had more to share.

"I have discovered something stronger than even bronze, but I have not shown it to anyone. I hoped to keep it hidden until a day that I could use it for great benefit. I believe that day has arrived." Jubal and Jabal smiled. Methuselah was all ears—mistrusting ears.

Noah and Uriel followed him to a table with a large meteorite on it. "Metal from heaven," said Tubal-cain. "I did not have to even smelt it. I call it 'iron.'"

"Help me move this table," he asked. He positioned himself to push the heavy metallic worktable.

Uriel stepped over and bumped it aside like it was a baby's crib.

Tubal-cain almost fell down and Uriel gave him a smile.

Below the table was a latched door. Tubal-cain pulled it open, revealing a hidden stash of weapons. He pulled up a sword made from the iron. Uriel could see that the Watchers had instructed him in the art of sword making. He wondered if Tubal-cain had been exposed to any black arts.

"These are swords. I see your guardian is already a master of them," said Tubal-cain to Noah.

He handed one to Uriel, who grasped it with interest. The angel tested its weight and slashed the air. *Good. Very good.*

"It's more durable than bronze, almost unbreakable. If we could find this ore on earth, we could defeat an army. Who knows, maybe we could even kill a god or two."

Tubal-cain was very deliberate in his words, which did not escape Noah's notice. He liked it. Killing the gods was exactly what he had in mind.

"I do not have an army," Noah said, "but what I do have is a squad of stealthy assassins."

"With these swords, we could use their own secrets against the gods," said Tubal-cain.

Uriel interrupted. "As our near mishap of this evening illustrates, we have nowhere near the competence for such a feat. If you think you can just saunter into the city of Erech, traipse right into the temple and challenge Anu to a duel, you are sorely misinformed and ill advised. You might as well jump off one of these cliffs right now, because that is what you would be doing."

Noah said, "Well, I guess that means you will have to train the rest of us, then, Uriel."

Tubal-cain handed out swords to everyone.

Uriel had known it was coming. He groaned.

"Enough bellyaching," said Methuselah. "It is for Noah's advantage."

"And I thank you for your measured counsel," Uriel replied. He turned to Noah. "What about the box?"

"What about it?" replied Noah.

"This is not your calling, Noah," said Uriel.

"Am I not the Chosen Seed?" said Noah, "to end the rule of the gods?"

Uriel was annoyed, "Not in that way."

"I will end their rule," said Noah, "one by one."

# CHAPTER 9

Lugalanu's dining table was grand, twenty cubits long with a spread fit for a king: a soup of gazelle spleen broth with lentils, chickpeas and leeks. He often ate mutton or goats, but tonight was special: horseflesh. Beef was rare, for there was little pasture land. Fresh radishes, beets and turnips, figs and dates graced the table, as well as the fine delicacy of turtle eggs to compliment them. Royal privilege allowed the variety of breads and bread cakes made from the plentiful grains grown in the kingdom. These bread cakes were offerings made for the Queen of Heaven. Lugalanu and his temple staff ate the remaining amount after Inanna had her fill. He loved them drenched in honey.

Barley was the most common grain in the kingdom, making barley beer the most common drink. Dark or clear, fresh or well aged, Sumerians drank volumes of beer.

Lugalanu drank plenty of it this evening, barely touching his food. He sat all alone at this grand table spread. He watched Emzara and some maidservants clean up the food.

The leftovers would be eaten by the servants, with the exception of the meats that could be smoked and stored for later use. Good food was one of the surest ways to maintain grateful servants. With well-fed bellies, servants would more easily tolerate the fits of rage and abuse that occasionally came over Lugalanu. It is said that a man becomes what he worships, and this was no less true for Lugalanu. He sought to emulate the noblesse oblige of Anu, but often mirrored the emotional outbursts of Inanna.

Tonight, he was depressed.

The object of his depression worked before him, cleaning the table and pouring him more beer. He stared at Emzara's beauty, her regal posture. He contemplated her moral purity. He was priest-king and it was his divine right to force her to be his wife. But he knew it would not be his victory. Thank Anu for the beer. It helped to calm him.

He watched her as she poured his beer. Servants wore simple white tunics, but his personal staff had an added element of decorative embroidery to set them apart. His eyes moved down to her stomach.

She felt the intensity of his gaze and spilled the beer on the table.

"I am sorry, my lord," she said.

"You are beginning to show," he said. It was not true. She was only a few weeks pregnant, and only the most observant would have been able to tell the thickness that was beginning to increase around her middle. He was trying to raise the topic of his offer again.

"I will wear loose clothes," she replied. She completed her pouring and shyly moved to finish the clean up.

He grabbed her arm. He felt her recoil and released his grip apologetically. With a touch of heartsickness in his voice, he asked, "Do I treat you well?"

"Yes, my lord," she said. He had treated her well for the short time she had been with him. He had appointed her as an aide to the Chief Maidservant in charge of Lugalanu's personal staff, Alittum, an experienced, agreeable and ambitious woman, who constantly sought to ingratiate herself to Lugalanu.

Emzara administered the other servants, and domestic chores such as cooking, cleaning, and finances. Though she had been given a new Sumerian name, as were all captured slaves, Lugalanu called her Emzara when they were alone. He sought a connection with that inner part of her that was not owned by the gods. Her Sumerian name was Nindannum, which meant "lady of strength." This name, given her by Lugalanu, also expressed his great admiration for her. Such name references to "ladies" were usually used only of goddesses.

Most slaves were branded with the name of the god on the back of their hands, but Lugalanu allowed Emzara the less popular form of wearing a bronze bracelet with the symbol. He sought to accommodate her personal devotion to Elohim by exempting her from any duties directly related to the worship of the gods or their divination and sorcerous activities.

Her special treatment did not go unnoticed by Alittum, nor the fact that Emzara was learning Alittum's own responsibilities. Therefore, Alittum made life miserable for Emzara, criticizing her every move. Unfortunately for Alittum, it had the undesired effect of making Emzara try so hard that she was already a model servant.

But Alittum was not here now. She had departed with the other table servants.

"If you were to remove your unborn, you could be my wife. You would birth kings and queens from your womb." He cloaked the desperate plea as an alluring offer.

She had the upper hand and she knew it. "Would you force me, my lord?"

Lugalanu glanced at the other servants cleaning the room They studiously attended their responsibilities, pretending not to hear anything said by their master. He waved his hand at them. They instantly scurried out the door.

Lugalanu and his favorite were alone. He could let down his composure. "I do not understand you, Emzara. In this world, the vanquished embrace their fate. Yet you do not." *It was true*, he thought. *The strong ruled the weak, and the weak accepted their station in life as their fate from the gods. After all, they were created as slaves for the gods.*

"I cannot," she responded. She believed in the rule of righteousness as opposed to the rule of power. Righteousness came from faith in Elohim, who created all humankind in his image. She knew this faith ran fully counter to the Sumerian belief that only the king was created in the image of the gods. She would die for her beliefs because life was of no value without them.

"That is what I like about you," he said, almost regretfully. It would only make the victory real to have all her personal strength and conviction willingly yield to him. All the more so since he did not tell her that he had engaged a sorcerer to cast a spell of enchantment upon her to fall in love with him. He participated in a ritual, building a reed altar and praying to the bright Morning Star, sacred to Inanna, goddess of fertility. He made an offering and prepared figurines that he dutifully burned, and created a potion that he slipped into her drink.

But none of it had worked. The incantations, spells, and charms of the manipulative magic, none of it seemed to have an effect on her.

He would continue to be patient.

He spoke with ostensible sadness, "Your son will be a servant of the goddess in her temple." He made it sound as if it was out of his hands and he could do nothing to change it. That was a lie.

She looked to him with hope. "But he will be alive," she said, looking for affirmation of his promise.

He gave her none. Of course, he could simply kill the child, rip it from her womb. He really should do so, because if this was the child of the Chosen Seed, then it was certainly possible that it would carry on the lineage that might bear the revelation should Noah fail.

The thought of these options encouraged him. He felt powerful. He, the human ruler of a city, a mere servant of the gods, might have in his hands the power to destroy those gods. Even though to do so could bring about his own destruction, it was still a power over those gods.

On the other hand, if this really was the bloodline of the coming King, then he also had the power over Elohim to end that bloodline and thwart the plans of the Creator himself. He smiled to himself. He would do nothing, and this would ensure his position, for the drug-like high could only be maintained by the power over choices, and that power was dissipated as soon as those choices were exercised.

The patter of approaching feet outside the door interrupted Lugalanu's musing. A panting servant slid around the corner, and bobbed up and down in a fit of genuflection.

"What is it?" Lugalanu barked, on the verge of one of his Inanna-like fits.

"My lords Anu and Inanna require your immediate presence in the throne room."

Lugalanu sobered instantly and sprang into action. He was out the door as quickly as his feet could carry him. He might hold the power to destroy the gods, but that event would not be today.

Emzara knew this kind of request came rarely, so she decided to risk the danger by secretly following him. She knew that a passive response to her situation would never give her control over her destiny. She had to take chances. She had to take control.

She grabbed a royal canister in order to get by the guards. She stayed just out of sight behind Lugalanu as he traversed the hallways back into the palace area. When he reached the royal outer court gates, Emzara slipped around to a servant's entrance in the inner court. After all, she was a servant. She had memorized the ins and outs of the servant's access through the entire Eanu and Eanna districts.

She stayed in the shadows behind the outer pillars and slipped her way up toward the altar of the sanctuary. She could get no closer to the thrones than twenty cubits, but the acoustics in the throne room were so perfect she could hear every word.

They were already in counsel with Lugalanu when she settled in the shadows.

"He escaped?" asked Lugalanu.

"He killed the entire guard of the slave mines!" yelled Inanna. "Curse this Noah ben Lamech and his audacity!"

Emzara suppressed a gasp.

The chimera bull and lion creatures glanced over in Emzara's direction. They had acute hearing.

The conversation stopped. Anu and Inanna followed the gaze of their throne guardians. One of them moved to investigate. But before it got down the steps, Emzara had slipped behind a pillar just in time.

A servant passed her hiding place, drawing their attention to him. He carried chalices of blood for the gods. He placed the libations on the altar and left.

The gods and their priest-king returned to their discussion.

"Are you sure he is the prophesied Chosen Seed?" Anu asked Lugalanu.

Inanna burst out, "He denied it! You heard it yourself."

Lugalanu said, "He appears to have the protection of Elohim over him."

The incident had taken place a week before, but they only now discovered the escape when their weekly shipment of copper did not arrive. A contingent of soldiers had been sent to investigate. Evidently all the slaves had remained and continued their labors awaiting new leadership. It pleased Anu that it was true after all: men's souls, not merely their bodies, could be owned.

"We can afford no risks," said Anu. "Send the Gibborim. They will find this Noah and they will kill him."

"Yes, my lord and god," said Lugalanu.

He shivered inside himself. The Gibborim were an elite corps of Nephilim, a unit of five highly trained assassins. They could hunt anything and kill it, and they were unstoppable. It was said that one corps of Gibborim had conquered an entire city in the northern hinterlands, killing everyone and eating the flesh of the victims for weeks.

The lion-man continued to stare in Emzara's direction. He had not taken his eyes off the location since she had gasped. With a snarl, he bounded off the dais and covered the distance through the shrubbery to the pillars in a couple strides.

When he got there, Emzara was already gone.

The evening fell. Lugalanu rode his four-wheeled chariot through the streets of the city drawn by muscle-bound war horses. everyone in the streets moved out of the way, hiding in the shadows and locking their doors, but not because of Lugalanu's mighty chariot stallions. It was the five assassin Gibborim that followed him. They were taller than most Nephilim, about ten cubits tall. They were tattooed head to foot, wore exotic armor, and carried their unusual weapons and supplies on their backs. They walked with eyes intensely focused on their objective.

Emzara followed their movement toward the gates of the city behind the procession, in the shadows. She slid behind a water trough as the procession stopped at the gates.

One of the Nephilim sensed something and turned, looking straight at the water trough. Emzara had slid off to the side in the dark of an alley. The Naphil turned back to its mission commander, Lugalanu.

"My Gibborim," said Lugalanu, "on you lies the hope of this kingdom." They listened to him with cold, unblinking reptilian eyes. They were instruments of death and destruction. The king made the seriousness of his charge clear, "If you do not destroy this Chosen Seed, he will destroy you and your seed. Bring me his head."

With barely an acknowledgment of his words, the Gibborim walked out of the gates.

Emzara had found her way to the wall, where she could see the giant fiends through a fissure in the rock. They broke into a run out under the moonlight. The earth rumbled beneath their feet. They were so powerful, they did not need beasts of burden. They were faster without them.

In despair, Emzara uttered a prayer to Elohim. If these monsters of evil were after her beloved Noah, he did not stand a chance. He was doomed. Only Elohim could rescue him now. She turned to find her way back to the palace.

To her shock, Lugalanu stood in her path looking straight at her. Her face went flush.

He stared at her. "You are curious of my intrigues?" he asked.

"My lord, it was my opportunity to slip away from the palace for the night air." She had carefully prepared the excuse. "I prefer to be near you than alone in the streets."

Lugalanu stared at her silently. She thought he did not believe her. Her ruse had been exposed.

"Emzara," he said with a scolding tone. She readied herself for punishment. "You are not a caged animal; you need only ask and I will extend your leash." He stared at her, oblivious to the incongruity of his statement.

She was thrown for a second. Her ruse had worked. He did not suspect a thing. She forced a sweet little smile of innocence.

He stepped up close to her, brushing her hair aside with a tender hand. "You see, Emzara, am I not a reasonable man?"

# CHAPTER 10

Noah and his band of warriors traveled seventy leagues north by northeast into the Great Desert, paralleling the valley plains and avoiding the cities. They found sequestered sand canyons and settled in for battle training with Uriel and their new sickle sword weapons. A labyrinthine network of channels cut through the canyon's sandy floor. Towering walls of sandstone surrounded them, walls almost forty cubits high swept by wind and water. Ancient waters, leaving ribbon-like waves of sedimentation, shaping grooves in the rock, had created the channels. The rocks were smooth to the touch. During the day, the light created a beautiful sight of orange, yellow, and red glowing layers.

Noah picked this location for the specific reason that they could lose anyone who might be after them. Both seasoned nomads and unseasoned travelers had died here, lost in the vast natural maze. But Noah had traversed these canyons in the past and knew them well. He knew them too well. His razor sharp memory both blessed and cursed him. Whatever he saw once with full concentration, he could remember with a detailed accuracy matched only by storytellers and scribes. If he were not the Patriarch he would probably have been an oral bard. The curse of his memory was that he could not forget the details of the pain he had experienced in his life: the expression of his best friend dying in his arms in battle, the gestures of his first wife that haunted him instead of fading away with time. And his superb memory did not help his impatience with others.

The men stood in a circle, gripping their iron sickle swords for fight. Noah, Methuselah, Jubal, Jabal, and Tubal-cain surrounded Uriel holding his double-handed swords in the center. Uriel barked, "Begin!" and one by one, starting with Noah, the men attacked Uriel, using the battle moves they had practiced for the last few weeks. Uriel had given them basic routines of sword-fighting moves to memorize and repeat endlessly. They contained repetitious exercises that drove the men to near exhaustion and boredom. That was the intent. They had to develop second nature impulses for a fight.

The technique was based on the Way of the Karabu, the ancient secret order of giant killers from Sahand. Methuselah had learned these skills as a younger man. He was rusty, being out of practice. But Noah was somewhat familiar with it, for Methuselah had taught him over the years. The other three men, however, were entirely new to this technique.

Several weeks of exercises were no substitute for the kind of seasoned training needed to become a master swordsman. But fortunately, these men were already accomplished fighters in their own right, which gave Uriel some unanticipated surprises. Jubal, a musician, may have had arms more slender than the others, but he proved to work his sword with fluidity and dance that outplayed the strength of the others. Uriel sometimes said that Jubal was a natural born Karabu.

Noah's sharp memory and strong will resulted in excessive devotion to mastering the forms. This resulted in a proficiency that impressed even Uriel. Tubal-cain's sheer muscle power made up for his lack of finesse, and Jabal's expertise with a staff gave him added skills that would no doubt benefit the group in a skirmish.

As Uriel brandished his weapon against each attack, he calmly tutored the men with corrections and observations of their moves. "Good thrust," here, "bad slash," there, "breathe deeply, feet spread." "Sweep more, Jubal," "Stay low, Noah," "Think of the sword as water. Wash over the enemy." The men grunted with exhaustion as Uriel deflected their every blow with a casual agility that frustrated them, making them feel they had not learned a thing.

"Cease!" yelled Uriel. He could see they were done for the day. Methuselah collapsed to the ground trying to gasp for air. Jubal and Jabal leaned on each other for support. "Well, that was invigorating," said Uriel.

"Invigorating?" countered Noah. "You have not even broken a sweat."

Uriel smiled. "I have had eons of practice. You have had only years, and they, mere weeks."

"If this is any sign of how difficult it will be to fight the gods and their supernatural minions," said Methuselah, still catching his breath, "perhaps we had better reevaluate our stratagem."

"Let us talk after a meal," said Noah.

Methuselah cooked a stew of roots and herbs on the campfire. They sat and listened quietly as Jubal breathed out a soft tune on his reed pipe. Unlike the harp, Jubal's personal favorite instrument, the reed pipe was more conducive for travel because of its small size and durability. Jubal valued this little bone-carved instrument as much as his sword. Without the beauty of music in his life, he would die a soul bereft of happiness.

Methuselah watched Noah scratching out markings on a piece of animal hide he had acquired from a carcass found on the desert floor. Noah used some dye made from animal blood with a homemade quill from a vulture's wing. He had been at the writing all evening with a torch over his shoulder. Methuselah's curiosity got the better of him. He tried to take a look but Noah would not let him see what he was doing.

Tubal-cain finally blurted out in his characteristic bluntness, "Noah, do you still want to kill the god Anu?"

"And his priest-king," added Noah. He remembered the look of Lugalanu and his proud assertions spouted at Noah. He was just as guilty of killing Noah's wife and unborn child as the god who corrupted him.

"I told you," said Uriel, "the gods cannot be killed."

"Then I will die trying," said Noah.

"You would sacrifice us all?" challenged Uriel.

"Everyone is free to leave at any time," said Noah.

Methuselah jumped in. "You are a proud man, Noah ben Lamech."

"A beautiful woman once told me that," said Noah. "She was murdered, along with my people, by the pride of gods."

"Would you make your sons orphans as well?" said Uriel.

That one made Noah pause. The one way to his heart was his family.

"Not if my guardian does his job," concluded Noah.

Noah was bent on using Uriel's commission to protect him as a way to manipulate Elohim's help in his quest. Surely, if Elohim wanted Noah alive for his purposes, then he would have to exercise some kind of supernatural protection over him, even if Noah was willing to go to Sheol and back to accomplish his goal. And if it did not mean that, then Noah would rather die and stay in Sheol anyway. Lugalanu had Noah's entire tribe wiped out with his wife and unborn child, and Anu had ordered it, so they must pay.

Methuselah spoke again, this time with pain in his every word. "Noah, do you think you are the only one who has lost his beloved to the ravages of this evil world?"

Everyone fell silent. Noah knew it was a rhetorical question, so he did not answer. He listened.

Methuselah continued, "Do not be so sure that revenge is a meal that will satisfy your hunger. It is more like a disease that eats away your soul. As the years go on, bitterness turns you into the very thing you detest. You begin a blessed man. But when Elohim takes away that blessing, you begin to believe you deserved it in the first place. You blame him and eventually you end up an old bellyaching ingrate without the ability to appreciate the good in anything. And you realize that you are the reason for your misery. You have become your own enemy."

Everyone knew that Methuselah spoke of himself, and they honored his vulnerability with their silence. They all stared at the flames until Methuselah's words of experience sank deep into them.

Uriel finally spoke, "If you want to defeat your enemy, then you must know your enemy," he said. "And the first thing you must know about the gods is that they are not what they seem."

Jubal stopped his music. Everyone sat up and looked at Uriel.

"What do you mean?" said Tubal-cain.

Tubal-cain and the twins did not know of Enoch's visions as Noah and Methuselah did.

Methuselah began, "My father Enoch first told us of the Watchers, the Sons of God."

Uriel explained, "They were in Elohim's divine council. They fell from heaven and made themselves gods on earth. Two hundred of them, led by Semjaza and Azazel. They landed on Mount Hermon in the region of Bashan in the north." The others were rapt in attention.

Uriel continued, "Along with those two hundred, a number of lesser angels or *mal'akim*, the lower messengers of Elohim, also came into the world."

"What do you mean, lower? Are they weaker?" asked Jubal.

Uriel shook his head. "To call these angels lower in rank than the Sons of God is misleading. Mal'akim are warriors who have the wisdom of sages and the power of several men."

Methuselah continued with the history. "Mount Hermon and Bashan have important lore behind them. The name means place of the Serpent."

Jabal nodded. "It is the Cosmic Mountain," he said. "The Gateway of the Gods. Some people say the mountain is also the gateway to Sheol."

"They are not wrong," Uriel said. "It is in the foothill village of Kur, guarded by the goddess of the underworld, Ereshkigal, sister of Inanna. If one makes it through the Seven Gates of Ganzir, they have access to the waters of the Abyss, which leads to the netherworld of Sheol." Noah took note of the connection of Ereshkigal to Inanna.

Methuselah's voice took on more force. "It was in Bashan that the first of the mighty warrior giants appeared. They became kings called the *Rephaim* and they spread out on the land to rule after the Watchers came down from heaven. These Rephaim had first ruled the cities then led their evil minions in the great Titanomachy." He took a deep breath. "They were hunted down and cast into Sheol by the archangels, where they remained to this day." Uriel nodded.

Methuselah continued, "The Watchers set up their rule as gods and began to teach mankind sorceries, astrology, warfare and other violations of the natural order. They have instituted an aggressive program of breeding. They want to create their own paradise. They saw the daughters of men and mated with them to create the Nephilim as their own bloodline. They have enslaved humanity as their servants to build them temples. They have structured their temples to look like the original cosmic Mount Hermon. They even call the temple shape 'holy mountains.'" He snorted with derision. Noah knew all this, but it was new information for Tubal-cain and the brothers Jubal and Jabal.

"What is their intent?" asked Tubal-cain.

"They are the seed of the Serpent, Nachash," said Uriel, "and they are at war with the seed of the Woman, Havah, the mother of all living. They have been effective in their strategy, for Elohim has seen that the wickedness of man is great on the earth and that every intent of the thoughts of his heart is only evil continually. So he prophesied that a Chosen Seed would come who would end the rule of the gods, and out of his bloodline would come an anointed King who would crush the head of the Nachash and his seed. Noah is that Chosen Seed."

The men all sat open-mouthed, looking at Noah. They could have cut the thick silence with a dagger. Uriel turned to Noah and said, "Noah's bloodline is the key to their defeat."

"Then help me defeat these Sons of God," said Noah.

"You will defeat them by building the box," said Uriel.

"What box?" asked Jubal.

"None of your business," Noah snapped. "That is a certain disagreement between me and my Maker. My main concern right now is to find a way to defeat these corrupt deities."

"The Sons of God cannot die," said Uriel. "But they have similar limitations on the earthly plane as we archangels do. Though they are divine, they are created beings, so they can be bound."

Noah stared inquisitively at Uriel. He realized that Uriel concealed much more than he revealed. "What do you mean by 'bound?'"

Uriel stared back at Noah thoughtfully. He decided he would reveal that detail later. He avoided a direct answer. "For some reason, they are weakened by water, for instance. If you plunge them in water, they lose their strength. More importantly, if they are trapped in the depths of the earth, they would not die, but they could be imprisoned."

Methuselah said, "To live forever trapped in rock?"

"Until the end of days," corrected Uriel.

Tubal-cain said, "That would be worse than death."

"And more difficult to accomplish," added Uriel.

Noah sat, deep in thought. Everyone was missing the point in focusing on the mechanics of binding. He watched Uriel like a falcon as he asked, "Is that what you are here to do, Uriel, bind the Sons of God?"

Uriel paused, then nodded. The others were confused. "Elohim is about to bring judgment down on the earth," Uriel explained to them. "Part of that plan is to bind the gods in the midst of that judgment, to imprison them until the Final Day."

"Only archangels can accomplish this binding?" asked Noah.

"It is one of our talents," admitted Uriel.

"Now we are talking," smiled Noah.

Uriel sighed. He wondered if he would ever get this man to build the box.

"You mentioned Ereshkigal is the sister of Inanna," said Noah.

Uriel nodded. Noah smiled with satisfaction. It was more satisfying revenge to kill the family members of your target of hatred before you killed them. "She is much weaker than Anu," he said.

Uriel nodded again. He knew where this was going.

"So, if we start with one of the weaker gods," Noah speculated, "we can work our way up the pantheon."

"Noah, this is not your calling," said Uriel.

"Think of it this way," said Noah, "we are helping you to fulfill your calling."

Before Uriel could respond, a strange bellow in the distance interrupted them. The hideous noise sounded like a beast from the pit of Sheol. The camels stirred in agitation.

"What is it?" asked Methuselah, looking to Uriel.

"The call of the Gibborim," said Uriel darkly.

"Gibborim?" asked Tubal-cain.

"The mightiest of the Nephilim, Seed of the Serpent. We are being tracked," said Uriel. He began packing up his things. "It was inevitable."

"Is there anything we can do?" asked Tubal-cain.

"Run for your lives," said Uriel.

Jabal gave a nervous laugh, and then realized Uriel was not jesting.

"We have to leave now, or you will all die," said Uriel.

The others began packing up immediately.

Uriel turned to Noah and said, "It is probably a squad of four to six of them. We do not stand a chance. If we stay, they will find us. You may face the gods sooner than you expect."

The five Nephilim stood at the southern edge of the sand canyons. The leader of the squad looked down at some camel droppings on the sandy floor. He took a deep breath through his nose, seeking a trace scent. Then he leapt forward into the canyon opening, followed by the others. The ground rumbled under their feet, a rolling wave of evil. They were tall and would be slowed down by some of the tight corners and low hanging formations of the canyons. But they were locked in on their prey, and it was only a matter of time before they found them. Just as the height and strength of the Nephilim were amplified, So too were their five senses, which were acute to an extreme. It was said they could see their target's eyes at nearly 700 cubits, smell blood at half that distance, and when on the hunt, could hear the silent breath of their victims. But they were also offspring of the Sons of God, born of sorcery, that gave them a sixth sense into the spiritual world. They were more than mere killing machines. They were killing demoniacs.

Noah and his men barreled out of the north canyon passage and found themselves at a crossroads. The desert lay before them, while to the east spread the Fertile Crescent valley. They gathered to take their bearings.

"Split up by twos," said Noah. "Take different routes and we will meet at a common destination."

"Where?" said Methuselah.

Before Noah could decide, Uriel pronounced it, "Mount Hermon."

The men looked at him with surprise, Noah, the most taken aback.

Uriel answered their expressions. "The mountain village of Kur, where the goddess Ereshkigal guards the gates to Sheol." Noah was surprised at his change of attitude.

"You said you wanted to start with a weaker god," said Uriel.

Noah smiled. Uriel was on board, but not entirely. The angel had his own agenda yet, for the box. But Noah now felt for the first time that he actually had a chance at revenge. He could not resist getting a dig in. "You changed your mind," he said on the sly.

"No!" snapped Uriel. "My charge is to protect you until *you* change *your* mind!"

Noah grinned. "So if I build the box, you will leave me alone?"

"It would be my pleasure," retorted Uriel. The others shared a smile amongst themselves.

Noah called Methuselah over to him and reached in his pack, pulling out the rolled piece of leather he had been marking on. He handed it to Methuselah. "In case, I do not reach you."

Methuselah unrolled the leather. It had cuneiform written all over it, along with a drawing of a large rectangular box. Noah had memorized the plans from his vision and had written them down.

Noah swiftly mounted his camel and whipped it around with a yell. Uriel followed him toward the southwest. They would try to shake the Nephilim from their trail in the harsh desert before reaching Mount Hermon.

Jubal joined Jabal and they raced northward. Methuselah and Tubal-cain went east. They all had much ground to cover if they wanted to stay ahead of the infernal hounds on their tail.

Tubal-cain mocked Methuselah, "You had better keep up with me, old man."

"It is you I am worried about, fat man," Methuselah shot back.

Tubal-cain looked hurt. Methuselah had got his goat, found the chink in his armor. "I am not fat!" he growled, "I have iron bones!" He kicked his camel and the two of them raced into the desert horizon. Methuselah was glad that this way he could keep an eye on this dubious character.

It took several days for the Nephilim to wind their way through the canyon maze and navigate through the layers of distraction laid out by Uriel. A supernatural tracker himself, Uriel had the advantage of knowing how to set false clues and dead-end trails. He knew they needed the time to gain enough distance before the Nephilim found their true exit point from the canyons.

The opening to the valley where Noah and his men had split up breathed with the sounds of life. Insects buzzing around, crickets chirping, distant howls and birdcalls combined in a cacophony of nature. Suddenly, all those sounds stopped. Dead silence. The ground started to rumble. Moments later, the five Nephilim reached the gap at a steady hunting pace.

The pack leader sniffed the air. He studied the hoof prints on the ground, then scanned the horizon. In an uncanny display of unspoken understanding, they split up into three groups, two taking the north passage, two to the east, and the leader bounding westward. After a short sprint, the pack leader let out his hideous Gibborim call. It echoed loud through the desert plain. The other Nephilim circled back and all joined the pack leader's pursuit.

All five of them were on Noah's trail.

# CHAPTER 11

Alittum noticed the special attention given to Emzara. The Chief Maidservant burned with jealousy and envy, though she kept it judiciously hidden. Lugalanu did for Emzara what he had promised; he extended her leash in the palace and city. Nindannum, the Sumerian name that Alittum used for Emzara, had already been exempted from the cultic duties related to the temple worship, which Alittum thought could only lead to ultimate betrayal of Anu. But now this so-called "lady of strength" had been given more privileges; her own quarters, a personal allowance, and a day of rest during the week, something usually reserved for chief administrators like Alittum.

Nindannum got out of the temple district into the surrounding community even more than Alittum. The Chief Maidservant was saddled with so much responsibility she never had time for herself. Nindannum shopped for the palace food in the marketplace, inspected the fields outside the city walls, and even got involved in trade with traveling caravans from other cities and countries. Nindannum was not at home in this world. Alittum could see that. She could also see through her demure composure. That was not shyness or submission. Nindannum protected herself. And she was plotting something, Alittum was sure of it.

Alittum could not conceive of anything beyond the obvious. She assumed Nindannum aimed to replace Alittum herself as Chief Maidservant. In every way she could think of, Alittum resisted. But what more could she do in competition with this upstart foreign slave? Alittum had submitted her body and soul to Lugalanu. She lowered herself to that of a dog, obeying every command of a soul depraved with absolute power. She let him use her, hoping it would endear him to her. But she feared that it only served to increase his contempt for her.

Alittum wondered if Lugalanu was closer to Nindannum than to her. In some ways his restraint toward Nindannum inspired him toward more abuse with Alittum. She could not imagine what Lugalanu could want of Nindannum. Did not she, Alittum, give him everything he wanted? Yet he treated Nindannum with such respect and esteem that it made Alittum's heart ache with loneliness.

Alittum considered ending her life to escape the despair. Hopefully, Lugalanu would regret his actions toward her. But then she became more constructive in her calculations. She reasoned that the best way to make him sorry would be the destruction of the object of his affections. If she could only eliminate Nindannum, and that detestable child in her belly, in such a way that it would not be detected, she might regain her station with Lugalanu. He might finally see her in a new light.

Alittum's experience afforded her great knowledge of every intricacy and detail of the palace and temple as well as the politics of court. If anyone had the resources to conduct a perfect palace crime, it was Alittum. Therein lay her plan, a plan that would begin by becoming Nindannum's best friend.

As a first step, Alittum visited a sorceress to put a spell of misfortune on Nindannum and to conjure the demoness Lamashtu who could kill Nindannum's unborn if given the right opportunity. She had heard through the gossip of the palace servants of such miscarriages, but had never seen it for herself. Now, she wanted to see it with all her liver, the very seat of her emotions. She had never considered herself an ambitious or vengeful person. She had never even used black magic before. It was too malicious for her personal integrity. But Nindannum's relentless pursuit of advancement forced Alittum's hand. She needed to protect her own status and legacy. Alittum purified herself through washing and oils, and sat through the incantation of the sorceress. She prayed for the utter ruin of Emzara, even as she prepared to reach out to her in feigned camaraderie.

Emzara's pregnancy was beginning to show. She knew she had little time if she wanted to escape this comfortable prison before her child was born and given up to false gods. She ran through all the possibilities in her head. She could hide out in a trading caravan leaving the city. But those were extensively searched for just that reason. So many slaves had tried to run away that the guards had become quite skilled in the art of uncovering stowaways. That was a sure path to a flogging. Many had died from the wounds of that punishment.

And what if she did get out of the city? Where would she go? She had no idea where Noah might be. She would be easy prey for the predators of the desert, both animal and human. She could not do it on her own. She needed help. But who could she trust? Alittum had become much more agreeable in recent weeks. She knew she was a threat to the Chief Maidservant because Lugalanu obviously favored her. But Emzara had fought so hard to affirm Alittum's station and defer her own that it appeared to calm Alittum of her fears.

It had occurred to Emzara that perhaps she should prepare for the kind of opportunity that she did not anticipate, such as the attempt of her husband to rescue her. She had been taught the basic plan of servants' access throughout the temple district, but she knew there was a network of more secret passageways. Only a select few of the leadership, like Alittum, knew the details of those hidden ways. If Emzara could learn those networks, she might be ready should an opportunity present itself.

But then her heart went sick. Her beloved Noah did not even know she was alive. As far as he knew, she was dead along with all their tribe. Even if he was not sure she was dead, how could he possibly discover her whereabouts in the very heart of darkness in Erech? And even if he could discover that, what difference would it make when he was being hunted by a band of assassin Nephilim? They were so skilled he would not stand a chance against them. He would need a guardian archangel for even a shekel of hope. She fought the impulse to cry. He was probably already dead. She prayed to Elohim instead.

When she finished praying, she felt more at ease. Prayers always took her mind off herself and her impossibilities and onto Elohim and His possibilities. She got up to return to her staff duties. A thought suddenly struck her. Whether Noah was dead or alive, whether he would save her or not, she should begin to think of others and not just herself. It might not be to her advantage to seek escape, but it might be to the advantage of others; those who were the slaves of the temple and palace, those who were beaten so badly they preferred to die in the wilderness seeking freedom in death to their own hell on earth. If she could learn the network of secret passageways, she might be able to establish a pathway to freedom for other slaves. She could become the means of redemption for others, a redemption that she could not achieve for herself.

It was surely the providence of Elohim when, the very next day, Alittum approached Emzara and asked to speak to her in private.

"Nindannum, how is your health?" asked Alittum.

"I am well, thank you," replied Emzara, holding her womb affectionately.

It struck Alittum that Nindannum displayed no signs of trouble. Surely, the Lamashtu demoness would have done something by now, even if just to harass her victim. Alittum would have to consult the sorceress as soon as she had some time. She brightened her countenance. "It is no secret that I have not treated you as you have deserved these past months," said Alittum. "I have been intimidated by your poise and presence. But now I see that you are a woman of true character and virtue, and I want to apologize for my inappropriateness, my impatience and shortness with you."

Emzara was shocked. She did not know what to say. "Alittum, I bear no complaint. I have nothing but gratitude for the privilege of being your aide and learning from your wisdom and experience."

Alittum could barely stomach the patronizing flattery. "Well, I think it is time for you to become aware of one more privilege."

Emzara sat up with piqued attention. Alittum continued, "It is of such privacy and significance that only the highest of temple and palace caste are allowed to know of it. I am talking of a system of secret passageways through the city."

Inside her gut, Emzara felt the rush of excitement. Elohim had answered her prayers.

Alittum concluded, "They connect all the main palace structures and lead outside the city as well."

"To what do I owe the honor of this revelation?" asked Emzara.

"To your own character," replied Alittum. "I feel that I could trust you with my life. So I knew that I would need for you to trust me with yours. But you must tell no one, not even Lugalanu."

*Strange,* thought Emzara. *Why would Lugalanu not want to know?* In fact, would he not have been the one to ask for her initiation?

Alittum answered Emzara's thoughts as if she read her mind. "If anything should happen through the use of those passageways — anything against the law — it would serve to protect you from any implication if Lugalanu knew not of your acquaintance with them."

*Could this be true?* thought Emzara. Could Alittum be offering her the very opportunity that she sought? Surely, this was from Elohim! She could not have asked for a more perfect opportunity.

Then Alittum added, "But be careful. These passageways also lead to the secret chambers of the gods, where no human is allowed to enter, save the king."

Emzara had heard of these chambers, but did not know much about them. Rumor said they were places where the gods engaged in sorceries, including the birth of the Nephilim from the daughters of men. The women who were forced to carry these infernal fetuses in the womb were never seen again. Emzara wondered what fate had befallen the innocent Shazira, the girl chosen as one among many to be the vessel of a demigod. Emzara suppressed a wave of nausea.

Alittum continued, "The chambers are said to contain the secrets of the universe. Wonders that humans cannot bear to behold: Astrology, sorcery, magic spells and enchantments. It is said that should a human learn such secrets she might become a challenge to the gods themselves." To Emzara, this seemed more like a tempting offer than a dangerous warning. She could feel a tug in her own soul toward the forbidden knowledge. Access to the heart of this evil empire could one day be used to bring about its downfall.

Alittum had carefully avoided reference to the punishment for such a breach of confidence. This kind of violation would no doubt require the ultimate price of one's life. Still, the focus on the possibilities had its affect on Emzara. The knowledge fed her hatred of injustice and her desire to right the wrongs of her world. It served her sense of significance, that she might be in the position to alter the course of history. It nurtured her pride.

# CHAPTER 12

The Great Desert was a vast hostile territory that would kill visitors unaccustomed to its harsh environment. Travelers faced a lack of water, scorching hot days, freezing cold nights and unpredictable sand storms at a moment's notice. Fortunately, Methuselah knew the terrain because he had been through its jaws in the past during his giant killing days with his father Enoch. They had crossed the barren terrain on their way to Bashan. They had endured the worst of dehydration and sandstorms, and a most peculiar mystical tree guarded by seductive demons. But he prayed they would not stumble upon that nightmare again because they barely made it out alive.

During that encounter with the demonic tree, Methuselah's company had been rescued by a Thamudi tribe that had settled in the region and became allies with them. But they had been on a mission from Elohim that required them to move onward. Later, when Noah was a young boy, the two tribes had met again. Noah had become fast friends with the chief's son, Salah al Din, whose name meant "righteousness of faith." Noah wondered how his former playmate had fared since they were last together.

Noah planned to go deep into the desert in an attempt to lose their Nephilim trackers. Jubal and Jabal would lose theirs by fleeing into northern lands where the new kingdom of Akkad had begun. Methuselah and Tubal-cain would cross the Mesopotamian plains to the east and shake off their Nephilim in the Zagros Mountains, doubling back to meet everyone at the village of Kur in Mount Hermon after two moons.

Noah had not anticipated that all five Nephilim would be on his trail. Uriel had surmised this misfortune by the time they arrived at the Thamudi fortresses.

The Thamud were a mysterious people. Rock dwellers, they literally sculpted their residences in the stone of the buttes. The outer carving looked like the facades of buildings in any city of the plain, but they were in fact entirely hollowed out of the rocks of the hills. The beautiful, huge creations housed a people of formidable fierceness. One had to be fierce to survive the unrelenting brutality of the desert. The settlement to which Noah returned sheltered about seven hundred souls, three hundred able warriors and their wives and children.

Noah and Uriel were greeted by a party led by none other than Chief Salah al Din. Noah's playmate had grown up to be the tribal chieftain.

"Mustafa!" Salah called to Noah. "Mustafa" meant Chosen One in his tribal dialect. Salah never tired of reminding Noah that he had embraced Enoch's revelation and believed Noah to be the Chosen Seed who would end the rule of the gods and bring rest to the land— even if Noah himself would not accept it. "It has been too long, old friend," Salah said as he embraced his visitor.

"How is that old goat, Methuselah?' the chieftain asked. "He and father were as close as you and I."

Noah tried to keep face with proper etiquette, "He complains too much, but he is still a strong arm for me. We all miss Diya al Din. Your father was a great man, and we will never forget his kindness to us."

Salah said, "Thank you, my friend. Our humble home remains your own."

He read their solemn expressions, sensing that something was wrong. Noah introduced him to Uriel and then broke the news. "I am sorry to tell you, Salah, that this visit is not a blessed one. My companion and I are being hunted by a party of Gibborim."

Salah knew of the Gibborim. He knew they only left death and destruction in their wake. But that could only mean one thing to Salah. "If the principalities and powers of darkness are on to you," he teased, "that must mean you may soon begin to accept your own identity."

Noah could not return the jest. He was too tired, and scared for Salah and his people. "We seek only supplies, Salah. And we will be on our way. We will not jeopardize your people's safety. We have our own quest to accomplish."

"Nonsense," said Salah. "Tonight, we will celebrate with feasting, and discuss your strategy."

Noah could not argue with Salah's stubborn kindness. He was too desperate at this point. He nodded. He and Uriel rode off with Salah to the Thamudi fortresses.

The banquet tables were laden with the best food that desert living could provide; crispy beetle appetizers, sand grouse, snake, roasted gecko lizards on sticks, as well as a delicacy of gazelle organs. And beer flowed freely. Salah held nothing back from his beloved friend. But he could see that Noah remained somber.

Salah leaned in close to Noah and said, "My friend, how are your people?"

Noah told him the whole story of the butchery of his entire clan, and his subsequent capture and escape. It broke Salah's heart. His eyes teared up with empathy.

"Tell me of your quest, and how I can be of service to you," said Salah.

Noah explained grimly, "I have decided that I *will* end this rule of the gods, one by one, by binding them and casting them into the depths of the earth. Our first destination is Mount Hermon."

Salah knew Mount Hermon's fame as the cosmic mountain where the Watchers had come down from heaven. He knew it was the portal to Sheol, guarded by the underworld gods Ereshkigal and Nergal. "But I thought only archangels could bind such divine monsters of power and cruelty," said Salah. Understanding suddenly hit him. He stared at Uriel. He had been entertaining an angel unaware in his very own citadel.

A mischievous grin settled over Salah's face. "So it has finally begun. The judgment of God is nigh." Uriel's face was unresponsive. He would give nothing away. "We have a saying out here in the wadi," added Salah. "Let justice roll down like waters."

Noah said, "But first, we must shake these Nephilim from our cloaks, or we will not live to accomplish our task."

"Demigods are rascals," Salah observed. "They embody the worst of both worlds."

Uriel knew this was true. The reason archangels had a harder time defeating Nephilim was that the Watchers' offspring were a violation of the divide between heavenly and earthly creation. Members of Elohim's divine council were heavenly beings. They inhabited the same realm as Elohim, just as humans occupied the earth. But Nephilim were the spawn of both heaven and earth. They fully inhabited the corporeal flesh, but were animated by an occult spiritual vitality that almost equaled a member of the heavenly assembly. An angel could traverse between worlds, but would become subject to the limitations of both. Uriel knew this from experience. But a Naphil lived in both worlds at once. In some ways Nephilim were stronger than mal'akim, but the mal'akim angels had one significant advantage: They were immortal, Nephilim were not. Nephilim could die. That point gave Uriel some small satisfaction.

Salah was intensely curious and had much he wanted to ask Uriel. "Tell me, Uriel, how do you bind an angel or a *Bene Elohim*?"

Uriel looked at Noah, who nodded in approval. He could trust Salah with his very life. Uriel pulled back his cloak, pushed up his sleeve, and touched an armband that looked like it was made of white hair. Uriel unraveled a small amount and let Salah feel it. It felt as fine as a spider's web and was barely visible.

"Hair from the cherubim of the throne of Elohim. It is indestructible," said Uriel.

Salah was amazed. Uriel would offer no more than he was asked, but Salah badgered him with an unending stream of questions. Fortunately for Salah, Uriel was pleasantly full from the meal and more open than usual.

"What exactly is a cherubim?" Salah began.

"Cherub," corrected Uriel. "Cherubim is the plural. They are the carriers of the throne chariot of Elohim. They were also guardians of the tree of life and the gates of Eden," said Uriel.

"What do they look like? Do they look like you?"

Salah's childlike innocence amused Uriel. "They are far more terrifying than me."

"That isn't saying much," Noah jested.

Uriel sobered up. "They have skin that shines like burnished bronze. They have four sets of wings, and four faces. Usually one face is of a human, one of a lion, one of an eagle, and one of the cherub itself. They are accompanied by the Flames of the Whirling Sword, divine beings that can smite anything that approaches their custody. The sound of a cherub's wings alone strikes terror into the hearts of its enemies." It was all so matter-of-fact for Uriel. He lived in the presence of these beings, not to mention the more terrifying presence of Elohim.

Salah had pestered Enoch years ago when his tribe had first met them, so he had a few more loose ends to clear up. "Now, what are the seraphim and how are they different from cherubim?"

"Seraphim are specially appointed Watchers, the reptilian ones, with six wings, that guard the throne of Elohim."

Salah kept right on moving without a pause. "So the seraphim are like the Serpent of Eden?"

"Yes. But the Serpent of Eden is an unfortunate misnomer. The Nachash is unquestionably serpentine in his character, justifying the legends surrounding him as one of the seraphim who guarded Elohim's throne. But he was not merely a serpent. His name in another sense meant 'brazen brightness,' and like other Watchers, he was a Shining One. His body was like beryl, his face like the appearance of lightning, his eyes like torches of fire, his arms and feet like burnished bronze. The 'Serpent of Eden' became a useful allusion, because he had been cursed by Elohim to crawl the earth away from his heavenly abode with the Sons of God."

"Why did he tempt the original pair in the Garden?" asked Salah.

"He is also called *the satan* which means 'the accuser' in God's heavenly court." Salah followed the explanation well. He knew that God's divine council of holy ones surrounded Elohim's throne and engaged in legal disputes of justice on earth.

Uriel continued, "But unlike a just prosecutor of crimes, the Nachash was a liar and murderer from the beginning. He was the father of lies, the tempter and deceiver of God's people. He seeks to use God's lawfulness against him." Uriel had a particular bitter memory of the satan's attempt in the past to sue Elohim in his own court. It was a diabolically brilliant strategy of manipulating legal procedure and technicalities against the Judge himself. But it did not quite work.

"But when the pair was cast out of Eden, the Nachash began his campaign to defile every corner of Elohim's good creation. He set up his parody of the mountain of Eden at Mount Hermon, in Bashan, the 'Place of the Serpent.' He was eventually joined by Semjaza, Azazel, and the other fallen Sons of God to pursue their nefarious grand design on Eden. It was the war of the Seed of Nachash with the Seed of

Havah, and it was for total conquest. No quarter given. To the victor, complete spoils. Their loss at the Titanomachy was but one battle."

"This is a long war not quickly resolved," said Salah overwhelmed by its implications. He remembered tales of the Titanomachy, the War on Eden.

"Indeed," said Uriel, abruptly changing tone. "And that is why we must be leaving. Your kindness is gallant. But the longer we stay here, the more certainly you become marked quarry for the Gibborim. They will not forgive your hospitality to us. I fear it may already be too late."

"Too late, you say?" said Salah. "Good. That is exactly what I was waiting for."

Noah and Uriel were completely taken by surprise.

"Close your mouths, will you? You are letting sand flies in. We have a job to do," said Salah. "We will take you as far as we can in our underground tunnels, which should further frustrate any scent. And when they arrive and do not forgive us for our hospitality, as you have indicated, then they will simply have to accept our hostility!"

"No," said Noah. "You cannot do this!"

"It is too late. You said so yourself," said Salah. "Admit it, Noah, I have bettered you. If you remember, I usually beat you in Seega. Face it, I am a superior strategist." Salah smiled with a self-satisfied grin. Noah grimaced at the thought. Salah was right. Many times, they had confronted one another in that ancient board game. Salah had routinely captured Noah's stones, sliding them off the board with playful jests that irritated Noah to death. But this was not the time for jesting.

"You will all die," said Noah.

Salah turned deadly serious. "Noah, I have waited all my life for this moment. Do not be so resigned to our defeat. We have a few tricks up our tunics. We know this desert better than this mangy pack of spoiled lizards venturing out of their plush valley. Do you still not realize what an honor it is to defend the Chosen Seed of Elohim against his foes?"

Salah turned to Uriel. "Uriel, my sympathies go out to you, knowing how difficult it must be to guard this thick-skulled baboon."

Uriel chuckled, "This is but the tip of the ziggurat."

Noah embraced his friend, the mighty warlord Salah al Din. He knew he would probably never see him again in life.

"Come with me, my friend," said Salah. "I want to give you a gift."

Noah and Uriel followed into a chamber filled with bubbling kettles and pots, simmering over several small fires. Salah showed him a cauldron full of thick black liquid. "We call it 'pitch.' We create it by a process of distilling bitumen from the ground." Noah had seen bitumen pits in some areas of Sumer but had not realized it had any practical benefit.

Salah explained how his tribe had learned that it was useful for many tasks, including creating long-burning torches and for waterproofing boats and homes.

Noah could not believe his ears. This was an answer to one of the problems with his calling. The directions for the tebah, the box, had included covering it inside and out with "pitch." Now he understood what that was.

Salah gave them some small pouches with the pitch sealed in them. "You may be able to use them some day to find your way in a dark place."

Noah and Uriel tucked their gifts away and bid their host a restful night. They retired to their chambers and entered the deepest sleep they had experienced in weeks.

The giants came at night. They did not even bother to use stealth. The ground rumbled, announcing their approach. It was sooner than Salah had anticipated. He was not as prepared as he hoped to be, but they would make the best of it. They were three hundred battle-seasoned warriors against five demonic Nephilim. Could it really be that impossible?

The Nephilim began their assault by catapulting huge boulders at the embedded fortresses. Three of the demonic soldiers held their shields up as cover while the other two jettisoned the large stones into the rock walls, using a sling made from the thick hides of elephants. Within a day, the outward structures crumbled to piles of rubble. Many of the interior chambers collapsed from the pounding force. The women and children moved further back into the tunnels for protection. The men prepared to fight these gigantic hellions in hand-to-hand combat.

The Thamud had dromedaries for their cavalry. Though camels looked clumsy compared to a horse, they were actually quite fast animals, able to run up to fifteen leagues in an hour in a sprint. They were not afraid of battle. The Thamud gave them light leather armor that kept them agile in a strike force. They could literally run circles around the Nephilim to tire them out. It became like a game of tag for them. The limber sprinting dromedaries dodged the lunging, clumsy monsters. The Nephilim would sometimes fall on their faces in the dust. Salah's soldiers laughed at them, ensconced in the stone bulwarks.

The harassing campaign did not last long.

The Nephilim figured out the patterns of the camel-bound warriors and began capturing them and crushing them. The remaining cavalry retreated to the fortress and readied themselves for the next attack.

Salah's forces kept up the harassment and held the Nephilim at bay for days. But the end was unavoidable. Cavalry, arrows, maces or spears could not stop the Nephilim. They eventually wore down the defenses and pushed the Thamud back into the underground shafts, burrowed over generations. The giants were smart enough not to allow themselves to be separated, where they could become victims of overwhelming odds if lured down various cut-off corridors. But it was here that they also made their mistake.

The Nephilim had wounds, but they were used to such minor inconveniences. They decimated Salah's men step by step. A mere forty humans were left, and they were in their final throes. The Naphil leader saw that Noah had not gotten out in time. The fleeing pair had stayed to fight with their desert allies in the hopes of stopping their pursuers. The Chosen human and his irritant archangel were finally cornered with the Thamud in a last stand cavern carved out of the desert rock. They stood in the center of the contingent guarding them with their lives, lives that would soon be extinguished.

Salah's captain noticed that there were only four Nephilim. Had they separated after all? It struck him immediately. They must have sent a scout to find the tunnel exit. He screamed at the top of his lungs, "THE EXIT! GET NOAH OUT!"

It was too late. The fifth Naphil came through the cave exit, dragging the bodies of guards he had killed. He screamed the war cry of the Gibborim. The men were trapped. There was no escape. They would have to fight to the last man and pray their deaths would be quick.

This close to the source, the lead Naphil could smell Noah's scent. It attacked and split the human unit in half, grabbing Noah and Uriel within mere seconds. The leader pulled back the stinking cloak.

It was not Noah or Uriel, but in fact Salah and his Captain wearing the prey's clothes. The Naphil screeched in anger. They had been deceived!

Salah laughed triumphantly and yelled his command to his soldiers. They waited at the key brick buttresses. At the signal, they released their latches. A series of cascading collapses brought down the entire ceiling, caving in on their heads. Every last one of them, human and Naphil, were covered in a grave of rock and sand that no living thing could survive.

The Thamud had sacrificed themselves to stop the Nephilim.

# CHAPTER 13

Emzara learned the network of secret passageways below the temple district and city with the patient help and support of Alittum. It was a complex system, like a spider web, with intersecting hallways, and dead end tributaries. An uninformed traveler of the passages would get seriously lost without proper directions.

She thought of her beloved Noah and how he would be proud of her, if he knew what she planned. She was nearing her child's birth. She became more heartsick for her child at the thought of birthing him without his father present. She prayed to Elohim that her child would not be raised within this wicked culture of idolatry. Lugalanu's statement about the child's temple devotion haunted her. It would be a fate worse than death to see her son in the grip of these despicable false gods. If only her beloved knew she was still alive. The fact that the Gibborim had not returned was a good sign. At the least, it meant that Noah was still alive because they had not caught him. Or, by the grace of Elohim, could he have killed them? She wanted to figure out some way to let him know she was alive, but she felt it could distract him from his own survival. That was more important to her right now.

She had always believed he was the Chosen Seed, but she was also a dutiful wife and would give her true opinion only when consulted. Her biggest influence in persuading Noah was in prayer. When Noah was blinded by his own stubbornness, she would ask Elohim to soften his heart. Elohim had a way of opening Noah's eyes better than anyone else could. She did not believe that Elohim had abandoned them. She was sure he was planning something very significant to make his point. It would take something big to transform Noah to accomplish his calling. Elohim was like that. Meanwhile, she would focus on making the best of her own situation for the glory of her God.

One day, Emzara asked Alittum how long it would take for guards to seek out a missing palace or temple slave. She couched it in the context of doing bookkeeping of staff numbers, but Alittum knew in that moment that Nindannum planned to help runaway slaves.

Alittum marveled at this in her thoughts. So that was her intention! Help disgruntled slaves who sought their freedom to escape. It was shamefully egalitarian of Nindannum and proved her lack of royal blood and culture. What fool would risk her life to die in the howling desert, when the kingdom would care for their every need? The gods required minimal devotion, and for what higher purpose would the peasants live in the wild? Themselves? Alittum found it laughable. Uncivilized folk needed to be molded and shaped by the noble class to know their station in life, otherwise they degenerate into this kind of decadent thinking. Alittum now had the opportunity that none of her useless spells and enchantments against Nindannum seemed to be able to achieve. Or was this the actual fruit of her magic?

Alittum encouraged Emzara in her fondness toward slaves. One day, Alittum "let out" the secret that she sometimes wished she could help slaves to freedom. Emzara took the bait and they quickly established an underground pathway to freedom. Emzara now trusted Alittum. But Alittum knew that she had to seal Emzara's confidence by volunteering to be the first to deliver slaves through their new arrangement.

Emzara and Alittum carefully chose their first two beneficiaries. One, a male slave in the palace named Daduri had been beaten mercilessly for incompetence. He had lost an eye and was in the infirmary, but had healed sufficiently to travel. The other was a twelve-year old female named Humusi, recently captured and appointed to be a temple slave. She was so defiant that the priestesses left her alone, until she could have a session with Inanna that would set her straight. What Inanna did in those disciplinary sessions Alittum did not know, but the rumors were ugly.

On the planned day of escape, Lugalanu noticed that Alittum and Emzara were acting skittish. He wondered if they were hiding animosity toward each other. Overwhelmed with royal edicts and law court rulings, he lost his temper with Alittum over a petty administrative detail. He grounded her to her chambers. He would visit her later and have his way with her. Of course he would envision Emzara in her place, but that would be of no consequence to Alittum. She was so needy and desperate for his love, that anything he gave her would be consumed like a crumb of food by a starving dog.

He pitied Alittum. She had no soul left to give any man, least of all him. But she was a good head-maidservant, and she did satisfy his more depraved fantasies. He decided not to replace her as Chief Maidservant with Emzara just yet.

The two women prepared their scheme. Alittum decided she would follow through with their plans, because Lugalanu was so caught up with his business that he would not even consider talking to Alittum for another day. He would probably forget that he even sent her to her chambers. In fact, this would make her more able to disappear through the passageways. She would not be missed if she was serving out her punishment.

The women did not anticipate Lugalanu's own plans.

While Emzara administered the household services, Lugalanu snuck into Alittum's chambers looking for her. Her chambermaid was alone in the room. Although the girl did not know exactly where Alittum was, a beating released enough information for Lugalanu to realize something was deeply amiss.

Alittum had prepared Daduri and Hamusi with some foodstuffs and tools for their trek out in the wilderness, once they were outside the city limits. They had taken one of the tunnel routes that led to just outside the palace walls, but they had gotten lost. Once they found their way again, Alittum kissed them and bid them good luck. She wondered how she could ever actually believe in this kind of ludicrous rebellion. Nindannum must have been possessed by evil spirits to think this was goodness. Alittum considered consulting an exorcist when she returned.

She returned from her secret passage into her chamber A fuming Lugalanu greeted her. A beaten Daduri and Hamusi lay at his feet in shackles.

"Alittum, how could you?" said Lugalanu. "What evil spirit has possessed you to do such a thing?"

The irony struck Alittum, making her flounder in her response. "My lord, I can explain. This is not what it appears to be."

"You are not what you have appeared to be," he spit out. "Is this what you have secretly pursued all these years? After all I have given you; my body, my soul, my trust, *this* is how you return my graces?"

"My lord," she cried. She wanted to tell him all about her plan, all about Nindannum and how this was just an act to expose Nindannum for what she was. It was too late.

He pulled out his dagger and drew near to her. He covered her mouth with his left hand, and gently slid the blade into her.

She dropped to the floor in pain, angrier at her own stupidity than with anything he had done to her all those years.

*It is just as well*, she thought. *I deserved it anyway.*

She slipped into oblivion.

Lugalanu found Emzara working on the dinner meal for the temple staff. He walked up to her with lifeless eyes. "Alittum is gone. After you birth your child, you shall be Chief Maidservant." Emzara saw his blood soaked shirt and stood in shock as Lugalanu walked away.

# CHAPTER 14

Mount Hermon was located in the northwest of the Fertile Crescent at the end of the Sirion mountain range. It was the area of Bashan, the "Place of the Serpent," near the Jordan River. It was the cosmic mountain where the Sons of God, the Watchers, came down from heaven. On its southernmost base lay the mountain community of Kur, dedicated to Ereshkigal, goddess of the underworld. Her temple, a ziggurat platform, was embedded into the slope of the mountain, with little more than the front face visible to the public. The mighty giant kings, the Rephaim, had built the temple and city, leaving it an oversized architectural wonder that dwarfed the inhabitants and worshippers.

It was evening and torches lit the temple for a display of glowing splendor in the midst of a pitch-black night. Priests blew long horns from within secret openings on the ziggurat to summon the people of the region for sacrifice. An unmistakable, deep reverberation penetrated to the very core of the soul and drew the people from leagues around. They came from all the outlying areas of Bashan to participate in the sacrifice. Entire extended families of multiple generations, carrying their torches, created a river of fires pouring into the temple complex. They camped in the nearby fields and gathered around the base of the temple for the liturgy.

Noah and Uriel could remain anonymous in the masses of this large congregation. Noah had allotted the passage of two moons for the six of his company to eventually convene at this location. Because the Gibborim had all gone after Noah and Uriel, that pair had been delayed. It was already the third new moon. They looked for their comrades in the teeming throng, but they were nowhere to be found. Noah wondered if the men had made it, or if they had given up, or if they had been captured by the gods of the city. The look of this bestial mob did not bode well for any positive option.

They tied up their camels inside the edge of the forest line near the temple, for their getaway.

They looked up at the sole stairway of brick that rose seventy cubits upward to the top temple chamber. On the chamber ledge sat a huge bronze statue of a seated Ereshkigal with her arms open to receive sacrifice. It loomed over a large fire pit called the *tophet* or "burning place."

They could see the ridge just below the altar, lined with a hundred parents and infants in their arms. They could also see the parents scratching the names of their children on the stone walls, to join the thousands that had accumulated over the years.

Uriel leaned in and whispered to Noah, "Inside the mountain temple is the entrance to the Seven Gates of Ganzir, the Gateway to Sheol."

The long horns blew again, summoning a line of hairless shaven priests with small cylindrical drums just below the line of parents and children. They pounded the drums in unison creating the sound of an amplified beat that signaled the dance.

The crowd below began to sway to the beat at first, and then slowly broke down into individual dancing, which further degenerated into erotic jerking spasms and snake-like body waves. It was as if their bodies had been taken over by another force.

It disgusted Noah.

Uriel reminded Noah to keep his look toward the temple mount. Otherwise they would be noticed. Noah found it difficult. Noah and Uriel wore cloaks to cover their weapons and maintain anonymity, as well as hide their repulsion with the debauchery of the masses around them.

On the temple mount, two priestesses with elongated skulls, exotic ornamented robes, and fully tattooed bodies approached the line of parents and children. In most cases, it was only one parent, a mother or father holding their infant, with an occasional pre-teen next to them. They were led up the small stairway to the temple mount.

A figure came out of the shadows of the temple columns completely covered in a hooded robe. The figure stood on the ledge in full sight of the people. Two priestesses stood beside it and pulled off the cloak to reveal the high priestess. The crowd cheered. Unlike the other priests and priestesses, she maintained long, flowing hair with an ornate headdress indicating royalty. She covered her fully tattooed body with jewels, necklaces, bracelets, rings and piercings.

The high priestess walked over to the fire pit. High, hot flames leapt out of it, licking the night air. The priestesses led the line of worshippers to the high priestess.

The first woman held her infant and began to cry. She reluctantly placed the infant, not two years old, into the hands of the two priestesses. They gave the crying child to the high priestess. She turned to the flames and held the baby high over her head. The crowd below went silent.

Noah shivered. It was eerie. The priestess controlled their very souls.

Her booming voice echoed down the steps of the ziggurat. The acoustics magnified the sounds with a supernatural vitality.

"Ereshkigal, mighty goddess of the underworld, we call you forth!"

The crowd responded with chanting, "Ereshkigal! Ereshkigal! Ereshkigal!"

Noah's eyes stayed locked on the infant held high above the flames. The chanting made him sick to his stomach. A tide of hatred rose within him. He could not let this happen. He grabbed the hilt of his sword.

Uriel stopped him. "We cannot stop this, Noah. Remember, these people are not forced. This idolatry is freely chosen."

He was right, of course. Mankind chose this. They chose to worship these gods and violate the natural order, the natural separation of things, the separation of heaven and earth. Ever since the murder of Abel by his brother Cain, the heart of man grew more and more desperately wicked and their sins grew more unspeakable. Noah's tribe was among the few groups of true humanity that did not imbibe in such monstrosities.

Noah released his sword hilt.

He noticed a little girl, not yet seven years old, watching him with curiosity. She stared at him with large eyes, while holding her father's hand. The father and mother stared enthralled at the altar above them.

The crowd continued the possessed chanting. "Ereshkigal! Ereshkigal! Ereshkigal!"

The surrendered infant cried, but its tiny voice was drowned out by the bloodthirsty mob. Noah dreaded what was going to happen next: abominable sacrifice. He closed his eyes tight. He could not bear to watch. The roar of the mob swelled around him. He opened his tear-filled eyes, trying with all his might not to weep.

The line of parents began handing their offspring over one by one for the slaughter of the innocents. As the people below grew disinterested with the repetition, they became more focused on themselves, and their dancing soon turned more wild and chaotic.

The little girl caught Noah's eye again. She stared at him as if she knew he did not belong here. He knew that she could see his eyes were not dry.

She smiled. He smiled back, but he could not hold it for long. He knew that one day it might be her fate to be led up those stairs. This little child with all her life before her, all her hopes and dreams, would be snuffed out, her innocent life burned from her body.

The drone of the long horns signaled the next sequence of events. Everyone's attention returned to the high platform. A young girl had been brought to the high priestess by two deformed dwarves and placed on the hands of the large bronze statue. She was laid down and held in place at her head and feet by the two misshapen creatures.

Uriel leaned in again toward Noah and whispered, "It comes."

Seconds after he spoke, a loud bellowing sound came from the fiery pit. A flock of bats scattered into the sky.

Out of the flames rose a Watcher, a Shining One like Anu, but with leathery reptilian wings. It burst out of the pit and into the sky like a creature bursting out of water for air. It wore the horned headdress of deity on its elongated head, and like Inanna was androgynous in appearance, though female in dress.

Uriel confided to Noah, "Ereshkigal, our target."

The multitude around them grew delirious with worship. Ereshkigal landed on the ground and hissed at the people below. They responded with cheers. Her wings spread out in glory as she stood over the child with coldblooded focus. She bared her fangs and feasted on her innocent blood.

Again the mob erupted with approval. Again, the long horns wailed.

Noah did not notice that the father had let go of the hand of the little girl watching him. The father and mother had become engrossed in worship. The girl drifted away from them toward Noah and Uriel.

But it was too late for her to find them.

Noah and Uriel made a hasty retreat. Their plan had been to corner Ereshkigal with distraction so Uriel could get close enough to bind the subterranean goddess. But none of their men were here. They might not get another chance like this for some time, because the goddess did not crawl out of her pit but once every new moon.

A figure stepped into their path and blocked them. Noah and Uriel poised to draw swords.

It was Methuselah, and he was angry.

"Your choice of location for hiding your camels was juvenile and pathetic. You might as well trumpet your presence to the goddess." Noah and Uriel glanced at each other like rebuked children. Methuselah finished, "And you are very late. The men are over there now."

Noah and Uriel followed the disgruntled Methuselah back to their secreted camels in the bush.

They were greeted first by Tubal-cain. "It is good to see you alive, cousin. We wondered if the Gibborim had followed you, since we never saw them on our trail."

They embraced. "It is a long story," Noah said.

Uriel smiled at the irony. They were stronger together than apart, and he would never let them separate again.

Uriel cut short their celebration, "It is only a matter of time before the Gibborim find us."

Methuselah chimed in, "The sooner we bind this abomination in the depths of the earth, the better."

"But how do we do it?" asked Tubal-cain.

"That has just become complicated," said Noah. He explained the plan he and Uriel had prepared, the need to catch the goddess unaware during sacrifice. They would have a long wait until the next moon, but there was nothing else they could do. She would not come out for another month. They certainly could not storm her gates with their paltry six-man hit squad.

Jubal and Jabal, ever the positive duo, spoke up. Jubal said, "But that will give us more time to plan and consider all possibilities." Jabal jumped in without hesitation, "Will we not need more time to find a crevice to cast her into the earth?"

"Yes," said Methuselah, ever the pessimist. "We may need more time than we have. It is easier said than accomplished."

"No," interrupted Noah, "we cast her into Sheol."

The men looked at Noah with surprise.

"She guards the gates of the Abyss to Sheol," said Noah. "Let us kick her into that crevice and let it keep her."

The men looked at each other, perplexed. They wondered if there was a single one of them that would support that death march.

Uriel did not calm their fears. "We must be careful not to follow her in," he said, "The dead who descend never return."

"What of the living?" asked Tubal-cain.

Uriel sighed. His hesitation only made matters worse. "The shades of the dead would eat the living," he answered, punctuating their doom, "eternally."

A pall fell over the group.

"Well," countered Methuselah with dripping sarcasm, "if that is not just the future I have sought for all these years, I do not know what is. Being eaten alive forever and ever."

Jubal and Jabal gulped. Tubal-cain stared off into oblivion.

Noah would have none of it. All he wanted was revenge. He had lost everything and had nothing more to lose, except the one thing that held barely by a thread in his heart: faith. He spoke with the confidence of an archangel, "Well, then, let us avoid Sheol—and go trap ourselves a god. At least we have plenty of time to prepare."

The men gathered their courage together.

The little girl Noah had seen in the crowd surprised them. She had wandered away from her parents and had followed Noah into the bush. She stood staring at them, as surprised as they were. She glanced fearfully behind her to see if she had been followed. She had not been.

Tubal-cain started to pull his sword by impulse.

Noah stopped him. "I know this little one," Noah said.

"She looks afraid," said Methuselah.

"Poor innocent child," said Noah. He realized he now had a bigger dilemma than when they had arrived. They could not leave this waif alone to die at the hands of her parents and their murderous idolatry. She was not a faceless part of the indiscriminate masses to him. She was an individual child with a soul, who apparently knew her destiny and was silently crying out for his help. But they could not take her with them. They were on a deadly journey. She would slow them down and become a liability to their higher purpose. It would take at least one man to watch over her, and that was one less warrior in the heat of combat with the minions of hell.

Noah was about to deliberate with his men, when his decision was made for him.

The child screamed at the top of her lungs, "EVIL MEN! EVIL MEN!" and ran back out into the crowd.

Noah's team scrambled.

A dozen men from the crowd ran past the girl toward where she pointed. She continued to scream, "OVER THERE! EVIL MEN! EVIL MEN!"

The first of the rushing worshippers broke through into the trees. They were taken out with a volley of arrows from Noah's band.

"What do we do now?" yelled Tubal-cain. There would be others right behind them in seconds.

"Change of plans," said Noah. "On your camels! Follow me!"

In a flash, Noah was upon his mount. The others followed suit. Noah burst through the brush directly out into the enemy's midst, surprising them. His men followed him like a pride of lions on the hunt.

The worshippers did not know what was happening. The crowd parted in fear as the men raced headlong into the masses. The people just wanted to get out of the way of a stampede of dromedaries trampling everyone in their path.

Noah led the stampede through the thinning crowd right up to the temple steps.

The long stairway to the heavens rose upward seventy cubits of stone. His men now knew what he planned. There was no time to consult. They followed him dutifully. By the time anyone in the crowd understood that these riders were hostile, Noah's raiding party was almost to the top of the ziggurat.

Below them, men yelled for arms and began climbing the long flight of stairs.

At the top of the temple mount, the humans scattered. The priests cowered.

Ereshkigal was already gone, disappeared back into the fire pit.

Methuselah yelled above the growing din, "I thought we were supposed to be secret about this!"

"Dismount!" yelled Noah, and the men obeyed. Noah walked up to the pit of flames and peered in, Uriel by his side.

"What is he doing?" Tubal-cain asked.

Methuselah replied, "The same thing he has done all his life, since he was a boy, rushing in before the angels!"

Methuselah looked back down the steps. The sight reminded him of a swarm of angry fire ants streaming up the stairway, almost upon them.

The men gathered around Noah.

Noah looked to Uriel. "Is this the entrance to Sheol?" he asked.

"No," said Uriel, "to Ereshkigal's lair. Sheol is deeper."

"Good. That buys us time," said Noah, and he jumped.

Methuselah turned just in time to see Noah disappear into the flames. "NOAH!" he screamed, too late.

Uriel followed Noah. Unthinking, Methuselah followed Uriel.

The first of the mad mob reached the top and were upon them. Tubal-cain plowed down the first few attackers. Jubal and Jabal did not think it through. They ran and leaped into the flames, disappearing from view. Tubal-cain fought on all alone, with a growing swarm of angry idolaters circling him, pressing in, the flames at his back. Tubal-cain muttered a prayer, "Elohim, I trust in you. Noah, I am not so sure of, but please have mercy on my ignorance."

Tubal-cain turned, and bolted for the open pit. He leapt into the fire, closing his eyes. He passed through the wall of flames, only an instant of sheering heat. The next moment, he struck a floor and rolled to break his fall. He took stock for a moment to make sure he was still alive, could still feel pain. He rubbed his knee, bruised from the fall. He was alive with pain. He looked up into the eyes of Methuselah, who stood smiling down on him.

Methuselah mocked, "Nice of you to join us, hippopotamus. I was not sure you could make the jump."

Tubal-cain looked around. They were on a large outer ledge that encircled the flames rising in the center of the pit. The fire obscured the presence of the ledge from those above. Tubal-cain got up and drew his sword, looking back up through the flames.

"Do not fret yourself, cousin," said Noah, "They will not follow us into the pit of sacrifice."

"No, they will not. Who would be so foolish as to do that?" quipped Methuselah.

Tubal-cain grinned at him. "I do believe you peed your tunic, you old grizzled lizard. How is your bladder doing?"

Methuselah looked down, "I did not pee my tunic!" The men chuckled.

"Enough, you lovebirds," Noah chuckled. "Let us keep moving." He set the tone for this band of warrior poets, and they followed. He drew his weapon; they drew theirs. They followed him cautiously around the ledge to an entranceway on the other side of the flames.

The carved stone ledge gave way to a long portico of marble floors lined with pillars on both sides, twenty cubits wide and a hundred cubits long. Torches lit the way to the end, where a set of large wooden gates inlaid with brass bid them stay away. So they moved forward.

They inched cautiously toward the gates.

Noah whispered to Uriel, "Is this the first of the Seven Gates of Ganzir?"

Uriel didn't reply, all his senses honed on surveying their environment.

When they had covered half the distance, they heard a distinct rattling sound, then soft scraping of claws on a marble floor. They stopped. Something hid behind the pillars. Some *things*. All around them.

"Draw together," Noah commanded. They did so, blades out, ready for anything.

The shadows moved from behind the pillars on both sides of them. Strange creatures stepped out into sight, but they did not attack. The men could now see their stalkers. They were scorpion-men. Monstrosities with the upper torsos of human soldiers, and the lower bodies of man-sized scorpions, they were armed with bladed weapons and ready tail stingers.

Noah and his men were surrounded. Their hands tightened on their weapons, glancing around, waiting for the first move.

The scorpion-men did not attack. They were waiting.

Noah thought to himself, *What more abominable creatures could these Watchers create? What kind of sorcery enabled them to produce such demonic crossbred mongrels like these? The bird-men soldiers, the lion-men and bull-men guardians, the Nephilim as well, all were unnatural violations of the created order. What was the plan of these Watchers?*

Suddenly, the huge doors at the end of the portico creaked open. Everyone's attention shot to two large beings about five and a half cubits tall gliding through the doors. It was Ereshkigal. The second Watcher stayed by the door as Ereshkigal strode toward Noah and Uriel. The shining being kept her wings taut behind her back and stood a safe distance behind the scorpion-men.

Noah noticed a look of familiarity cross Uriel's face. Ereshkigal kept her eyes trained on the archangel; the one she knew had the power to bind her. "Uriel," she croaked, "I thought I smelled you."

Uriel responded, "Ramel, I see you have built quite a kingdom for yourself on earth, along with Sariel." He glanced at the other Watcher by the door. "I take it he goes by the name Nergal?"

In the mythology the Watchers had established, Nergal was the name of Ereshkigal's husband. He had become her spouse after he had insulted her for not being able to attend a banquet of the gods. Anu sent him down to the underworld to receive punishment from Ereshkigal. Nergal turned the tables on the chthonic queen, overpowering her on her own throne. This reputation stained Ramel's pride and he resented it. But he could do nothing about it for the present. It took a few generations to change a myth. He would have to tolerate the mockery of his humiliation by the other gods. He could not leave this underworld domain because he was Ereshkigal, the goddess guardian of the gates of Sheol.

Ereshkigal sneered with contempt at the archangel's condescension. "My earthly kingdom with all its limitations is still more satisfying than the assembly of Elohim. You should have joined us in the rebellion."

Uriel said, "Unlike you, I have no interest in dressing up as a goddess."

Ereshkigal belittled him. "You prefer being a slave. Why are you here?"

Noah blurted out, "To bind you into the depths of the earth." Uriel closed his eyes with embarrassment.

"Indeed?" said Ereshkigal, turning her gaze to Noah standing just behind Uriel. "And who is this presumptuous little one?"

"Noah ben Lamech, son of Enoch, destroyer of gods."

Uriel rolled his eyes. He wished Noah would just shut up.

Ereshkigal chuckled at Noah's audacity. An unexpected thought crossed her mind. She turned back to Uriel. "I have word that Semjaza and Azazel seek Elohim's Chosen Seed. Is this your doing, Uriel?" Her eyes kept trained on Uriel, ignoring Noah.

She knew only that the Chosen Seed would be a son of Enoch the prophet. None of the other gods bothered to tell her anything. She had to fight for every bit of information, being isolated in her miserable cosmic mountain.

"As you said, I am a servant," said Uriel sidestepping the question.

Ereshkigal looked into Uriel's eyes for some kind of revelation. But she could not find it. "Of course," she concluded, "And so you shall die as a slave."

She turned on her heel and walked back to the gates where Nergal waited. Casually, she ordered the scorpion-men, "Kill them all. Save the bodies."

The creatures raised their swords. They surrounded the men, one to one. But twenty circled Noah and Uriel. They knew the most important and difficult kill would be these two.

The scorpion-men attacked. These were the first opponents Noah's men had encountered who also had swords. The creatures were capable, as well as armored with helmets and shields. But their weapons were bronze, unlike the iron swords that Noah and his warriors wielded.

What Tubal-cain lacked in fighting skills, he more than made up with his brawn. He shattered the swords of his foes. Jubal and Jabal did a dance of brotherhood protecting each other back to back, dodging stingers and blades alike. One sting from the tail of a scorpion-man and the victim would die in minutes.

Uriel cut off stingers and sword arms with his usual finesse, but he had to work at it a bit more than usual. These creatures were among the best fighters he had encountered.

Tubal-cain cut the tail off a scorpion-man before it hit Methuselah. "You are too slow, grandmother!" In the instant he took to breathe those words, Methuselah turned and impaled one of the infernal insects about to strike Tubal-cain. "Fast enough to save your hide, chubby infant!"

Noah broke through the circle of attackers and reached the gates.

The creatures surrounded Uriel, pressing in tight. With Noah out of the way, this was just what Uriel needed to perform his signature move. He held out his blades and spun like a whirlwind. He cut down the last of his ten adversaries in mere moments. When he looked up, he saw Jabal about to be hit from behind. Uriel threw a sword like a javelin and pierced the creature against a column. It screamed in agony.

Noah's company were the only ones left standing. They gathered together. The corpses of scorpion-men littered the floor. Noah asked if everyone was whole, and they took account, catching their breath. This battle had taxed them. Some cuts and bruises, but all alive and well.

Noah turned to Uriel and asked, "Who are Semjaza and Azazel?"

"Fallen Sons of God. They led the rebellion. And now, they masquerade as the gods Anu and Inanna." The men continued to catch their breath.

Tubal-cain jumped in with disgust, "So the goddesses are all males in female disguise?"

"Do not let their pretended sex fool you," said Uriel. "They are all Sons of God, and Semjaza and Azazel are the mightiest."

"Well," said Noah, "I guess that means you and I have a common quest then."

"We have not even captured our first Watcher. And you are ready to face the mightiest of them all." Uriel's tone dripped with sarcasm. "And I will not let you forget the box."

"All right, all right," Noah complained. "Let us get through these seven gates and see if we will be proven strong enough to capture our first Watcher." Noah was capable of returning the sarcasm in his tone.

Jabal called to Uriel as he pulled the sword out of the scorpion-man's chest. It slumped to the ground. Jabal turned and tossed the weapon to the archangel, who caught it with a nod of appreciation. But Jabal did not see the reflexive spasm jolt through the body of the scorpion-man. His tail swept up and stung Jabal in the arm. Jabal screamed in pain. Tubal-cain cut off the creature's head.

The poison spread quickly.

Jubal caught Jabal before he could fall to the ground. "My brother!" Jubal shouted.

The men gathered quickly around him. Jubal pulled the stinger out of Jabal's arm. The wound was already full of pus. They watched the black poison travelling up Jabal's arm towards his heart.

"My brother," whimpered Jabal.

Noah looked to Uriel. "What can be done?"

Uriel shook his head. The Watchers with their occultic sorcery and poisons created these creatures.

Jabal looked up at Noah, fading fast. "Cousin," he gasped.

"Yes, cousin," replied Noah.

"Take care of our motley gang, brothers all." His soul had become knit as one with them, and now that thread was being unraveled.

His vision blurred.

"I will," said Noah.

"And *you* are in Elohim's care," said Jabal, between convulsions.

"Yes, cousin," said Noah reluctantly. Jabal breathed his last in his brothers' arms.

In that moment, Noah knew that he did not believe his own words. In Elohim's care? How could he say or believe such a thing? He had led this young man out of the slave mines with the promise of glory and revenge. He had trained him and mentored him over hundreds of leagues of hostile environments, fought with monstrous enemies. He had even brought him into the very portico of hell, only to see him die at the random hit of the stinger of a dead scorpion. What kind of care is that? What kind of purpose or meaning could be behind that? He felt abandoned by Elohim. Could Elohim be any more distant? Could Noah's alienation feel any more complete?

Methuselah led in a prayer over the body of Jabal. Men and angel knelt and gave their comrade's soul back to Elohim and his body back to the dust from which it came. The ritual made Noah feel worse. He held back tears of anger at his Maker's unwillingness to make sense out of this senseless tragedy.

After a moment of silence, they gathered to eat some food. The battle had starved them. They knew they were about to enter a seven-fold series of testing that would tax them to their limits and probably even lead to their deaths. They needed their full strength.

After their meal, Uriel took a firm grasp of the gargantuan door and heaved. The huge gate creaked opened just enough for the men to get inside. Uriel led, followed by Noah, Tubal-cain, Methuselah and Jubal.

They stood inside a huge wide cavern. Long stalagmites and stalactites filled the floor and ceiling. Glowing phosphorescent moss lit the space all around them, multicolored and quite glitteringly beautiful. Uriel had opened the gate by himself, but it took all the men to close it behind them. They did not want to be surprised by anyone sneaking up behind them.

Noah noticed that they appeared to already be at their destination. He said, "Just one gate? Where are the others?"

"Just one," said Uriel.

Noah said, "I thought there were seven gates of Ganzir that we would have to go through."

"Are you complaining?" said Methuselah.

Uriel laughed ironically. "That is the problem with myth, it tends to exaggerate."

"The bards call it poetic hyperbole," added Methuselah. "It aids in emphasizing a point. If you prefer, we could re-enter this gate seven times to satisfy your penchant for the grandiose."

Tubal-cain smiled, enjoying that he was not the target of Methuselah's barbs this time.

"Why did you not tell us this earlier?" asked Noah.

Uriel shrugged. "There were more important things to deal with than the petty details of an exaggerated legend."

Noah shook his head and led them on.

They moved cautiously to the center of the great cavern, past the jutting stalagmites, along a well-worn path, until they arrived at the shore of a small lake. The substance of the lake was black and viscous, like pitch, though not as thick. A perpetual flame flitted across the surface burning the top layer as fuel.

The sound of hands slowly clapping drew their attention across the black lake to two thrones of stone. Ereshkigal and Nergal sat upon the thrones. Ereshkigal stopped her mocking applause.

"Well done, Chosen One, and your gangly squad of 'mighty men,'" said Ereshkigal. "Welcome to the gates of Sheol. Few there are who see it in life."

Uriel glanced at the black lake. "The Abyss. Doorway to Sheol."

The men looked closer at the black fiery liquid. Tubal-cain stepped back.

"Sadly for you, Uriel, you will not have your chance to bind us," declared Ereshkigal. "And for you, Chosen Seed, this is the end of your quest. You have failed."

Uriel looked up and around them with a sudden intuition of an attack.

The ceiling above them rumbled like an approaching stampede. Everyone drew weapons.

Nergal finally spoke with a calculated coolness, "And now you will all know the pain of dying at the hands of Nephilim, as you rightly should."

Behind the men, the huge gates blew inward, kicked off their hinges by powerful feet. Two Nephilim assassins jumped inside the doorway, weapons drawn. Noah's team stepped back, blocked by the Abyss behind them.

The ceiling above them continued to shake with the force of a quake. The men looked up to see three holes burst open in the ceiling thirty cubits above them, one at a time. Rocks came crashing down from the holes, carrying with them the three forms of Nephilim landing in a cloud of rubble and dust. Like birds of prey, they rose from their crouched landing and drew their weapons. These were the same savage creatures that had stalked Noah and Uriel in the desert. Salah had told Noah about rigging the cave to collapse. If Salah was not able to carry out that plan, Noah knew his friend would have fought to the death. If he had been successful, then these monsters probably dug their way out of their own graves. Either way, Noah knew that Salah and his Thamudi tribe were all dead, wiped out by these creatures of hell.

The lead Naphil growled and the five of them advanced slowly, ready to pounce.

Tubal-cain blurted out what everyone was thinking, "Noah, what shall we do?"

Noah knew it was hopeless. These five Gibborim had decimated an entire city of warriors in their pursuit of Noah and Uriel. Two Watcher gods were at their backs. They did not stand a slash of a chance.

"We have no choice. We fight to the death," said Noah.

The Nephilim drew closer. The men gripped their swords and prepared to die.

"There is a choice," said Uriel. "We enter Sheol."

This did not go over well with a single one of them.

"And double our jeopardy?" said Noah.

"Only double?" Methuselah mocked.

"Nephilim will not follow us into Sheol," said Uriel.

"Why not?" asked Noah.

"Because they are too afraid of it," answered Uriel.

This was not lost on Methuselah who had to spit it out, "You would take us where Nephilim fear to tread?"

"You will have to trust me on this one," said Uriel. "Believe it or not, I am more able to help you down there than in here."

It was too late for debate. The Nephilim charged. In seconds they would all be dead.

Noah yelled, "Follow me!" and ran to the edge of the lake, making a flying leap into the black Abyss.

"Not another leap of faith," complained Methuselah. But he said it as he followed the others into the thick black liquid—Uriel, then Tubal-cain, and Jubal.

The Gibborim reached their spot just as Methuselah made his splash. The giants stopped in fear, looking into the blackness. Two of them backed up, not wanting to get close.

Ereshkigal damned Elohim and yelled at the Gibborim, "You are done here! Return to your masters." By this she meant Anu and Inanna, or Semjaza and Azazel. The squad of Nephilim backed away, gathering together for their return. But one of them stood staring into the black liquid. Just as his comrades noticed this, he sheathed his sword, glanced at them, and dove into the Abyss. The leader screeched as if he had lost a son. But the others did not move an inch. They knew their comrade was leaping to his sure death. They turned and left the cavern for their return trip to Erech.

# CHAPTER 15

Noah, Uriel, Methuselah, Tubal-cain and Jubal sank into the depths of the inky black fluid of the Abyss. It terrified them. They could not open their eyes. They did not know how long they could hold their breaths before their lungs would fill with thick black death.

They broke through the oily liquid into a new layer of water. Now they sank swiftly. Noah opened his eyes to see Uriel next to him like a loyal dog. The others were near. Tubal-cain passed him up with his heavier weight. Noah slowed himself to make sure they all passed him up so he could keep them in his sight. They continued to sink.

He did not see the Naphil who had broken through the oily layer into the water above them. The pursuer was not just sinking, but swimming to catch up with Noah.

Unseen by all of them, the shadowy form of a sea monster approached them in the distance: Rahab.

Uriel's sixth sense caused him to look up.

The Naphil was almost upon Noah. His hand stretched to grab Noah's head, his blade ready to plunge into Noah's body.

Uriel shouted, bubbles trailing upward.

Noah could not hear through the water, but the bubbles made him look at Uriel, wondering what he was trying to say.

The Naphil grabbed for Noah's head.

Rahab came out of the darkness. The huge dragon body swept through the water. Its jaws gaped open, with large razor teeth the size of swords. Rahab clamped down on the Naphil with a hundred tons of pressure, crushing the humanoid and carrying it away. The torrent in the water almost drew Noah up into its undertow. Uriel grabbed his ankle and pulled him back down.

The great dragon turned and circled back around. It was not finished. There were five pieces of sinking bait ready for snacks. It was too late for the men. They were out of breath. They could last no longer in this watery world. Their lungs had used up all the oxygen they could store. It was time to inhale water, drown and be eaten.

Suddenly, one by one, they broke through into Sheol and fell almost fourteen cubits down onto the ground, sputtering and coughing out water from their lungs.

It was as if the Abyss was a ceiling or firmament of Sheol, an upside down underworld, where they fell down out of the water onto dry land below.

They gasped for breath. Jubal spit it out first, "What was that *thing*?"

"Rahab," said Uriel, "sea dragon of the Abyss."

"*One* of the dragons," Methuselah corrected him. "The other one has seven heads."

"Thank you for the consolation," derided Jubal. "I feel much better."

"Thank Elohim for the Nephilim after all," muttered Tubal-cain. "One moment more, and we would be a meal."

Noah wondered, "But the size of its mouth. Why did it not grab me with the Naphil?"

Uriel shook his head and boiled with sarcasm, "Hmmm. You do not think that has *anything* to do with Elohim protecting you for his purpose of building the box, do you?"

The rest of them could see Uriel's anger. They all remained uncomfortably silent while getting up to look around.

Sheol: Land of the dead, the underworld. Visibility was very poor and breathing was even harder. They would have to conserve their energy.

Noah remembered the black pitch Salah had given them and the words he had spoken, "Some day to find your way in a dark place." He and Uriel pulled out their pouches filled with the thick tar. They made torches, covered them in pitch and lit them with a flint stone carried by Tubal-cain.

The light let them see more of the dreary, lifeless world they were in. It was an inversion of the upper world: inside-out rocks, upside-down trees, their tangled gnarly roots coming out of the ground.

A howling inhuman screech made them stand up and draw their weapons. They listened for more.

Suddenly, a creature jumped out of the rocks and ran straight at Noah. It looked humanoid in shape, but had lost its distinctive identity as human. It was sexless and without eyes or hair. It only had a large mouth on its head, a large, raving mouth full of outsized ugly pointy teeth, gnashing and gnawing, ready to eat its target.

Noah swept out his sword and cut off its head. It fell to the ground, but continued to grope around for its prey.

Tubal-cain kicked the thing onto its back and stomped down on one arm. Jubal stomped down on the other arm. "What is it?" asked Tubal-cain.

"A shade," said Uriel.

"It does not die?" asked Tubal-cain.

"It is already dead," Uriel answered.

"Call it 'the living dead,'" said Methuselah.

"Come to eat us alive forever?" asked Jubal.

"Yes," said Uriel. "Which is why your best defense is decapitation."

Methuselah leaned in to take a closer look at the thing squirming under their feet. "Disgusting," he said. The body was made of rotting flesh that was falling from its skeleton. He could see that it was animated by maggots and worms that filled the cavities and muscles.

An old saying came to his mind and he repeated it aloud, "Where the worm dies not."

Suddenly, two more shades jumped out from behind the rocks. Jubal and Uriel immediately cut off their heads. "How many are there?" asked Tubal-cain.

Before Uriel could answer, eight more shades came at them. The living men hacked and slashed, taking the shades down.

Uriel stood up on a rock looking at a valley below them. It teemed with an endless mass of shades coming in their direction.

"Lots," said Uriel. "Run."

They raced into the wasteland of twisted rocks and gnarled tree roots. But every turn they made, they were blocked by gangs of shades chomping after them. They changed course, only to be blocked by more marauding shades. At last, they broke through the maze of rocks and out onto a vast flat land of dried cracked mud.

Uriel led them out onto the flats. As they ran, the men saw shades bursting out of the ground. Their hands grabbed for the men, their mouths hungrily gnashing and grinding their teeth. Very quickly, the number of shades bursting from the ground overwhelmed them on all sides. There was nowhere to go. They were surrounded. They circled in defense one last time. The massive hive of hungry screeching shades pushed in on them.

"Prepare to be an eternal meal!" yelled Tubal-cain.

Uriel was not about to let that happen. He sheathed his sword, reached in his cloak and pulled out a ram's horn he had secreted from them until now. He put it to his mouth and blew for all his life. The deafening sound rolled out in shockwaves, blowing down shades with concussive force. It spread out in a ring around them.

"You are full of surprises," said Noah.

"I take back my criticisms of you," said Methuselah.

"It will not last," said Uriel.

Methuselah wondered briefly if Uriel was talking of his effect on Methuselah or on the shades.

The effect did not last. The downed shades were soon over-run by a new wave of shades, climbing over the others, mouths munching, tightening their circle once more. Uriel gave another hearty blow. The sound waves pushed the swarms back again. But this time, not as far. It had decreasing effect.

Uriel put the trumpet to his lips a third time. But before he could blow, they were all thrown off their feet by a massive earthquake. The ground exploded upward all around them. Seven giant ten-cubit tall warriors burst out of the ground. They rose from the earth like rulers standing to make judgment. They looked like Nephilim, but were taller and more regal. The shades laid down in submission before them.

"What are they?" asked Noah.

"Rephaim," replied Uriel. "Souls of the giant warrior kings. Demigods like the Nephilim, only more powerful. These were imprisoned here at the Titanomachy."

Memories flooded into Methuselah's mind. One of those Rephaim had killed his wife's family and he had given it a permanent limp with his blade.

"Is that who you were calling on your trumpet?" said Noah.

"No," said Uriel.

Methuselah put in his two shekels, "I have a feeling we would prefer to be eaten by the shades."

Uriel made one last blow on his ram's horn.


It was a quiet evening in the city of Kur on Mount Hermon. The new moon sacrifice was still weeks away. The villagers were in their homes asleep past the midnight hour. Hardly anyone noticed the faint echo of Uriel's trumpet resounding from the depths of Sheol.

Higher up the mountain on the north slope, just below the tree line, the nightlife fell silent. The crickets stopped. Wild rodents froze in their tracks, their eyes darting around in fear.

A blindingly brilliant light abruptly burst from the heavens above to the forest floor. It cut through the night like a dagger, and just as suddenly, it was gone. Darkness filled in the breach.

In a matter of seconds, three dark riders on horseback burst out of the brush from where the light had burned its path to the earth. The savage looking warriors, with armor that looked similar to that of the Nephilim, urged their fierce stallions onward. They rode with deliberation down the mountain toward the ziggurat on the south side.

# CHAPTER 16

Lugalanu stared into the flames of his hearth. He was heartsick, and his mind drifted into the consideration of new directions for his life.

A maidservant interrupted his thoughts. "My lord?" she said for the third time. It was the first he heard. He looked up at her and she nodded. In a flash he was up out of his chair and rushing down the hallway to the maidservant's quarters.

He arrived in time to hear the wail of a newborn child filling the darkly lit chamber. He rushed over to the quarantined area and whisked the curtains aside. Emzara lay cradling a baby boy in her arms. She was drenched with sweat, beaming ear to ear. Lugalanu smiled at her.

She had rejected the *ashipu* shaman and his birth magic, and refused to cradle the traditional bronze amulet to fend against infant death. The amulet carried an image of a pazuzu on one side and an incantation on the back for warding off Lamashtu, a demoness believed to cause miscarriage. Emzara clung instead to Elohim as her protector and provider. She needed no other.

"His name shall be Canaanu," said Lugalanu in anticipation of their naming ceremony.

"I shall call him Ham," she said. They had agreed she would have the right to call him her own name in secret, just as he had allowed her to retain her own family name within their private company.

The other maidservants cleaned up the bed sheets and tidied the room in preparation for Emzara's recovery. Lugalanu drew close to Emzara and whispered affectionately into her ears, "Emzara, if you were my wife, I would take no other bride."

"Why do you desire me so?" she asked.

"Why do you resist me so?" he responded.

Two priestesses of Inanna arrived with a bassinet. Their bald elongated heads and tattooed bodies still repulsed Emzara. Especially when she considered what they were there for and what they would do to her only son. That son was her only link to her beloved husband who she was not supposed to know was still alive, who may never discover that she was still breathing.

Emzara's eyes filled with pain. Lugalanu had been good to her, but she had no choice in this matter. Slowly, she raised the child to the priestesses, who took him and gently placed him into the bassinet.

"He will be a servant of the goddess Inanna," Lugalanu said. "He will serve in her temple for the rest of his life."

"At least he will live," she sighed in resignation.

"At least," said Lugalanu. It was a great pain to him to do this. He had fallen deeply in love with this woman. Even though he detested everything the child was, even though his instinct was to kill it, as one would obviously destroy every last seed of one's enemy, he would not do so. He knew that would forever destroy his chance to win Emzara.

He was beginning to wonder if he was only deceiving himself. He had been so confident he could woo Emzara over the last year. He would take ten years to do so if he had to. A hundred years even. It represented the one thing that was unattainable in his reality, and it became the one thing he wanted more than anything else; more than the riches, more than the power, more than his exalted status with the gods and rulership of the people. As he looked into her eyes, he could see the goodness, the truth, the beauty that had evaded him his entire life, and he wanted it to all be willingly surrendered to him. The one true thing he could not have was the one thing he was willing to devote the rest of his life to get. He would wait. He would remain patient, no matter how many years it took.

A messenger entered the room and approached Lugalanu. The priest-king lost his temper, "Must I be constantly interrupted? May I have one moment of peace?"

"I am sorry, your lordship. But the Gibborim have returned." Lugalanu looked up, surprised. He did not see that Emzara's eyes went wide with anticipation.

Lugalanu asked, "Was their mission objective achieved?" He had forgotten that Emzara saw him commission the Nephilim that day months ago. He certainly did not know she was aware Noah was still alive. So he spoke in generalities, referring to official matters that he expected she would not understand.

Emzara hid her emotions in response to the news of her beloved.

"No, my king," said the messenger.

Emzara's heart leapt for joy. He got away? Her Noah had escaped the mighty Gibborim?

"That is, there was no capture," the messenger continued. "Their quarry, I am told, fell into Sheol."

Emzara's heart broke. She trembled. It was all she could do to keep from weeping. But her life depended on it, and the life of her son too, so she held back with all her might.

"Sheol," repeated Lugalanu. "Hmmm. The jaws of Sheol are never satisfied, and he who goes down does not come up. I suppose I could not ask for better news."

Emzara could not ask for more crushing news. Everything she stayed alive and fought for was just murdered in front of her eyes. Questions flooded her soul. Was Elohim truly in control? What about the Revelation? How could he let such evil prosper and have victory, while the righteous perish? Had she wasted her entire life believing in a God whose will could be thwarted?

Her faith hung on by a slender thread. She did not understand Elohim, but she trusted him. This was another opportunity to express that trust, if it was as real as she had claimed.

The priestesses took baby Ham through the underground tunnel into Inanna's temple district. There, in a special room, they immediately began the process of cranial modification for servants of Anu. Newborns have soft pliable skulls whose plates were not fused for the first couple years of their lives as their skulls accommodated brain growth. The priestesses placed two curved pieces of wood on the front and back of Ham's little head. In effect, they maintained the original egg-like protrusion of the skull after birth. The pieces of wood were held tightly in place by connecting twine cables wound around a knob that could be tightened to increase pressure. They had to be careful not to crush the infant's skull.

Ham's frightened crying would soon be mitigated as he got used to the contraption. As he aged, less constrictive means could be used to finalize the head binding process until he was about two years old.

Herbal potions to kill all the hair on the body would not be necessary until the child was at least a teen and became more involved in the duties of the temple. Body piercing and tattooing would finalize the child's dedication to temple service around age sixteen or so. The entire process was rather monkish. Emzara would not be allowed to see her son until he was publicly dedicated at age sixteen. Even after that, he would be withheld from her. Priests and priestesses were not allowed to fraternize with the court servants. The caste system was harshly enforced throughout the kingdom. The only way Emzara would ever be able to have satisfying contact with her son would be if she became royalty by accepting Lugalanu's hand in marriage.

The Tigris and Euphrates Rivers poured into the Lower Sea at the edge of the earth. The body of water teamed with life. Seagoing vessels traded with distant lands. Others fished for the river cities close to the sea, like Eridu. Eridu was the oldest Sumerian city and was ruled by its patron god of the Abyss, Enki. It was the city of the first kings when kingship came down from heaven. Eridu's status had dwindled over the years as kingship transferred to other cities, ever since Inanna's treachery toward Enki.

Legend said that Enki had originally been given guardianship of the Tablet of Destinies, a tablet containing the universal decrees of heaven and earth, including godship, kingship, war, sex, music as well as magic, sorceries and occultic wisdom. Enlil, the Lord of the Air, who reigned over the city of Nippur up the river, collected the information on this tablet. Enlil had given it to Enki for safe-keeping, but Inanna was envious of Enki and crafted a plan to wrest the Tablet away from him and bring it to Erech.

She took her "boat of heaven" down the river and visited Enki, who laid out a feast of celebration for her. Enki fed Inanna butter-cakes and beer, but Inanna was calculating and got Enki drunk enough for him to hand over the Tablet to her. She then fled back to Erech with it on her boat of heaven. By the time Enki had come to his senses and sent his vizier after Inanna, it was too late. She had delivered the Tablet of Destinies to Erech, which became the new center of culture and civilization. Enki brooded bitterly at being double-crossed so boldly by Inanna. One day, he would have his revenge on her. But he would have to be patient. Besides, he was not the only one betrayed by the machinations of the goddess. Her reckless pursuit of power would surely one day result in more than one deity seeking vengeance against her.

One of those deities who might consider joining in revenge against Inanna was Enlil, Lord of the Air. Originally, he had shared patronage with Inanna over the city of Nippur, before the Titanomachy. Even though she had been humiliated after her failure in that war, losing the city to his kingship, he still carried the scars of her conniving skullduggery against him. He would never be satisfied until she was bound in the earth.

Ninhursag, the earth goddess, also had a grudge against Inanna. Ninhursag was patron deity of Kish, which lay farther up the Euphrates, past Erech and Nippur in the northern regions. But because of her cavorting liaison with Enki, she also had a temple in Eridu. The Watchers' myths, which sought to replace Elohim's creation story, gave Ninhursag the titles Ninmah, "Great Queen," and Nintu, "Lady of Birth," claiming she created man out of the clay of her womb. She knew Inanna had her eye on Ninhursag's throne, because she was the one "female" deity of the four high gods And Inanna envied Ninhursag's amorous entanglement with Enki.

The hierarchy of the pantheon was always at risk for challenge, and it was no secret Inanna was the most ambitious of them all. She had managed to make herself consort of Anu, which was clearly positioning. Anu did not seem to care. He enjoyed dominating her passionate temper. She was creative and bizarre. Anu took pleasure in the bizarre.

Inanna, it seemed, was building up a cadre of enemies within her own camp that did not bode well for her future.

The Lower Sea was a couple leagues downriver from Eridu, with its western shoreline along the winding desert coast. Just off this shoreline, the bodies of Methuselah, Tubal-cain, and Jubal floated dead in the water.

A fourth figure broke the surface and grabbed the bodies. He swam toward shore with a mighty strength.

Uriel dragged the bodies onto the sand. He massaged their lungs and squeezed their stomachs until they coughed up the water in their lungs and gulped air. Jubal, being the youngest and healthiest, came to first. One by one, Uriel revived them all.

They were alive. At first, they did not know where they were or how they got there. But it started to come back to them. They had been captured by the Rephaim in Sheol and imprisoned by their gigantic captors. But they had not been privy to the details of the negotiations for their release.

"Why did they let us go, Uriel?" asked Tubal-cain.

"They cannot hold archangels in Sheol. And I would not leave without you."

Methuselah spat sand from his mouth. "Where is Noah?" he asked.

"They required a ransom for those released," Uriel replied.

Methuselah did not follow this logic. "Noah is trapped in Sheol? Why on earth would you leave behind the one man who should not have been left behind? I would have given myself in his place." His anger with this so-called guardian rushed up.

"Noah gave himself in your place," said Uriel. "I could not stop him. He told the Rephaim he was the Chosen Seed."

The men could not believe what they heard. They refused to accept it.

"We have to go back," said Tubal-cain.

"No." Uriel responded as quickly as they had.

Methuselah would have none of it. "Are you shirking your responsibility, or are you planning on storming Sheol by yourself, you crazy angel?" he shouted.

"No," replied Uriel. "I have a few crazy associates who are going to help me."

Methuselah looked behind them. On the beach, three warrior horsemen waited. They got off their steeds and walked toward the men like wraiths of judgment. Jubal and Methuselah gasped in fear. But the men had nothing to fear. Their wrath was for the Rephaim holding the Chosen Seed in the pit of Sheol.

The three warriors walked right past them. Uriel joined them. They walked into the water up to their waists and dove in, disappearing from view. Before he dove after them, Uriel turned and shouted to the men, "Go to the Hidden Valley as Noah commanded. Methuselah, you have the plans."

Methuselah responded, "Uriel, if you find one of the Rephaim with a limp, give him my special regards." He was referring to the Rapha named Yahipan. He had permanently wounded the giant many years before in the uprising called the Gigantomachy. Uriel knew the personal loss that Methuselah had suffered at the hands of Yahipan. He would be sure to deliver the message with deadly accuracy.

With that, Uriel turned back and disappeared beneath the surface.

Methuselah pulled out the leather piece tightly packed in his cloak. He opened it up and looked at the cuneiform Noah had scratched into it.

"You heard the archangel, men. We have a commission, now let us fulfill it," barked Methuselah.

# CHAPTER 17

The pit was unimaginably deep. It was only about ten cubits in diameter, its walls black, and solid, unbreakably hard, unscalable rock. It dropped down immeasurable leagues. It was so deep, one could not see the bottom. But there was a bottom eventually, and it was the furthest depth of Sheol. It was Tartarus, a place of imprisonment at the uttermost distance from the presence of Elohim. Perpetual darkness, impenetrable silence, and absolute isolation. It was said that Tartarus was as far below Sheol as the earth was below the heavens.

Noah was incarcerated at the very bottom of those depths. He had a flat stone to sleep on. A single oil lamp, refueled only when food was occasionally lowered down in a basket, gave a little patch of light. Noah was, after all, still alive. It would not do well for the forces of darkness to have the Chosen Seed dead, for he would only be replaced by someone else. His captors were so certain of their prison, they took nothing from him, leaving even his dagger on his person.

Noah looked up toward the heavens, which he could only imagine were so far away it would not matter what he yelled. But he yelled anyway. "ELOHIM! WHY HAVE YOU DONE THIS TO ME?!"

His voice did not echo up the leagues of empty cavern walls as one would expect. Instead, it was stifled like whispers in a coffin, as if the words could not go beyond his own hearing, as if the words did not extend beyond his lips. He sat in a vortex where sound and reality swirled right back into him in absolute solitary confinement. Noah had complained for so long about wanting to be left alone. Now he had his wish—to the utmost. He was finally, totally and utterly, *alone*.

And he realized what a complete selfish fool he had been.

He looked up at the wall. He could only see a few cubits into the darkness with the lamp he had. Like a desperate rat, he jumped up, trying to grab a foothold, anything. He fell to the ground in a crumple, weeping. He looked at the brass wrist brace he had worn to remind himself of his wife. He ripped it off and threw it against the wall. The sight of it only multiplied his torment tenfold in this hell.

He pulled at his clothes, ripping them to pieces in a frenzied anger of self-pity. He looked up to heaven again. He was going mad, but he still had his pride.

"I HATE YOU! DO YOU HEAR ME, GOD OF ENOCH! I HATE YOU!"

There was no response.

"ARE YOU DEAF AND DUMB? ARE YOU BLIND?!"

Still no answer.

"WHAT DO YOU WANT FROM ME? WHAT HAVE I EVER DONE TO DESERVE THIS? ANSWER ME! WHAT HAVE I DONE TO DESERVE ALL THIS? WHAT HAVE I…"

And suddenly, from deep within his bowels, a groan of despair and resignation overwhelmed him. He fell to his knees weeping in deep sobs. The words he now said were the same, but they now meant the opposite of his original intent. Accusation turned to confession. "What have I done? What have I done to deserve this? I deserve this. I deserve all this."

He wept his very soul into the void. He was broken. He could say no more. He could only sob bitter tears of repentance.

"Noah," the whisper said.

Noah stopped.

What had he heard?

He listened for more.

Nothing.

But he *had* heard it.

He knew that voice.

He quickly rummaged through his discarded clothes and pulled out his dagger.

He went to the wall, carrying his small lamp to light the surface. He began to scratch the rock. Carefully, he carved cuneiform lines that were directions. Then he scratched out the picture of the tebah, the box from his calling in a dream that would not let him go.

He scratched feverishly. He would not stop. Not even for the food lowered in the basket by some minion of hell leagues above him. He just kept scratching.

Noah did not know how long he had been there. His beard had grown out. He looked up at the wall, dimly lit by his little lamp. The entire wall all around, three hundred and sixty degrees, up to the height of his reach, was covered with scratching. It was the blueprint and directions for the box carved over and over again. The blade in his hand had been worn to the hilt. Noah's mind was emptied of its obsession. He was bled dry of his pride. He collapsed to the floor in a broken heap.

From above, he heard a distant sound grow louder. It cut through the darkness and split the void. He knew that sound. It was the unmistakable resonance of Uriel's trumpet. He looked up into the void. He could see nothing.

But he kept looking up in faith.

Moments later, the end of a rope dropped to the floor. It was followed eventually by the figure of Uriel, rappelling down the wall. He landed on the ground with a thud.

Noah looked up at him.

Uriel looked back up from where he came and muttered, "Now *that* is a deep pit."

"You came back for me," Noah blubbered, barely able to speak.

Uriel smiled with a big grin. "You know Elohim. He hounds you until you freely obey." He had that hint of irony that Noah had learned to love so dearly.

Noah burst out laughing in tears.

Uriel could see that Noah was a new man. He shared the laugh with Noah, helped his weak companion to his feet, and embraced him.

"What took you so long?" said Noah with an impish smirk on his face.

Uriel grinned back. "There was a little matter of the Rephaim I had to take care of."

"You took care of seven Rephaim?" asked an amazed Noah.

Uriel gave him a parental scolding look. "Of course not. I had help."

Uriel grabbed Noah and helped him onto his back. The angel seized the rope, readying for his long climb back to reality. "We cannot save ourselves, Noah," he said. "But then I gather you understand that now."

"Hurry up, will you?" snorted Noah. "I have a box to build."

Uriel grinned and began his ascent with mighty archangelic speed and power.

Noah was so fatigued, he fell asleep on the climb up. When they arrived at the top, Uriel fell to the ground exhausted. His muscles were cramping, worn out from the climb. He tried to catch his breath and took a huge drink from a wineskin in his belt.

The impact of Uriel's collapse woke Noah. He looked around the cave they were in.

Three of the giant Rephaim lay with their faces to the ground, bound by cords Noah could not see – no doubt the barely perceptible Cherubim hair he had once been shown by Uriel. Three angelic warriors stood on the necks of the giants. They stepped down and approached Noah. Uriel had to stay seated on the ground.

"Who are they?" Noah asked.

"Archangels," huffed Uriel.

The warriors came and hugged the awkward Noah as if he were family.

"This is Mikael, Gabriel, and Raphael," said Uriel.

The three nodded as they were introduced. They were as handsome and muscle-bound as Uriel—more so. The thought went through Noah's mind that his guardian was the least impressive of the bunch. Strange, if he was supposed to be so important as the Chosen Seed. Noah opened his mouth to direct a verbal stab in Uriel's direction, but all that came out was, "Thank you for your efforts."

"Just do not let it happen again," said Mikael with a touch of humor. "Uriel is already in trouble for his guardianship of you."

"Or lack thereof," joked Gabriel.

"Hey," complained Uriel, "I did just carry him out of Tartarus. That should count for something."

"You bound the Rephaim," said Noah surprised.

"I told you," said Uriel, "It's a special talent we have. Though not without its difficulties."

Noah's forehead crinkled with concern. "Uriel, I thought you said you took care of seven Rephaim. There are only three of them on the ground."

"I did not say seven," corrected Uriel, "You did. It was a detail I considered too petty to correct at the time. But now, I believe it is exceedingly relevant to our safety. We should make good our escape."

Before they could even move, a bellowing inhuman screech filled the air. A stampeding Rapha burst through the cave opening, headed right at Noah. It limped as it ran.

Mikael and Gabriel leapt into action. They dove at the Rapha's shins and tackled it to the ground inches from Noah. The Rapha's fist came pounding down toward Noah's head. Uriel pushed Noah out of the way. If Uriel had been at his full strength, it would not have hurt so badly, but he was still weakened from his climb up from that infernal pit with Noah on his back. His muscles were too weak to deflect, he had to absorb. He blacked out.

Now it was Noah's turn. He pulled Uriel out of the way of the second strike from the beast.

Gabriel leapt on the creature's back and pulled its head back like a tethered stallion. Raphael and Mikael dragged him away from Noah by his feet.

The Rapha reached over his head and grabbed Gabriel. He threw the angel against the cave wall with a thundering crash.

These Rephaim were harder than the Nephilim on earth because they were dead and had greater strength in the underworld than in the land of the living. But so did the archangels. Mikael and Raphael whipped their cords out. They bound the beast before it could regain its balance to get up.

Uriel walked up to the limping Rapha now bound. He remembered Methuselah's words to him before he had dived back into the abyss. Give this one his regards. He could not kill this thing, but there was one thing he could do to bring it misery. He reached with both hands and grabbed the Rapha's eyeballs. With a mighty grip and yank, he ripped out both eyes from their sockets. He threw them into the deep pit out of which he had crawled. The Rapha screamed in agony.

Uriel leaned in and whispered in the monster's ear, "That was for Methuselah ben Enoch, you son of iniquity."

The other angels watched Uriel with shock.

He pulled Noah toward the entrance of the cave. Noah was afraid of him. That act had seemed brutally out of character for Uriel. But neither the man nor the other angels had been on the journey with Uriel and Methuselah those many generations earlier. If they had been, they would not have considered his action inappropriate at all.

They stepped outside the cave.

They were up a mountainside. A thousand cubits below them countless shades scrambled from the mountain base toward them. The three missing Rephaim trampled over the shades, crushing them indiscriminately on their way up toward the cave entrance. Their hideous screams pierced Noah's and Uriel's ears.

Uriel pulled Noah to the side of the ledge. He looked up. It was a rock climb of at least sixty cubits. Before Noah could register anything, Uriel grabbed him and lifted him up to a rock with a grunt and yelled, "Climb!" Normally, Uriel would have been able to throw Noah ten cubits upward, but not in his present exhausted state. Noah climbed for all he was worth. Breathing hard, Uriel looked up at the wall before him. Well, at least he did not have to carry Noah again. But he had to keep moving. He grabbed a rock and climbed.

Even in his fatigued condition, Uriel passed Noah. He arrived at the top, just as the Rephaim reached the cave entrance, climbing like spiders toward their prey. They would be only seconds in finishing the climb. Uriel reached down and grabbed Noah's cloak, pulling him up and over the ledge onto the mountaintop. The ceiling of the watery Abyss hung just ten cubits over their heads.

Uriel felt there was no way he would be able to do it. He would have to throw Noah up the distance to the Abyss.

The Rephaim were already on the ledge and sprinting for them.

Uriel whispered a prayer to Elohim and grabbed Noah. With every last ounce of strength left in him, he heaved Noah the ten cubits up to the water. The two Rephaim hit him and tackled him to the ground, crushing him in a heap.

In but a moment, one of them would help the other leap the distance to the water ceiling.

But they would not be leaping. They were dragged off Uriel by three very riled archangels.

# CHAPTER 18

Noah desperately kicked for the surface through the dark waters of the Abyss. He did not have much air to spare in making it to the top. He did not know where he was or where he would end up. He just had to make it to the surface. His lungs burned. He panicked. The shadowy form of Leviathan swimming in the distance only added to his despair. The fearsome offspring of Rahab. Could it get much worse than this? What difference would it make anyway? He would be drowned by the time the monster reached him.

Noah had the urge to give up.

Suddenly he felt a shoving from below. Uriel had followed him. He kicked with superhuman force, thrusting Noah upward. Noah knew Uriel was weak, but the angel seemed to find a hidden source of unending bursts of energy. Noah would have to make a joke about that if they made it out alive.

And he did make it.

He burst through the surface, gasping for air. Uriel appeared beside him moments later, sputtering out the next command, "Swim!"

There was a trading ship sailing their direction. The sailor in the crow's nest spotted Noah and Uriel as the ship drew near them.

Noah kicked his way toward the ship with everything in him.

Uriel kept looking over his shoulder for the sea monster.

The monster's spiny snakelike back broke the surface not a hundred cubits out. It glistened in the sun, gliding toward them, all seven of its heads focused with predator intensity. Seven sets of eyes. Seven sets of razor teeth. It had all the time in the world.

It was said of Leviathan that on earth there was nothing like it. A creature without fear. Nothing could match its ferocity or its power. Javelins and harpoons all broke upon its armored scales. Even its belly was covered with protection like sharp potsherds. It was said that Leviathan could belch from some of its mouths flame like a burning torch. From its nostrils it could spew smoke as from a boiling pot or burning rushes. It could crush the hull of a warship into splinters. It was said that Leviathan ruled the Abyss with seven times the terror of Rahab.

Knowing all this about the predator, Uriel stayed behind treading water. He could barely keep himself afloat. He gasped anxiously. He was no match for the jaws of Leviathan even if he had not been so drained of all his vitality. But he would divert its attention from Noah. He could at least do that. He would be a willing sacrifice in mere moments.

But that moment did not come.

He turned around in the water. Leviathan was nowhere to be seen. It had not gone past him, either. He saw Noah being helped up the side of the merchant ship. Uriel swam to the craft, waiting for the worst to come. Leviathan was a creature of chaos, but it was intelligent. It operated with calculation. This did not make sense. Something wicked was coming.

Uriel made it to the ship. The sailors helped him up.

The mast man shouted, "LEVIATHAN!" All hands on deck moved like the wind.

Uriel and Noah looked out on the starboard side. Strange. It must have passed under them and circled back.

The armored spine of the dragon broke the surface coming at them. Was it gathering momentum for a strike? A warship would not have a chance against this beast, let alone a merchant trading vessel laden with carnelia, lapis lazuli and pearls instead of soldiers and weapons. The creature was three times the length of the ship and six times its weight. It would snap the craft like a handful of toothpicks.

The sailors did not wait to find out. They trimmed the sail to catch the windward blow. Some joined the slaves at the oars to row for their lives. It was all quite futile. They could not outrun the sea dragon and they could not withstand its mighty force. But they refused to resign themselves to fate. They would struggle for life to the very end.

The Captain of the ship demanded Noah and Uriel's attention. "What curse is this you have brought upon us all? We will all die! I am a simple merchant!" Terrified anger pulled tight the olive dark skin of his face. His black hair shook as he gestured. "I have not wronged the gods! Why are you here in the middle of the sea? Are you demons?!"

It was one long stream of hyperventilation that matched Uriel's own laboring for breath.

Uriel collapsed to the deck. He could do nothing more. There was nowhere else to run. He rested his head against the mast. His collapse actually stopped the Captain's string of complaints.

The Captain turned his attention to Noah. He spewed a fresh litany of accusations at him. The lookout above interrupted him, yelling down, "CAPTAIN! IT IS BELOW US! LEVIATHAN IS BELOW US!"

The Captain froze.

Noah tilted his head. Below us? What does he mean below us?

Uriel struggled to get up. They ran to the side of the boat to peer into the water below. The sight struck everyone silent. The ship tacked northward toward the gulf inlet at a breezy pace. Directly below the ship, at thrice its size, gliding along just cubits below the flat hull of the boat swam Leviathan, matching the pace of the ship as if it was escorting the craft back to land.

Leviathan was guarding the seagoing vessel.

The Captain looked at Noah and blurted out a new stream of words. This time, however, the tone was of adoration. "Who is this man whom the gods favor? Where do you come from? Who is your god that we may worship him? Are you a god that you tame Leviathan?"

Noah listened, astonished.

Uriel grinned. "It appears I am not your only guardian."

Noah felt overwhelmed. Words of poetry rose in Noah's heart: The pillars of heaven tremble and are astounded at his rebuke. By his power he stilled the sea; by his understanding he shattered Leviathan. By his wind the heavens were made fair; his hand pierced the fleeing serpent. Behold, these are but the outskirts of his ways, and how small a whisper do we hear of him! But the thunder of his power who can understand? And Noah knew that Elohim was his guardian who controlled even the sea dragon of chaos.

The Captain interrupted his pious thoughts, "We are going inland up the river for trade. Will you voyage with us?"

"I see you are a lucky charm as well," quipped Uriel under his breath to Noah.

Noah said to the Captain, "We will go as far as Erech."

Noah paused. He could see that Uriel thought he might still be sidetracked by his old desire for revenge. But he quickly put that thought to rest. "From there," he said, "we trek into the Zagros Mountains."

Uriel sighed with deep relief. They were going to look for the Hidden Valley where Methuselah and Noah's tribal survivors had been sent. Noah was going to find them and build the box. If they were even alive.

# CHAPTER 19

The merchant vessel docked on the river port wharf of Erech, just inland from the coast where Ur and Eridu stood near the marshlands. The river made a wide delta at this point, about seven hundred cubits across, creating sufficient room for a well traveled trading port. The Euphrates flowed long from the northern mountains down to the Lower Sea in the south. The river, along with its eastern sister river the Tigris, was one of the four main tributaries that flowed from Eden. Together, they were the lifeblood of the Mesopotamian cities along its banks. Like all river civilizations, life ebbed and flowed with the seasonal effects of the river. Even civilization would ultimately ebb and flow with the rivers, for the loose winding curves of water were already beginning to alter course through the flat plain powered by the changing seasonal flooding.

It was spring. The river was high and the surrounding irrigation canals for agriculture were flooded in preparation for fertilizing the soil after the dry summer and winter months.

The surroundings puzzled Noah. By his reckoning, it had been summer when they had stormed the Gates of Ganzir on Mount Hermon and plunged into the Abyss on their journey in Sheol. How long had he been down there? It felt like weeks, but not a year.

The Captain hugged Noah and Uriel to bid them farewell. He had given them Indus Valley robes to wear, along with a small amount of money for their blessing upon his ship. It was the least he could do in gratitude. Noah had told him all about his God Elohim and how he created the heavens and the earth and humankind. He told him of the Fall and of faith, about the idolatry of the gods of the land, and about the judgment that drew nigh. The Captain and his entire boat were convinced and put their faith in Elohim.

They showered gifts of gratitude upon Noah and Uriel, which helped the pair in more than one way. First, they needed supplies and second, with their attire, they would not look like strange foreigners sauntering around the city.

As they walked down the plank of the ship to the dock the first thing they noticed was that everyone was shaved hairless and had elongated skulls with skin tattoos. Noah remembered that this kind of physical alteration was reserved for temple and palace servants of the gods, not the average citizenry. Yet as they walked the dock, it appeared that every inhabitant of the city now participated in the sacred identity with Anu. How could this have all happened within a few months? It did not seem possible.

He also noticed the presence of many horses and the distinct absence of onagers for travel use. He knew horses were just being introduced into the region and that the various cities were breeding them. But there were so many here. It just did not make sense that this kind of change could have happened without years of development and planning.

His gaze dwelt on the architecture. It was not the same. The buildings seemed taller than he remembered. He did not recognize the look of some of the city. Then he realized they had been walking down the very street where he had been paraded on the cart as captive of the gods. It was the same street, but it looked different. He had not had time to notice details of architecture while he was being pelted with rotten vegetables while transported on a cart of shame. But even so, this was different. The buildings seemed built up.

At the end of the street, they came upon the brick-making pit. Emaciated slaves crawled in it, creating mud bricks in the hot sun with sand, straw and mud. Stone was non-existent in the area, so mud brick was the main means of building structures along with some wood from the cedar forest. But again, Noah noticed that there were more slaves here than he had ever seen before. The brick making area was three times the size he remembered, and he guessed there were over a thousand slaves down there. Was his memory failing him?

A contingent of bird-men soldiers marched past them in the streets. Noah and Uriel pulled their cloaks up to cover their faces. They found a stable and bought two horses for their journey ahead. They stepped out into the street and saw the temple district of Inanna at the end of the street. Noah felt drawn to it as if bidden by some unseen force.

They arrived at the end of the market street by the entrance to the temple. Another large contingent of bird-men soldiers passed by. The military presence of these creatures seemed excessive to him. But the sight before them would raise that level of excess to new heights.

Across the street stood the entrance to the temple of Inanna. Its curved oval walls rose high over the street, casting a shadow on the long line of hundreds of male temple patrons. Minstrels played lute and pipe. Caged portholes embedded in the walls near the entrance hosted dancing women. But these were unnatural women. They were four-armed blue goddesses from the Indus Valley. They swirled swords in fluid motions to the music. Strings of human skulls hung from the floors of their cages. It was both perverse and violent, just like Inanna.

It made him sick to his stomach. Yet he knew this depravity was not entirely alien to his own soul. Evil was inside all men, including him. Their inclinations had simply been fed and nurtured instead of suppressed and overcome by faith. This moral decadence was not as bizarre as it appeared. It took humility for Noah to recognize that what disgusted him also strangely drew him, and if he made choices that began simple and small and grew over time, he could end up like any of these deluded slaves of sin. Evil was not "other." It was with him, *within* him.

Noah said simply, "I see her worship is popular." Then he added, "I was wheeled through these streets when I was first captured. But this is different. More wicked. More vile." He shook his head at his own understatement, for it was as if the entire city was possessed by demons.

"I need to tell you something, Noah," said Uriel, breaking him out of his trance. "How long were you in Tartarus?"

"Days?" said Noah. "Weeks. I lost track."

"In the depths of Sheol, it is as if time stops," said Uriel.

"Yes," said Noah. "Exactly." Then he noticed Uriel staring at him without responding.

"What are you saying?" Noah asked.

"While you were in Tartarus, up here on earth one hundred years have passed."

Noah became dizzy as the reality hit him in the gut. "One hundred years?" He could not believe it. His breath shortened. He could feel his heart pounding in his chest. He wanted to run, but there was nowhere to go.

"Yes," said Uriel. "The world has worsened. Every intent of the thought of man's heart is continually evil."

Another unit of bird-men soldiers marched past them. Uriel added, "And the gods are preparing for war."

"With whom?" asked Noah.

"With Elohim—and the seed of Eve," said Uriel.

Before Noah could appreciate the full impact of that statement, an earthquake surprised them. They lost their footing just a little. But people around them went about their normal lives as if nothing had happened.

Uriel said to Noah, "Birth pangs of Elohim's wrath."

Noah saw that the heavens were not the same. It was like the entire universe was transforming around him in preparation for something terrible.

"We have not much time," said Uriel. "We must reach the Hidden Valley."

Noah and Uriel mounted their horses and headed toward the Zagros Mountains.

# CHAPTER 20

Behind its outer walls, the Temple of Inanna was another world. When they entered the bronze gates from the dusty barren city streets, patrons became submerged in a world of sensuality, a garden of earthly delights. Lush flora filled the open courtyard: exotic fruit trees with dates, figs, and pomegranates. Tamarisk and palm trees rose above the floor in a canopy of leaves. The complex artificial irrigation channels of the city watered this botanical paradise of flowers and vegetation. A wisp of incense mixed with perfume wafted through the air, teasing the nostrils. The temple and palace gardens replicated a memory of Eden. It was as if gods and kings sought to retain their ancestral past even as they perverted it into its mirror opposite.

Strange hybrid creatures inhabited this anti-Eden: an obese woman with the head of a cow, another with reptilian skin, a dwarf with a tail and hooves, a deathly thin giantess with spindly arms and legs. There were dog-headed and pig-headed women. There were even woman-headed dogs and pigs. The violation of the created order had spread so deep, the judgment of God could not be closer.

Past the priestly and servant antechambers loomed the sanctuary that housed the stone statue of Inanna. The idol towered over seven and a half feet, carved from diorite, a dark grey volcanic rock imported from the northern regions. A libations and purification priest, called an *isib*, carefully attended to the new image that adorned the sacred space.

The original idol had fallen over and broken in half in the last major earthquake. This would not bode well for Inanna's reputation, so the priests had a new statue created in the idol workshop. From there, a holy procession brought the idol down to the river. It was placed in a reed hut specially erected for the "opening of the mouth" and "washing of the mouth" rituals. These ceremonies ritually purified the stone, and called down the deity to enliven the statue with her spirit. The mouth would first be washed multiple times with varying combinations of water, honey and ghee. A priest then engaged in various incantations of birthing the goddess in the image. It was not that they believed the image itself to be the goddess, but that it embodied the deity's presence and dominion. Noah would have seen it as another mimicry of Elohim's representative image in mankind ruling on earth. In effect, the statue was "born in heaven and made on earth." The damaged statue was mourned and cast into the river. The new one, embodied with the deity in a kind of resurrection from the netherworld, was brought back up into the sanctuary for its residence.

Images were ideal for the plan of the gods. They provided a means whereby they could keep the focus of humankind on an object of this world instead of the unseen presence of Elohim. At the same time, the idols would root that concrete connection to themselves. Anu and Inanna were loath to make themselves too visible to the population. They knew that physical absence reinforced a sense of mystery and reverence in the worshippers. The less they showed themselves to the masses, the more awe they inspired. Stone idols were simply helpful reminders.

The isib priest poured out liquid offerings and checked the idol's braces and security. It had already withstood the latest rumbling of earth, but he wanted to be sure it would be able to withstand a more rigorous quake. Like all those in the service of the gods, the isib had an elongated skull, was shaved of all hair, and carried the tattoos and piercings of the deity on his body beneath his multicolored linen robes. He was being groomed by Lugalanu himself to become a *sanga*, the next highest level of priest, an administrator with an eye toward becoming an *ensi*, the high priest.

A female temple servant slipped unnoticed into the room and whispered to the isib.

"Ham."

Ham, son of Noah, the child taken from Emzara a hundred years before, had grown into a well-educated son of Lugalanu, the priest-king. Though this was not official, it might as well have been, for Lugalanu had groomed him from birth for such a noble end. Ham knew that Lugalanu loved his mother Emzara and was still trying to persuade her to marry him, and that this was why he loved Ham as his own. He still could not understand just why his mother was so stubborn after so many years. Her attitude kept her, by temple regulation, from being in communication with her own son. If she would only marry the priest-king, she would be allowed to visit with her son because of her exalted status. She could then avoid the difficulty of secret rendezvous.

Ham turned to see his beloved Neela hiding in the shadows. They had married recently. His new rank as isib allowed him the privilege of matrimony disallowed to the eunuchs and lesser temple priests. Though his court name was Canaanu, both Emzara and Neela had earned the privilege of calling him Ham in private.

Ham held out his arms and bid her come. Neela whisked over and they embraced with a deep kiss. She was fifty years his junior, full of spunk and excitement for life. Something about Neela's desert descent made her stand out from the Mesopotamian passivity. She was curious, passionate, and headstrong, but she filled his life with such playfulness and hope that he could not live without her. And she could sense his every mood.

"My love, you are weary," said Neela. "What is Lugalanu waiting for? He should initiate you into the high priesthood and be done with it."

"Neela. First of all, the initiation only occurs on the New Year Festival, and I am still an office away from ensi. I must become a sanga first. That will take years."

"Years," she repeated with contempt. "Bah! Why must it take so long? You are a leader among men."

Ham smiled. "I thank you for your support, dear wife, but there is an order to things. You know full well we hurt ourselves if we violate the order of the gods. There are secrets I have not yet been initiated into."

"What secrets?" she said.

"How can I know if I have not been initiated, silly? And if I did, I certainly could not tell you."

He smiled and kissed her again.

She teased him, "To become a priest of Inanna, the Queen of Heaven, is no small thing for such a humble servant."

He teased right back, "But to be husband of Neela, the Queen of my heart, is an altogether exhaustive thing."

"Well, then, we exhaust each other," she smiled.

She could see he was not all there. "Are you thinking of your mother?" she asked.

He could not respond with the obvious yes.

The arrival of the Temple Guard interrupted them. Lugalanu stepped through the guards and into the room.

Neela immediately bowed and backed out toward the back room exit. Ham knelt before his king.

"Lord Lugalanu, I am your servant."

"Canaanu, my isib of Inanna, how do you fare?" Lugalanu replicated the lighthearted attitude of Anu in his own dealings with inferiors. Like god, like son.

"Well, my lord," replied Ham.

"Excellent, excellent," he said, looking around the sanctuary. "I applaud you. The goddess' temple is well kept, and I see you have taken special care of the new image of our high and mighty Queen of Heaven."

Ham detected a slight sarcasm in the tone. He knew that Lugalanu wearied of kowtowing to Inanna's intemperate volatility. But it was not something they talked about. Lugalanu knew it would be injudicious to instill such conflict of interest with the very priest he was preparing for her service.

Ham did not know that Lugalanu only made him a priest of Inanna in order to persuade Emzara to love him. Unfortunately, it had not worked out the way he had hoped. Lugalanu had suffered every day since then. Lugalanu had thought it might force Emzara to compromise, but it only hardened her resolve. He hoped that watching her son become increasingly involved in the priesthood of a god she hated would at least burn on her soul with a pain equivalent to what she caused him.

"Canaanu," said Lugalanu. His tone changed, becoming more serious. "All these years, you know I have considered you a son."

It was a plea for his love. Ham looked downward submissively.

"If I may, exalted one, then why would you keep your son from his mother?"

The inquiry was certainly respectful in tone, but it was still a cloaked challenge. Lugalanu liked that about Ham. "You are so much like your mother. You know full well the servants of Inanna do not mingle with the servants of Anu. It is not in my authority to challenge the covenants of the kingdom."

Hierarchy in the priestly caste was strictly enforced as a code of holiness. It was ironic that the kingdom built upon violation of the separation of the created order should maintain its own rigid separations and distinctions of sacredness. Of course the king was fully capable of determining exemptions as he pleased, so his motives were not as honest as they appeared.

Lugalanu continued, "Nevertheless, you are being groomed to become a high priest of the Queen of Heaven, so it is time for your introduction to the secrets of the Watchers."

Ham caught his breath. This was an opportunity he had coveted for years. Initiation into the secrets of the Watchers was both a sacred privilege and a dangerous responsibility. These gods, who had come from heaven to earth, had revealed many secrets to mankind, secrets of sorcery, apothecary, charms and enchantments, witchcraft, as well as astrological worship and the making of idols and their ritual incantations. They had also revealed the art of metal making for both ornament and war. The thought of admission into this cabal of mystery made Ham's entire being well up with exhilaration.

He followed Lugalanu out of the room toward his destiny.

They both did not realize that Neela had been hiding behind the statue of Inanna the entire time and had heard it all. Her pride in her husband made her beam with excitement. Her curiosity overwhelmed her. What were these wonderful "secrets of the Watchers?"

# CHAPTER 21

Lugalanu led Ham down a circular stairwell deep into the recesses of the earth below the temple complex of Eanu. The spiral brick staircase spun downward like a chambered nautilus sea shell. Lugalanu lit an occasional wall torch for their return trip.

Neela followed them in the shadows. She kept a safe distance to avoid detection, and she scurried along barefoot to silence the sound of her steps.

At the bottom of the dizzying staircase lay a series of twisting pitch-dark corridors. Fortunately for Neela, the hallways continued to be lit by Lugalanu's torch like a path of bread crumbs. Fear rose in her liver. There were so many turns, she began to lose her bearings. She worried that she could not find her way out if she found herself alone and without the lit torches. She could become a prisoner of the darkness, possibly even die down here. But it was too late to turn back. She had passed the point of no return and would have to continue on in hope she would be all right.

She had lived with risk all her life. As a little orphan servant girl of eight in the city, she found her way past all the guards, priests, and priestesses to the very top of the White Temple itself. Anu had found her so amusing and curious that instead of punishing her, he had rewarded her by appointing her to the temple staff of Inanna. For this act of kindness, Neela gave eternal gratitude to Anu, because it was how she found her way into the sight and passions of Ham. She continued in her stealth pursuit with a renewed sense of enthusiasm in her heart.

Lugalanu and Ham passed a secret corridor that brought back emotional memories for Lugalanu. Down that passage was the sealed burial chamber of his father, Lugalanuruku, the previous priest-king of Erech. He was named after his father, though he was the offspring of a Sacred Marriage rite with the high priestess. The ritual ensured fertility of the land. Priestesses were considered royalty and so their children were often successors to the throne, though they would not abdicate their temple status.

He would never forget the grand celebration of the funeral that heralded his own ascension to the throne. His father had died of unknown sickness when he was young. Neither the *ashipu* magic shaman nor the *ashu* medical doctor could cure him. He was anointed with oil and interred in the large vault on an elaborate bed-like pallet along with his beloved wife, who joined her husband in death.

The funeral procession had begun at the palace gates. A small band of musicians led the funerary lamentation playing lyres, lutes, and harps. The deathbed with its king and queen followed the musicians, surrounded by six personal guards. Behind them trailed twenty ladies-in-waiting and fifty other servants. The crowd of citizens lined the streets to catch a glimpse of their deceased grand ruler. Once the procession arrived at the temple, they were escorted by an entourage of priests out of the public eye and down into the secret recesses below the ziggurat.

They were led into the large crypt, where the priest-king was laid in his sarcophagus. Then the entire train of guards and palace servants filled the chamber, drank a poison, lay down and embraced their fate in union with their lord and master. They were to follow him into the afterlife where they would continue to serve him. The guards were fully clothed in armor and the servants in golden headdresses with necklaces of cornelian and lapis lazuli. A second vault next to them contained some gold and other riches along with two chariots and onagers, also killed with poison. The crypts were then sealed and their occupants left as the city mourned publicly. Considering how gloomy and hopeless the "land of no return" was, Lugalanu was grateful to still be a part of the land of the living.

He imagined how grand and glorious his own burial would be with Emzara poisoned beside him along with his own staff of attendants.

Lugalanu and Ham finally reached their destination, a large set of doors in the dead end of an unassuming passageway. It was large enough to accommodate Nephilim.

Ham gulped with a mixture of excitement and fear.

Lugalanu turned to him and said, "You are about to enter the inner sanctum of the gods. Few humans will ever see what you are about to see. At no point are you to express anything other than wonder and awe. Should you be appalled or revolted by what you see, remember, you do not understand the wisdom of the gods. Their ways and their thoughts are as high above you as the heavens are above the earth. Is that understood?"

"Yes," said Ham. A shiver went down his spine. He wondered just what might cause him to be "appalled or revolted."

They entered the door and closed it behind them. They travelled through a hallway lined with seven cubit tall, recessed doorways. Lugalanu stopped at one of them and opened it. They stepped inside a long, narrow room, an infirmary sectioned off by rows of brick walls, creating small stalls for beds.

"This is the breeding room for the sacred women who bear the Nephilim for the gods," Lugalanu explained.

As they walked down the hallway of stalls, Ham saw beds full of very pregnant women, one to a stall. The women were restrained with leather straps or metal shackles, depending upon their level of risk. It seemed more like a prison than a breeding room.

Lugalanu answered Ham's unspoken question in a whispered tone, "These are the ones nearest to giving birth. At earlier stages of pregnancy they have much more freedom. But the final stage can be violently painful so they have to be restrained for their own good."

"What happens after birth?" Ham asked, innocently enough. He had known of women chosen for this holy high honor, but had never seen them again.

"Unfortunately, it kills them," said Lugalanu matter-of-factly. Lugalanu had always felt sorry for the women and their plight. He tried to comfort Ham with what he comforted himself often, "Death is just a doorway into higher service of the gods. In some ways, they are better off than us."

The women looked drugged, not as giddy and hopeful about their future as Lugalanu seemed to suggest. One of the women screamed in pain just as Ham and Lugalanu passed her stall. She writhed desperately in the bed, straining against her bonds. A few midwives ran to her with a bucket and rags. Ham stared with fascination, wanting to see what happened, but Lugalanu pulled him away.

He escorted Ham back out into the hallway. The piercing scream of the woman giving birth rang in Ham's ears and echoed through the corridors.

The next doorway led them into another long hallway of stalls. These compartments did not hold pregnant women. Instead there were various versions of human-animal chimeras that Ham already knew well, seeing them around the palace and temple grounds. They too were chained to the walls with straw for beds. These were new kinds he had not seen before and they appeared to be in varying stages of mutation or development. Some looked like they had body parts attached surgically, such as a human body with a pig's head in one stall and a huge pig's body with a human head in the next. Others appeared to be an essential fusion of kinds, such as a humanoid whose body was completely covered with hair and whose face looked as much like a wolf as it did a man. It lunged at Ham, snarling for his blood. Ham jumped back, but the chain jerked the wolf man back into its stall.

Other hybrid fusions looked more like developmental failures of miserable creatures with human bodies and malformed appendages or misshapen body structures. These were chimeras gone wrong. It was all a den of sorcery, an experimental chamber of breeding horrors.

Ham remembered Lugalanu's words, and suppressed his reaction with a sense of awe and wonder—and morbid curiosity. He could see the practical use for the bird-men soldiers and other creatures like the pazuzu and the crossbred throne guardians. But these monstrous miscegenations suggested a deeper strategy at work in the minds of the gods. Just what, he did not know.

Lugalanu could see the wheels churning in Ham's mind. He said simply, "You will learn soon enough, and it will all become clear."

They exited the chamber of horrors and stopped at a final doorway. Lugalanu wanted the importance to sink into Ham's consciousness. "This is the holy of holies. The secrets of the Watchers reside here. The very knowledge of heaven." He opened the door.

Inside was a large vault of potions and vials, jars and vases, strange structures whose technology seemed far advanced from Ham's known world. Ham had been taught the rudiments of Mesopotamian science. He knew taxonomic categories of plants and animals, astronomical and astrological systems, and drugs for use with medicine and sorcery. But the things in this room were like nothing Ham had ever seen.

He looked upon the rudimentary forms of biological and genetic experimental science, mysteries beyond his education. Because the Sons of God were divine beings, they had occultic knowledge of which humans could only dream. But as earth bound creatures, they were limited to the resources at hand. Drugs and potions created a certain amount of magic, but they knew biological alteration was more fundamental than that. So they sought the manipulation of that basic nature through a primitive form of genetics.

Ham became fixated on a series of glass jars before him. He had heard of glass when it was first introduced to the economy, but he had not seen any of it until now. He stared, fascinated. But what the jars held was even more spell-binding. Ten jars contained fetuses of varying development and at varying stages of transformation from human to something shiny, slender, and reptilian – like the gods.

"Are you impressed with my creations?" a voice said, behind Ham.

Ham started out of his trance-like stare. He turned to see the mighty Anu standing behind him. He dropped to the floor in worship. "Greatly, my lord and god, greatly," he gulped, his heart beating out of his chest.

Anu offered his hand to help him up. Ham did not know what to do. He had never touched the hand of a god.

Lugalanu whispered with humor, "Your god awaits."

"Please, stand," said Anu.

Ham took Anu's hand with fear and trembling, and stood before his god. The skin was cold, clammy and slightly scaly. But Anu was kind, gentle, and patient with Ham's nervousness. He smiled.

"You are to become an ensi high priest?"

"Eventually, almighty one. My next promotion is to sanga." Ham's voice cracked with trembling.

Anu smiled warmly. "Your loyalty shall be rewarded soon enough. And I hope you will find your initiation satisfying and calming to your fears." His voice was so compassionate Ham felt as if he spoke telepathically to his heart and mind.

"It is my intent to be found worthy of such a holy honor," said Ham.

"Well then, welcome to the secrets of the Watchers," said Anu.

"My Lord, if I may," began Ham.

Lugalanu had watched the exchange carefully. He could spot Emzara's feisty inquisitiveness in her son starting to show itself.

"How can I begin to understand such wonderful sorceries?"

Anu welcomed the curiosity. "That is where faith comes in. What were you taught in school about the creation of the heavens and the earth?"

Ham recited from memory the rote words he had learned from the temple scribes about *Inanna's Tale of the Huluppu Tree* and the *Eridu Genesis*, "The sky god, Anu, carried off the heavens, and the air god, Enlil, carried off the earth. The Queen of the Great Below, Ereshkigal, was given the underworld for her domain. And Anu, Enlil, Enki, and Ninhursag fashioned the dark–headed people of Sumer."

"Well done," smiled Anu. "And now I will tell you the truth. That creation story is a lie."

Ham's stomach dropped. What could he be saying? The Most High God and the Lord of the Air, did not separate the heavens from the earth?

"What you have been taught is a myth that is intended to protect humankind from what they could not understand. There are some truths that are so sacred only the most wise and most loyal are to be entrusted with them."

Ham swallowed. Lugalanu saw him sweating. He had cultivated this young man with great care. He had confidence that Ham would rise to the honor of this high calling.

Anu continued, "What do you know of the deity called Elohim?"

"A distant god of a lost Garden in Eden?" It was all he could muster, as if it was all he knew. But it was not all he knew.

Emzara had actually taught him much about Elohim, for she worshipped him in secret. She had constantly admonished Ham to worship him as well whenever they had their clandestine meetings. It was all rather distasteful to him. She spoke of Elohim creating the heavens and the earth; and of Adam of the earth and Havah his wife, the mother of all the living; of how they were images of Elohim on earth much like the statues of Anu and Inanna in the temple were images of the deities. She spoke of the Serpent, Nachash, the Shining One, a Watcher himself, who drew them away from Elohim in disobedience and how Elohim expelled them from the Garden, away from his presence. She had told him how Elohim revealed that a Chosen Seed would come who would end the rule of the gods and bring judgment upon the gods, and rest to the land. And that a king would come from his lineage that would ultimately destroy the seed of the Serpent.

It seemed like conspiratorial myth to Ham. Worse, it was treason to the gods. It was the one thing Ham worried deeply about regarding his dear mother. He wondered what inspired her to be so fanatically devoted to such delusionary rambling. What made her satisfied with slavery and poverty over the rich pleasures and glories of the Kingdom of Anu? And her commitment to a dead man who, she kept reminding Ham in secret, was his real father. The only father that Ham knew was his adopted father Lugalanu, who loved him and took care of him. *That* man was his father, and that man stood with Ham right now in the presence of deity, supporting his rite of passage into the secrets of the gods.

Anu brought Ham out of his thoughts. "Elohim is the true creator of heaven and earth."

The words jolted Ham out of the blue. He did not see it coming. Was Anu telling him right now that his mother was right? How could that possibly be? His entire view of the world was just turned inside out.

"But Elohim is an evil god," continued Anu. "He is a jealous and bitter old spirit." Anu paced around the room and launched upon a diatribe against the deity. "This so-called 'creator of heaven and earth' has hidden from mankind the secrets which you see before you this day. He has sought to keep humankind in bondage to ignorance, jealous of allowing them to become enlightened like himself. He has sought to keep everyone and everything separate. He separated light from dark, he separated heaven from earth, human from animal, male from female, *man from god*." Anu was histrionic in his delivery, but it served to underline his righteous indignation with such injustice.

"That is a rather selfish deity, would you not agree?" asked Anu.

"Yes, my lord," said Ham without thinking.

Anu stopped his pacing near the doorway. He sniffed the air. After a quizzical look, he returned to his pacing.

He had just missed discovering Neela, who hid on the other side of the open door. Anu had been close enough for her to reach around and touch him. She had managed to escape detection.

Anu concluded his tirade, explaining his plan. "But I bring new hope and change. I want to undo the separation, to erase the distinctions between creatures. I want to make all things into One." Anu bent down and looked into one of the jars of fetuses on the shelf. "By combining my seed with human seed, I will fundamentally transform humankind. I will create man in my image rather than in Elohim's image. I will give man his proper destiny. I will make man into a god."

All of Emzara's words came flooding into Ham's mind, causing doubts and fears. The prophecy of the Chosen Seed ending the rule of the gods and bringing the judgment of Elohim down upon their heads.

Anu drew Ham's attention to the jars of fetuses. "The Nephilim are the offspring of our union with the daughters of men. But I have been working on another way of combining our flesh with human flesh, in a way that may not be so obvious as our giant progeny." Anu could not describe in detail the molecular genetics to which he was referring. Mankind's knowledge and technology were not advanced enough yet for Ham to understand this. He would have to simplify the language. "Our goal is to breed a Naphil that would look like a normal human being. It would not be a giant, it would have ten fingers and ten toes, but it would have the heart and soul of a Naphil. It would be a demigod. It would carry in its blood the ability to breed a race of Nephilim that would spread across the land."

"Are these demigods among us?" asked Ham.

"Not yet," said Anu.

Ham cautiously ventured out, "And what of the Chosen Seed? Is the Revelation true? How can we fight it?"

For the first time in his sermon, Anu became visibly perturbed. It was not a secret that the Revelation was spreading about by word of mouth, first in the temple and palace and then within the city walls. It would soon be unavoidably known by every single soul.

"That is why the gods are seeking to create an alliance between all the cities," he answered, "to overcome our differences in a coalition of common purpose. Together, we will create an army of legions for war against the Seed of Havah."

Lugalanu saw these disclosures overwhelming Ham. He put his arm around him in support. "This is why we need leaders of your will to power," he said.

Anu continued, "If we cannot breed out this coming king, we will find the Chosen Seed by killing every last remnant of the nomadic tribes of humanity who do not worship the pantheon."

The seriousness of it all settled upon Ham.

Anu had moved near the door again. But this time, he spun like a coiled snake and reached around the doorway, pulling out a choking Neela by the neck.

"What is this eavesdropper slithering in the dark? A slender conspirator?!" shouted Anu, his voice booming with supernatural reverberation.

Neela stared mesmerized into Anu's penetrating cold blue eyes. He saw into her very soul. He sniffed her with relish and satisfaction, justified that he had caught her scent earlier. He released his grip around her neck.

Ham fell to his knees before Anu.

"My god, forgive me! She is my wife. I did not know she followed me."

Anu looked down on Ham, groveling at his feet.

"My god, she has not a conspiratorial bone in her body. She is recklessly curious. That is all. I beg of you, if you must punish, punish me instead."

This surprised Anu. Such love for such puny worth.

"Her curiosity brought her into your service many years ago. You honored her for it. Please remember your goodness in your name."

Anu tilted his head with interest. He had a vague recollection. He inhaled her scent deeply this time. A smile spread across his face. "The White Temple. I do remember. This is now the second time this little mouse has managed to scurry her way under the eye of the cobra."

Neela quivered. Immediate death no longer hovered over her. But it did not matter. She was a disobedient child caught with her hand in the fig jar.

Anu slowly smiled, and his warm lightheartedness returned. Neela could feel it in her own body relaxing.

"A curious wife you have, my priest. She is a willing subject. She will serve us both well."

Ham breathed a sigh of relief. But then a chill went through him when Anu took yet another intoxicating inhale of her scent into his nostrils.

# CHAPTER 22

Noah and Uriel rode their horses at a canter into the Zagros Mountains about seventy leagues northeast of Erech. When they had escaped Sheol, the other archangels stayed behind to finish their task of binding the Rephaim. Uriel had explained to Noah that the archangels would get reinforcements and seek out the last of the human tribes in the West. A war was coming, a war of gods and men. The fallen Watchers had been planning it for a long while. They had seduced most of the people of the land into their sorceries and idolatries and were now determined to exterminate the rest. The only chance humanity had was for the angels to organize them to defend themselves. But getting the last of the human tribes to agree on anything was a nearly impossible project. Nevertheless, they had to try. It might take months to accomplish this goal, but other angels were sent out as well.

The one advantage of a war for the archangels was that if they could get all the Watchers together in an allied effort, it would enhance the angels' opportunity to bind the fallen into the heart of the earth as Elohim had commanded. Noah and Uriel discussed the possibilities of such an impossible task for a goodly portion of their trek through the plains and into the mountains. There were two hundred of the gods and they were not all mustered at Erech. Nevertheless, the most important leaders were and those were the priority for the archangels.

"Where is this Hidden Valley you keep speaking of?" Noah asked.

"If I told you, it would not be hidden," Uriel chortled.

Uriel had often reminisced about the old days when he, Methuselah, and Noah's mother and father had ended up in the Hidden Valley, hemmed in on all sides by natural formations making it virtually invisible to explorers. He would speak of their adventures being hunted by the cursed Cain's wolf tribe, and how they had triumphed over that man of wrath to live another day. There would be no lineage of demon dogs left in the Hidden Valley. He assured Noah they were all taken care of.

After days of riding, they sought one of the few secret passageways into the valley.

Noah said, "Strange that we are so close to the cities of the plain, yet they are unaware. Right under their filthy noses."

"I am sure the entrance is near here, as far as my memory serves me," said Uriel.

A deep bellowing roar interrupted them. It shook the very trees around them to the roots. Noah gaped at Uriel. This was a beast very large and very near.

"Did I forget to tell you, this is the realm of Behemoth?" quipped Uriel. "Do not worry, he is much too big to get through the pass."

"Well, that is comforting," shot back Noah snidely. "Have you ever seen Behemoth?" he asked.

Uriel said, "He is like Leviathan, but on land."

"Well, I hope you are happy," said Noah. "You succeeded in ruining my day."

"It is not that bad," added Uriel. "Behemoth only has one head."

"Oh, that makes it all better," said Noah.

Uriel *had* seen Behemoth. Uriel was there at the creation and was privileged to be a part of the morning stars who sang praises to Elohim when he laid the foundation of the earth, struck its line, determined the measurements and sunk its bases. He had gloried when Elohim created a firmament in the midst of the waters to separate the waters above from the waters below. He watched with awe as Elohim made the waters swarm with great sea monsters like Rahab and Leviathan, and let the earth bring forth living creatures according to their kind, creeping things and beasts of the earth, including Behemoth. The irony was not lost on him that creation was both wonderful and fearsome.

Uriel yelled, "Run for your life!" and kicked his horse.

Noah wondered if he was jesting again.

The colossal beast broke out of the forest near them. The hair on Noah's neck stood up and a shiver of terror surged down his spine. The creature was the size of a tall building, and it ran after them at full speed, the ground shaking beneath its trampling feet.

Noah only got a glimpse of its monstrous ugliness. In a flash, he galloped for his life after Uriel. All he saw was its huge trampling legs, its tail like a cedar tree, an ugly hump, and its bull-like head. Uriel was right. It was as terrible as a sea dragon on land.

The gargantuan gained on them.

Noah could see Uriel bearing straight for a vine covered wall of the rock bluff. He wondered what the angel was doing, placing them between a rock wall and a hard place.

Uriel yelled to him, "Trust me!"

Noah saw Uriel disappear into the wall vines without smashing to pieces. It was a hidden entrance. He glanced back to see Behemoth was almost upon him as he split the vines with his horse. The monstrosity hit the narrow opening and it felt like the entire mountain around them rattled. Uriel was right again. The beast was much too huge to fit through the pass. Thank Elohim.

Noah stared back at the raging creature. He could see one of its eyes was destroyed and laid over with scars.

Noah had learned of Behemoth from Methuselah. He never forgot the story his grandfather told him of the day he lost his precious wife Edna to this hideous monster. The creature protected its territory with ferocity. When Methuselah, Edna, and Noah's parents had first discovered this location, they did not know about Behemoth. It had attacked and killed Edna. Its size and strength were so overwhelming that Methuselah had only had the chance to blind it in one eye with a javelin before escaping into the pass. Nothing could pay back the devastation this monster wrought upon Methuselah. The event broke him. He was never the same again. At least Methuselah had been able to leave a permanent scar to remind the monster of the man who planned to one day return and kill it.

But Behemoth was still alive.

Noah wondered if that meant that Methuselah had not made it back here as they had agreed. It did not bode well for Noah's plans. Had Methuselah been killed by this land dragon?

They arrived at the end of the pass, where it opened up to the Hidden Valley. They both gasped, looking out onto a world seemingly lost in time. A lush valley of plants, trees, and animals spread before them, a place that could only be described as a jungle paradise.

"It reminds me of Eden," said Uriel.

"If it was," said Noah, "I would be dead by the sword of the Cherubim." He chuckled to himself, and they entered a pathway through the foliage.

Uriel knew it was coming, but did not anticipate such hostility.

A young warrior swung out of hiding on a vine. He knocked Noah off his horse to the ground, pushing Noah face down to the earth.

Uriel was off his horse in an instant. He stopped still when he saw the warrior with a dagger to Noah's throat. Beyond that first one, three others stood with bows drawn on Noah and Uriel. These warriors were good. They were trained well in stealth. They obviously had heard Behemoth's announcement of approaching intruders. They wore animal skins and they were all young, only about a hundred years old or so.

Lying on the ground, Noah stopped struggling when he felt the edge of the blade against his throat in a tight hold.

The warrior was strong. He belted out to his comrades, "They seem human enough!"

The lead archer spit through his aim, "Of course they do, Shem. Clever disguise for clever abominations."

Noah's eyes went wide. Those words were familiar; the name, the voice. He tried to get a better glimpse of his captor. "Shem? Shem ben Noah?"

It confused the young warrior with the dagger. The archer's surprise gave way to recognition.

Noah looked up at the young man with arrow aimed at his heart. "Japheth?" he pleaded.

Japheth, ever the impulsive one, responded first. "Father! I did not recognize you!"

Shem lowered his dagger, and turned Noah around. They looked into each other's eyes. No further doubt remained that they were father and son.

"It has been so long." Shem wrapped Noah in a big bear hug.

Japheth dropped his bow, ran and jumped onto the two of them, and they tumbled to the ground in a family wrestling match.

They rolled to a stop on the jungle floor.

"We thought you were dead!" shouted Japheth.

Noah looked them up and down with pride. "You have grown into such fine warriors."

"Uh, Noah," interrupted Uriel.

The three of them looked over at Uriel, still under the aim of the archers.

"May I request you share some of that familial love?" Uriel joked.

"Forgive me," laughed Shem. "Men, put down your arms."

The archers lowered their weapons with sighed relief.

"Father, where have you been?" asked Japheth.

"That is a long story," said Noah. "And I am hungry."

The warriors led Noah and Uriel to a large clearing in the center of the valley. As they broke through the jungle brush, Noah and Uriel stopped. The sight took their breath away. There were elaborate wooden homes, a couple hundred strong, scattered around in a small village, with families going about their business. A sight that amazed Noah towered behind the village. It was a huge wooden skeletal structure the size of a large rectangle building. A pile of cut, trimmed and cleaned trees, enough to build a small city sat within walking distance of the massive construction.

"Tebah?" said Noah.

Methuselah, Tubal-cain and Jubal ran to them from the village, shouting greetings.

They exchanged long overdue embraces, grabbing each other's wrists. Noah could not keep his eyes off of the structure.

"You are building the box?" he asked.

"Your sons and tribe are," said Methuselah, "in your name."

Methuselah pulled out a piece of leather with scratchings all over it. He handed it ceremoniously to Noah.

"You gave me the directions before your little vacation in Sheol all those years ago. Must this old man shame your dullness of memory?"

Noah grinned widely and hugged Methuselah again. "Old man, I missed you terribly." He looked at Tubal-cain. "I trust my cousin here has kept you in your place with his molten word and wit."

Methuselah harrumphed. "My dirty loin cloth, he did. I am too nimble for such a corpulent whale."

"I fear our feeble senior has lost more than his bowels," retorted Tubal-cain, circling his finger around his skull in a "crazy" gesture.

"I must say," Methuselah changed the attack, "I am impressed to see that your guardian angel has actually done his job for once in protecting your obstinate rump."

"It's good to be back with family," snorted Uriel, and they all laughed.

Uriel said to Methuselah, "I believe it was you who told me many years ago, you would like to retire here."

"Elohim has granted my wish," said Methuselah.

Noah looked around at the village. "Do not tell me," he said, "all these villagers are the remnant orphans of my tribe grown of age?"

"You have been away for a hundred years," Uriel reminded him.

Japheth added delightfully, "Elohim did say to be fruitful and multiply."

Suddenly, a small tremor shook the valley. It made them solemn again.

Tubal-cain said, "I have been timing them. They are increasing. Fortunately the mountain range around us absorbs most of the rattle, but out on the plain is another story."

"Birth pangs of Elohim's wrath," said Noah, repeating the words he had heard Uriel tell him in Erech.

Shem said, "We have been preparing the materials and waiting for you to return as Patriarch to finish your calling."

Noah looked at Shem's belt to see the leather case holding the whip sword Rahab at his side. He saw Betenos' bow on Japheth's back. Noah said to his sons, "I did not fulfill my promise to train you in your grandparents' weapons."

"Considering the nature of your delay, father" said Japheth, "we forgive you."

Methuselah interjected, "I did the best I could."

Shem concluded, "We are trained, we are speedy, and we are ready."

Noah looked at them with proud tears of joy. "Well, then, let me finish my calling."

"First," said Methuselah, "I want to show you something."

Methuselah took Noah alone to an ancient terebinth tree by a small brook in a dark corner of the forest. They stood before a pile of rocks placed by the tree long before. "Terebinth," said Methuselah. "They are considered sacred objects of communication with the divine.

"This is where she sleeps," he continued. "Your grandmother Edna. My happiness. It has been good for me to be back. It has reminded me that one day, we shall be united again."

Noah asked, "Why did you never remarry, Grandfather?"

Methuselah sighed with sadness. "Because I foolishly found my significance in being loved by her, rather than in us both being loved by Elohim."

Noah put his arm around his grandfather.

Methuselah said, "I wish you had met her. You would have loved her. You are a lot like her. Full of life, zeal, and a good warrior."

Noah said, "It is hard to imagine: 'Grandmother, the giant killer.'"

They laughed. "Let me tell you," said Methuselah, "She was a giant killer of a wife."

"Grandfather, it is hard to believe any woman could handle you," said Noah lightheartedly.

Methuselah chuckled, "I am surprised I could handle her."

"Why have you not killed Behemoth?" asked Noah, referring to the source of his unhappiness.

Methuselah completed Noah's sentence slyly, "Yet."

Noah looked at him curiously.

Methuselah explained, "While we reside in this valley, that vile creature acts as a guard dog for our security. I would be a fool to settle my score without consideration of the consequences. But when the wrath of Elohim comes, I will have my satisfaction."

Noah wondered if he meant that Elohim's wrath would *be* that satisfaction or if Methuselah still had designs on the beast. He did not want to feed the hurt, so he avoided asking.

# CHAPTER 23

It had taken years to prepare for building the tebah. Methuselah had led the tribe as they grew of age. He patiently taught them the construction skills they needed to build the box. They had honed their talent by building elaborate village homes of wood that provided the added blessing of luxurious living. They found a peculiar tree of very hard wood in the valley they called "gopher wood." It was a long process to cut down the trees and create long, cured and glued planks. The boards were then sealed with a prime coating of tree pitch. The pitch was made by bleeding the sap from pines, burning the pine wood into charcoal, grinding that to powder, and mixing that powder into large vats of boiling pine resin. They then painted the wood with the tree-made pitch to seal it with an initial coat.

The day Noah took charge of construction, they had already built the skeletal structure for the box based on the directions of the holy writ given from God to Noah, and then to Methuselah on leather. Everything stood ready. They needed only to begin the process of final construction. It could be completed within months if things went well.

They had perfected a means of holding the beams together by pounding wooden pins into them. They had found bitumen pits nearby for the final layer of pitch to cover the wood of the completed box with a one or two inch thickness. Noah drove them hard to finish quickly, but he never asked of any man what he was not willing to do himself. Often, men sought him with some question to be answered, only to find him hammering in wooden pegs or helping to saw a plank to fit better. They all worked in shifts from sun up to past sundown, using torches made from the bitumen pitch after dark fall.

As Noah looked out onto the valley from the top of the box, he remembered what Uriel had said when they first arrived, how it had looked like Eden. He pondered what it was like for the Man and Woman to be in such communion with Elohim, their fellow creatures, and the world around them, full of splendor and glory. He wondered what it would be like to be in Elohim's presence and the presence of his divine council of ten thousands of holy ones surrounding his throne and worshipping in the Garden that was his temple. He grieved over how the primordial sin of the first pair had plunged them into darkness, and separated them from their Maker, the Most High, and how the world could have all gone so wrong so quickly.

It was crazy to be building a huge barge like this in the middle of the Zagros Mountains, leagues away from any river or body of water. But Elohim said he was going to judge the land and all its inhabitants and this would be his vessel of salvation; this tebah. Elohim had become sorry he had created mankind, for all flesh had corrupted their way on the earth, and the land was filled with violence through them, and the violence raised its voice to the ears of Elohim in heaven. So he had determined to make an end to all flesh. He would send a deluge of water to blot out man whom he had created from the face of the land, man and all the animals in its wake. This floating box would be Elohim's redemption of a righteous few. Noah did all that the Lord commanded him.

Inside the barge, the structure was organized into three decks lined with a multitude of pens. Ventilation was a long top housing that ran the length of the box, a roofed opening a cubit high, with a hatch for bad weather. The people wondered why the boat was so large, far exceeding the capacity for their few hundred bodies on board. Then Noah told them that God was going to bring animals of every kind from the remotest parts of the land in pairs and in sevens to reside on the boat with them. They did not believe this, until the day when animals of all kinds started to arrive in the valley in numbers, ready to board the box. The carnivores were surprisingly domesticated and would not eat flesh, instead grazing like the herbivores beside them. Methuselah joked that Uriel had hypnotized them with magic. Lions, tigers, and wolves lounged right next to lambs, oxen, and camels. It was another miracle but it would not be the last.

How would they take care of the refuse of all these animals filling up the box? Their excrement alone would pile up within days and create toxic fumes that could kill all the life on board. Tubal-cain and Jubal created a way to use the waste to their advantage. They built a large, closed-off holding tank at the stern of the boat that rose through all three floors. They had discovered that the gases released by the rotting defecation were flammable. So they created a piping system from the refuse tank throughout the craft. Small holes in the pipes allowed them to light the releasing gas. This created a perpetual light source for as long as the animals defecated, which would be as long as Elohim had them on the boat.

What caused Noah the most consternation was the change in the heavens. The earthquakes shook the pillars of the earth and went wide enough to even rattle the pillars of the firmament. The sky changed colors. Even the sun would turn blood red as it set in the gates of the West. Noah noticed an increase of storm clouds on the horizon, distant thunder portending a coming apocalypse. But this was not a time to brood. They finally finished the construction of the box and filled it with the animals.

It was a time to celebrate.

# CHAPTER 24

Ham slipped quietly through the underground tunnel between the two temples. This was not the tunnel for temple staff. It was one of the secret passageways known only to him and few others. He was on a covert mission. The tunnel soon joined a passageway into the temple hallways near Lugalanu's private staff quarters. He looked both ways. It was clear. He scurried up to a locked door and softly rapped on the wood with a deliberate coded knock. A young maidservant opened the door and let him in.

Ham's words were immediate and frustrated, "Mother, please."

Inside, Emzara stood with three fugitive slaves, each carrying small bundles for travel. They saw Ham and withdrew in fear.

"Now, see, my son, you have frightened them. It is all right, children. Ham will not betray you."

Ham snapped testily, "Do not be too sure of yourself. Three fugitives at once? Must you tempt fate so?"

"These three are images of God and they have names. Ham, meet Rami, Biran and Hannah."

The first two were young men. Hannah was pregnant. The three bowed before Ham, who gave Emzara an angry look.

"My given temple name is Canaanu, mother."

"Oh, do not fret yourself," said Emzara. "It is not a sin for them to know the true identity of their liberators, the house of Noah ben Lamech." They knew Ham was the holy sanga, the administrative priest just under the ensi high priest. Ham had received the promotion earlier and was being groomed to become the ensi under Lugalanu.

Ham nodded awkwardly. He did not hate them, but he was not used to treating servants as special human beings in God's image as his mother did. In his understanding, slaves were but shadows of men who were in the image of kings, and only kings were in the image of the gods. But that was an ongoing dispute he had with his mother and it was not going to be settled any time soon.

"Mother, every time I visit you in secret, I endanger my temple status. But you increase my peril when you smuggle out servants like this. You know what the penalty is."

Emzara knew. The penalty was death, quick and sure, without legal proceedings. She remembered Alittum's horrible demise, but thought it was worth the rescue of the innocent.

"I am helping them to freedom and new life," replied Emzara, "away from *here*." Her words came bitterly. "Here" was still not in her heart and soul as it was in Ham's.

She strode past Ham, drawing the fugitives along. At the door, she handed them each bread cakes. They wrapped the cakes and placed them in their bundles. She looked at each of them and gave them an embrace and a prayer, "May Elohim guide you and protect you to safety."

She opened the door and checked for clear, then led them out into the hallway. Ham followed her, irritated.

"Why can you not accept your place in this world?" he whispered harshly to her.

"Because we are not of this world, you and I."

"*This* world," sputtered Ham, "has granted us riches, privilege, royalty. Would you prefer being a wandering nomad in the wilderness?"

Emzara stopped in the middle of the hallway and glared at Ham with moist eyes. She did not say a word, but he knew what she thought. Of course she would prefer to be so.

"Forgive me," said Ham. "Your past is not my own."

He could see she held back a torrent of emotion. "You are the son of Noah ben Lamech, son of Enoch," she said.

"I am the adopted ward of Lugalanu, priest-king of Anu. *He* has raised me. *He* has been a father to me."

"*Your father* ended in Sheol by the hand of Lugalanu."

Emzara continued onward, as if walking away from him.

He followed after her with zeal and complaint. As much as he loved her, Ham could not understand his mother's hardness of heart. In the world they inhabited, men killed other men in war and took their wives with every battle. The fact that Lugalanu would not force her and waited for her was nothing short of grace in Ham's understanding.

"He has begged for your forgiveness. Sought atonement. But you have spurned him."

Emzara's heart had bled for her son from the day he was taken from her. She did not hold it against him. How could he know the goodness that was hidden from him? She had taught him of Elohim as best she could with the few visits she could get through the years. But what chance did she have with a system of idolatry that controlled his every waking moment from the education he received to the entertainment he imbibed? Nevertheless, she knew he was in God's image. She knew he had a conscience. He was Ham *ben Noah*.

"We become the choices we make in this life, Ham. I pray you consider the choices you are making—and their consequences," she whispered.

Ham sighed. She had that look that could penetrate his soul. It was at moments like this that he would question everything he knew. Though she was a bit crazy, she had something deep inside her that was utterly and truly real. And he wanted it. But he just could not forsake the life he had worked so hard to achieve, a life of such royal pedigree and future. And for what? A phantasm of a man who was supposed to be his father, and a god who did not show himself but only spoke to foolish prophets?

They arrived at the secret passageway and moved the stone enough for Hannah to slip through with her pregnant belly.

Before they could continue, they heard hurried footsteps down the hall. Ham reflexively pushed the stone closed as they turned to face a dozen temple guards pointing spears at the four of them.

Ham gathered his confidence and chastised the guards, "What is the meaning of this foolishness? Down with your weapons! I am the sanga priest."

They did not put down their weapons. They jammed the blades closer to their throats and chests.

Lugalanu marched through their midst and up to the new captives. He looked disappointedly at the slaves who had already wet themselves with fear. "I was wondering where you two were," he said with sarcasm.

"Take them…" he was interrupted in his words by Emzara's look. He almost said "take them to the block," the chopping block where their heads would roll from their shoulders. Instead he said, "Take them away." Emzara's goodness still had a way of melting him.

Three guards moved the slaves roughly away as Lugalanu led the others down the hallway to his own quarters.

It seemed like an eternity to Emzara, She wondered if they were being led to their execution. Instead, they found themselves alone in Lugalanu's private quarters.

He turned and stared silently at both Emzara and Ham, as if they were a couple of children about to be punished with the rod. But this was far more serious. Not a rod but an axe would be their fate.

Finally, Lugalanu spoke up, "I will not report this to the gods. Neither of you will be executed."

A shock went through both Ham and Emzara. He was sparing their lives?

Indeed, he was sparing their lives. Lugalanu had been waiting for this one thing. He could not have asked for a better opportunity than to catch them both in such a compromising position, placing them at his mercy. Quite frankly, he was tired of being merciful. He knew Emzara had been having secret contact with Ham throughout the years. He knew that Ham loved her and would not turn her in for her treachery of freeing slaves. But for Ham this was surely a loyalty to blood, rather than treason to the gods. Besides, revenge against Elohim's Chosen Seed would not be complete in death, but in conversion of his seed. It had been to Lugalanu's advantage to let them develop their secret familial love for one another.

"In seven days' time, we will celebrate Akitu," he said. "Canaanu will be initiated into the high priesthood. You will no longer call him Ham." He looked with firmness at Emzara. "And you will consent to be my loyal and willing wife."

Then it all made sense to her. In order to save Ham's life, Emzara would without question give her own, even if it was to such humiliation and defilement. Ham would perform his duty completely, to protect his mother. Lugalanu would own them both. It would not be a true willingness of her own, but she knew it would be close enough for Lugalanu's purposes, after all these years. Emzara's eyes went moist with tears. What had she done?

Akitu was the New Year harvest festival that began on the first of the year in the month of Nissan. It consisted of twelve days of ritual and celebration. It was a time for the priest-king to have his scepter of power renewed by the gods, as well as time for the initiation of priests. Ham would become the ensi high priest below Lugalanu at this very festival, but one week away.

This year was going to be a special Akitu. The pantheon of gods planned to come from all the cities of the plain and meet in Erech in divine council—the seven who decreed fate. The Tablet of Destinies would be brought out and the gods would decide the fates for the coming year. They were also bringing their armies to encamp around the city, fully dressed for war. Why? Was this just for pageantry or did the gods have plans they had not yet revealed?

Another earthquake shook the temple. Dust fell on Emzara's head from above. It seemed the very foundations of the earth were being shaken. Did these signs in the sky above and the earth beneath have something to do with this gathering?

# CHAPTER 25

Noah's tribe celebrated for several days with feasting and dancing. It was early evening. A fatted calf roasted on a fire spit as Noah and his men deliberated in council. Methuselah slouched beside him, along with Shem, Japheth, Tubal-cain, and Jubal.

Earlier in the day, a stranger had arrived in the Hidden Valley. He turned out to be an angel with a message for Uriel, who was finally revealing to the men the import of the dispatch.

"The judgment of Elohim is nigh," said Uriel with a sobered look. "The archangels have mustered the last of the human tribes. They will be at the city walls of Erech by the time of the New Year Festival."

"How many?" asked Noah. He saw Uriel hesitate.

"About two thousand strong."

Noah closed his eyes in despair.

"Do you jest?" blurted Tubal-cain. "The armies of six gods will be assembled on the plains surrounding Erech. That would be upwards of twenty thousand soldiers."

Silence gripped them all. They were too stunned to know what to say next. But not Shem.

"We are ready for war," said Shem with a confident voice.

Japheth picked up Noah's sword from where it leaned against the table. He raised it high. "A sword for the Lord, and for Noah ben Lamech."

"No," stopped Noah. "The family of Noah will enter the tebah as Elohim has commanded."

Shem frowned indignantly. "You would withdraw? You would have us be cowards?"

"Obedience to Elohim is not cowardice," said Noah. He spoke with a new wisdom.

"What has changed in you, father?" asked Japheth. "You have always been a man who would die for righteousness and freedom of your soul. But now…"

"But now," interrupted Noah, "I will *live* for the righteousness of Elohim and the freedom of future generations."

Methuselah, Tubal-cain, and Jubal knew exactly what Noah was talking about, and they knew he was right. They fully understood that the most selfless, most courageous thing for Noah to do, the *only* courageous thing to do would be to save himself for his bloodline to survive. He was the Chosen Seed of Havah, through whom would come the King of victory over the Seed of Nachash. It must continue according to Elohim's plan.

Noah's sons were not so quick to wisdom. "I do not understand this," complained Shem. "I do not understand Elohim and his plans."

"Neither do I," said Noah. "But I do trust him. And that is all I have in this world."

They all could see that the leader standing before them was a different man than the one some had journeyed with to Sheol and back. None of them were the same.

The arrival of three horsemen from the tribe interrupted the discussion. They were scouts seeking intelligence on the armies assembling at Erech. One of them carried a pregnant woman on his horse. He helped her down. The scout looked somberly at Noah. "The armies of the gods are encamped outside the city walls. It is worse than we anticipated."

Noah stared at the pregnant woman dressed in servant's clothes and bearing the brand of Anu on her wrist. "And who is this?" he asked.

"We found her in the wilderness outside the city," replied the scout.

Noah's tenderness reached out to her. "What is your name, child?

"Hannah."

"What were you doing outside the city limits?"

She was a bit fearful still. "Escaping from the temple palace."

"By what means?"

She handed Noah the hand drawn map of the underground tunnels and the direction to the Zagros. "A woman in the temple employ."

Methuselah jumped in, "Would that not be treason? Who could that be?"

"Nindannum," she replied. "Chief maidservant of the priest-king Lugalanu."

"Is this Nindannum a captured slave?" Noah knew chief stewards and maidservants were usually older.

"Yes," Hannah said. "She often whispers of her husband killed by the high priest's forces. Noah ben Lamech."

Noah's breath stopped. Sudden silence gripped the gathered men.

Noah's knees gave out. Shem and Japheth caught him. But they almost lost their own footing as well with the shock.

"Emzara is alive?" asked Noah, as if to Elohim himself.

Hannah did not know who she was talking to, but she was excited to have a connection. "She has a son," she blurted out.

"What is his name?" asked Noah.

"He is called Canaanu in the palace. But his mother calls him Ham."

Noah sat down. "My wife, my son," he said to himself. "Ham." The word flowed affectionately from his lips.

"My baby!" screamed Hannah. She gripped her huge pregnant belly in pain, and then clutched a magic amulet around her neck. The water broke at her feet.

Hannah was taken into a house of birthing. Midwives surrounded her, attending to her needs behind a curtained area lit by candlelight.

She screamed and struck out at one of the midwives, who fell to the floor from the force of the blow. But she continued to grasp her little magic amulet and mumbled a birth incantation to the moon-god. It was to no avail.

"The infant is too large," cried one of the midwives. "We cannot deliver it."

Hannah's belly had been abnormally large and it appeared that her birth would be a serious danger to both mother and child.

Noah, Methuselah and Uriel stood in the room by the doorway. "Do all you can," said Noah. "The tribe is praying."

The midwives did the best they could to calm Hannah and make her comfortable. The outcome was in Elohim's hands.

Uriel could tell that Noah's thoughts were far away, on something else. He looked angrily at Noah. "Do not do this, Noah."

"Emzara is my wife, Uriel."

"It is not Elohim's will."

"Elohim's will is that my family find refuge in the box. Do you suggest I go without them?"

Methuselah butted in, "If you try to rescure her, you will be captured and executed."

"Methuselah," chided Noah, "I am surprised at you. Where is your faith?"

An inhuman scream of pain from Hannah interrupted them. The midwives backed away, staggering through the curtain.

Noah and the others could see Hannah's body spasming violently. Then she stopped dead. Before anyone could move, they saw her belly rip open. What should have been her infant rose out of her torn body. It was twice the size of a normal infant. But it was not human. It was a Naphil. It made an unholy screech and began to feed on the corpse of its own mother.

Noah drew his sword and strode swiftly to the bed.

Behind him, Shem yelled, "Abomination!"

Noah whipped aside the remaining shred of curtain. The Naphil infant was ugly as it was evil. It had snake eyes and a hairless reddish gray skin color with six fingered hands. It screeched at Noah, baring its newborn monstrous teeth.

Noah swung his sword and cut off the creature's hideous little head.

He turned back to Uriel with a justified expression. In measured tone, holding back a flood of righteous wrath, he declared, "I will not leave my wife and son to this wickedness."

"We are going with you," said Shem.

"In the name of all that is holy," added Japheth.

For the first time since creation, Uriel had nothing to say.

Noah, Shem, and Japheth mounted their horses at the edge of the village. Uriel, Methuselah, Tubal-cain, and Jubal saw them off. Noah grasped the map that Hannah had followed out of the temple and city. The exit point was a small cave opening in a butte outside the city. "We will enter the city through the servant's escape route."

Uriel looked up at him. "I have discharged my duty. I protected you to accomplish your calling. The box is built. I must now help lead the armies of man to a war that you will certainly be caught in the middle of."

Noah smiled. "Fear not, Uriel, Elohim is the God of the impossible."

Uriel would not let that one go. "He is God of impossible *men*."

Noah grinned, grabbed wrists with him. "My guardian, my protector."

"My friend," finished Uriel with the first tear in his eye Noah had ever seen.

He rode away with his sons into the forest.

Uriel turned to Methuselah and Tubal-cain.

"The time has come. We ready for the morning."

# CHAPTER 26

They reached the plains outside Erech at a quick pace. Noah, Shem, and Japheth found the outcropping of rock that was on the map. They hid their horses and slipped into the entrance. After going through the Gate of Ganzir and the Abyss, this long dark tunnel seemed a minor inconvenience to Noah.

Outside, past the river, the armies of the gods camped in military order. They filled the fields around the city and river like a massive hive of soldier ants.

Twenty cubits below the milling armies, Noah, Shem, and Japheth slithered through the catacomb tunnels on their way to rescue Emzara and Ham from their prison of paganism. From the moment he had discovered that Emzara was alive, Noah could not sleep. He could barely eat. His mind burned with desire to be united with his beloved. What had she endured all these years without him? He could barely contain the pain of knowing that she was alone in a world of evil without his protection and love to give her life—for her to give him life. Did they torture her? Would he have to carry her through great loss of her own dignity? And a son. A son! She named him Ham. Ham *ben Noah*. What had he grown into? Was he a soldier? A servant? A craftsman? Had he been corrupted by the world that enslaved him? The questions would not stop invading his mind as he traversed the shadows of the hewn caves lit by their pitch-covered torches.

Then Noah stopped. He thought he heard something. He looked back at Shem and Japheth. They nodded. They had heard it too. They strained to listen for another sound. There was none.

"The rock must be settling from the mass of godless minions above us," said Noah. He waved them on.

Without warning, Shem and Japheth were both lifted off the ground by their necks.

Noah turned to see an eight cubit tall Naphil grasping his sons by their throats. They clutched at the six fingered hands choking them to death.

Noah drew his sword. It was pitifully small compared to the ogre before him. The creature was a Naphil, but not a soldier of any kind. Its skin seemed as dirty as the rock around them. It seemed more like a cave troll, something sent to live down here to do precisely what it was doing to Noah and his sons, catch intruders and eat them.

The monster snarled at Noah and stepped forward. His sons had seconds before their larynxes would be crushed.

Noah yelled a battle cry and prepared to fight to his death.

The Naphil arched back in response to Noah's scream. It stumbled backward and dropped Shem and Japheth. It tumbled to the ground. The young men landed hard and rolled out of the way, gasping for breath. They marveled that a mere scream should frighten a Naphil. How could that be?

The Naphil clawed at its own neck, grasping at some invisible object. It whirled.

Noah saw the true cause of their good fortune: Uriel had jumped on its back. He was strangling it with the unbreakable binding cord he used on Watchers.

The Naphil spun around, unsuccessfully trying to grab the archangel just out of his brawny reach. It backed up against the tunnel wall trying to crush its nemesis into the rock. But its nemesis was not human. Like a lock-jawed crocodile, Uriel would not let go. The Naphil grew weaker. But these creatures did not die easily. They could go without air much longer than any human.

The Naphil had lost control of its defenses while focusing on its attacker.

Noah, Shem, and Japheth grabbed their swords. They found their opening to thrust the weapons into the Naphil's abdomen and sternum. The Naphil gave a choked scream. It fell to its knees, and then to its face on the ground. Uriel quickly drew his two daggers and plunged them into the monster's ears on both sides and right into its brain.

For the first time in battle, Noah saw Uriel catching his breath. Fighting a Naphil was extremely difficult, even for an archangel.

Uriel looked up at Noah and said blithely, "I knew you would still need me."

Shem and Japheth massaged their necks.

"I thought I got rid of you, pestering guardian angel," smiled Noah. But he sobered quickly. "What about the war?"

"Methuselah will make a fine general," said Uriel. "He is almost as old as I am."

Shem and Japheth were able to smile again.

"Well, we have to hurry," said Noah. "It appears the escape route is no longer a secret."

Two soldiers guarded the hallway outside Emzara's quarters. She would not have the freedom she previously treasured.

The secret passageway opened a crack, just a few cubits away from them. It caught their attention. They readied their spears and approached the opening. Anything that came through that passage would not live long enough to know what happened to it.

But nothing came.

Cautiously, they slipped into the darkness with their weapons ready.

They were both clubbed to the ground by Shem and Japheth.

"What do they teach these numskulls?" whispered Shem.

Noah hushed him. He led them into the hallway. They sought the doorway that matched the one on the map. Noah's heart pounded with excitement and a heightened awareness of danger. When they found the door, they used the special knock that Hannah had shown them.

Emzara was visiting with Ham when they heard the rap on the door. Emzara clicked her tongue for the maidservant to answer the door. Ham slipped silently behind one of the large pillars by the fireplace. Who could be visiting like this? Since they had been caught, no one had used the secret knock or tunnels until now. It would have been stupid. Was this a trick?

The maidservant brought Noah and his sons into the room. Emzara knew it was not a trick. It was a miracle from God in heaven above.

"Utnapishtim, you are alive!" she gasped.

"My Naamah," said Noah. They walked straight into each other's arms. They kissed boldly, desperately. She could not stop saying over and over again, "You are alive. You are alive."

Noah pulled her back. "And our sons."

Then Emzara noticed them behind Noah. They stepped forward with tearful eyes.

Emzara fainted.


When she awoke, she saw the faces of Shem and Japheth staring at her.

"My sons," she said, "back from the dead."

They moved in close to kiss their mother. She ran her hand down their rough cheeks. She held onto their arms.

"You have grown," she said simply.

Noah could not help it. His joy brought out his humor again. "You have aged," he threw in.

It was true. She had—gracefully, but she had. She looked closer at him. "You have not."

It disturbed her. Was he a phantasm? Was this all a dream-vision?

"It is a long story," said Noah. "But I will never let you go again."

She saw the beaten copper bracelet on Noah's wrist and smiled. "My husband, you never did."

She looked past them to the pillar in the corner. "Ham."

Noah, Shem, and Japheth turned. Ham stepped cautiously from behind the pillar.

"Ham, these are your father and brothers, Shem and Japheth."

Shem and Japheth gave an uneasy nod. But Ham stared at Noah.

It was strange for all of them. Ham was hairless, with temple tattoos, and an elongated head. The men before him were hairy, bearded humans in animal skins worthy of slaves. Noah had prepared them for this possibility. And it did not matter to him.

"My son. My son," said Noah. He stepped up to Ham, looking at him. He was not sure what to do.

Ham broke down in tears.

Noah moved closer and embraced his lost son, the son he could not save, the son he was not around to raise, to teach how to lead and fight, and how to love; the son who was stolen from him and violated by an evil god.

Ham cried like a child in Noah's arms. It was as if he had reverted to the childhood he lost.

Noah shared his tears. "We have come to bring you home."

Japheth jumped in a bit too eagerly. "A war of gods and men is brewing. The human tribes are amassing for assault on the city."

Ham snapped out of his emotion almost instantly. "Are they led by the Chosen Seed?"

The others exchanged uneasy looks. Ham could not understand what it meant.

"I am the Chosen Seed," said Noah.

Ham stepped back in shock. "*You* will end the rule of the gods?"

"Exactly my reaction," said Uriel, stepping out from behind everyone.

"Meet Uriel," said Noah, "my guardian angel."

It was almost too much for Ham all at once.

Noah continued, "The judgment of Elohim is coming upon the land. This family is to be spared, and you are a part of this family."

Ham looked away in retreat.

"Husband," said Emzara, "our son's past is not our own. He is a stranger to Elohim."

Ham felt like a total outsider at that moment. Then Noah smiled at him and slapped him on the back. "Sometimes, I too feel a stranger to Elohim. We shall get along well, you and I."

Ham blurted out, "My wife, Neela. She is in the temple of Inanna."

Noah looked at them all and gave a shrug. "Well, then, we shall have to go get her."

They needed to move quickly. Ham went to retrieve his wife from her bedchamber. Emzara led Noah, Uriel, Shem, and Japheth to the courtyard of Inanna. They did not want to chance another encounter with a Naphil guarding the tunnels below. They decided to do the one thing that no one would expect. They would simply walk right out the front door of Inanna's Temple district, right under their filthy noses.

They met in the garden area. Neela was overwhelmed to meet her true Father- and brothers-in-law, men of whom she had only heard stories. Now, here they were before her, in the flesh, ready to take her away from everything she had known and into a new world of danger and the unknown. She hesitated at first. But she loved her husband so terribly that she would go to the very gates of Sheol if he asked her. He was a good man, a devoted husband and lover. She could see that the way he treated his mother was proof of a man she could trust, who would love his wife and family as deeply as he loved life. It was the only point of departure from his obedience to the gods. Still, she wondered how he could give up the royalty, the privilege, and the security of this, the only life that they had known.

They crossed the open courtyard under the moonlit night. Ham was well known by sight, which would create enough of a diversion for them to take the gate guards by surprise.

A Naphil warrior jumped down from the gate into their path.

Uriel drew his swords and stepped in front of Noah.

The Naphil snarled and held his mace at the ready.

The circle tightened. They all drew their weapons, pulling Neela and Emzara into the middle for protection. Shem's sword Rahab unfurled in his hands, ready to strike like a cobra. Japheth's bow was drawn and ready for attack.

It was futile.

Nephilim started jumping from the courtyard roof all around them, hemming them in—ten Nephilim in all.

Noah looked to Uriel. The angel shook his head. It would be a slaughter.

Ham backed away from them, drawing Neela with him.

Everyone noticed. Noah felt a stab of pain deep in his kidneys.

Shem spit it out first, "Ham? You betrayed us?"

Shem stepped toward Ham, preparing to whip Rahab in his direction.

Noah shouted, "Shem!"

A Naphil stepped in between them, blocking the attack.

It was all over before it had even begun.

Ham stated simply, "My name is Canaanu." He pulled Neela close to him and walked away.

# CHAPTER 27

A pair of Nephilim dragged Noah roughly up the long stairway to the heavens of Anu's temple. The chains hanging from his limbs made the climb exhausting. Swirling clouds and flashes of occasional lightning with booming thunder made a sea of turmoil on the horizon. It was getting closer. An earthquake shook the city and temple. Noah and his guards stumbled, regaining their balance.

At the top of the White Temple, the guards ushered Noah into the sanctuary and into the presence of Anu and Inanna. They sat on thrones, guarded by their bull-man and lion-man aladlammu. Noah expected them, but he was not prepared to see what was off to the side of the thrones.

Uriel hung from the ceiling. He was upside down, bound and chained like a animal for slaughter. He was so badly beaten, Noah could barely recognize him.

Anu saw Noah's reaction. "If he were human, he would be dead. But alas, he is not human."

Noah remembered that angels could not die. They could suffer, feel pain, and even experience limitations of the flesh this side of the heavenlies, but they could not expire. Uriel barely held to consciousness. He let out a groan.

The sound pierced through Noah's soul. This archangel, this warrior who had sacrificed all for Noah, now hung like a captured animal for slaughter because of the recklessness of Noah's own choices. What had he done?

"Noah ben Lamech," Anu interrupted Noah's thoughts, "the Chosen Seed. I was ready to wage war to find you. Yet, here you are, delivered if you will, by the very hands of Elohim."

Noah hated this evil miscreant with every fiber of his being.

Anu's chin rose pompously in contempt, a common pose for him. He gestured flamboyantly with his hand. "Welcome to my holy temple. I am Anu, the supreme god, king of kings, and lord of lords. My consort, Inanna, Queen of heaven and earth." He paused ceremoniously with an arrogant grin. "But you already knew that."

Then, the mocking stab, "So, where is *your* god?"

Noah would not dignify the remark. Instead, he prophesied, "I know who you are, Semjaza and Azazel, fallen Sons of God. You have laid the nations low, you sit on the mount of assembly, you have made yourselves like the Most High. But you will be brought down to Sheol."

Inanna broke in bitterly, "He imagines himself a prophet now, and privy to the Watchers' secrets."

Anu chuckled in mockery, "I shall call you 'Atrahasis,' 'exceedingly wise one.' Or would you prefer, 'Ziusudra,' 'He of immortality,' since you fancy yourself a slayer of gods?"

"WHERE IS YOUR GOD?" Inanna interrupted with a roar, her voice echoing like thunder through the temple mount and in Noah's ears.

Noah would not answer.

Another groan from Uriel drew their attention. His parched lips parted enough to force out a few words with great effort. "Elohim—is—coming."

Anu would not tolerate any more of Uriel's insolence. He rose from his throne and strode over to Uriel's vulnerable form. He picked up one of his swords and promptly cut off Uriel's head.

Noah screamed, "NOOO!" He lunged toward Anu ready to kill him with his bare hands, but the Nephilim held him back from his futile gesture.

Inanna snickered, "That will shut him up."

Anu spoke to two servants watching Uriel, "Throw the body in the dungeon. Keep it away from the head. Archangels have a nasty habit of regeneration." He reconsidered. "On second thought, give me the head. I will keep it with me."

One of the servants brought Uriel's head to Anu. He grabbed it by the hair and looked into Uriel's face. He turned it to show it to Noah.

Noah gasped. Uriel's eyes found Noah's. He was still alive. He could not speak because his vocal cords had been severed from his lungs. But their eyes made a connection far deeper than words.

The servants cut down Uriel's body and took it away. Anu placed the head on the floor next to him.

Lugalanu and Ham entered from the rear of the temple. They were dressed in the royal robes of the priest-king and soon-to-be ensi high priest. At Lugalanu's other side was his new consort, Emzara, bedecked in splendid queenly robes.

Ham could not look at Noah. But Emzara would not take her eyes off him. Noah knew exactly what she was saying to him: she was and always would be only his alone. A silent tear of vengeance slid down Noah's cheek.

Anu announced, "Ah, my faithful priest-king and his entourage."

Lugalanu and Ham took their place beside the thrones and bowed to Anu and Inanna.

Anu proclaimed with characteristic self-importance, "Tomorrow is Akitu, the New Year festival. The gods of the land will convene in divine council. Canaanu will become a high priest of Inanna. Lugalanu will marry this woman, Nindannum, who I understand has some relation to you, my captive?" It was a rhetorical question designed to twist the dagger in Noah's liver rather than receive an answer.

Emzara's expression plead with Noah for rescue. But rescue was not forthcoming.

"As rite of passage," continued Anu, "the new high priest's charge will be to sacrifice the Chosen Seed to the pantheon."

Emzara looked at Ham with horror. She had not known this monstrous plan.

Ham could only look down in shame. But he knew his place and his need for affirmation of devotion. He looked back up. He raised his chin high in royal emulation of Anu's own conceit. Lugalanu beamed with pride.

Noah's eyes blurred with the sting of betrayal. He could not believe his son would do such a thing. It defied his comprehension. His son had been ripped from his family culture and tradition, raised in a world of slavish idolatry, but still, how could one do such a thing to his own flesh and blood?

Inanna had the last word, "Let us put an end to this ridiculous Revelation of 'the man who would end the rule of the gods.' If Elohim is so high and mighty, let him come to end this himself."

# CHAPTER 28

The dungeon lay below the temple complex. It seemed fitting that the location of imprisonment in this realm would be below the edifice of religious power. Noah, Shem, and Japheth were locked in separate small cells with iron bars. The cells instilled a sense of enclosing fear and isolation, containing barely enough room to stand, let alone sit. But Noah and his sons stood—and prayed.

"Almighty Elohim," said Noah, "creator of heaven and earth. Forgive our sins. Hear our prayers. May we, your servants, be found acceptable in your sight. I have not always done what you have asked of me, and it has taken your heavy rod of chastisement to bring me back in line with your purposes. I do not ask for our survival, but for your will to be done."

A door opened and slammed shut around the corner, interrupting them. They could not see what it was. They strained to hear and figure out what was happening.

Out of their sight, around the hallway corner, two guards led a cloaked figure through an opened cell door. Inside the cell lay the headless body of Uriel. The guards picked it up and carried it out like a wounded soldier. It moved sluggishly. Though it could not die, it required the head for coordinated movement.

The guards exited the way they came. The cloaked figure turned to glance behind them.

It was Neela. She knew Noah and his sons were nearby, but she did not know where. She could not hear anyone. So she hastened and left.

Noah and his sons heard the prison hall door slam shut. They finished their prayer. Shem and Japheth said in one accord, "In the name of Elohim, creator of heaven and earth, your will be done."

An earthquake rocked their dungeon vigorously. Noah heard his iron cell door creak loudly. The iron twisted, misshapen by the immeasurable tons of rock above them. It bent outward, leaving a gap large enough for Noah's arm.

Noah thought that this might be Elohim's own hand twisting open the gates that held them. He smiled, reached out, and grabbed his misshapen doorway. He yanked. But it remained firmly in place, maybe even more so. He yanked again. He soon realized that it would not open. The iron had twisted but not enough to free him. They would not escape after all. *Elohim answers prayers, but not always the way we wish.* This was certainly not new to him or his sons.

In the guarded halls of the temple complex, Lugalanu stood with his palace diviner before an altar. Upon it lay a slaughtered lamb, its blood dripping down the small drain channels of the altar. Lugalanu sought interpretation of omens through extispicy and hepatoscopy, the practice of examining an animal's entrails and liver for divining the future. The diviner priest slit the belly of the unblemished lamb and reached in to pull out its guts. He placed them on another stone for examination. beside the liver, still hot from the slaughtered lamb. The smell of the organs repulsed Lugalanu and he stepped back to avoid the drifting odor.

The diviner looked for abnormalities or anomalies that would signify a negative answer to Lugalanu's question of whether Emzara would be his queen in his new seat of power. He poured water over the intestines and liver to clear the blood away and scrutinized them closely. Another diviner aided him, manning a cart with clay tablets of interpretation on them. All manner of irregularities had been recorded by scribes for archival reference. Some of the tablets were even in the shape of a liver with descriptions of interpretations pressed into the clay with cuneiform styluses. Though all the intestines were included in the divination process, the liver was among the most important because it was considered the source of blood and life.

Lugalanu fidgeted impatiently.

The diviner was perturbed. The priest-king always did this to him. He waited until the last moment to seek the ancient wisdom and then expected the diviner to make up for the lateness of his own irresponsibility by rushing the process. He decided to draw it out a little longer just to make his point.

Lugalanu paced.

The diviner finally looked up to give Lugalanu his answer.

"Yes."

Lugalanu passed through the heavily guarded entrance of Emzara's quarters. He found her seated on a couch, staring into the flames of the fireplace. She did not move, she did not look up. She just continued to stare into the flames licking the brick flu.

Eventually, she slowly stood to acknowledge his presence. But she kept gazing into the fire.

"On the morrow, you will be a queen," said Lugalanu. "I expect you to act appropriately."

Emzara had only one thought in her mind. "You knew all along who I was," she said.

She looked at him and saw it was true.

Lugalanu had sought all these years to win her love, but now that it would never be, it did not change his intent. "I gave you the choice. I offered you my very soul." He paused dramatically. "The bearer of the Chosen Seed's royal bloodline will bear my seed instead. Whether by free will or by force."

Lugalanu turned and left Emzara staring into oblivion.

She stood still for what felt like a lifetime. The sum of her days added up to this very moment, in captive quarters below a temple of idols in the dust of death.

She gathered herself together and marched into her bedchamber, shutting the door behind her. She walked over to the side of the bed and withdrew a dagger from hiding. She sat on the bed and pulled back her sleeve. The dagger trembled in her hand.

She wept uncontrollably.

## CHAPTER 29

The Akitu New Year Festival was a twelve-day celebration. The first day would involve the final arrival of the people into the temple district and city streets. The second day brought elaborate purification rituals and washings for both priests and temple. On the third day, statues of the gods were carved out of cedar and tamarisk wood. The fourth day was considered the true starting point, because it was the actual first day of the year. After recitations, prayers and rituals, the priests would recite their creation epic to the people. The story would connect their past with their future and reinforce the kingdom of the gods.

The fifth day was the zenith of the festival. After prayers, and exorcisms of evil spirits, the priest-king was ritually humiliated in private before the gods. He was stripped of his kingly symbols of crown, ring, scepter, and mace, and then slapped by a *sesgallu* priest. He was then re-established in his kingship by having the kingly elements returned to him by Anu himself. This enthronement ritual of reversion to chaos and renewal of order was then followed by the arrival of the other gods into the temple of Anu. A public sacrifice for the sins of the people came after that. Though the decreeing of the destinies and dazzling procession of the gods through the streets in bejeweled chariots would not happen until day eight, the gods began their council assembly on day five. After the procession on the eighth day, the priest-king would engage in *hieros gamos*, the Sacred Marriage rite of sex with his queen, in place of Inanna, to insure fertility in the coming year. Emzara dreaded the Sacred Marriage, for it was her decreed appointment with Lugalanu.

But this was day five.

The land around the city swarmed with the armies of the gods. An elaborate tent for the reigning deity and his king sat in the center of each army. Since Inanna had her residence at Erech, she did not have her own forces. The soldiers in the armies had remained relatively civil. Raping of women was held to a minimum, for it was considered somewhat vulgar when invited to a city's festival as this. Under normal situations of course, it was perfectly fine, but not as guests of the high god Anu in his own city. They would soon enough find their outlet to loot and desecrate.

Inside the walls, the city overflowed with pilgrims and worshippers from leagues around. The marketplaces were full of vendors selling vegetables, fish, lizards, scorpions and other exotic desert delicacies.

The district around the temple complex resounded with bacchanalian celebration. Wine flowed, food was consumed in gluttonous amounts, resulting in much vomiting and diarrhea. The food was deliberately full of parasites enabling the digestive systems to respond by evacuating the contents soon after eaten, thus leaving room for continued consumption.

Immorality of all kinds filled the streets. Spontaneous dancing broke out, led by the blue dancers and their traveling minstrels. The human dancers jerked and spasmed as if taken over by spirits. Their eyes turned upward, showing only the whites, and they uttered strange guttural sounds as if performed by a distant ventriloquist.

There were other delights as well. Sorcerers lined the streets with potions and rituals, enabling the citizens to be possessed by a god, a great honor to plebeians who might otherwise never find themselves in the physical presence of deity. Of course, there were exorcists as well for those stubborn "deities" who would not find themselves ready to leave so soon after a possession. Astrological readings, magical potions of fertility and abortion, alchemy, spells, and enchantments—everything an idolater could desire in this panoply of paganism.

In the White Temple above, the day had already begun with Lugalanu's private ritual enthronement. Then three entourages of deity climbed each of the three stairways and arrived at the top terrace. They were greeted by Anu and Inanna, dressed in elaborate finery of divinity for the day: customary horned diadems of deity, and gaudy jewelry beneath their vulture winged robes. It took exaggeration and ostentation to incite the veneration of humans, but it worked every time. She had redesigned her simple horned crown into an elaborate headdress of huge brightly colored horns the size of small goats themselves. Even Inanna's unusually garish display did not stand out from the others as much as usual on this day. But her makeup did. Her exaggerated distortion of eyebrows, bright excessive eye shadow, overwrought angular lipstick made her look a bit like a serious clown to Lugalanu, but he would never dare to reveal such thoughts for fear of his certain death at her spiteful hands.

The three arriving divinities were Enki from Eridu, Ninhursag from Kish, and Enlil from the holy city of Nippur. Along with Anu, these were the four high gods. They were visually as stunning as Anu and Inanna. Each stood well over five cubits tall, with sparkling golden serpentine skin with serpentine eyes, oblong elongated skulls, and wearing royal vulture feathered robes and horned headdresses. The other minor gods had already arrived with less fanfare: Nanna the moon god from Ur and his son Utu the sun god from Larsa. Their status was significantly less than the other gods, and their armies as well, so they avoided drawing attention to themselves. Together these were the "Seven who decree the fates."

An earthquake shook the temple and grounds.

The deities stumbled and regained their balance. Except Enki, who lost his footing and fell down, crushing to death a servant who had been behind him.

Below on the temple grounds, a large crack spread a hundred cubits from the base of the ziggurat. Dozens of such openings were beginning to appear all over the city.

The black mass of impending storm had ebbed to within leagues of the city.

"Today, this will all cease," said Anu to his fellow divinities in the White Temple.

"Elohim is a jealous, senile old deity," retorted Enki, "with a penchant for childish tantrums."

Ninhursag got to the point. "What is the sacrifice? I need blood."

Anu and Inanna glanced at each other with a smile. Anu offered, "Nothing less than the Chosen Seed himself."

The other Watchers looked at them with surprise, eager to hear more.

"From the Revelation?" asked Enki.

Anu nodded.

Enlil jumped in, "How did you manage such privilege?"

Ninhursag added quickly, "Why did you not tell us?"

Anu paused, then slyly said, "I am the supreme god, am I not?"

Each of the Watchers received a chalice of blood from a servant. Anu raised his in toast to himself and merely nodded to his own glory. The others toasted and they drank their blood deeply. Ninhursag gulped it down in one motion.

An earthquake stopped them all again. Enki lost control of his cup and it shattered on the ground, splattering blood everywhere. "Blast this infernal turmoil!"

Ninhursag muttered under her breath sarcastically, "Is that how the Tablet of Destinies slipped through your fingers as well?" Enki gave her an angry look.

She turned to Anu. "Well, Supreme God, I suggest you sacrifice with haste or we may all lose our divine privilege."

Anu clapped his hands. Within seconds, the sound of deep long horns bellowed from the heights of the temple, followed by a series of huge kettledrums at the base. He bade the gods follow him to the ledge overlooking the city.

Below them, they saw the masses assembling. The crowds looked up, and cheered their presence to the percussive beats of the kettledrums.

Anu reached into a sack tied to his waist. He pulled out the head of Uriel, holding it high to look out upon the land before them. Uriel's silent eyes could only tear up with righteous anger.

Ninhursag muttered to Inanna, "I see he has found a way to make a toy out of an archangel. Clever."

Anu threw Uriel's disembodied head behind him into the White Temple.

It rolled up to his throne and thudded to a stop. Unknown to Anu, Uriel's headless body lay right behind his throne, a few cubits away, hidden there by Neela. The archangel's ram's horn trumpet was tied to the belt on the beheaded form.

Outside, Anu focused on speaking to the people below. His voice amplified thunderously throughout the city. It was one of the Watchers' special gifts.

"People of the land! Behold the divine council of your gods!"

The people cheered.

Another earthquake occurred. Another crack in the earth, but this time, it opened as a crevice and water from below sprayed the crowd.

Anu took advantage of this coincident timing. "What you see before you is the might and power of the pantheon!"

The crowd cheered again.

Anu bid Enlil step forward and speak. His voice too carried with a powerful resonance. "I am Enlil, god of the air, and I bring you storm!"

Above, the sky flashed with lightning followed by a crack of thunder. The people roared.

Enlil glanced at Ninhursag with surprise. They could not have had better luck than this. Of course they had the power to manifest certain physical disruptions in nature, but not to this level of spectacle. Only Elohim had that kind of control.

Ninhursag stepped forward. She could feel the vibrations coming. She waited a moment, then shouted triumphantly, "I am Ninhursag, goddess of the earth, and I bring you quake!" Seconds later, the earth rumbled and the crevice below opened wider.

Enki saw he only had seconds. He jumped forward and shouted rapidly, "I am Enki, god of water, and I bring you the deep!"

He timed it well, because the water already began pouring out of the crevice before he finished. It splashed up in a wave that pulled a cluster of people back into the crevice to drown. The crowd did not care; they went wild. These were the gods of the land, and they were showcasing their glorious power.

Inanna jested about the timing of these storm events, "Maybe Elohim is supporting us after all." She knew it was not true. Not in a thousand millennia would Elohim support their rebellion. He was a tyrant without an ounce of mercy. So if the old malcontent intended to crack apart the heavens and earth, they might as well use this opportunity to claim credit for it.

Inanna shouted to the people, "Behold, the Chosen Seed! A sacrifice to appease the gods!"

The crowd roared again as Inanna gestured below to a Stone Temple right next to the ziggurat, about fifteen cubits down. The Stone Temple stood right next to Eanna as a support structure that was used for the messy work of sacrifice so the White Temple could stay clean. On the Stone Temple stood a newly arranged sacrificial altar display consisting of Noah stretched out on frame made of angled and crossed wooden poles. Behind him, Shem and Japheth were tied back to back on a post, kindling around their feet. Across the way from them, Lugalanu stepped forward with a reluctant Emzara. She wore the regal Sumerian wedding dress of white linen robes with gold lined patterns, lapis beads, all scented with cedar oil. The night before, she had been shaven completely of all her hair as was the custom for a priestess, and for the wife of the king as well. On her head she wore a lapis-lazuli headdress with ostrich feathers and precious gems inlaid with gold.

Neela watched the pageantry from a small assembly structure at the back of the Stone Temple terrace. Ham stepped forward next to Lugalanu. The king performed a prayer and incantation before the younger man to initiate him into the high priesthood. The crowd applauded. Then Lugalanu handed Ham the sacrificial dagger, a long sharpened slate blade.

The crowds below cheered for the sacrifice. Ham looked over at Noah, tied to the frame.

Up above on the temple parapet, Inanna fumed impatiently to the other gods. "All this pomp and ritual bores me. I wish they would just hurry up and kill them all."

"Patience, my dear," said Anu. "We will be drinking Chosen blood soon enough."

Ninhursag chimed in, "These humans are loathsome creatures."

Inanna added, "I would just as soon see them all crushed to death as see them worship me."

Enki wondered with genuine amazement, "And they worship us so freely instead of Elohim." Inanna gave him a dirty look.

Anu spoke to the spectacle below them, "So begins a New Year of abundance and fertility! Of marriage and sacrifice!"

The crowds shouted in support. "Of gods and war!" They went into a frenzy, shouting Anu's name, which pleased him greatly in sight of all the others.

Inside, Uriel's head no longer sat on the floor near his throne.

Another seismic quake sent shock waves through the city. It was the biggest one yet. A part of the ziggurat foundation crumbled. Several new crevices ripped open, gushing water. They sucked people into the depths. Some screamed for their loved ones who were taken. Others went back to their enraptured worship.

Everyone heard the horn blast of Uriel coming from the White Temple area. It boomed out over the land to heaven itself.

Uriel's head had found his body. The angel had regenerated. He ran full tilt toward the line of Watchers at the edge of the Temple.

The Watchers turned, too late.

Uriel hit Anu and Inanna. They were at the top of the stairway. The three of them tumbled down ten stairs at a time. Uriel held onto Anu with a vise grip. Had they been human, the impact would have broken every bone in their bodies. But they were not human.

Inanna fell alone. She steadied herself before Uriel and Anu did. In the tumble, her gaudy horned headdress and vulture winged robe flew off her, revealing a bizarre costume of black leather. When she rose with dagger firmly gripped in hand, she looked like what she was, the goddess of sex and war.

Uriel and Anu shook off their dizziness about twenty cubits below her.

The sound of a distant trumpet drew everyone's attention to the desert horizon.

Ten or fifteen leagues out, Uriel could see the armies of the human tribes break over the far ridge. He knew then that the archangels had accomplished their task. They had rallied the last of humanity.

Another trumpet sound drew Uriel's smile. He would know Gabriel's trumpet anywhere.

Anu bellowed with a voice of thunder, "ALL GODS TO WAR!"

The gods raised their own war horns and blew.

The army encampments outside the city walls transformed into rapidly moving hives of armed soldiers organizing and flowing toward the attacking forces on the distant ridge.

Anu was absorbed in his call to war. So he was not ready for Uriel's second running leap. The righteous angel hit him square-on. They flew off the edge of the staircase and down into the crevice below, disappearing from sight.


Lugalanu saw the falling bodies. He knew he had to move fast. He yelled to Ham, already in position before Noah's weak hanging form, "CANAANU, KILL HIM!"

Emzara withdrew her dagger from where she concealed it in her wedding dress. Back in her bedchamber, she had decided not to take her own life in exchange for the privilege of taking Lugalanu's instead.

She raised the blade high to plunge it into him with as much force as she could muster.

Lugalanu saw her motion and grabbed her hand before she could deal the death blow. He jerked away the knife, hit her in the jaw, and threw her violently to the ground.

She hit her head and almost lost consciousness.

Ham saw it all. He also saw the truth of what was before him. This was what his mother had spoken of for many years. This was what he could not understand nor see in agreement with her. Yet, suddenly, it was all clear to him, as if scales had fallen from his eyes. All the riches, all the power, all the sensual delights, all of it was a big lie. In that instant, he knew the truth he had known all his life, but had suppressed; the truth that his mother had sweat blood trying to get him to see. It was the truth that Elohim himself had just confirmed with clarity: This world system was evil.

Ham did not want it anymore.

He turned to Noah and confessed in tears as he cut him loose, "My name is Ham ben Noah. Father, forgive me."

Neela had gone to Emzara's rescue, laying over her as a covering, a desperate attempt to divert the blows onto herself.

Lugalanu yanked her off of Emzara and cast her aside. She flew over the edge of the Stone Temple precipice.

Ham screamed and ran over to the ledge, "NOOOOO!"

Lugalanu raised the knife blade high over Emzara's prone figure. She lifted her arm over her head in a hopeless attempt to shield her head.

"This is your last rejection of me, Nindannum!" he screamed, and plunged.

Midway through the stroke, a spear impaled him from behind. In pain, he turned to see Noah holding the spear, a determined look in his eyes.

"Leave my family alone, you son of iniquity," growled Noah. He pulled Lugalanu around and pushed him over the ledge and out of sight. He fell right past Ham helping Neela up from her precarious hold on the edge. She had somehow grabbed the ledge in her fall.

Down in the crevice, below the churning waters, Uriel fought for control over Anu. He thanked Elohim for the fact that the Watchers were weakened by water. Uriel had his opponent up against a ledge of rock, trying to pin him. But he underestimated Anu's strength underwater. Anu slowly regained an upper hand.

Uriel saw his moment. A large wall of rock above them crumbled. It tumbled down toward them. Uriel released his grip, surprising Anu. He kicked himself away from the wall and Anu. Anu did not have time to avoid the falling debris that cascaded down upon him. He was buried in the depths under tons of sinking landslide.

Uriel kicked toward the surface. Suddenly, he was lifted by a torrential upsurge. The swelling water gushed out of the crevice, launching Uriel out onto land. He rolled to his feet.

Neela and Ham released Shem and Japheth from their post. Noah embraced Emzara with the fervor of eternal devotion.

Ham pulled the sword Rahab from beneath his cloak and handed it to Shem. Shem looked at his brother startled. Then he grinned. This was indeed a son of Noah.

They heard a whistle from below and ran to the ledge. They saw Uriel waving them down.

Ham turned to Noah and asked, "Are we to join the war, father?"

"No," said Noah. "We obey Elohim. We must get back to the tebah."

"The tebah?" queried Ham. "A box? What box?"

"I will explain on the way," said Noah. They all dashed off, running down the stairs inside the Stone Temple.

Inanna saw them escaping. She let out an ugly howling screech that resounded above the din and chaos. Below her, the people had scattered to the deceptive safety of their homes or places away from the temple. Up above, the gods had gone, on their way to lead their troops. Inanna jumped the distance between Eanu and the Stone Temple, fifteen cubits down. She landed on the Stone Temple terrace, her supernatural legs absorbing the impact. She ran to the edge of the terrace and jumped again, landing this time on a ledge ten cubits below.

At her feet lay the silent unmoving figure of Lugalanu with the spearhead sticking out through his belly. She reached down and held him in her arms with an uncharacteristic gentleness. He opened his eyes weakly. She grabbed the shaft of the spear and pulled it out through his body. He screamed in pain and blacked out.

Inanna bit her own arm, drawing blood. She let the blood drip out of her lesion onto Lugalanu's fatally wounded torso. It sizzled when it came into contact with the mortal body. The flesh began to regenerate. The blood of a god surged through him and revived his body. Inanna put her mouth to Lugalanu's cold blue lips and blew a gush of air into his lungs.

He gasped and coughed awake. He was revived.

"Now, my little pet," she said to him "muster a company of soldiers. We have a Chosen Seed to catch and kill."

# CHAPTER 30

The armies of man broke over the ridge and lined up in formation, awaiting command. The Mesopotamian plain spread out before them. This drier region that was called the desert of Dudael. It would be the battlefield. They all knew it would shortly be drenched with flowing blood of warfare. None of them had any pretentions, with odds of ten to one glaring them in their faces.

Three generals galloped forward on their horses, each accompanied by an archangel. Each led a battalion of about seven hundred soldiers, Tubal-cain and Raphael commanded the left flank division, Jubal and Gabriel were over the right flank division, and Methuselah and Mikael led the center division.

They met in the center to counsel. "Have you fought Nephilim?" Mikael asked Methuselah.

Methuselah raised his eyebrow. "In my day, I was quite the giant killer. Now, I think I am just an archangel's irritant."

Everyone knew he was talking about Uriel. They all smiled.

Mikael said, "Well, then you should do well on this day."

"Will you lead us?" asked Tubal-cain.

"No," said Mikael. "You will. We archangels have gods to bind."

They could see the armies of the gods moving into formation on the dry plains before them: Phalanxes of humans, followed by battalions of falcon-headed, hawk-headed, dog- and wolf-headed soldiers. Behind them, platoons of Nephilim finished off a demonic army of genetically mutated beasts. They were twenty thousand strong.

Then the three lead generals of the gods came forward from the rear. They were Enki, Ninhursag, and Enlil, mounted on special harnesses on the backs of monstrous Nephilim.

Mikael mocked, "Three of them. Apparently, Uriel has more than made up for his sloppy guardianship of Noah. He has already bound Anu."

"He is relentless, that Uriel," smiled Methuselah.

"Let us pray he was successful in aiding Noah's escape," said Mikael with hope.

"Where are the other three gods?" wondered Raphael.

Nanna the moon god was with Inanna on her chase. None knew that Utu had fled from the city, like the coward he really was, leaving his armies without a leader. Utu had led forces with Inanna in the great Titanomachy of the past. He had also fled that battle, when he had seen their forces losing.

Noah and Emzara, Ham and Neela, Shem and Japheth, and Uriel halted their mounts on the outskirts of the city. They had commandeered some horses and slipped unmolested into the underground tunnels Emzara and Ham knew so well. They had not run into any other underground Nephilim, thank Elohim. They could see the armies facing off against each other for war on the desert of Dudael behind them.

A swirling black mass of funnel clouds churned directly overhead. It appeared that the wrath of God was truly upon them.

"I should be there leading them to battle," said Noah.

Emzara touched him lovingly on the arm.

He concluded, "Elohim's will be done."

"Now *that* is finally obedient faith," cracked Uriel.

Noah gave him a side glance, "Will you now finally leave me alone?" he retorted.

"Not on your life," said Uriel. They shared a smile, but not for long.

"Father, to the south," said Shem.

They all looked. An ominous dust cloud moved in their direction a few leagues behind them. Uriel's eagle eyes could see it was a company of two hundred chimera soldiers on horseback, a dozen pazuzu flying overhead, and a handful of Nephilim rumbling in the lead.

"Assassins," said Uriel. He could just see the figures riding on the backs of the bull and lion aladlammu creatures. "Inanna, Nanna the moon god, and Lugalanu."

The earth trembled again. Lightning and thunder overhead gave a frightening emphasis to their impending doom.

"Elohim be with us," said Noah. "We are going to need him more than ever."

He yelled and kicked his horse into a race for the Zagros Mountains and the Hidden Valley. The others matched pace with him.

# CHAPTER 31

Each side weighed its options, observing and analyzing their opponents. It would be a full day before any assault would occur on the Dudael battlefield. The desert plain was framed in the north with the armies of man, and in the south with the armies of the gods. They stood arrayed for battle a mere thousand or so cubits distance from one another. The human tribes were on the higher ground so they bore an advantage. It was not much of an advantage, but anything would help in this hopeless cause. They did not want to lose this benefit, so they waited to draw their opponents uphill. But the gods were too smart for that. The armies of the gods were defending a city; they would not need to leave their defensive position.

A comparison of these two armed forces could not reveal a more imbalanced opposition. The armies of man that had come together in this emergency confederation wore animal skins, some protective leather. They carried axes, maces, and spears, and a passion to worship Elohim against the gods. The cities had created professional armies whose sole purpose was to do battle. Their warriors were universally equipped with a new kind of armor to protect them in fighting. They wore copper helmets over leather caps to protect their skulls from fracture and blunt trauma. They draped leather capes over their bodies, with small bronze circlets attached to create a more impenetrable cloak. They were trained and disciplined to fight in a phalanx unit of eight men wide and six files deep, covering each other with leather shields and spears. Some units had even been trained with the newly introduced sickle swords. The humans faithful to Elohim were not only outnumbered by this standing army, they were out-armed and out-trained.

In spite of this military advantage, the gods would not engage in pre-battle negotiations. They would not risk getting too close to an archangel who could bind them and cast them into the earth. There would be no quarter asked and no quarter given. It would be a war of ultimate annihilation, winner kill all—to the last soul.

The soldiers did not want to fight at night, but it seemed they would be fighting in darkness anyway. The skies overhead were fast becoming blackened piles of storm clouds, shadowing the entire region.

The armies of the gods would not leave their position for an uphill climb. But the armies of man were not descending. It was a stalemate of strategies. The archangels and Noah's generals were in fact, deliberately delaying their engagement in order to facilitate Noah's flight to the Hidden Valley. Finally, after a second day of stalling, they had figured that by Elohim's grace, Noah would be close enough to his destination by now. They could wait no longer. They led their forces in a slow march downfield. They would conserve every ounce of energy they could for battle. They would not allow too far a run to tire them. The armies of the gods marched forward as well, in synchronized lock step.

When they were within a few hundred cubits of each other, they stopped. Mikael, Gabriel, and Raphael blew their trumpets. The armies of man shouted a war cry for all they were worth.

The armies of the gods shouted back.

The archangels blew their trumpets again. Methuselah shouted "A sword for the Lord and for Noah!" The forces broke into a run toward the enemy.

But the armies of the gods did something unanticipated. Enki, Enlil, and Ninhursag blew their trumpets and the phalanxes of human soldiers on the front lines split apart. From behind them, came droves of bird-men and dog-men soldiers. The gods sent their elite squads out against the first line of humans. It would be a slaughter, a demoralizing tactic that would be considered risky for enduring battles. But in this case, no one expected an enduring battle. The mutant warriors were of such caliber, they would level the first human troops quickly and maintain enough strength for the second tier fighting. Against these numbers, the faithful human forces would be pulverized.

The charging armies met with a crash of bone and metal. Spear met mace, axe met sword, human met demigod. The gods on their Nephilim crushed their opponents with ease. The archangels plowed through their enemies like so much chaff. It would take some time, but the humans would ultimately be overwhelmed by the hybrid beast soldiers, who were created and mutated for just this purpose. They were soulless fighting machines.

Methuselah called down their second of three waves of forces. He had prayed that their previous fighting would weaken these elite chimera monsters. But it was not to be.

As soon as Methuselah made his call, the gods made theirs. A company of Nephilim dressed for war ran out to battle; a hundred of them. They were fierce, diabolical, unstoppable, and they hit the newly arriving human forces like a tidal wave. But these Nephilim did not just kill their enemies; they killed everything in their path, including their own soldiers.

Suddenly, another huge quake shook the entire valley, throwing everyone to the ground. It split the battlefield down the middle with a huge crevice. Water gushed out of it from the fountains of the deep. It sucked soldiers of both sides into the Abyss to their deaths.

Then, from the enemy side came the sound of long horns. As suddenly as the Nephilim had charged, they returned to their own battle lines, leaving the human armies confused. Why would they retreat in a moment of sure victory?

Methuselah stood up on the height of ridge, trying to assess their options. Then he saw what the enemy waited for. From behind the enemy lines, a thousand men carried a very large ornamented box, one hundred cubits long and thirty cubits square, onto the field. It was made of cedar wood and covered with pitch, with large occultic spells and charms inscribed all over the sides of the box. When they set it down, water spilled out of its cracks onto the ground. It was immensely heavy. All the warriors stopped fighting, to see this monstrosity set near the battleground. Methuselah could not imagine what it might be.

But they would not find out for another half day, because the malice of the gods led them to draw out the inevitable and build a mounting dread in their human opponents before they would unleash their next wave of terror.

Noah and his family had pushed their horses to the breaking point as they fled to the Hidden Valley. The animals were frothing from the exertion. Emzara's horse had already died beneath her, so she rode with Noah.

An unstoppable force of evil, their hunters had stayed on their tail. They were close enough to the family to see them approaching the opening to the Zagros Mountains.

That was when the pazuzus attacked. A swarm of the hideous black flying hellions had left the chasing party and raced toward Noah's band. They dropped out of the sky upon the fugitives in a rage, talons flashing and slashing.

Neela was the first under attack. A pazuzu lifted her off her horse. Ham hacked off its beastly legs, and Neela dropped back onto her steed. His back swing caught another one by its wing, sending it crashing to the ground to be trampled by the horses. Ham had worked with these creatures and had a good sense of their movements and attack patterns.

Japheth did not. Three of the dog-faced creatures attacked him together. They gouged his head and shoulders with their razor talons. Blood oozed freely from the multiple wounds.

Uriel was just ahead of Japheth. He grabbed a bow and quiver of arrows and spun around on his horse. Riding backward, he picked off pazuzus like target practice. With his superhuman speed and preternatural aim, he rapidly downed six of the flying fiends in quick succession.

Then he ran out of arrows.

Shem swung Rahab over his head like a twirling rope fan, slicing half a dozen pazuzus in half with ease. He was actually enjoying it.

Then, for no apparent reason, the remaining few pazuzus gave up and returned to the sky above them.

But the damage had been done. They had been dramatically slowed down. Inanna's assassin squad was almost upon them. Noah worried what they would do about Behemoth, who was surely blocking their path through the gorge.

# CHAPTER 32

The battle of gods and men resumed with the huge box towering behind the city lines. Yet another skirmish further weakened the human forces. Methuselah had sent forth their last battalion of soldiers. They were totally committed, and most were dead. The angels alone held their ground and kept the forces at bay. But they needed to turn their attention to their calling, that of binding the Watchers. When they left the human forces to do that, the tide of the battle turned fully against Methuselah's men.

Tubal-cain and Jubal fought near each other, comrades in battle to the end. Their tactics and skills were diametrically opposite. Tubal-cain bashed, crushed, and clobbered two at a time with his muscle-bound brawn, while Jubal danced a free flowing stream of slicing, dicing, and slashing. He had picked up the Karabu technique well and was quite good at it. They were a complimentary team. Jubal longed to be fighting next to his dear departed brother. He suspected he would see him soon. Tubal-cain wondered if he had already eaten his last meal, because he was starving.

Mikael zeroed in on Enlil and his Naphil. Mikael's agile sword matched the Naphil's swift axe, thrust for thrust. Mikael waited for the right moment. It came when the Naphil dodged an attack and fell off balance for just an instant. That was all Mikael needed. He dove in between the Naphil's long legs and rolled beneath him. He cut its heel tendons on both sides. Surprised, the Naphil fell to the ground, twisting and landing on his back, pinning Enlil.

In a split second, Mikael was upon the god. Enlil had been knocked dizzy by the fall.

Mikael swiftly cut off the Naphil's head. He pulled Enlil out from under the creature. Hoisting the groggy Watcher on his shoulders, he ran for the huge crevice in the midst of the field and jumped right in with his hostage.

Gabriel and Raphael teamed up against Enki and Ninhursag. But when Enki saw the fall of Enlil, he grabbed his horn and sounded a wailing call.

The large box on the field had five men up top. They wielded their sledgehammers in response to Enki's horn. They slammed out the large pins that held the hinges of the box front.

The door crashed open. A huge flood of seawater flushed out of the box and onto the battlefield. It washed away monsters and men. Lurking in that gargantuan box of salty brine was something else: Leviathan.

The sea dragon slithered out onto the field, a literal fish out of water—a gigantic and very angry fish—with multiple heads, monstrous teeth, serious armored scales, and a powerful tail. The writhing twisting serpent flipped around, crushing everything in its wake and dispersing all in its path. Its jaws snapped viciously, chomping chimeras and humans left and right, forward and behind. None escaped its fury.

Tubal-cain and five other warriors circled a Naphil. The giant's durability wore them down. Then Leviathan was released quite close to them. Tubal-cain could see its impenetrable armored scales, smell its decrepit fishy stench, and feel the heat of its fiery breath. Not only did the creature crush, chomp and slaughter, but it breathed fire from some of its mouths when out of the water and in contact with the air. One burst of flame burnt a company of combating warriors to a crisp in seconds. It would all be over shortly.

Methuselah saw the end was near. He released their final secret weapon to counter the monster on the battlefield: Behemoth. This was the monstrosity that killed his beloved Edna, and Methuselah had vowed to one day return and kill the monster. The creature had taken away the grace in his otherwise lonely life. But when Methuselah had faced the bitterness in his soul, he had realized that his redemption would be found not in killing the monster, but in capturing it and turning it into a benefit for Elohim's purposes.

Even though it was blind in one eye, the brutish beast required ten angels and thirty men to capture it in the mountains. The angels had used their supernatural binding cords to muzzle it and incarcerate it in a large cedar cage on wheels.

That cage now rolled wildly down the hill into the heat of battle, heading directly for Leviathan.

Warriors dove out of its way. Some did not see it coming and were crushed under its massive wheels. The aim had been accurate. The cage crashed right into Leviathan. The sea beast's massive tail swung around, exploding the wooden structure to pieces, releasing the roaring Behemoth.

A shiver of hope went through Methuselah. Behemoth was not as big as Leviathan, but it was at home both on land and in water. That should have placed its aqueous nemesis at a disadvantage. Perhaps it would match Leviathan's ferocity with its own bones of bronze, tail of cedar, and teeth of iron.

But it was not to be.

A wave of dread washed over Methuselah. It did not attack Leviathan. He watched the one-eyed Behemoth strike out for the easier prey, the last living soldiers on the battle ground. Now, two gigantic monsters smashed everything around them like a team of destroyers. Their gamble had not paid off. Their plan had failed.

*It was all over*, thought Methuselah.

Down in the battle, Tubal-cain saw his moment and charged. The Naphil had only a sword. It was unaware of one of the dragon's heads right behind him, turning in their direction. Tubal-cain knew they needed another few moments of diversion, so he burst out of the circle and engaged the Naphil one on one. It was a foolish action that only a man who knew that all was lost with no other chance would make. It was enough to divert the Naphil.

It turned to faced Tubal-cain. The burly metalworker's robust human size was like an infant in comparison with the demigod.

Tubal-cain managed a few good hits against the giant. Then it swung its blade and cut off Tubal-cain's arm in one clean cut.

Tubal-cain cried out in pain and dropped to his knees.

The Naphil looked down, planning an execution style finish to this courageous but failed little warrior. It did not realize that Tubal-cain had not dropped out of pain, but out of calculation. Behind the Naphil, two heads of Leviathan swiveled in their direction, mere cubits away.

The Naphil heard the deep guttural sound of air gurgling and metabolically interacting with chemicals inside Leviathan's innards, but he did not turn toward the noise. He raised his sword high to finish off the prone Tubal-cain. The wounded warrior fell prostrate to avoid the wall of fire that spewed from Leviathan's mouths. An inferno of flame engulfed the Naphil and others around him.

Tubal-cain may have lost his arm, but he had not lost his wits, thanks to the adrenaline of battle surging through his body. The burning blast flared just above where he lay, singeing his hair, and giving him a heat rash he would not care for if he lived until tomorrow. But he did not expect a tomorrow. He had only today. He raised the stump of the arm and allowed the flame to cauterize the wound, giving him more time to fight. It would be a bit more difficult with the lack of his sword arm. *Oh well*, he thought, *Elohim can give me a new one when I rise to meet him.*

Behemoth trampled and attacked downhill toward the last of the armies of the gods. At least now it was killing only the enemy. The writhing serpent Leviathan slid closer to the large chasm, closer to the battling titans of archangels and Watchers, its heads snapping up bodies as it went.

Enki and his Naphil were vicious in battle. Gabriel was taking a pounding. Enki did not see Mikael come up out of the crevice from behind him. Mikael had taken care of Enlil. Now he jumped Enki, leaping as Gabriel attacked. The two of them were a mighty team, but Enki was fighting for his eternity. Even though he was near the crevice, he was not going to let these two god-lickers ruin his future.

Tubal-cain and Jubal each saw the wrestling match of god and angels from their two different locations. Tubal-cain fought on foot, in spite of the pain of his newly cauterized wound. Jubal sat on the back of a horse he recently acquired from a now headless opponent. They were within distance of the match. They caught each other's eyes and nodded. They smirked in recognition, knowing what they had to do. It was now a personal contest between them, who could get there first.

Tubal-cain bolted forward on foot. Jubal kicked his horse and galloped for the divine beings in battle.

The grappling tangle of flesh that was Enki, his Naphil, Mikael, and Gabriel were evenly matched. The tie breaker came in the form of Tubal-cain and Jubal. They hit the tangled bodies almost simultaneously. Tubal-cain was sure he had reached the target a flash before Jubal. It was exactly the amount of force needed to throw the balance in favor of the angels. The whole lot of them tumbled over the edge and into the wide fissure.

Tubal-cain had enough breath left in him to shout to Jubal as they were plunging downward, "I BEAT YOU!"

Jubal had the last word, knowing where they were heading, "LET ELOHIM DECIDE!"

Tubal-cain had the last thought, Yes, but you had a horse, and I was on foot.

The turbulent waters of the great deep swallowed them up.

Tubal-cain and Jubal were not the only ones who would not leave that crevasse. Mikael and Gabriel bound Enki in the depths of the Abyss with the Cherubim hair from their armbands.

Above, at the precipice of the rift, the snapping jaws of Leviathan moved closer to Ninhursag on his Naphil. The god fought with Raphael. The mouths of six of the seven dragon heads were full of soldiers. One of the heads started choking. It had swallowed a Nephilim and two soldiers whole. But one head focused on Ninhursag and his Naphil. It was ready for another bite.

Raphael had one chance. He took it. He leapt right up into the arms of the Naphil, jamming his sword into the creature's chest. It screamed in pain and fell backward, with Ninhursag still in the harness, right into the jaws of Leviathan. The jaws snapped shut on both Watcher and Naphil.

Another earthquake tumbled the field like waves. Leviathan flipped into the crevice and descended into the deep.

It started to rain.

# CHAPTER 33

Methuselah had not been able to tell Noah about the capture of Behemoth. So it was a gratifying surprise when they entered the Hidden Valley without the deep roar and imposing presence of the humongous guardian blocking their path. Unfortunately, it also meant that there was nothing to block the path of their pursuers.

The earth convulsed as Noah and his band arrived at the Hidden Valley village. Lightning and thunder increased in frequency. The sky was black with storm clouds. The floodgates of heaven opened upon them and dropped rain like a waterfall.

The wives of Shem and Japheth stood at the opening of the tebah. The village was empty of all life. Noah was thankful that the rest of the village must be safe inside the box. They just needed to get to the door in time and close themselves in.

They did not reach the door in time.

Inanna and her squad of soldiers and Nephilim broke through the brush and into the clearing. Lugalanu immediately broke away from the squad. He jumped down from his mount, and circled around the structure on foot.

Another quake suddenly split the ground beneath the feet of Inanna's hellions. Many of them went down alive into Sheol, bird-men, dog-men and Nephilim alike. Nanna and his bull-man ride were swallowed up into the Abyss.

*If only all the Watchers would fall so easily*, thought Uriel. He shoved Noah toward the box, and yelled, "GET IN AND LOCK THE GATE! NOW!" He turned to face the enemy, drawing his double swords.

Noah and his family ran for it. They reached the door. But Noah, Shem, and Japheth stopped to cut down the few soldiers that caught up with them.

Noah turned and saw Uriel dispatch two Nephilim and five bird-men soldiers with uncanny swiftness. The power of Elohim transfigured the angel and he became a shining star. And that shining star blocked Inanna's approach to the boat.

Noah whirled to pull the rope to the door ballast. It would lift up the huge heavy doorway.

The rope had been cut.

They could not pull it up themselves. It was far too heavy.

More soldiers were almost upon them.

To their surprise, Elohim himself closed the door and shut them in, leaving the world outside to its destiny.

They did not ask questions about the miracle. They quickly reinforced the door and applied pitch to the edges for sealant.

That done, Noah turned and saw his family, seven of them—he made eight: Emzara, Shem and his wife Sedeq, Japheth and his wife Adatanes, and Ham and his wife Neela.

*Strange,* he thought. "Where is the rest of the village?"

Sedeq and Adatanes looked down.

"Where is the rest of the village?" he repeated.

"Did not Uriel tell you?" said Sedeq.

"Tell me what?" His voice grew more stressed.

Adatanes was bolder than Sedeq. "They fought with the armies of man."

"They what?" He could hardly contain himself.

"They fought with the armies of man against the gods," she repeated.

"You are telling me the entire tribe of men, women and children went to die in the battlefield?" This was madness.

Adatanes told him their story. After Noah left to rescue Emzara, the angel of the Lord, *Mal'ak Yahweh* as he was called, came to their village. He had come riding on a cloud in the presence of his holy ones and he spoke the word of Elohim to them.

She continued, "He told us that he was coming to judge the earth and that it was his will that only the family of Noah board the boat when the floods came. It was not easy on the ears to hear this. But there was something about Mal'ak Yahweh. It was as if he went to each member of the tribe and comforted them individually with assurance. I cannot tell you how, father-in-law, but he spoke to each of us, and we knew he would bring the world to rights."

"Well, if that is not just like him," complained Noah. "He still seems to enjoy speaking directly to everyone but me."

Sedeq and Adatanes giggled.

"Do not be impertinent young ladies," snapped Noah.

"Forgive us," said Adatanes. "It is just that, well, Mal'ak Yahweh said you would say those very words."

"If I live to be a thousand, I will never understand his ways," he finished. "But perhaps that is what makes him God and me his humble servant."

He opened his arms wide and bid his family to join in as he beseeched Elohim, the Lord their God to have mercy upon their souls and that they would have favor in his sight.


Outside the boat, Uriel and Inanna fought like titans. Blow by blow they were equals, but Inanna was not alone. She was on her lion-man joined by three Nephilim with maces and axes.

The waters burst forth from the fountains of the deep and gushed out through the chasms opened in the earth. The contenders carried their battle to the rooftops of the flooding village. Uriel dispatched one Naphil, but he was ultimately overcome by the other two. They pinned him to the roof of one of the homes.

Inanna strode up to him in the pouring rain and thunder. She spit out with every ounce of bile that filled her demonic soul, "You have thwarted my will for the last time, you worthless slave of Elohim."

Another earthquake rocked the valley, causing them all to look up.

A huge wall of water crashed through the valley. It hit the box and burst around it. It descended upon Inanna, her chimera mount, Uriel, and the Nephilim and they were instantly washed away in a churning tidal wave of doom.

Inside the boat, Noah's family grabbed hold of some timbers. The force of the water hit the boat and shook it loose from its mooring to the ground. The barge started to drift in the massive tide.

On the battlefield of Dudael, the sheets of torrential rain and flood waters washed away the armies of both gods and men. They had been utterly wiped out to the last person. It was complete and total annihilation. They were all dead -- except for one last regiment of bird-men soldiers.

On the ridge above the plain, Methuselah and his personal guard of a handful of soldiers were the last of the human tribes. They saw the regiment of bird-men ascending toward them. Methuselah smiled. He had prayed for this very thing. He had asked Elohim that he be alive to see the end, and to have a good death, one that would be glorious. He felt the rumbling behind him as a thousand soldiers approached his group of ten from below. He raised his arms to heaven and yelled with all the passion in his soul, "EDNA, I AM COMING!"

And then he spoke the name he had learned so many years ago from his forefather Adam, the special covenant name of his god, reserved for a future time of revealing. No one would hear it now, so he was free to worship without restraint. "YAHWEH ELOHIM! THY WILL BE DONE!"

Behind him, a huge fifteen cubit high wall of water appeared, as if bidden by Methuselah. It surged over the desert of Dudael, swallowing up everything. Methuselah and his guards disappeared under the enormous wave as it crashed upon the last of the armies of the gods and drowned them all like ants in a rainstorm.

It took seconds for the deluge to wipe the battlefield clean. A few seconds more, and the city was completely enveloped. The water smothered everything that breathed. It dissolved man-made structures as if they were sand castles.

The torrential wave made its way across the plain, extinguishing everything in its path. All flesh that moved on the land died, everything in whose nostrils was the breath of life died. Elohim blotted out every living thing that was on the face of the ground.

Only Noah was left, and those who were with him in the box.

# CHAPTER 34

The box had been built effectively. It floated barge-like in the water, about two thirds of it below the waterline. It was a drift ship or a current rider, not a sailing vessel. Elohim would be its rudder.

Inside, Noah's family settled in for a long voyage. They did not know exactly how long it would be, but Elohim had told them it would rain for forty days and forty nights. They knew the terrible truth that he was going to blot out all living things in the land. They knew they would be the only survivors. They knew they would start anew Elohim's plans for the human race.

Noah was already organizing the work details. The barge was full of animals of every kind. Though many had been nestled into hibernation by Elohim's hand, there were still many that had to be taken care of and fed. It would be a consuming job for these mere eight people. They had to get to work immediately. The sounds of bleating, mooing, squealing, braying, growling, and whinnying already filled the air in a cacophony of need. It would be a long journey indeed.

Noah's family did not hear Lugalanu, hiding just down the hallway and around the corner from them. He had snuck into the boat when everyone's attention had been on the battle. He carried a long dagger in his hand and waited for his moment.

He found it.

Lugalanu gripped his blade tightly and walked down the hallway toward the family. He had no need to conceal himself or surprise anyone. He was fully capable of taking them all out in a fury. He muttered to himself with satisfaction, "It is not so easy to kill a demigod."

Noah looked up from the table where they counseled. He saw Lugalanu approaching them, dagger clutched in one hand, eyes full of rage.

Everyone followed Noah's gaze. His sons pulled the women behind them to prepare for a battle. Unfortunately, the few weapons aboard were not at hand. They had not anticipated such a moment.

But Lugalanu had not anticipated what happened next.

He was halfway to the family. Suddenly, a lion jumped out of a stall, blocking his way. It growled, ready to pounce. *A nuisance*, thought Lugalanu, but killing it would be an opportunity to excite his blood rage before he took the family.

Then another lion joined it. And a tiger. And then a panther. Soon, feline predators with bared teeth and protracted claws entirely obstructed his path.

It made him pause.

A snort behind him made him look back.

A big black bull stomped its feet, preparing to charge. Behind it a huge gorilla joined in.

Lugalanu's eyes went wide with fear. The animals knew he was their enemy and they were going to protect their own.

The bull charged. It hit Lugalanu in full stride, goring him on its horns and throwing him to the floor. The predators all pounced. Lugalanu disappeared beneath their teeth and claws.

Lugalanu had believed his own lie. He was no demigod. He was very human.

And then he was no more.

Noah's family clung to each other in protection.

Elohim worked in mysterious ways.

Outside, all was darkness and rain and tempestuous waters. Seventy cubits from the boat, Inanna broke the surface, shorn of all clothing and accouterments. No more masquerade. Azazel was a pure, undefiled predator. He cut through the water like a shark toward the boat. His eyes focused on the craft with intense determination. He was weakened in the water, but he was one of the strongest of the divine *Bene Elohim,* and had a will of iron.

But even a *Bene Elohim* was no match for the jaws of the mighty Rahab. She burst through the water from below and clamped down on his body with her iron jaws. The speed of Rahab made it leap out of the water a dozen cubits before splashing back down in a fountain of spray. The monster sank fast and carried Azazel deep into the murky abyss.

It rode a violent current with its victim into the convulsive swirling sea below. Then a large wall of rock and sediment buried them, freezing Azazel in Rahab's jaws, unable to move but bound alive forever.

In the boat, Noah's family had already begun their arduous task of feeding the animals and cleaning the stalls.

Neela offered some hay to a couple of sheep. They grabbed it and munched to their heart's content.

She stopped, a stabbing pain in her belly. A wave of nausea overcame her. She quickly found a pail and wretched.

Ham rushed to her, comforting her with a loving hand on her back.

Noah noticed her retching and was concerned. "What is wrong, Neela?" he asked.

"She must be seasick," Ham offered.

"I hope you get over it soon, because we have a long drift ahead of us," said Noah.

"It is not seasickness," interrupted Neela. "I am with child."

Ham grinned wide with happiness. Emzara hugged her first, followed by the rest of the family.

Noah said happily, "Well, we will have a world to repopulate, and it appears Ham and Neela have beat us all to the task." Everyone laughed and got back to their work.

Neela sought hard to conceal her own fears. She had secrets she could not reveal—secrets of the Watchers. Semjaza and Azazel had achieved their goal of cross-breeding a normal human being that would carry the Nephilim genetic traits in a recessive form, to blossom in later generations once the lines had spread throughout the land.

Neela knew that the first of those demigods had been created, and it grew inside her.

*Chronicles of the Nephilim* continues with the next book, *Enoch Primordial*, the prequel.

See the next page for a discount on the next two books in the series.

CHAPTER 35: DISCOUNT BOX SET

# So, You've Read *Noah Primeval.* Now Get the Next 2 Books in the Series for 30% OFF!

### Limited Time Offer
### Various Ebook versions

## 30% Off Box Set

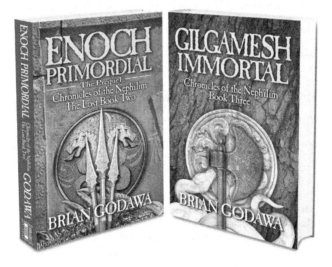

### Enoch Primordial & Gilgamesh Immortal
### Books 2 & 3 Ebook Box Set
By Brian Godawa

https://wp.me/P6y1ub-inT

# APPENDIX A:
# THE SONS OF GOD

Deut. 6:4

"Hear, O Israel: The LORD our God, the LORD is one."

Psa. 82:1

God has taken his place in the divine council; in the midst of the gods he holds judgment.

A major premise of my fictional novel *Noah Primeval* is that the gods of the ancient world were real spiritual beings with supernatural powers. Thus, the mythical literature and artistic engravings of the gods that have been uncovered by Mesopotamian archeology reflect a certain amount of factual reality. The twist is that these gods are actually fallen divine angelic beings called "Sons of God" (*Bene Elohim*) in the Bible. These Sons of God had rebelled against God's divine council in heaven and came to earth in order to corrupt God's creation and deceive mankind into worshipping them in place of the real God. While this is not polytheism, neither is it absolute monotheism. It is Biblical theism, which will become clear shortly.

Though I have clearly engaged in imaginative creative license and fantasy in the novel, it is not without Biblical theological foundation. The purpose of this essay is to make an argument that in principle the Bible does in fact suggest a paradigm that reflects something similar to the theological interpretation presented in the novel. For that reason I might call *Noah Primeval* a theological novel.

Jewish monotheism and Christian Trinitarianism affirm the oneness of God's being. Christianity contains an additional doctrinal nuance of three persons, Father, Son and Holy Spirit, who share the same substance while maintaining separate persons. In this way, the Christian is able to both affirm God's oneness (unity) *and* his threeness (diversity). Simply put, God is three persons in one being, *not* three beings.

Jews, Muslims and atheists who seem to assume that a monotheistic worldview cannot provide for diversity within the divine realm have often accused Christians of being polytheists. I call this Jewish/Muslim viewpoint, "absolute monotheism" as opposed to Biblical theism. What would shock most readers of the Bible is that the same Old Testament quoted by the *Shema* about God being "one," also describes a cosmic worldview that includes a hierarchy in heaven of divine beings, a kind of governmental bureaucracy of operations that counsels with God, and carries out his decrees in heaven and earth. Biblical scholars refer to this hierarchy as the divine council, or divine assembly and it consists of beings that are referred to in the Bible as *gods*.

Before examining the texts about the divine council it is important to understand that the English word "God," can be misleading in Biblical interpretation. The most common Hebrew word translated in English as "God" in the Bible is *Elohim*. But God has many names in the text and each of them is used to describe different aspects of his person. *El*, often refers to God's powerful preeminence; *El Elyon* (God Most High) indicates God as possessor of heaven and earth; *Adonai* means God as lord or master; and *Yahweh* is the covenantal name for the God of Israel as distinguished from any other deity. *Elohim*, though it is the most common Hebrew word for God in the Old Testament, was also a word that was used of angels (Psa. 8:5; Heb. 2:7), gods or idols of pagan nations (Psa. 138:1), supernatural beings of the divine council (Psa. 82:6), departed spirits of humans (1Sam. 28:13), and demons (Deut. 32:17).[1] Scholar Michael S. Heiser has pointed out that the Hebrew word Elohim was more of a reference to a plane of existence than to a substance of being. In this way, Yahweh was *Elohim*, but no other elohim was Yahweh. Yahweh is incomparably *THE* Elohim of elohim (Deut. 10:17).[2]

## Of Gods and Elohim

A common understanding of absolute monotheism is that when the Bible refers to other gods it does not mean that the gods are real beings but merely *beliefs* in real beings that do not exist. For instance, when Deuteronomy 32:43 proclaims "rejoice with him, O heavens, bow down to him, all gods," this is a poetic way of saying "what you believe are gods are not gods at all because Yahweh is God." What seems to support this interpretation is the fact that a few verses before this, (v. 39) God says, "See now, that I, even I am he, and there is no god [elohim] beside me." Does this not clearly indicate that God is the only god [elohim] that really exists out of all the "gods" [elohim] that others believe in?

Not in its Biblical context it doesn't.

When the text is examined in its full context of the chapter and rest of the Bible we discover a very different notion about God and

---

[1] Geoffrey W. Bromiley, "God, Names of," *The International Standard Bible Encyclopedia, Revised.* Wm. B. Eerdmans, 1988; 2002, p. 504-508.

[2] Michael S. Heiser, *The Myth That is True: Rediscovering the Cosmic Narrative of the Bible*, unpublished manuscript, 2011, p 25-29. Available online at www.michaelsheiser.com. I have read quite a few scholars on the divine council, but Michael Heiser has been the most helpful and represents the major influence on this essay.

gods. The phrase "I am, and there is none beside me" was an ancient Biblical slogan of incomparability of sovereignty, not exclusivity of existence. It was a way of saying that a certain authority was the most powerful *compared to* all other authorities. It did not mean that there were no other authorities that existed. We see this sloganeering in two distinct passages, one of the ruling power of Babylon claiming proudly in her heart, "I am, and there is no one beside me" (Isa. 47:8) and the other of the city of Nineveh boasting in her heart, "I am, and there is no one else" (Zeph. 2:15). The powers of Babylon and Nineveh are obviously not saying that there are no other powers or cities that exist beside them, because they had to conquer other cities and rule over them. In the same way, Yahweh uses that colloquial phrase, not to deny the existence of other gods, but to express his incomparable sovereignty over them.[3]

In concert with this phrase is the key reference to gods early in Deuteronomy 32. Israel is chastised for falling away from Yahweh after he gave Israel the Promised Land: "They sacrificed to demons not God, to gods they had never known, to new gods that had come recently, whom your fathers had never dreaded" (Deut. 32:17). In this important text we learn that the idols or gods of the other nations that Israel worshipped were real beings that existed called "demons." At the same time, they are called, "gods" and "not God," which indicates that they exist as real beings, but are not THE God of Israel.

Psalm 106 repeats this same exact theme of Israel worshipping the gods of other nations and making sacrifices to those gods that were in fact demons.

---

[3] Michael S. Heiser, "Monotheism, Polytheism, Monolatry, or Henotheism? Toward an Assessment of Divine Plurality in the Hebrew Bible" (2008). Faculty Publications and Presentations. Paper 277, p. 12-15,
http://digitalcommons.liberty.edu/cgi/viewcontent.cgi?article=1276&context=lts_fac_pubs
&sei-
redir=1#search=%22heiser+Monotheism,+Polytheism,+Monolatry,+or+Henotheism%22
accessed March 23, 2011.

Psa. 106:34-37
They did not destroy the peoples, as the LORD commanded them, but they mixed with the nations and learned to do as they did.
They served their idols, which became a snare to them.
They sacrificed their sons and their daughters to the demons.

One rendering of the Septuagint (LXX) version of Psalm 95:5-6 reaffirms this reality of national gods being demons whose deity was less than the Creator, "For great is the Lord, and praiseworthy exceedingly. More awesome he is than all the gods. For all the gods of the nations are demons, but the Lord made the heavens."[4] Another LXX verse, Isa. 65:11, speaks of Israel's idolatry: "But ye are they that have left me, and forget my holy mountain, and prepare a table for [a demon], and fill up the drink-offering to Fortune [a foreign goddess]."[5]

The non-canonical book of 1 Enoch, upon which some of *Noah Primeval* is based, affirms this very notion of gods as demons, the fallen angels of Genesis 6: "The angels which have united themselves with women. They have defiled the people and will lead them into error so that they will offer sacrifices to the demons as unto gods."[6]

[4] Randall Tan, David A. deSilva, and Logos Bible Software. *The Lexham Greek-English Interlinear Septuagint*. Logos Bible Software, 2009. Baruch 4:7 in the Apocrypha echoes this Scriptural theme as well when speaking of Israel's apostasy: "For you provoked him who made you, by sacrificing to demons and not to God."
[5] Lancelot Charles Lee Brenton, *The Septuagint Version of the Old Testament: English Translation* (London: Samuel Bagster and Sons, 1870), Is 65:11. Randall Tan and David A. deSilva, Logos Bible Software, *The Lexham Greek-English Interlinear Septuagint* (Logos Bible Software, 2009), Is 65:11.
[6] James H. Charlesworth, *The Old Testament Pseudepigrapha: Volume 1*, 1 En 19:1 (New York; London: Yale University Press, 1983).

The New Testament carries over this idea of demonic reality of beings behind the idols that pagans offered sacrifices to and worshipped: "No, I imply that what pagans sacrifice they offer to demons and not to God. I do not want you to be participants with demons (1Cor. 10:20)." In Revelation 9:20, the Apostle John defines the worship of gold and silver idols as being the worship of demons. The physical objects were certainly without deity as they could not "see or hear or walk," but the gods behind those objects were real beings with evil intent.

Returning to Deuteronomy 32 and going back a few more verses in context, we read of a reality-changing incident that occurred at Babel:

> Deut. 32:8-9
> When the Most High gave to the nations their inheritance, when he divided mankind, he fixed the borders of the peoples according to the number of the sons of God. But the LORD's portion is his people, Jacob his allotted heritage.

The reference to the creation of nations through the division of mankind and fixing of the borders of nations is clearly a reference to the event of the Tower of Babel in Genesis 11 and the dispersion of the peoples into the 70 nations listed in Genesis 10.

But then there is a strange reference to those nations being "fixed" according to the number of the sons of God.[7] We'll explain in a moment that those sons of God are from the assembly of the divine

---

[7] The astute reader will notice that some Bible translations read "according to the sons of Israel." The ESV reflects the latest consensus of scholarship that the Septuagint (LXX) and the Dead Sea Scrolls (DSS) segment of this verse is the earlier and more accurate reading than the later Masoretic Text (MT) of the same. See Heiser, Michael, "Does Deuteronomy 32:17 Assume or Deny the Reality of Other Gods?" (2008). Faculty Publications and Presentations. Paper 322, p 137-145. http://digitalcommons.liberty.edu/lts_fac_pubs/322/

council of God. But after that the text says that God saved Jacob (God's own people) for his "allotment." Even though Jacob was not born until long after the Babel incident, this is an anachronistic way of referring to what would become God's people, because right after Babel, we read about God's calling of Abraham who was the grandfather of Jacob (Isa. 41:8; Rom. 11:26). So God allots nations and their geographic territory to these sons of God to rule over, but he allots the people of Jacob to himself, along with their geographical territory of Canaan (Gen. 17:8).

The idea of Yahweh "allotting" geographical territories to these sons of God who really existed and were worshipped as gods (idols) shows up again in several places in Deuteronomy:

Deut. 4:19-20

And beware lest you raise your eyes to heaven, and when you see the sun and the moon and the stars, all the host of heaven, you be drawn away and bow down to them and serve them, things that the LORD your God has allotted to all the peoples under the whole heaven.

Deut. 29:26

They went and served other gods and worshiped them, gods whom they have not known and whom He had not allotted to them.

"Host of heaven" was a term that referred to astronomical bodies that were also considered to be gods or members of the divine council.[8] The *Encyclopedia Judaica* notes that, "in many cultures the

---

[8] H. Niehr, "Host of Heaven," Toorn, K. van der, Bob Becking, and Pieter Willem van der Horst. *Dictionary of Deities and Demons in the Bible DDD.* 2nd extensively rev. ed. Leiden; Boston; Grand Rapids, Mich.: Brill; Eerdmans, 1999., 428-29; I. Zatelli, "Astrology and the Worship of the Stars in the Bible," *ZAW* 103 (1991): 86-99.

sky, the sun, the moon, and the known planets were conceived as personal gods. These gods were responsible for all or some aspects of existence. Prayers were addressed to them, offerings were made to them, and their opinions on important matters were sought through divination."[9]

But it was not merely the pagans who made this connection of heavenly physical bodies with heavenly spiritual powers. The Old Testament itself equates the sun, moon, and stars with the angelic "sons of God" who surround God's throne, calling them both the "host of heaven" (Deut. 4:19; 32:8-9).[10] Jewish commentator Jeffrey Tigay writes, "[These passages] seem to reflect a Biblical view that... as punishment for man's repeated spurning of His authority in primordial times (Gen. 3-11), God deprived mankind at large of true knowledge of Himself and ordained that it should worship idols and subordinate celestial beings."[11]

There is more than just a symbolic connection between the physical heavens and the spiritual heavens in the Bible. In some passages, the stars of heaven are linked *interchangeably* with angelic heavenly beings, also referred to as "holy ones" or "sons of God" (Psa. 89:5-7; Job 1:6)[12].

---

[9] "Astrology", *Encyclopaedia Judaica* Michael Berenbaum and Fred Skolnik, eds. 2nd ed. Detroit: Macmillan Reference USA, 2007, p. 8424.

[10] See also Deut 4:19; Deut 17:3; 2King 23:4-5; 1King 22:19; Neh 9:6.

[11] Jeffrey Tigay, *JPS Torah Commentary: Deuteronomy* (Philadelphia: The Jewish Publication Society, 1996): 435; as quoted in Michael S. Heiser, "Deuteronomy 32:8 and the Sons of God," Bibliotheca Sacra 158 (January-March 2001): 72; online: http://thedivinecouncil.com/.

[Copyright © 2001 Dallas Theological Seminary;, online: http://thedivinecouncil.com/

[12] See also Job 38:4-7; Neh. 9:6; Psa 148:2-3, 1King 22:29 & 2King 21:5. In Isa 14:12-14 the king of Babylon is likened to the planet Venus (Morningstar) seeking to reign above the other stars of heaven, which are equivalent to the sons of God who surround God's throne on the "mount of assembly" or "divine council" (see Psa 89:5-7 and Psa 82).

Daniel 10:10-18 speaks of these divine "host of heaven" allotted with authority over pagan nations as spiritual "princes" battling with the archangels Gabriel and Michael.

Some Second Temple non-canonical Jewish texts illustrate an ancient tradition of understanding this interpretation of the gods of the nations as real spirit beings that rule over those nations:

Jubilees 15:31-32

(There are) many nations and many people, and they all belong to him, but <u>over all of them</u> he caused <u>spirits to rule so that they might lead them astray from following him</u>. But over Israel he did not cause any angel or spirit to rule because he alone is their ruler and he will protect them.

Targum Jonathan, Deuteronomy 32, Section LIII[13]

When the Most High made <u>allotment of the world unto the nations</u> which proceeded from the sons of Noach [Noah], in the separation of the writings and languages of the children of men at the time of the division, He cast the lot among the <u>seventy angels, the princes of the nations</u> with whom is the revelation <u>to oversee the city</u>.

---

[13] See also 1 Enoch 89:59, 62-63; 90:25, 56:5; 3Enoch 48C:9, DSS War Scroll 1Q33 Col. xvii:7, Targum Jonathan, Genesis 11, Section II; Philo, On the Posterity of Cain and His Exile 25.89; Concerning Noah's Work as a Planter 14.59; On the Migration of Abraham 36.202; 1 Clement 29; Origen, First Principles 1.5.1. Thanks to Don Enevoldsen for some of these passages. Walter Wink footnotes a plenitude of texts about the 70 angel "gods" over the 70 nations in the Targums in Walter Wink. *Naming the Powers: The Language of Power in the New Testament* (The Powers : Volume One) (Kindle Locations 2235-2242). Kindle Edition.

In conclusion, the entire narrative of Deuteronomy 32 tells the story of God dispersing the nations at Babel and allotting the nations to be ruled by "gods" who were demons, or fallen divine beings called sons of God. God then allots the people of Israel for himself, through Abraham, and their territory of Canaan. But God's people fall away from him and worship these other gods and are judged for their apostasy. We will now see that Yahweh will judge these gods as well.

## Psalm 82

Bearing in mind this notion of Yahweh allotting gods over the Gentile nations while maintaining Canaan and Israel for himself, read this following important Psalm 82 where Yahweh now judges those gods for injustice and proclaims the Gospel that he will eventually take back the nations from those gods.

> God [elohim] has taken his place in the divine council;
> in the midst of the gods [elohim] he holds judgment:
> "How long will you judge unjustly
> and show partiality to the wicked? *Selah*
> Give justice to the weak and the fatherless;
> maintain the right of the afflicted and the destitute.
> Rescue the weak and the needy;
> deliver them from the hand of the wicked."
>
> They have neither knowledge nor understanding,
> they walk about in darkness;
> all the foundations of the earth are shaken.
>
> I said, "You are gods [elohim]
> sons of the Most High, all of you;

nevertheless, like men you shall die,

and fall like any prince."

Arise, O God, judge the earth;

for you shall inherit all the nations!

So from this text we see that God has a divine council that stands around him, and it consists of "gods" who are judging rulers over the nations and are also called *sons of the Most High* (equivalent to "sons of God"). Because they have not ruled justly, God will bring them low in judgment and take the nations away from them. Sound familiar? It's the same exact story as Deuteronomy 32:8-9 and Isaiah 24:21-22.

Isaiah 24:21–22

On that day the LORD will <u>punish the host of heaven, in heaven, and the kings of the earth, on the earth</u>. They will be gathered together as prisoners in a pit; they will be shut up in a prison, and after many days they will be punished.[14]

One of the Dead Sea Scrolls written in the first century B.C., reinforces this ancient Jewish interpretation of Psalm 82 as punishment focused on the divine council of gods, with Satan as their chief, allotted judicial authority over the nations:

its interpretation concerns Satan and the spirits of his lot [who] rebelled by turning away from the precepts

---

[14] Interestingly, this passage of Isaiah is not clear about what judgment in history it is referring to. But the language earlier in the text is similar to Psalm 82 and to the Flood when it says, "For the windows of heaven are opened, and the foundations of the earth tremble. 19 The earth is utterly broken, the earth is split apart, the earth is violently shaken. 20 The earth staggers like a drunken man; it sways like a hut; its transgression lies heavy upon it, and it falls, and will not rise again." So this may be another passage that uses a Flood reference tied in with the Watchers and their punishment.

of God to … And Melchizedek will avenge the vengeance of the judgements of God … and he will drag [them from the hand of] Satan and from the hand of all the sp[irits of] his [lot]. And all the 'gods [of Justice'] will come to his aid [to] attend to the de[struction] of Satan.[15]

The idea that the Bible should talk about existent gods other than Yahweh is certainly uncomfortable for absolute monotheists. But our received definitions of monotheism are more often than not determined by our cultural traditions, many of which originate in theological controversies of other time eras that create the baggage of non-Biblical agendas.

According to the Evangelical Protestant principle of *Sola Scriptura*, that the Bible alone is the final authority of doctrine, not tradition, believers are obligated to first find out what the Bible text says and then adjust their theology to be in line with Scripture, not the other way around. All too often we find individuals ignoring or redefining a Biblical text because it does not fit their preconceived notion of what the Bible *should* say, rather than what it actually says. The existence of other gods in Scripture is one of those issues.

In light of this theological fear, some try to reinterpret this reference of gods or sons of God in Psalm 82 as a poetic expression of human judges or rulers on earth metaphorically taking the place of God, the ultimate judge, by determining justice in his likeness and image. But there are three big reasons why this cannot be so: First, the terminology in the passage contradicts the notion of human judges and fails to connect that term ("sons of God") to human beings anywhere else in the Bible; Second, the Bible elsewhere explicitly reveals a divine

---

[15] *11QMelch* Geza Vermes, *The Dead Sea Scrolls in English*, Revised and extended 4th ed. (Sheffield: Sheffield Academic Press, 1995), 361.

council or assembly of supernatural sons of God that are judges over geographical allotments of nations that is more consistent with this passage; Third, a heavenly divine council of supernatural sons of God is more consistent with the ancient Near Eastern (ANE) worldview of the Biblical times that Israel shared with her neighbors. We'll take a closer look at each of these following.

**Human or Divine Beings?**

Though the sons of God in Psalm 82 and elsewhere in the Old Testament have been understood as supernatural, angelic, or divine beings through most of Jewish and Christian history, it is fair to say that there has also been a minor tradition of scholars and theologians who have interpreted these beings as human rulers or judges of some kind or another.[16] They claim that the scenario in which we see these sons of God is a courtroom, the liturgy they engage in is legal formality, and the terminology they use is forensic (related to lawsuits), thus leading them to conclude that these are poetic descriptions of the responsibility of natural human authorities over their subjects on earth. And they would be supernaturally wrong.

The setting, liturgy and language are indeed all courtroom-oriented in their context, but that courtroom is God's heavenly courtroom because that is how God reveals his own judgments to his people and the nations. Let's let Jesus exegete this passage for us.

---

[16] Some prominent examples are: The Jewish Rabbinic Targums and Babylonian Talmud as referenced in "The Sons of God and Nephilim of Genesis 6: Aliens, Demons, or Humans?" By Gary DeMar (Unpublished manuscript); Ramban (Nachmanides), *Commentary on the Torah: Genesis*, trans. Charles B. Chavel (New York: Shilo Publishing House, 1971); William H. Green, "The Sons of God and the Daughters of Men," in *The Unity of the Book of Genesis* (New York: Charles Scribner's Sons, 1910); Meredith G. Kline, *Kingdom Prologue: Genesis Foundations for a Covenantal Worldview*, (Overland Park: KS; Two Age Press, 2000); James B. Jordan, *Primeval Saints: Studies in the Patriarchs of Genesis* (Moscow, ID: Canon Press, 2001).

In John 10, learned Jews in the Temple challenge Jesus about his identity as Christ. Jesus says that he and the Father are one, a clear claim of deity in the Hebrew culture, which results in the Jews picking up stones to stone him because he, being a man, made himself out to be God (10:33). Their particular Rabbinic absolute monotheism did not allow for the existence of divinity other than the Father. Jesus responds by appealing to this very passage we are discussing: "Jesus answered them, "Is it not written in your Law, 'I said, you are gods'? If he called them gods to whom the word of God came—and Scripture cannot be broken—do you say of him whom the Father consecrated and sent into the world, 'You are blaspheming,' because I said, 'I am the Son of God'?" (10:34-36).

If the judges in Psalm 82 "to whom the word of God came" were considered to be men rather than gods by Jesus, then his appeal to the passage to justify his claims of deity would be nonsensical. He would essentially be saying "I am a god in the same way that human judges were human representatives of God." But this would not be controversial, it would divest Jesus of all deity, and they would certainly not seek to stone him. No, Jesus is affirming the divinity of the sons of God in Psalm 82 and chastising the Jews that their own Scriptures allow for the existence of divine beings (gods) other than the Father, so it would not be inherently unscriptural for another being to claim divinity. Of course, Jesus is the species-unique Son of God (John 1:18),[17] the "visible Yahweh" co-regent over the divine council (Dan. 7). But Jesus' point is that the diversity of deity is not unknown in the Old Testament.[18]

---

[17] Heiser points about that the Greek word for "only begotten" son of God is *monogenes*, which is better translated as "unique," in the same way that Isaac was not Abraham's only son, but was referred to as his "only son" in this sense of uniqueness (Heb 11:17). Heiser *The Myth That is True*, p. 28-29.

[18] Michael S. Heiser, "Deuteronomy 32:8 and the Sons of God" http://www.thedivinecouncil.com/DT32BibSac.pdf, accessed March 23, 2011, p 20-21. See

Jesus is arguing for the Trinitarian concept of divine diversity as being compatible with Old Testament monotheism, which was not compatible with man-made traditions of absolute monotheism that Rabbinic Jews followed. Remember, in the Bible, the concept of "god" (elohim) was about a plane of existence not necessarily a "being" of existence, so there were many gods (many elohim) that existed on that supernatural plane, yet only one God of gods who created all things, including those other elohim or sons of God.

This is precisely the nuanced distinction that the Apostle Paul refers to when he addresses the issue of food sacrificed to idols—that is, physical images of deities on earth. He considers idols as having "no real existence," but then refers to other "gods" in the heavens or on earth *who do exist*, but are *not the same* as the One Creator God:

> 1 Cor. 8:4-6
>
> Therefore, as to the eating of food offered to idols, we know that "an idol has no real existence," and that "there is no God but one." For although there may be so-called gods in heaven or on earth—as indeed there are many "gods" and many "lords"—yet for us there is one God, the Father, from whom are all things and for whom we exist, and one Lord, Jesus Christ, through whom are all things and through whom we exist.

> 1 Cor. 10:18-20
>
> Consider the people of Israel: are not those who eat the sacrifices participants in the altar? What do I imply then? That food offered to idols is anything, or that an idol is anything? No, I imply that what pagans sacrifice

---

also, "Michael S. Heiser, "Mormonism's Use of Psalm 82," The FARMS Review, 19/1, 2007, http://www.thedivinecouncil.com/John10Psa82excerpt.pdf accessed March 23, 2011.

<u>they offer to demons and not to God</u>. I do not want you
to be participants with demons.

In 1 Corinthians, as in Revelation 9:20 quoted earlier, gods are
not merely figments of imagination without existence in a world
where the Trinity is the sole deity residing in the spiritual realm.
Rather, physical idols (*images*) are "nothing," and "have no real
existence" in that they are the representatives of the deities, not the
deities themselves. But the deities behind those idols are real demonic
beings; the gods of the nations who are not THE God, for they
themselves were created by God and are therefore essentially
incomparable to the God through whom are all things and through
whom we exist.

The terminology used by Paul in the first passage contrasting the
many gods and lords with the one God and Lord of Christianity
reflects the client-patron relationship that ANE cultures shared. As
K.L. Noll explains in his text on ancient Canaan and Israel, "Lord"
was the proper designation for a patron in a patron-client relationship.
There may have been many gods, but for ancient Israel, there was only
one Lord, and that was Yahweh."[19]

This is certainly difficult for a modern mind to wrap itself around
because we have been taught to think that there are only two
diametrically opposed options: Either absolute diversity as in
polytheism (many gods of similar essence) or absolute unity as in
absolute monotheism that excludes the possibility of any other divine
beings less than the One God.[20] As we have already seen, the Bible

---

[19] K.L. Noll, *Canaan and Israel in Antiquity: An Introduction*, New York: NY; Shefffield
Academic Press, 2001, p. 212.

[20] Another possibility, henotheism, is the belief that there are many gods but one god is
supreme over them all. But this is nothing more than an exalted polytheism because that
supreme god is not a different species, whereas Biblical theism or *monolatry* maintains
Yahweh as being of a different substance, essence, or species than the other gods it speaks
of.

seems to indicate that there are other "gods" who are not of the same species as God the Father or God the Son, yet they do exist as supernatural entities with ruling power over the nations outside of God's people. Some scholars have used the term *monolatry* of this view rather than monotheism, because monotheism excludes the existence of any other gods, while monolatry allows for the existence of other gods, but demands the worship of one God who is essentially different from all other gods.[21]

Psalm 89 fills out the picture of the heavenly divine council as opposed to an earthly human one that is composed of these sons of God who are comparably less than Yahweh:

> Psa. 89:5-7
>
> Let the heavens praise your wonders, O LORD,
> your faithfulness in the assembly of the holy ones!
> For who in the skies can be compared to the LORD?
> Who among the heavenly beings (Hebrew: *sons of God*) is like the LORD,
> a God greatly to be feared in the council of the holy ones, and awesome above all who are around him?

Here, the sons of God are referred to as an assembly or council of holy ones that surround Yahweh in a heavenly court "in the skies," not in an earthly court or council of humans, thus reinforcing the supernatural distinction from earthly judges. Israel is sometimes called, "a holy nation" (Ex. 19:6), a "holy people" (Isa. 62:12), "holy ones" (Psa. 16:3), and other derivatives of that concept, but the Hebrew word for "holy ones" (*qedoshim*) is used often in the Bible to

---

[21] Michael S. Heiser, The Divine Council In Late Canonical And Non-Canonical Second Temple Jewish Literature (Madison, WI: University of Wisconsin, 2004), 10.

refer to these supernatural sons of God, as the "ten thousands of his holy ones," surrounding God's heavenly throne.[22] Daniel calls these heavenly *holy ones* "watchers" in Daniel 4 (verses 13, 17, and 23) and the New Testament book of Jude quotes the non-canonical book of Enoch regarding God coming with ten thousand of his holy ones who were also these "watchers" or sons of God from heaven (Jude 14).[23] The Dead Sea Scrolls of Qumran also used the term "holy ones" in many passages to refer to angelic beings from God's heavenly throne, making this a common Semitic understanding congenial with the worldview of Daniel.[24]

So there is Biblical unanimity in describing a heavenly host of ten thousands of sons of God, called gods, watchers, and holy ones who surround God's throne in the heavens as an assembly, and who counsel with God and worship him, and some of whom were given to rule over human nations in the past (also called "demons"), but have lost that privilege at some point. These gods are clearly *not* human

---

[22] Deut 33:1-4; Job 5:1; 15:15; Psa 89:5, 7; Dan 8:13; 14:7; Zech 14:5; Jude 14. Michael S. Heiser points out that even though the MT of Deut 33:1-4 appears to reference the congregation of Israel as "holy ones," the Septuagint version of this verse, which the New Testament authors seem to quote, applies the term to "angels" at Sinai through whom God gave the law (Acts 7:52-53; Heb 2:1-2; Gal 3:19) Heiser, *The Myth That is True*, p. 149-152. In Daniel 7 it appears that the holy ones in God's divine council in heaven (7:27) are spoken of in fusion (7:21-22, 25) with the "saints" or holy ones in earthly Israel (7:18). The beasts of earthly kingdoms ruled over by their Watcher Princes are at war with Israel and its Watchers led by Michael. And in Deut 33:2-3 the term "holy ones" is used of both Israelites *and* supernatural beings in the same paragraph.

[23] And behold! He cometh with ten thousands of His holy ones, To execute judgment upon all, And to destroy all the ungodly. (Enoch 1:9)
And his activities had to do with the Watchers, and his days were with the holy ones. (Enoch 12:2)
And it came to pass after this that my spirit was translated And it ascended into the heavens: And I saw the holy sons of God. (Enoch 71:1)

[24] See these DSS passages: 1QM 1:16; 10:11–12; 12:1, 4, 7; 15:14; 1QS 11:7–8; 1QH 3:21–22; 10:35; 1QDM 4:1; 1QSb 1:5; 1Q 36:1; 1QapGen 2:1. John Joseph Collins, Frank Moore Cross and Adela Yarbro Collins, *Daniel: A Commentary on the Book of Daniel, Hermeneia—a critical and historical commentary on the Bible* (Minneapolis: Fortress Press, 1993), 313-314. The sectarian Jews from Qumran who safeguarded the Dead Sea Scrolls believed they were united with the angels in heaven, so they occasionally used the term "holy ones" to refer to those humans, but this reinforces the usage of the term as related to the angelic beings.

judges on earth; they are supernatural elohim in the heavenly divine council.

## Biblical Narratives of the Divine Council

The idea of a divine council of sons of God surrounding Yahweh as a hierarchical assembly is not merely mined from poetic passages in the Psalms; it is explicitly described in narratives that seem to settle any question of the matter. The two main passages are 1Kings 22 and Job 1-2.

In 1 Kings 22, the evil King Ahab of Israel seeks out prophets to tell him that his wicked intentions of invading Ramoth-gilead will be condoned by Yahweh. Many of the prophets encourage Ahab to do so with God's blessing. The prophet Micaiah however describes this vision of what actually happened:

> 1 Kings 22:19-22
>
> And Micaiah said, "Therefore hear the word of the LORD: I saw the LORD sitting on his throne, and all the host of heaven standing beside him on his right hand and on his left; and the LORD said, 'Who will entice Ahab, that he may go up and fall at Ramoth-gilead?' And one said one thing, and another said another. Then a spirit came forward and stood before the LORD, saying, 'I will entice him.' And the LORD said to him, 'By what means?' And he said, 'I will go out, and will be a lying spirit in the mouth of all his prophets.' And he said, 'You are to entice him, and you shall succeed; go out and do so.'

So, here we see an explicit description of how the Divine council of God operates. The sons of God, called "host of heaven" surround God's throne and God throws out a question that they then deliberate through council until God accepts one of the ideas offered by a spiritual being. God then gives that spirit the authority to go and perform the will of the council led by Yahweh.

Job 1 and 2 picture a very similar scene of God's heavenly assembly "presenting themselves" in a legal procession "before the Lord" with the added element of the prosecuting "adversary" (the Hebrew word *ha satan* means "the adversary"):

> Job 1:6-12
> Now there was a day when the <u>sons of God came to present themselves before the LORD</u>, and the adversary also came among them... And the LORD said to the adversary, "Behold, all that he has is in your hand. Only against him do not stretch out your hand." So the adversary went out from the presence of the LORD.

> Job 2:1-6
> Again there was a day when <u>the sons of God came to present themselves before the LORD</u>, and the adversary also came among them to present himself before the LORD... And the LORD said to the adversary, "Have you considered my servant Job, that there is none like him on the earth, a blameless and upright man, who fears God and turns away from evil?...And the LORD said to the adversary, "Behold, he is in your hand; only spare his life."

Once again, God counsels with his divine assembly of sons of God, asking questions and deliberating, in this case with the adversary. And then God gives the adversary the responsibility of carrying out the will of God's overseen council meeting. These sons of God are the same heavenly host who were present when God was creating the foundations of the earth and sang for joy as in the Psalm passages we already looked at (Job 38:7). These could not possibly be human rulers in an earthly court.

The last passage that describes a scene exactly like the previous two is in Zechariah:

> Zech. 2:13-3:7
> Be silent, all flesh, before the LORD, for he has roused himself from <u>his holy dwelling</u>. Then he showed me Joshua the high priest <u>standing before the angel of the LORD</u>, and Satan ["<u>the adversary</u>"] <u>standing at his right hand to accuse him</u>... Now Joshua was standing before the angel, clothed with filthy garments. And the angel said to <u>those who were standing before him</u>, "Remove the filthy garments from him."...And the angel of the LORD solemnly assured Joshua, "Thus says the <u>LORD of hosts</u>..."

In this vision of Zechariah he sees into God's holy dwelling where Yahweh has brought his heavenly host standing before him and the satan standing ready to accuse Joshua before the heavenly court. Yahweh is called "Lord of hosts" because he is surrounded by that heavenly host of the sons of God (Remembering that the name of God used in a passage reflects a distinct aspect of his identity or character related to that passage).

Scholars point out that this vision of Zechariah is exemplary of another thread throughout the Old Testament of the covenant lawsuit. As we have seen in Job, 1Kings and Zechariah, there are legal procedures that the divine council engages in when deliberating judgment upon Israel or another guilty nation or king.[25] We have seen the summoning of the host and defendant, a presentation or standing before God, the judge's call for testimony from the council, accusation of an adversary or the prophet himself, and judgments carried out by council members. These same elements are assumed in other passages with a more implicit presence. Examples would be Isaiah's vision of the heavenly throne of seraphim with the plural imperatives by God "Who will go for us?" (Isa. 6) or "Comfort my people and cry out" (Isa. 40), or in Ezekiel's throne room vision (Ezek. 1). In these passages, God asks a question to an unknown group of beings. That group is no doubt the divine council around his throne. Jeremiah and Amos have even indicated that the mark of a true prophet versus a false prophet is that the true prophet has actually stood in the divine council and received his directions from God and his holy ones, while the false prophet has not (Jer. 23:18, 22; Amos 3:7).

## Ancient Near Eastern Parallels

We have seen that the term *sons of God* is used interchangeably in the Bible with other words such as gods, demons (in some cases), heavenly host, host of heaven, watchers, holy ones, assembly, and divine council. But there is a third reason why the sons of God are not human judges but divine heavenly beings, and that is because the same divine council or assembly of gods shows up in ancient Near Eastern

---

[25] Herbert B. Huffmon "The Covenant Lawsuit in the Prophets" *Journal of Biblical Literature*, Vol. 78, No. 4 (Dec., 1959), pp. 285-295; Wheeler Robinson, H., "The Council of Yahweh," *Journal of Theological Studies*, 45 (1944) p.151-158.

stories from Israel's neighbors. In other words, Israel shared a common cultural environment with her contemporaries that provides a context for interpreting the intended meaning of the Biblical text.[26] If we want to understand the meaning of a mysterious term or concept in the Bible we must exegete the broader cultural context within which Israel operated. Though this is not finally determinative of Biblical meaning, it carries great weight considering that Israel shared much in common with her neighbors in terms of language, worldview, symbols, and imagination.

Thorkild Jacobsen, one of the foremost authorities on Mesopotamian religion explained the origins of the divine council as a projection of the terrestrial conditions of the primitive form of human governmental democracy that existed in ancient Mesopotamia.[27] Though this worldview of divine world and cosmos ruled by the gods through a divine assembly was not monolithic and unchanging, scholar Patrick D. Miller has argued that it nevertheless remained fairly constant, and was clearly a part of the Biblical worldview as well.[28]

The Mesopotamian/Sumerian worldview that Abraham was immersed in before his calling by Yahweh involved a divine council of gods that functioned in part as a court of law that ruled over the affairs of men, including the authority to grant kingship to both gods and men. The divine council met in assembly under the god of heaven and "father of the gods," An (later, *Anu*), but also with him was Enlil, the god of storm. Either of them would broach a matter to be considered which

---

[26] John Walton called it a "common cognitive environment." John H. Walton. *Ancient Near Eastern Thought and the Old Testament: Introducing the Conceptual World of the Hebrew Bible*. Grand Rapids, MI: Baker, 2006; p 21.
[27] Thorkild Jacobsen, "Primitive Democracy in Ancient Mesopotamia," *Journal of Near Eastern Studies*, Vol. 2, No. 3 (Jul., 1943), 167.
[28] Patrick D. Miller, "Cosmology And World Order In The Old Testament The Divine Council As Cosmic-Political Symbol" *Israelite Religion and Biblical Theology: Collected Essays by Patrick D. Miller*, NY: Sheffield Academic Press, 2000, p 425.

would then be discussed and debated by the "great gods" or "Anunnaki," whose number included the fifty senior gods as well as "the seven gods who determine fate."[29] As Jacobsen put it, "Through such general discussion—"asking one another," as the Babylonians expressed it—the issues were clarified and the various gods had opportunity to voice their opinions for or against."[30] The executive duties of carrying out the decisions of the assembly seemed to have rested with Enlil as a kind of co-regent with An.

The *Enuma Elish*, the Akkadian creation myth of the Babylonians who presided over Israel's exile also depicted a divine council of gods convened around the supreme god Marduk whose operations reflected the same heavenly bureaucracy.[31] But as Heiser points out, the consensus of scholars is that the Ugaritic pantheon of Canaan was the closest conceptual precursor to the Israelite version of the divine council.[32] The linguistic parallels are numerous and their comparison yields fruitful understanding of the Hebrew worldview, both in its similarities and differences.

Among the many parallels that Heiser draws out between the Canaanite and Israelite divine council are the following:

> Ugaritic terms of the divine council include, "assembly of the gods," and "assembly of the sons of God." The Hebrew Bible uses the terms, "sons of God," "assembly of the holy ones" (Psa. 89:6), and "gods" "in the council of God" (Job 15:8).

---

[29] The seven gods who determine fate are portrayed in the novel *Noah Primeval* as An, the god of heaven, Enlil the god of storm, Enki the god of water, Ninhursag the earth goddess, Nanna the moon god, Utu the sun god and Inanna the goddess of sex and war.

[30] *Jacobsen*, "Primitive Democracy," 168-169.

[31] Min Suc Kee, "The Heavenly Council and its Type-scene," *Journal for the Study of the Old Testament* Vol 31.3 (2007): 259-273.

[32] Heiser, The Divine Council, 8.

In Ugaritic mythology, El was the supreme god and Baal was his vice-regent who ruled over the other gods of the council. In the Hebrew Bible, El/Elohim/Yahweh is the creator God, but he also has a vice-regent, the Son of Man/Angel of the Lord who was a visible incarnation of Yahweh who ruled over the divine council (Dan. 7). Christians would eventually argue that this "second Yahweh" was in fact the pre-incarnate Messiah, Jesus.

In Ugaritic mythology, El lived in a tent on a cosmic mountain in the north (*Sapon*) "at the source of two rivers," where the divine assembly would meet to deliberate and El would dispense his decrees. The mountain was a connection between heaven and earth, that is the earthly temple and its counterpart in heaven. In the Hebrew Bible, Yahweh's sanctuary is also in a tent (tabernacle) on a cosmic mountain, Zion (Psa. 48:1-2), that is in the heights of the north (*Sapon*). This mountain is poetically linked to Eden, which is the source of rivers (Ezek. 28:13-16) and its precursor, Mount Sinai was where God dispensed his word with his heavenly host (Deut. 33:1-2; Ps. 68:15-17).[33]

Though there are more congruencies between Canaanite and Hebrew concepts of the divine council than listed here, there are certainly many incongruencies as well, not the least of which was the polytheistic worldview of Canaan versus the monolatrous worldview of Israel. Gerald Cooke's classic article, "The Sons of (the) God(s)"

---

[33] Heiser, *The Divine Council*, 34-41.

lists the distinguishing characteristics in the Hebrew divine council of sons of God:

> The full mythological representation is absent: the individualization, personalization and specification of function which characterized this idea-complex in other cultures of the Near East finds little parallel in the Hebrew-Jewish records... The recognition or assignment of functions in the heavenly company is never specific as in non-Israelite mythologies: they appear only in the more general functions of praising Yahweh and his holiness, serving as members of the royal court, entering into counsel with Yahweh, exercising judgment over the peoples, and doing Yahweh's bidding. Nor are the interrelations of the gods treated in Israelite tradition as in other traditions. Members of the heavenly company remain essentially characterless functionaries even when they appear singly as "the spirit," "the satan," or a "messenger." Yahweh's relationship to the lesser beings appears only in the formalized title "sons," which seems to describe only the classification of these beings as divine; Yahweh is never associated in paternal relationship with any particular one(s) of these beings, as are many of the gods of pagan pantheons; if Yahweh's "fatherhood" vis-à-vis these divine beings can be spoken of at all, it has only the formal meaning found in the idea of the "father" (i.e., head and leader) of a group of prophets; members of the heavenly company are never called "sons of Yahweh"; worship of any of the heavenly court besides the supreme

Judge, Yahweh, is never countenanced by prophetic Yahwism. Members of the heavenly company never threaten his authority as supreme Judge and King.[34]

So the similarities between the worldviews need not mean absolute identity, but rather a common linguistic understanding that may help modern interpreters to understand the Bible in its own historical and cultural context. As Miller concluded, "The mythopoeic conception of the heavenly assembly, the divine council, is the Bible's way of pointing to a transcendent ordering and governing of the universe, of which all human governments and institutions are a reflection, but even more it is the machinery by which the just rule of God is effective, that is, powerful, in the universe."[35]

---

[34] Gerald Cooke, "The Sons of (the) God(s)," *Zeitschrift für die alttestamentliche Wissenschaft*, n.s.:35:1 (1964), p 45-46.
[35] Miller, "Cosmology And World Order," p 442.

# APPENDIX B:
# THE NEPHILIM

Gen. 6:4

The Nephilim were on the earth in those days, and also afterward, when the sons of God came in to the daughters of men, and they bore children to them. Those were the mighty men who were of old, men of renown.

Num. 13:33

And there we saw the Nephilim (the sons of Anak, who come from the Nephilim), and we seemed to ourselves like grasshoppers, and so we seemed to them."

The meaning of the Biblical word *Nephilim* has been a matter of unending controversy in Church history. That the word is still not translated into an English defined word but *transliterated* in most Bible translations is evidence of the fact that no agreement can be made over its original meaning. The two passages quoted above are the only two places in the Bible where the Hebrew word *Nephilim* is used. What would surprise some Bible readers is that these are not the only places where the Nephilim are *talked about* in Scripture. *Nephilim* has a theological thread that begins in Genesis 6 and goes through all the way to the New Testament.

The main opposing interpretations of this word come down to whether it is a reference to mighty leaders of some kind or to giants of abnormal human height. In my novel, *Noah Primeval* I take the perspective that these are giants and that these Bible passages are not merely obscure and unconnected factual references to an historical oddity, but rather that they are part of a diabolical supernatural plan of "sons of God" who are fallen from God's divine council of heavenly host. While my novel is obviously speculative fictional fantasy, it is nevertheless loosely based upon what I believe is a theological thread revealed in the Bible that becomes clear upon closer inspection of the text.

Taking a look at the first passage, Genesis 6:4, in context we read:

> Gen. 6:1-4
>
> When man began to multiply on the face of the land and daughters were born to them, the sons of God saw that the daughters of man were attractive. And they took as their wives any they chose. Then the LORD said, "My Spirit shall not abide in man forever, for he is flesh: his days shall be 120 years." The Nephilim were on the earth in those days, and also afterward, when the sons of God came in to the daughters of man and they bore children to them. These were the mighty men who were of old, the men of renown.

Genesis 6 is the opening lines to the story of Noah's flood. It talks about man reproducing upon the face of the earth and "sons of God" taking women as wives. I have already documented extensively elsewhere that the phrase *sons of God* in the Bible is a proven attribution to supernatural members of God's divine council. But some still attempt to change that meaning of the phrase in this passage to mean either men in the "righteous lineage" of Seth as contrasted with the daughters of men in the "unrighteous lineage" of Cain, or to mean kingly rulers on the earth who were engaging in polygamy.

In either case, these interpretations correctly acknowledge the negative connotation of the intermarriage and the violation of a separation, but they both seek to define the sons of God as natural men on earth. What both of these "humanly" interpretations miss is that the passage does not talk about a violation of separation of status or bloodline, but upon heavenly and earthly essence. The text links the "daughters of men" to the multiplication of "man" in general, *not* to a particular bloodline or royalty.

The Sethite view seeks to base its argument on an early reference in Genesis after Cain has killed Abel, and God grants a new son, Seth, to replace Abel for Eve. "To Seth also a son was born, and he called his name Enosh. At that time people began to call upon the name of the LORD (Gen. 4:26)." They believe that these ones calling upon the name of the Lord are those in the line of Seth as opposed to people in the line of Cain.

But the text does not restrict the righteousness in any way to Seth's lineage. It speaks in general of people calling upon God. In fact, the word used of "man" in Genesis 6 is "adam" which makes the population growth of Genesis 6:1 a generic reference to humankind fulfilling God's mandate to *the* Adam as mankind's representative to populate the earth, not to the exclusive lineage of Cain. The daughters are after all, "daughters of *adam*," in the text, not daughters of Cain.

Michael Heiser sums up the arguments against the human interpretation:

> First, Genesis 4:26 never says the only people who "called on the name of the Lord" were men from Seth's lineage, nor does it say that Seth's birth produced some sort of spiritual revival. This is an idea brought to the

text from the imagination of the interpreter. Second, if these marriages are human-to-human, how is it that giants (*Nephilim*) were the result of the unions? Third, the text never calls the women "daughters of Cain." Rather, they are "daughters of men [humankind]." Fourth, nothing in Genesis 6:1-4 or anywhere else in the Bible identifies those who come from Seth's lineage with the descriptive phrase "sons of God."[1]

There is simply no explicit reference in the Bible to sons of Seth being sons of God or daughters of man being only daughters of Cain. One must bring a preconceived theory to the text to make it fit. But in so doing, one must ignore the more explicit Biblical passages about the sons of God as God's heavenly host. And in so doing, one must affirm a racial righteousness based on human blood lineage. The emphasis in the text is on the separation of heavenly and earthly flesh.[2]

The New Testament agrees with the supernatural interpretation of divine/human cohabitation because it actually alludes to this very violation of fleshly categories and resultant punishment in 2 Peter and Jude, letters that show a strong literary interdependency on one another. If you compare the two passages you see the sensual violation of human and angelic flesh that is located in Genesis 6:

2Pet. 2:4-10

For if God did not spare <u>angels when they sinned</u>, but cast them into hell (*tartarus*) and <u>committed them to chains of gloomy</u> darkness to be kept until the judgment; if he did not spare the ancient world, but

---

[1] Michael S. Heiser *The Myth That is True: Rediscovering the Cosmic Narrative of the Bible*, unpublished manuscript, 2011, p 70. Available at www.michaelsheiser.com.
[2] For a refutation of the sons of God as human rulers, judges or potentates, see Appendix A, "The Divine Council and the Sons of God."

preserved Noah, a herald of righteousness, with seven others, when he brought a flood upon the world of the ungodly; if by turning the cities of <u>Sodom and Gomorrah</u> to ashes he condemned them to extinction, <u>making them an example of what is going to happen to the ungodly;</u>... then the Lord knows how to rescue the godly from trials, and to keep the unrighteous under punishment until the day of judgment, and especially those who <u>indulge in the lust of defiling passion</u> and despise authority.

Jude 6-7
And angels who did not keep their own domain, but abandoned their proper abode, he has kept in eternal chains under gloomy darkness until the judgment of the great day— just as Sodom and Gomorrah and the surrounding cities, which likewise indulged in gross immorality and pursued strange flesh, serve as an example by undergoing a punishment of eternal fire.

Both these passages speak of the same angels who sinned before the flood of Noah, and who were committed to chains of gloomy darkness. 1 Peter 3:19-20 calls these imprisoned angels "disobedient." According to our study, the angelic sons of God are spoken of as sinning in Genesis 6, so these must be the same angels referred to by the authors of the New Testament. But just what is their sin?

Both Peter and Jude link the sin of those fallen angels with the sin of Sodom and Gomorrah, which is described as indulging in "gross immorality" by pursuing "strange flesh." The Greek words for "gross immorality" (*ek porneuo*) indicates a heightened form of sexual immorality, and the Greek words for "strange flesh" (*heteros sarx*) indicate the pursuit of something different from one's natural flesh. This "strange flesh" cannot be a reference to homosexuality for several reasons. First, homosexuality is not the pursuit of *hetero* or different gender, it is the pursuit of *homo* or same gender. Secondly, homosexual behavior involves the *same* human male flesh (*sarx*), not different flesh as it would with angels. Thirdly, when the New Testament refers to the unnaturalness of homosexual acts it uses the Greek phrase, *para physin*, which means "contrary to nature" (Romans 1:26). The Bible certainly does condemn homosexuality as sin, but the sin of Sodom that that Jude and Peter focus on is not so much homosexuality, as interspecies sexuality between angels and humans.[3]

Angels on earth can have a physical presence. The angels who visited Sodom were clearly spoken of as enfleshed in such a way that they were physically present to have their feet washed and even eat food with Abraham and with Lot (Gen. 18:1-8; 19:3). Bible students know that the men in Sodom were seeking to engage in sexual penetration of these same angels who visited Lot in his home. So here, men seeking sex with angels is not merely a homosexual act, it is a violation of the heavenly and earthly flesh distinction that the Scriptures seem to reinforce. So Peter and Jude link the angels sinning before the flood to the violation of a sexual separation of angels and humankind. The New Testament commentary on Genesis 6:1 affirms the supernatural view of the sons of God as having sex with humans.

It has been long known by scholars that the letter of *Jude* not only quotes a verse from the non-canonical book of *1 Enoch* (v. 14 with 1

---

[3] This observation is qualified by the fact that in Genesis 19, the Sodomites do not apparently know that the two men are angels. In Judges 19, the same exact scenario as Sodom is played out with Benjaminites in Gibeah seeking homosexual copulation with a visiting Levite (angels are not involved). Jude seems to draw out the angelic/human copulation angle in his interpretation. In full Biblical context, it may be most consistent to say that the sin of Sodom includes both homosexuality *and* angelic/human violation.

Enoch 1:9),[4] but that Jude 6-7 and 2 Peter 2:4-10 both paraphrase content from *1 Enoch*, thus supporting the notion that the inspired authors intended an Enochian interpretation of "angels" called the Watchers (sons of God) having sexual intercourse with humans. *1 Enoch* extrapolates the Nephilim pre-flood story from the Bible as speaking of angels violating their supernatural separation and having sex with humans who bear them giants.[5]

Any question regarding the authenticity of this interpretation in Jude and Peter is quickly answered by another commonality that the New Testament authors share with the Enochian interpretation. Their combination of the angelic sexual sin with the sexual sin of Sodom is a poetic doublet that does not occur in the Old Testament, but does appear in multiple Second Temple Jewish manuscripts circulating in the New Testament time period. Jude and Peter are alluding to a common understanding of their culture that the angelic sin (and its hybrid fruit of giants) was an unnatural sexual violation of the divine and human separation. Here are some of those texts:

---

[4] Richard J. Bauckham, Vol. 50, *Word Biblical Commentary: 2 Peter, Jude*. Word Biblical Commentary. Dallas: Word, Incorporated, 2002. Here is the Jude passage: "[T]hat Enoch, the seventh from Adam, prophesied, saying, "Behold, the Lord comes with ten thousands of his holy ones, to execute judgment on all and to convict all the ungodly of all their deeds of ungodliness that they have committed in such an ungodly way, and of all the harsh things that ungodly sinners have spoken against him." Here is 1 Enoch 1:9, the text from the actual book that Jude quotes: "And behold! He cometh with ten thousands of His holy ones to execute judgement upon all, and to destroy all the ungodly: And to convict all flesh of all the works of their ungodliness which they have ungodly committed, and of all the hard things which ungodly sinners have spoken against Him.

[5] See 1 Enoch 6-19 and 86-88, especially 7:1-2; 15-16; 106:17. Richard Bauckham observes, "This was how the account of the "sons of God" in Gen 6:1–4 was universally understood (so far as our evidence goes) until the mid-second century A.D. (*1 Enoch* 6–19; 21; 86–88; 106:13–15, 17; *Jub.* 4:15, 22; 5:1; CD 2:17–19; 1QapGen 2:1; *Tg. Ps.-J. Gen.* 6:1–4; *T. Reub.* 5:6–7; *T. Napht.* 3:5; *2 Apoc. Bar.* 56:10–14)." Bauckham, Richard J. Vol. 50, *Word Biblical Commentary : 2 Peter, Jude*. Word Biblical Commentary. Dallas: Word, Incorporated, 2002, p 51. Other Second Temple Jewish writings support this ancient interpretation of pre-diluvian Nephilim/human offspring as giants: 3 Baruch 4:10; Wisdom 14:6; 3 Maccabees 2:4; Sirach 16:7.

## Sirach 16:7-8

He forgave not the giants of old,
[the fruit of the angelic sin]
Who revolted in their might.
He spared not the place where Lot sojourned,
Who were arrogant in their pride.[6]

## Testament of Naphtali 3:4-5

[D]iscern the Lord who made all things, so that you do not become like <u>Sodom</u>, which departed from the order of nature. Likewise the <u>Watchers departed from nature's order</u>; the Lord pronounced a curse on them at the Flood.[7]

## 3 Maccabees 2:4-5

Thou didst destroy those who aforetime <u>did iniquity</u>, among whom were <u>giants</u> trusting in their strength and boldness, bringing upon them a boundless flood of water. Thou didst burn up with fire and brimstone the men of <u>Sodom</u>, workers of arrogance, who had become known of all for their crimes, and didst make them <u>an example to those who should come after</u>.[8]
[notice "making an example for those after" that is also referenced in Jude 7]

---

[6] *Apocrypha of the Old Testament, Volume 1,* ed. Robert Henry Charles, Sir 16:7–8. Bellingham, WA: Logos Research Systems, Inc., 2004, 372.

[7] Charlesworth, James H. *The Old Testament Pseudepigrapha: Volume 1.* New York; London: Yale University Press, 1983, 812

[8] *Apocrypha of the Old Testament, Volume 1.* ed. Robert Henry Charles, 3 Mac 2:5. Bellingham, WA: Logos Research Systems, Inc., 2004, 164.

**Jubilees 20:4-5**

[L]et them not <u>take to themselves wives from the</u> <u>daughters</u> of Canaan; for the seed of Canaan will be rooted out of the land. And he told them of the judgment of <u>the giants,</u> and the <u>judgment of the</u> <u>Sodomites,</u> how they had been judged on account of their <u>wickedness,</u> and had died on account of their <u>fornication, and uncleanness, and mutual corruption</u> <u>through fornication.</u>[9]

This is critical for understanding the Nephilim as unholy giant progeny because the Nephilim are the result of this sexual union between angel and human.

Some respond that angelic beings cannot have sex with humans because of Jesus' statement in Matthew 22. Jesus is confronted by Sadducees who are trying to force Jesus to deny the future Resurrection of the dead. They construct a hypothetical of a woman with multiple husbands due to their multiple deaths, and then ask him whose wife she is at the Resurrection,, hoping to stump Jesus on the horns of a dilemma. Jesus replies, "You are mistaken, not understanding the Scriptures nor the power of God. "For in the resurrection they neither marry nor are given in marriage, but are like angels in heaven (Matt. 22:29-30)." Because of this, it is alleged that angels cannot have sexual intercourse with humans.

But this is not at all what Jesus is concluding. Firstly, Jesus is not talking about sexual intercourse, but the religious law of marriage connections between husband and wife. Secondly, he is not talking about what angels *cannot* do, but what they *do not* do. Angels in heaven who obey God do not marry. This has no implication on what

---

[9] *Pseudepigrapha of the Old Testament Volume 1.* ed. Robert Henry Charles. Bellingham, WA: Logos Research Systems, Inc., 2004, 42.

a fallen angel is capable of physically doing when coming to earth. Thirdly, Jesus is talking about angels in heaven, their natural abode, not angels on earth who left that abode to engage in unnatural liaisons with human flesh (as we saw in 2 Peter 2 and Jude). The angels in heaven that Jesus is talking about are not the angelic sons of God who left heaven, came to earth, and violated God's separation of those domains by having intercourse with human women.

Returning to Genesis 6:1-4, let's take a look at the second part of the passage:

> Gen. 6:3-4
>
> Then the LORD said, "My Spirit shall not abide in man forever, for he is flesh: his days shall be 120 years." The Nephilim were on the earth in those days, and also afterward, when the sons of God came in to the daughters of man and they bore children to them. These were the mighty men who were of old, the men of renown.

Some believe that the Nephilim were not the result of the sexual union between the sons of God and the daughters of men, but rather Nephilim were simply mighty warriors who happened to be around during those times before and after the incident of the sons of God. But this view would make nonsense of the text by inserting something (Nephilim) that has no connection to what is being talked about, namely the sexual unions and the flood. The pericope of verses 1-4 are a lead up to the proclamation of the flood in verses 5-8. The contextual reading of this concise unit of text begins talking about the sexual union of the sons of God with the daughters of men, then makes a reference to God's announcement to destroy the world in 120 years, which then references the Nephilim in context with that judgment, and then bookends the pericope with a reference back to the supernatural sexual union again, thus linking everything between those "bookends" as a sidebar explanation of what it was all about, which leads to the flood in verse 5-8. The Nephilim were around before and after *the flood*, not just the intermarriage incident, and they were the offspring result of that union.[10] Numbers 13:33 confirms this interpretation by saying that the Anakim at the time of Joshua were descendants of the Nephilim, so the Nephilim were clearly around before *and after* the flood.

But the question remains, what does the Hebrew word *Nephilim* mean? Some scholars looking at the root word claim that it means "fallen ones" because that is what the Hebrew means, "to fall". But there is a problem, and that is that the Septuagint (LXX) which is sometimes quoted by the New Testament authors as authoritative, translates this word as "giants."[11] Did those ancient Hellenized Jews not know the true meaning of the word? Or did they know something we do not?

Biblical scholar Michael S. Heiser has revealed a Biblical reference that virtually seals the proof that *Nephilim* are giants, not "fallen ones." In his article "The Meaning of the Word *Nephilim*: Fact vs. Fantasy"[12] he explains that Hebrew is a consonantal language,

---

[10] C. Westermann concludes, "There is every reason to think that the Nephilim in 4a refers to mythical semi-divine beings, the fruit of the marriages of the gods with humans, who are connected with the overstepping of the bound presumed in the divine judgment of v. 3. "They came to (them)": " 'to come to' refers in this connection only to the male who visits a woman's quarters, 30:16; 38:16" (E.A. Speiser, AncB). This sentence states expressly that children were the fruit of the union of the sons of the gods with the daughters of men, and clearly, they must be something special; they could not be just plain ordinary mortals." Claus Westermann, *A Continental Commentary: Genesis 1-11*, (Minneapolis, MN: Fortress Press, 1994), p 378.

[11] Genesis 6:4; Randall Tan, David A. deSilva, and Logos Bible Software. *The Lexham Greek-English Interlinear Septuagint*. Logos Bible Software, 2009.

[12] Michael S. Heiser, "The Meaning of the Word *Nephilim*: Fact vs. Fantasy" http://www.acidtestpress.com/

which means it only spells words with consonants and leaves the reader to fill in the vowels. The ancient language of Aramaic is also consonantal and has an influence on the Hebrew text at various places. There are many Aramaic words in the Bible, and some chapters, such as Daniel 2-7, are written in Aramaic. In later copies, vowel markers were added to the consonants in order to aid in pronunciation. He then explains that the Hebrew word NPHL which is translated into English as *Nephilim* has different meanings depending on the morphology or form of the word. Evidently the morphological form of the word in Genesis and Numbers is not that of the Hebrew meaning "fallen ones," but that of the Aramaic meaning "giants." And the Bible clinches this argument in Numbers 13:33:

> Num. 13:33
> And there we saw the Nephilim (the sons of Anak, who come from the Nephilim), and we seemed to ourselves like grasshoppers, and so we seemed to them."

Heiser shows that the first spelling of Nephilim in the verse is the Hebrew spelling, but the second spelling of Nephilim is a variation that is clearly the Aramaic spelling of "giants." And should there really be any question when the text then describes these Anakim who are descendants of the Nephilim as being gigantic in stature such that they felt like small grasshoppers?

Now, let's take a look at the Anakim and the other giants that the Bible speaks about. The Anakim or "sons of Anak" are unquestionably defined as giants throughout the Bible because of their tall height (Num. 13:33; Deut. 1:28; 2:10, 21; 9:2). One of the most famous of all those

Anakim giants was Goliath.[13] He stood at 9 feet 9 inches tall.[14] His coat of mail alone weighed about 125 pounds, the weight of his spearhead was 15 pounds (1 Sam. 17:4-7). There is no doubt Goliath was unnaturally huge in stature. And his brother Lahmi was of the same genetic material (1 Chron. 20:5). Philistia had a big problem with these Anakim giants, as 1 Chronicles 20:4-8 attests to no less than four of them who had to be killed by King David's men in an apparent campaign against the giants.

But if we go back in time from David to Joshua and the conquest of the Promised Land, we see that the giant Anakim that David was fighting were merely the leftovers from Joshua's own campaign to wipe them out:

> Josh. 11:21-22
> Then Joshua came at that time and cut off the Anakim
> from the hill country, from Hebron, from Debir, from
> Anab and from all the hill country of Judah and from
> all the hill country of Israel. Joshua utterly destroyed
> them with their cities. There were no Anakim left in
> the land of the sons of Israel; only in Gaza, in Gath,
> and in Ashdod some remained.

As it turns out, the Anakim were not the only giants in the land. Evidently the land in and around Canaan was crawling with giants that were called by different names in different locations, such as the Emim, Rephaim, Zamzummim, Horim, Avvim and possibly Caphtorim:

---

[13] Joshua 11:21 says that the only Anakim left by the time of David were in Gaza, Ashdod and Gath, Goliath's home.

[14] David Tsumura, *The First Book of Samuel, The New International Commentary on the Old Testament* (Grand Rapids, MI: Wm. B. Eerdmans Publishing Co., 2007), 441.

Deut. 2:10-11, 20-23

(The <u>Emim</u> formerly lived there, a people <u>great and many, and tall as the Anakim</u>. Like the Anakim they are also counted as <u>Rephaim</u>, but the Moabites call them <u>Emim</u>... (It is also counted as a land of Rephaim. Rephaim formerly lived there—but the Ammonites call them <u>Zamzummim</u>— a people <u>great and many, and tall as the Anakim</u>; but the LORD destroyed them before the Ammonites, and they dispossessed them and settled in their place as he did for the people of Esau, who live in Seir, when he destroyed <u>the Horites</u> before them and they dispossessed them and settled in their place even to this day. As for <u>the Avvim,</u> who lived in villages as far as Gaza, <u>the Caphtorim,</u> who came from Caphtor, destroyed them and settled in their place.)

King Og of Bashan is described as one of the last of "the remnant of the Rephaim" whose bed was over 13 feet long and made of iron (Deut. 3:11). That is no kingly bed alone; that was a large strong iron bed to hold a giant.

The Rephaim have an interesting Biblical history that connects them literarily to the Nephilim in the Bible. First, the Nephilim are described as *gibborim*, or "mighty men," "men of renown" in Genesis 6:4. This word *gibborim* is used extensively throughout the Old Testament of warriors such as David's "mighty men" (2 Sam. 16:6) and even of the giant Goliath (1Sam. 17:51) and many others.[15] The

---

[15] Josh. 1:14; 6:2; 8:3; 10:2, 7; Judges 11:1, 1Sam. 2:4; 14:52; 2Sam.23:16-17, 22; 2King 5:1; 24:14; 1Chr. 7:5, 7, 11, 40, and many others. Nimrod was noted as being the first Gibborim mighty warrior on earth after the flood: Gen. 10:8; 1Chr. 5:24.

Nephilim were mighty warriors. The Rephaim were mighty warrior kings.

In the Bible, *Rephaim* were Anakim giants, descendants of the Nephilim (Deut. 2:11; Num. 13:33), who were so significant they even had a valley named after them ("Valley of the Rephaim," Josh. 15:8). But there is more to the Rephaim than that. Og, king of Bashan, was a Rephaim giant, and all his portion of the land of Bashan was called "the land of the Rephaim" (Deut. 3:13), an ambiguous wording that could equally be translated as "the 'hell' of the Rephaim."[16] Bashan was a deeply significant spiritual location to the Canaanites and the Hebrews. And as the *Dictionary of Deities and Demons in the Bible* puts it, Biblical geographical tradition agrees with the mythological and cultic data of the Canaanites of Ugarit that "the Bashan region, or a part of it, clearly represented 'Hell', the celestial and infernal abode of their deified dead kings," the Rephaim.[17]

Mount Hermon was in Bashan, and Mount Hermon was a location in the Bible that was linked to the Rephaim (Josh. 12:1-5), but was also the legendary location where the sons of God were considered to have come to earth and have sexual union with the daughters of men to produce the giant Nephilim.[18]

There are two places in the Bible that hint at the Rephaim being warrior kings brought down to Sheol in similar language to the Ugaritic notion of the Rephaim warrior kings in the underworld:

---

[16] K. van der Toorn, Bob Becking and Pieter Willem van der Horst, *Dictionary of Deities and Demons in the Bible DDD*, 2nd extensively rev. ed., 162 (Leiden; Boston; Grand Rapids, Mich.: Brill; Eerdmans, 1999).

[17] "Bashan," *DDD*, p 161-162. "According to *KTU* 1.108:1–3, the abode of the dead and deified king, and his place of enthronement as *[Rephaim]* was in *[Ashtarot and Edrei]*, in amazing correspondence with the Biblical tradition about the seat of king Og of Bashan, "one of the survivors of the Rephaim, who lived in Ashtarot and Edrei" (Josh 12:4)."

[18] The non-canonical book of Enoch supports this same interpretation: "Enoch 6:6 And they were in all two hundred [sons of God]; who descended in the days of Jared on the summit of <u>Mount Hermon</u>, and they called it Mount Hermon, because they had sworn and bound themselves by mutual imprecations upon it."

Is. 14:9

Sheol beneath is stirred up to meet you when you come;

it rouses the shades [The Hebrew word *Rephaim*] to greet you,

all who were leaders of the earth;

it raises from their thrones

all who were kings of the nations.

Ezek. 32:21

They shall fall amid those who are slain by the sword... The mighty chiefs [*Rephaim*] shall speak of them, with their helpers, out of the midst of Sheol: "They have come down, they lie still, the uncircumcised, slain by the sword."

Hebrew scholar, Michael S. Heiser concludes about this connection of Rephaim with dead warrior kings in Sheol and Bashan:

> That the Israelites and the biblical writers considered the spirits of the dead giant warrior kings to be demonic is evident from the fearful aura attached to the geographical location of Bashan. As noted above, Bashan is the region of the cities Ashtaroth and Edrei, which both the Bible and the Ugaritic texts mention as abodes of the Rephaim. What's even more fascinating is that in the Ugaritic language, this region was known not as Bashan, but *Bathan*—the Semitic people of Ugarit pronounced the Hebrew "sh" as "th" in their dialect. Why is that of interest? Because "Bathan" is a

common word across all the Semitic languages, biblical Hebrew included, for "serpent." The region of Bashan was known as "the place of the serpent." It was ground zero for the Rephaim giant clan and, spiritually speaking, the gateway to the abode of the infernal deified Rephaim spirits.[19]

## List of Giants

The Bible reveals that there are many different clans that either were giants or had giants among them that were ultimately related in a line all the way back to the Nephilim of Genesis:

Nephilim (Gen. 6:1-4; Num. 13:33)

Anakim (Num. 13:28-33; Deut. 1:28; 2:10-11, 21; 9:2; Josh. 14:12)

Amorites (Amos 2:9-10)

Emim (Deut. 2:10-11)

Rephaim (Deut. 2:10-11, 20; 3:11)

Zamzummim (Deut. 2:20)

Zuzim (Gen. 14:5)

Perizzites (Gen. 15:20; Josh. 17:15)

Philistines (2 Sam. 21:18-22)

Horites/Horim (Deut. 2:21-22)

Avvim (Deut. 2:23)

Caphtorim (Deut. 2:23)

The following are implied as including giants by their connection to the descendants of Anak in Numbers 13:28-29:

---

[19] Michael S. Heiser *The Myth That is True*, p 169. Available online at www.michaelsheiser.com.

Amalekites

Hittites

Jebusites—The word means "Those who trample"

Amorites (Amos 2:9-10 links the Amorites as giant in
size and strength)

Hivites (Has the same consonants as a Hebrew name
for snake)

Here were the towns, cities or locations that were said to have had
giants in them:

Gob (2 Sam. 21:18)

Hebron/Kiriath-arba (Num. 13:22; Josh. 14:15)

Ar (Deut. 2:9)

Seir (Deut. 2:21-22)

Debir/ Kiriath-sepher (Josh. 11:21-22)

Anab (Josh. 11:21-22)

Gaza (Josh. 11:21-22)

Gath (Josh. 11:21-22)

Ashdod (Josh. 11:21-22)

Bashan (Deut. 3:10-11)

Ashteroth-karnaim (Gen. 14:5)

Ham (Gen. 14:5)

Shaveh-kiriathaim (Gen. 14:5)

Valley of the Rephaim (Josh. 15:8)

Moab (1 Chron. 11:22)

Many significant individuals are described in the Bible implicitly
or explicitly as giants being struck down in war against Israel:

Goliath (1 Sam. 17)

Lahmi, Goliath's brother (1 Chron. 20:5; 2 Sam. 21:19)

Ishbi-benob (2 Sam. 21:16)

Saph/Sippai (2 Sam. 21:17; 1 Chron. 20:4)

Arba (Josh. 14:15)

Sheshai (Josh.15:14, Num. 13:22)

Ahiman (Josh. 15:14, Num. 13:22)

Talmai (Josh. 15:14, Num. 13:22)

An unnamed warrior giant (1 Chron. 20:6)

And unnamed Egyptian giant (1 Chron. 11:23)

Og of Bashan (Deut. 3:10-11)

The ubiquitous presence of giants throughout the narrative of the Old Testament is no small matter. When God commanded the people of Israel to enter Canaan and devote certain of those peoples to complete destruction (Deut. 20:16-17), it is no coincidence that most of these peoples we have already seen were connected in some way to the Anakim giants, and Joshua's campaign explicitly included the elimination of the Anakim/Sons of Anak giants. Could these giants that were from the lineage of the Nephilim (who were the offspring of the Sons of God) be the very Seed of the Serpent that would be at enmity with the promised messianic Seed of the Woman (Gen. 3:15)? You will have to read the sequels to *Noah Primeval* to find out.

# APPENDIX C:
# LEVIATHAN

In my novel *Noah Primeval*, I have a sea dragon called "Leviathan" that is crucial to the plot of the story. While it is a monster of the waters, a symbol of chaos, it nevertheless is providentially used by Elohim and tamed for his own purposes. I found this character in the pages of the Bible itself and had always been befuddled by its presence. It kept popping up in strange places like the book of Job and the Psalms. Was this a mythical creature in holy writ? Was God's power over Leviathan as described in Job just a poetic way of saying God is in control and nothing is too powerful for him? I would soon find out that this recurring sea dragon was so much more.

Job 41 is devoted to this strange creature. Here is that chapter in its entirety:

> "Can you draw out Leviathan with a fishhook
> or press down his tongue with a cord?
> Can you put a rope in his nose
> or pierce his jaw with a hook?
> Will he make many pleas to you?
> Will he speak to you soft words?
> Will he make a covenant with you
> to take him for your servant forever?
> Will you play with him as with a bird,

or will you put him on a leash for your girls?
Will traders bargain over him?
Will they divide him up among the merchants?
Can you fill his skin with harpoons
or his head with fishing spears?
Lay your hands on him;
remember the battle—you will not do it again!
Behold, the hope of a man is false;
he is laid low even at the sight of him.
No one is so fierce that he dares to stir him up.
Who then is he who can stand before me?
Who has first given to me, that I should repay him?
Whatever is under the whole heaven is mine.
I will not keep silence concerning his limbs,
or his mighty strength, or his goodly frame.
Who can strip off his outer garment?
Who would come near him with a bridle?
Who can open the doors of his face?
Around his teeth is terror.
His back is made of rows of shields,
shut up closely as with a seal.
One is so near to another
that no air can come between them.
They are joined one to another;
they clasp each other and cannot be separated.
His sneezings flash forth light,
and his eyes are like the eyelids of the dawn.
Out of his mouth go flaming torches;
sparks of fire leap forth.
Out of his nostrils comes forth smoke,
as from a boiling pot and burning rushes.

His breath kindles coals,
and a flame comes forth from his mouth.
In his neck abides strength,
and terror dances before him.
The folds of his flesh stick together,
firmly cast on him and immovable.
His heart is hard as a stone,
hard as the lower millstone.
When he raises himself up the mighty are afraid;
At the crashing they are beside themselves.
Though the sword reaches him, it does not avail,
nor the spear, the dart, or the javelin.
He counts iron as straw,
and bronze as rotten wood.
The arrow cannot make him flee;
for him sling stones are turned to stubble.
Clubs are counted as stubble;
he laughs at the rattle of javelins.
His underparts are like sharp potsherds;
he spreads himself like a threshing sledge on the mire.
He makes the deep boil like a pot;
he makes the sea like a pot of ointment.
Behind him he leaves a shining wake;
one would think the deep to be white-haired.
On earth there is not his like,
a creature without fear.
He sees everything that is high;
he is king over all the sons of pride."

As this chapter describes, this is no known species on earth. From
the smoke and fire out of its mouth to the armor plating on back and

belly, this monster of the abyss was more than a mere example of showcasing God's omnipotent power over the mightiest of creatures, it was symbolic of something much more. And that much more can be found by understanding Leviathan in its ancient Near Eastern (ANE) and Biblical covenantal background.

In ANE religious mythologies, the sea and the sea dragon were symbols of chaos that had to be overcome to bring order to the universe, or more exactly, the political world order of the myth's originating culture. Some scholars call this battle *Chaoskampf*—the divine struggle to create order out of chaos.

Hermann Gunkel first suggested in *Creation and Chaos* (1895) that some ANE creation myths contained a cosmic conflict between deity and sea, as well as sea dragons or serpents that expressed the creation of order out of chaos.[1] Gunkel argued that Genesis borrowed this idea from the Babylonian tale of Marduk battling the goddess Tiamat, serpent of chaos, whom he vanquished, and out of whose body he created the heavens and earth.[2] After this victory, Marduk ascended to power in the Mesopotamian pantheon. This creation story gave mythical justification to the rise of Babylon as an ancient world power most likely in the First Babylonian Dynasty under Hammurabi (1792-1750 B.C.).[3] As the prologue of the Code of Hammurabi explains, "Anu, the majestic, King of the Anunnaki, and Bel, the Lord of Heaven and Earth, who established the fate of the land, had given to Marduk, the ruling son of Ea, dominion over mankind, and called Babylon by

---

[1] Hermann Gunkel, Heinrich Zimmern; K. William Whitney Jr., trans., *Creation And Chaos in the Primeval Era And the Eschaton: A Religio-historical Study of Genesis 1 and Revelation 12* (Grand Rapids: MI: Erdmans, 1895, 1921, 2006), xvi.

[2] "He cast down her carcass and stood upon it.
After he had slain Tiamat, the leader...He split her open like a mussel into two parts; Half of her he set in place and formed the sky... And a great structure, its counterpart, he established, namely Esharra [earth]."
(Enuma Elish, Tablet IV, lines 104-105, 137-138, 144 from Heidel, *Babylonian Genesis*, 41-42)

[3] Heidel, *Babylonian Genesis*, 14.

his great name; when they made it great upon the earth by founding therein an eternal kingdom, whose foundations are as firmly grounded as are those of heaven and earth."[4] The foundation of Hammurabi's "eternal kingdom" is literarily linked to Marduk's foundational creation of heaven and earth.

Later, John Day argued in light of the discovery of the Ugarit tablets in 1928, that Canaan, not Babylonia is the source of the combat motif in Genesis,[5] reflected in Yahweh's own complaint that Israel had become polluted by Canaanite culture.[6] In the Baal cycle, Baal battles Yam (Sea) and conquers it, along with "the dragon," "the twisting serpent," to be enthroned as chief deity of the Canaanite pantheon.[7]

Creation accounts were often veiled polemics for the establishment of a king or kingdom's claim to sovereignty.[8] Richard Clifford quotes, "In Mesopotamia, Ugarit, and Israel the *Chaoskampf* appears not only in cosmological contexts but just as frequently—and this was fundamentally true right from the first—in political contexts. The repulsion and the destruction of the enemy, and thereby the

---

[4] W.W. Davies, The Codes of Hammurabi and Moses: With Copious Comments, Index, and Bible References (Berkeley, CA: Apocryphile Press, 1905, 2006), 17.

[5] John Day, *God's Conflict with the Dragon*. Day argues that the Canaanite Baal cycle implies a connection with creation, since it is a ritual fertility festival (cyclical creation) falling on the New Year, traditionally understood as the date of creation. But his strongest appeal is the argument in reverse that the Canaanite myth makes a connection between creation and *Chaoskampf* because the Old Testament does so.

[6] "Then the word of the LORD came to me, saying, "Son of man, make known to Jerusalem her abominations and say, 'Thus says the Lord GOD to Jerusalem, "Your origin and your birth are from the land of the Canaanite, your father was an Amorite and your mother a Hittite." (Ezek. 16:1-3)

[7] Most recently, David Tsumura has argued against any connection of such mythic struggle in the Biblical text in favor of mere poetic flair: David Toshio Tsumura, *Creation And Destruction: A Reappraisal of the Chaoskampf Theory in the Old Testament* (Winona Lake, IN: Eisenbrauns, 2006).

[8] Bruce R. Reichenbach. "Genesis 1 as a Theological-Political Narrative of Kingdom Establishment." *Bulletin for Biblical Research* 13.1 (2003).

maintenance of political order, always constitute one of the major dimensions of the battle against chaos."[9]

The Sumerians had three stories where the gods Enki, Ninurta, and Inanna all destroy sea monsters in their pursuit of establishing order. The sea monster in two of those versions, according to Sumerian expert Samuel Noah Kramer, is "conceived as a large serpent which lived in the bottom of the "great below" where the latter came in contact with the primeval waters."[10] The prophet Amos uses this same mythopoeic reference to a serpent at the bottom of the sea as God's tool of judgment: "If they hide from my sight at the bottom of the sea, there I will command the serpent, and it shall bite them" (Amos 9:3). One Sumerian text, *The Return of Ninurta to Nippur*, refers to "the seven-headed serpent" that must be defeated by the divine Ninurta to illustrate his power to overcome chaos.[11]

Perhaps the closest comparison with the Biblical Leviathan comes from Canaanite texts at Ugarit as John Day argued. In 1929, an archeological excavation at a mound in northern Syria called Ras Shamra unearthed the remains of a significant port city called Ugarit whose developed culture reaches back as far as 3000 B.C.[12] Among the important finds were literary tablets written in multiple ancient languages, which opened the door to a deeper understanding of ancient Near Eastern culture and the Bible. Ugaritic language and culture shares much in common with Hebrew that sheds light on the meaning of things such as Leviathan.

---

[9] Clifford. *Creation Accounts*; footnote 13 p 8.

[10] Samuel Noah Kramer. *Sumerian Mythology: A Study of Spiritual and Literary Achievement in the Third Millennium B.C.* Philadelphia, PA: University of Pennsylvania Press, 1944, 1961, 1972; p 77-78.

[11] *The Return of Ninurta to Nippur*, Black, J.A., Cunningham, G., Robson, E., and Zólyomi, G., The Electronic Text Corpus of Sumerian Literature, Oxford 1998-. < http://www.gatewaystobabylon.com/myths/texts/ninurta/nippurninurta.htm>

[12] "Ugarit," Avraham Negev, *The Archaeological Encyclopedia of the Holy Land.* 3rd ed. New York: Prentice Hall Press, 1996.

A side-by-side comparison of some Ugaritic religious texts about the Canaanite god Baal with Old Testament passages reveals a common narrative: Yahweh, the charioteer of the clouds, metaphorically battles with Sea (Hebrew: *yam*) and River (Hebrew: *nahar*), just as Baal, the charioteer of the clouds, struggled with Yam (sea) and Nahar (river), which is also linked to victory over a sea dragon/serpent.

| UGARTIC TEXTS | OLD TESTAMENT |
|---|---|
| 'Dry him up. O Valiant Baal! | Did Yahweh rage against the rivers, |
| Dry him up, O Charioteer of the Clouds! | Or was Your anger against the rivers (*nahar*), |
| For our captive is Prince Yam [Sea], | Or was Your wrath against the sea (*yam*), |
| for our captive is Ruler Nahar [River]!' | That You rode on Your horses, |
| (KTU 1.2:4.8-9)[13] | On Your chariots of salvation? |
|  | (Hab. 3:8) |
|  |  |
| What manner of enemy has arisen against Baal, |  |
| of foe against the Charioteer of the Clouds? | In that day Yahweh will punish Leviathan the |
| Surely I smote the Beloved of El, Yam [Sea]? | fleeing serpent, |
| Surely I exterminated Nahar [River], the | With His fierce and great and mighty sword, |
| mighty god? | Even Leviathan the twisted serpent; |
| Surely I lifted up the dragon, | And He will kill the dragon who lives in the sea. |
| I overpowered him? | (Isa 27:1) |
| I smote the writhing serpent, |  |
| Encircler-with-seven-heads! | "You divided the sea by your might; |
| (KTU 1.3:3.38-41)[14] | you broke the heads of the sea monsters on the |
|  | waters. |
|  | You crushed the heads of Leviathan. |
|  | (Psa 74:13-14) |

Baal fights Sea and River to establish his sovereignty. He wins by drinking up Sea and River, draining them dry, which results in Baal's supremacy over the pantheon and the Canaanite world order.[15] In the second passage, Baal's battle with Sea and River is retold in other words as a battle with a "dragon," the "writhing serpent" with

---

[13] Wyatt, *RTU2*, pp 69-70.
[14] In Wyatt, *RTU2*, pp 79. Charioteer of the Clouds also appears in these texts: KTU 1.3:4:4, 6, 26; 1.4:3:10, 18; 1.4:5:7, 60; 1.10:1:7; 1.10:3:21, 36; 1.19:1:43; 1.92:37, 39.
[15] KTU 1.2:4:27-32.

seven heads.[16] Another Baal text calls this same dragon, "*Lotan,* the wriggling serpent."[17] The Hebrew equivalents of the Ugaritic words *tannin* (dragon) and *lotan* are *tannin* (dragon) and *liwyatan* (Leviathan) respectively.[18] The words are etymologically equivalent. Not only that, but so are the Ugaritic words describing the serpent as "wriggling" and "writhing" in the Ugaritic text (*brh* and '*qltn*) with the words Isaiah 27 uses of Leviathan as "fleeing" and "twisting" (*bariah* and '*aqalaton*).[19] Notice the last Scripture in the chart that refers to Leviathan as having multiple heads *just like the Canaanite Leviathan.* Bible scholar Mitchell Dahood argued that in that passage of Psalm 74:12-17 the author implied the seven heads by using seven "you" references to God's powerful activities surrounding this mythopoeic defeat of Leviathan.[20]

The Apostle John adapted this seven-headed dragon into his Revelation as a symbol of Satan as well as a chaotic demonic empire (Rev 12:3; 13:1; 17:3). Jewish Christians in the first century carried on this motif in texts such as the *Odes of Solomon* that explain Christ as overthrowing "the dragon with seven heads... that I might destroy his seed."[21]

Thus, the Canaanite narrative of Lotan (Leviathan) the sea dragon or serpent is undeniably employed in Old Testament Scriptures and carried over into the New Testament as well.[22]

---

[16] Though this verse is spoken by the goddess Anat, Baal's sister, as if she accomplished these exploits, it is described as Baal's actions in other texts (KTU 1.5:1:1-35) that lead scholars to conclude that Anat's claims are a kind of sympathetic unity of action between her and Baal.

[17] KTU 1.5:1:1-4. Wyatt *RTU2*, p 115.

[18] Walter C. Kaiser, Jr. *The Ugaritic Pantheon* (dissertation). Ann Arbor, Mich: Brandeis University, 1973, p 212.

[19] Michael Fishbane, *Biblical Myth and Mythmaking*, Oxford University Press, 2003, 39.

[20] Mitchell Dahood S.J., *Psalms II 51-100 The Anchor Yale Bible* (Yale University Press, 1995) 24.

[21] Odes of Solomon 22:5. James H. Charlesworth, *The Old Testament Pseudepigrapha and the New Testament, Volume 2: Expansions of the "Old Testament" and Legends, Wisdom, and Philosophical Literature, Prayers, Psalms and Odes, Fragments of Lost Judeo-Hellenistic Works* (New Haven; London: Yale University Press, 1985).

[22] See also Isa 51:9; Ezek 32:2; Rev 12:9, 16, 17;

And notice as well the reference to the Red Sea event also associated with Leviathan in the Biblical text. In Psalm 74 above, God's parting of the waters is connected to the motif of the Mosaic covenant as the creation of a new world order in the same way that Baal's victory over the waters and the dragon are emblematic of his establishment of authority in the Canaanite pantheon. This covenant motif is described as a *Chaoskampf* battle with the Sea and Leviathan (sometimes called *Rahab*[23]) in this and other Biblical references.

Psa. 74:12-17

You broke the heads of the sea monsters in the waters.

You crushed the heads of Leviathan;...

You have prepared the light and the sun.

You have established all the boundaries of the earth;

Psa. 89:9-10

You [Yahweh] rule the raging of the sea;

when its waves rise, you still them.

You crushed Rahab like a carcass;

you scattered your enemies with your mighty arm.

Isa. 51:9-10

Awake, awake, put on strength, O arm of Yahweh;

Awake as in the days of old,

the generations of long ago.

Was it not You who cut Rahab in pieces,

Who pierced the dragon?

Was it not You who dried up the sea,

---

[23] An Akkadian equivalent of "Rabu" can be found on the Babylonian Map of the World describing a sea serpent. Wayne Horowitz, *Mesopotamian Cosmic Geography*, Winona Lake; IN: Eisenbrauns, 1998, 35; "Rahab," *DDD*, 684.

The waters of the great deep;

Who made the depths of the sea a pathway

For the redeemed to cross over?

Isa. 27:1

In that day the LORD with his hard and great and strong sword will punish Leviathan the fleeing serpent, Leviathan the twisting serpent, and he will slay the dragon that is in the sea.

The story of deity battling the river, the sea, and the sea dragon Leviathan is clearly a common covenant motif in the Old Testament and its surrounding ancient Near Eastern cultures.[24] The fact that Hebrew Scripture shares common words, concepts, and stories with Ugaritic scripture does not mean that Israel is affirming the same mythology or pantheon of deities, but rather that Israel lives within a common cultural environment, and God uses that cultural connection to subvert those words, concepts and stories with his own poetic meaning and purpose.

*Chaoskampf* and creation language are used as word pictures for God's covenant activity in the Bible. For God, describing the creation of the heavens and earth was a way of saying he has established his covenant with his people through exodus into the Promised Land,[25] reaffirming that covenant with the kingly line of David, and finalizing the covenant by bringing them out of exile. The reader should understand that the Scriptures listed above, exemplary of *Chaoskampf,* were deliberately abbreviated to make a further point below. I will now add the missing text in those passages in underline

---

[24] Psalm 18, 29, 24, 29, 65, 74, 77, 89, 93, and 104 all reflect *Chaoskampf.* See also Exodus 15, Job 9, 26, 38, and Isa 51:14-16; 2Sam 22.

[25] John Owen, *Works*, 16 vols. (London: The Banner of Truth Trust, 1965-1968), Vol. 9 134.

to reveal a deeper motif at play in the text—a motif of creation language as covenantal formation.

Psa. 74:12-17

Yet God my King is from of old,

working salvation in the midst of the earth.

You divided the sea by your might;

[A reference to the Exodus deliverance of the covenant at Sinai]

You broke the heads of the sea monsters in the waters.

You crushed the heads of Leviathan;...

You have prepared the light and the sun.

You have established all the boundaries of the earth;

Psa. 89:9-12; 19-29

You rule the raging of the sea;

when its waves rise, you still them.

You crushed Rahab like a carcass;

you scattered your enemies with your mighty arm.

The heavens are yours; the earth also is yours;

the world and all that is in it, you have founded them.

The north and the south, you have created them...

I have found David, my servant;

with my holy oil I have anointed him,

so that my hand shall be established with him...

and in my name shall his horn be exalted.

I will set his hand on the sea

and his right hand on the rivers...

My steadfast love I will keep for him forever,

and my covenant will stand firm for him.

I will establish his offspring forever

and his throne as the days of the heavens.

Isa 51:9-16
Was it not You who cut Rahab in pieces,
Who pierced the dragon?
Was it not You who dried up the sea,
The waters of the great deep;
Who made the depths of the sea a pathway
For the redeemed to cross over?...
[Y]ou have forgotten the LORD your Maker,
Who stretched out the heavens
And laid the foundations of the earth...
"For I am the LORD your God, who stirs up the sea and its waves roar (the LORD of hosts is His name). "I have put My words in your mouth and have covered you with the shadow of My hand, to establish the heavens, to found the earth, and to say to Zion, 'You are My people.'"
[a reaffirmation of the Sinai covenant through Moses]

Isa. 27:1; 6-13
In that day the LORD with his hard and great and strong sword will punish Leviathan the fleeing serpent, Leviathan the twisting serpent, and he will slay the dragon that is in the sea...
In days to come Jacob shall take root,
Israel shall blossom and put forth shoots
and fill the whole world with fruit...
And in that day a great trumpet will be blown, and those who were lost in the land of Assyria and those who were driven out to the land of Egypt will come and

worship the LORD on the holy mountain at Jerusalem. *[the future consummation of the Mosaic and Davidic covenant in the New Covenant of Messiah]*

In these texts, and others,[26] God does not merely appeal to his power of creation as justification for the authority of his covenant. More importantly, He uses the creation of the heavens and earth, involving subjugation of rivers, seas, and dragon (Leviathan), as poetic descriptions of God's covenant with his people, rooted in the Exodus story, and reiterated in the Davidic covenant. The creation of the covenant is the creation of the heavens and the earth which includes a subjugation of chaos by the new order. The covenant is a cosmos—not a material one centered in astronomical location and abstract impersonal forces as modern worldview demands, but a theological one, centered in the sacred space of land, temple, and cult as the ancient Near Eastern worldview demands.[27]

It has been noted by scholars that the motif of *Chaoskampf* is absent from Genesis 1 where God creates the heavens and the earth, painting a very different picture of the Hebrew creation story than its ANE neighbors. However, its very absence in that text is most likely a part of the covenantal polemic in the text. For a close look at the original Hebrew shows us that the word for dragon that we have been talking about (*tannin*) is in fact used of the "great sea creatures" (*tanninim*) that God created on Day five:

Gen. 1:21-22
So God created the great sea creatures (*tanninim*) and every living creature that moves, with which the waters

---

[26] See also Psa. 77:16-20; 136:1-22.
[27] N.T. Wright, *The New Testament and the People of God* (Minneapolis, MN: Fortress Press, 1992), 306-307.

swarm… And God saw that it was good. And God blessed them, saying, "Be fruitful and multiply and fill the waters in the seas, and let birds multiply on the earth."

The ancient Near Eastern audience would read this text and know full well what was being implied against their cultural familiarity with the sea dragon. Apparently, the ANE notion of struggle against the dragon is subverted in this text by depicting God creating the dragon by the mere words of his mouth, rather than wrestling with a preexistent monster for control over the sea. And then God blesses that dragon as one of the many "good" creations that he commands to reproduce. This picture amounts to the reduction of the dragon to a mere domesticated pet in the language of Genesis 1.

In this text, the conspicuous absence of the struggle of *Chaoskampf* is evidence of its subversion to the greater purposes of the Hebrew creation story. Sometimes Leviathan is used as a covenantal expression for the establishment of God's world order out of chaos, and sometimes, it is used as a symbol of God's authority over pagan religious expressions. In any case, its Biblical meaning is connected to its ancient Near Eastern symbolic context, not to a modern interpretation of a merely physical sea monster.

# APPENDIX D:
# MESOPOTAMIAN COSMIC GEOGRAPHY
# IN THE BIBLE

In my novel, *Noah Primeval*, I depict the universe as it was thought to be through the eyes of ancient Mesopotamians, as a three-tiered universe with a flat disc earth, surrounded by waters, which includes the watery Abyss and beneath that, the underworld of Sheol. Above the earth is a solid dome of the heavens, beyond which is the waters of the "heaven of heavens" where God's throne sits on the waters. A generic illustration of this cosmography is the old public domain image depicted below. I decided to use this cosmic geography as creative literary license to capture the way the ancients saw and experienced the world. This essay explains the Scriptural expression of this worldview as held by the Biblical writers.

*Cosmography* is a technical term that means a theory that describes and maps the main features of the heavens and the earth. A Cosmography or "cosmic geography" can be a complex picture of the universe that includes elements like astronomy, geology, and geography; and those elements can include theological implications as well. Throughout history, all civilizations and peoples have operated under the assumption of a cosmography or picture of the universe. We are most familiar with the historical change that science went through from a Ptolemaic cosmography of the earth at the center of the universe (geocentrism) to a Copernican cosmography of the sun at the center of a solar system (heliocentrism).

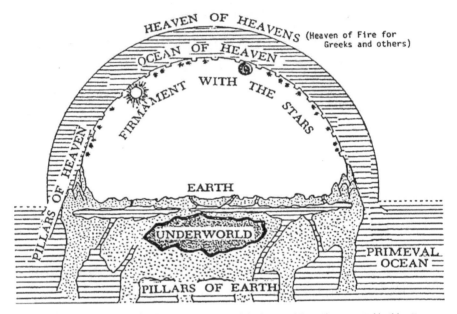

This antique drawing represents the Mesopotamian picture of the universe used in this story.

Some ancient mythologies maintained that the earth was a flat disc on the back of a giant turtle; animistic cultures believe that spirits inhabit natural objects and cause them to behave in certain ways; modern westerners believe in a space-time continuum where everything is relative to its frame of reference in relation to the speed of light. Ancients tended to believe that the gods caused the weather; moderns tend to believe that impersonal physical processes cause weather. All these different beliefs are elements of a cosmography or picture of what the universe is really like and how it operates. Even though "pre-scientific" cultures like the Hebrews did not have the same notions of science that we moderns have, they still observed the world around them and made interpretations as to the structure and operations of the heavens and earth.

332

A common ancient understanding of the cosmos is expressed in the visions of 1 Enoch, used in the novel *Noah Primeval*. In this Second Temple Jewish writing, codified around the third to fourth century B.C., and probably originally written much earlier, Enoch is taken on a journey through heaven and hell and describes the cosmic workings as they understood them in that day. Here is just a short glimpse into the elaborate construction of this ANE author:

1 Enoch 18:1-5

And I saw the storerooms of all the winds and saw how with them he has embroidered all creation as well as the foundations of the earth. I saw the cornerstone of the earth; I saw the four winds which bear the earth as well as the firmament of heaven. I saw how the winds ride the heights of heaven and stand between heaven and earth: These are the very pillars of heaven. I saw the winds which turn the heaven and cause the star to set—the sun as well as all the stars. I saw the souls carried by the clouds. I saw the path of the angels in the ultimate end of the earth, and the firmament of the heaven above.[1]

The Bible also contains a picture of the universe that its stories inhabit. It uses cosmic geographical language in common with other ancient Near Eastern (ANE) cultures that shared its situated time and location. Believers in today's world use the language of Relativity when we write, even in our non-scientific discourse; because Einstein has affected the way we see the universe. Believers before the 17th century used Ptolemaic language because they too were children of

---

[1] James H. Charlesworth, *The Old Testament Pseudepigrapha: Volume 1*, 1 En 18 (New York; London: Yale University Press, 1983).

their time. It should be no surprise to anyone that believers in ancient Israel would use the language of ANE cosmography because it was the mental construct within which they lived and thought.[2]

## The Three-Tiered Universe

Othmar Keel, leading expert on ANE art has argued that there was no singular technical physical description of the cosmos in the ancient Near East, but rather patterns of thinking, similarity of images, and repetition of motifs.[3] A common simplification of these images and motifs is expressed in the three-tiered universe of the heavens, the earth, and the underworld.

Wayne Horowitz has chronicled Mesopotamian texts that illustrate this multi-leveled universe among the successive civilizations of Sumer, Akkad, Babylonia, and Assyria. The heavens above were subdivided into "the heaven of Anu (or chief god)" at the very top, the "middle heavens" below him and the sky. In the middle was the earth's surface, and below that was the third level that was further divided into the waters of the abyss and the underworld.[4]

Let's take a look at the Scriptures that appear to reinforce this three-tiered universe so different from our modern understanding of physical expanding galaxies of warped space-time, where the notion of heaven and hell are without physical location. Though the focus of this essay will be on Old Testament context, I want to start with the

---

[2] The book that opened my mind to the Mesopotamian cosmography in the Bible was *Evolutionary Creation: A Christian Approach to Evolution* by Denis O. Lamoureux, Eugene; OR, Wipf & Stock, 2008. I owe much of the material in this essay to Mr. Lamoureux's meticulous research on the ancient science in the Bible. But one need not accept his evolutionary presuppositions to agree with his Biblical scholarship.

[3] Othmar Keel, *The Symbolism of the Biblical World*, Winona Lake; IN: Eisenbrauns, 1972, 1997, 16-59.

[4] Wayne Horowitz, *Mesopotamian Cosmic Geography*, Winona Lake; IN: Eisenbrauns, 1998, xii-xiii.

New Testament to make the point that their cosmography did not necessarily change with the change of covenants.

> Phil. 2:10
> That at the name of Jesus every knee should bow, of those who are <u>in heaven</u>, and <u>on earth</u>, and <u>under the earth</u>.

> Rev. 5:3, 13
> And no one <u>in heaven, or on earth, or under the earth,</u> was able to open the scroll, or to look into it... And every creature <u>in heaven and on the earth and under the earth</u> and in the sea...

> Ex. 20:4
> "You shall not make for yourself a carved image, or any likeness of anything that is in <u>heaven above,</u> or that is <u>in the earth beneath,</u> or that is in the <u>water under the earth</u>.

> Matt. 11:23
> Jesus said, "Capernaum, will you be <u>exalted to heaven?</u> You will be <u>brought down to Hades</u>. [the underworld].

Both apostles Paul and John were writing about the totality of creation being subject to the authority of Jesus on his throne. So this word picture of "heaven, earth, and under the earth" was used as the description of the total known universe—which they conceived of spatially as heaven above, the earth below, and the underworld below the earth. And not only did the inspired human authors write of the universe in this three-tiered fashion but so did God Himself, the author and finisher of our faith, when giving the commandments on Sinai.

One may naturally wonder if this notion of "heaven above" may merely be a symbolic or figurative expression for the exalted spiritual nature of heaven. Since we cannot see where heaven is, God would use physical analogies to express spiritual truths. This explanation would be easier to stomach if the three-tiered notion were not so rooted in a cosmic geography that clearly was their understanding of the universe (as proven below). A figurative expression would also jeopardize the doctrine of the ascension of Jesus into heaven which also affirms the spatial location of heaven above and the earth below, in very literal terms.

> Acts 1:9-11
> He was lifted up, and a cloud took him out of their sight. And while they were gazing into heaven as he went, behold, two men stood by them in white robes, and said, "Men of Galilee, why do you stand looking into heaven? This Jesus, who was taken up from you into heaven, will come in the same way as you saw him go into heaven."

> John 3:13
> No one has ascended into heaven except he who descended from heaven, the Son of Man.

> John 6:62
> Then what if you were to see the Son of Man ascending to where he was before?

John 20:17

Jesus said to her, "Do not cling to me, for I have not yet <u>ascended to the Father</u>; but go to my brothers and say to them, 'I am <u>ascending to my Father</u> and your Father, to my God and your God.'"

Eph. 4:8-10

Therefore it says, "When <u>he ascended on high</u> he led a host of captives, and he gave gifts to men." (In saying, "<u>He ascended</u>," what does it mean but that <u>he had also descended into the lower regions, the earth</u>? He who <u>descended is the one who also ascended far above all the heavens</u>, that he might fill all things.)

The location of heaven being above us may be figurative to our modern cosmology, but it was not figurative to the Biblical writers. To suggest that they understood it figuratively would be to impose our own modern cultural bias on the Bible.

Now let's take a closer look at each of these tiers or domains of the cosmos through the eyes of Scripture in their ANE context.

## Flat Earth Surrounded by Waters

I want to start with the earth because the Scriptures start with the earth. That is, the Bible is geocentric in its picture of a flat earth founded on immovable pillars at the center of the universe. Over a hundred years ago, a Babylonian map of the world was discovered that dated back to approximately the ninth century B.C. As seen below, this map was unique from other Mesopotamian maps because it was not merely local but international in its scale, and contained features that appeared to indicate cosmological interpretation.[5] That map and a translated interpretation are reproduced below.[6]

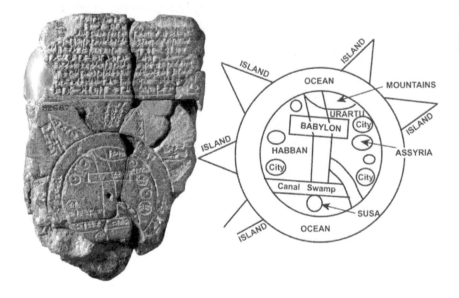

The geography of the Babylonian map portrayed a flat disc of earth with Babylon in the center and extending out to the known regions of its empire, whose perimeters were surrounded by cosmic waters and islands out in those waters. Of the earliest Sumerian and Akkadian texts with geographical information, only the Babylonian map of the world and another text, *The Sargon Geography,* describe the earth's surface, and they both picture a central circular continent surrounded by cosmic waters, often referred to as "the circle of the earth."[7] Other texts like the Akkadian *Epic of Gilgamesh,* and Egyptian, and Sumerian works share in common with the Babylonian map the notion of mountains at the edge of the earth beyond which is

[5] Horowitz, *Mesopotamian Cosmic Geography*, 25-27.
[6] Photo is public domain (Courtesy of the British Museum). Illustration is my own based on Horowitz, *Mesopotamian Cosmic Geography*, 21.
[7] Horowitz, *Mesopotamian Cosmic Geography*, 320, 334. This interpretation continued to maintain influence even into the Greek period of the 6th century B.C. (41).

the cosmic sea and the unknown,[8] and from which come "the circle of the four winds" that blow upon the four corners of the earth (a reference to compass points).[9]

The Biblical picture of the earth is remarkably similar to this Mesopotamian cosmic geography. When Daniel had his dream *from God in Babylon*, of a tree "in the middle of the earth" whose height reached so high that "it was visible to the end of the whole earth," (Dan. 4:10) it reflected this very Babylonian map of the culture that educated Daniel. One cannot see the end of the whole earth on a globe, but one can do so on a circular continent embodying the known world of Babylon as the center of the earth.

"The ends of the earth" is a common phrase, occurring over fifty times throughout the Scriptures that means more than just "remote lands," but rather includes the notion of the very physical end of the whole earth all around before the cosmic waters that hem it in. Here are just a few of the verses that indicate this circular land mass bounded by seas as the entire earth:

Isa. 41:9
You whom I took from the ends of the earth, and called from its farthest corners

---

[8] A Sumerian hymn to the god Enlil, Lord of the Wind, represents these ends of the earth within the context of the god's rule over all the earth: "Lord, as far as the edge of heaven, lord as far as the edge of earth, from the mountain of sunrise to the mountain of sunset. In the mountain/land, no (other) lord resides, you exercise lordship. Enlil, in the lands no (other) lady resides, your wife, exercises ladyship." Horowitz, *Mesopotamian Cosmic Geography*, 331.
"Circle of the earth" in Egyptian understanding meant the disc of the earth unto the horizon "(These) lands were united, and they laid their hands upon the land as far as the Circle of the Earth." "Inscription on the second pylon at Medinet Habu," J.H. Breasted, *Ancient Records of Egypt*, Part Four, University of Chicago, 1906, p 64.
[9] Horowitz, *Mesopotamian Cosmic Geography*, 195-97, 334.

Psa. 65:5
O God of our salvation, the hope of all the ends of the earth and of the farthest seas

Zech. 9:10
His rule shall be from sea to sea, and from the River to the ends of the earth.

Mark 13:27
And then he will send out the angels and gather his elect from the four winds, from the ends of the earth to the ends of heaven.

Acts 13:47
'I have made you a light for the Gentiles, that you may bring salvation to the ends of the earth.'

Job 28:24
For he looks to the ends of the earth and sees everything under the heavens.

Remember that Mesopotamian phrase, "circle of the earth" that meant a flat disc terra firma? Well, it's in the Bible, too. "It is he who sits above the circle of the earth, and its inhabitants are like grasshoppers" (Isa. 40:22). Some have tried to say that the Hebrew word for "circle" could mean *sphere*, but it does not. The Hebrew word used here (*ḥûg*) could however refer to a vaulted dome that covers the visible circular horizon, which would be more accurate to say, "above the vault of the earth."[10] If Isaiah had wanted to say the earth was a sphere he would have used another word that he used in a previous chapter (22:18) for a ball (*kaddur*), but he did not.[11]

Two further Scriptures use this "circle of the earth" in reference to God's original creation of the land out of the waters and extend it outward to include the circumferential ocean with its own mysterious boundary:

> Prov. 8:27, 29
> When he established the heavens, I was there; when he drew <u>a circle on the face of the deep</u>… when he <u>assigned to the sea its limit</u>, so that the <u>waters might not transgress</u> his command, when he marked out the foundations of the earth.

> Job 26:10
> He has inscribed a circle on the face of the waters at the boundary between light and darkness [where the sun rises and sets].

Even when the Old Testament writers are deliberately using metaphors for the earth, they use metaphors for a flat earth spread out like a flat blanket.

---

[10] "*hûg*" Harris, R. Laird, Robert Laird Harris, Gleason Leonard Archer, and Bruce K. Waltke. *Theological Wordbook of the Old Testament.* electronic ed. Chicago: Moody Press, 1999, p 266-67.

[11] Even the Septuagint (LXX) does not translate the Hebrew word into the Greek word for sphere. "Isaiah 40:22," Randall Tan, David A. deSilva, and Logos Bible Software. *The Lexham Greek-English Interlinear Septuagint.* Logos Bible Software, 2009.

Job 38:13
Take hold of the skirts of the earth, and the wicked be shaken out of it.

Job 38:18
Have you comprehended the expanse of the earth?

Psa. 136:6
To him who spreads out the earth above the waters.

Isa. 44:24
"I am the LORD, who spread out the earth by myself."

## Geocentricity

In the Bible, the earth is not merely a flat disk surrounded by cosmic waters under the heavens; it was also the center of the universe. To the ANE mindset, including that of the Hebrews, the earth did not move (except for earthquakes) and the sun revolved around that immovable earth. They did not know that the earth was spinning one thousand miles an hour and flying through space at 65,000 miles an hour. Evidently, God did not consider it important enough to correct this primitive inaccurate understanding. Here are the passages that caused such trouble with Christians who took the text too literally because it did not seem to be figurative to them:

Psa. 19:4-6
Their voice goes out through all the earth,
and their words to the end of the world.
In them he has set a tent for the sun,

which comes out like a bridegroom leaving his chamber, and, like a strong man, runs its course with joy. Its rising is from the end of the heavens,
and its circuit to the end of them.

Psa. 50:1
The Mighty One, God, the LORD, speaks and summons the earth from <u>the rising of the sun to its setting</u>.

Eccl. 1:5
The sun rises, and the sun goes down,
and hastens to the place where it rises.

Josh. 10:13
And the sun stood still, and the moon stopped,
until the nation took vengeance on their enemies...
<u>The sun stopped in the midst of heaven</u> and did not hurry to set for about a whole day.

Matt. 5:45
Jesus said, "For he makes his <u>sun rise</u> on the evil and on the good."

Two objections are often raised when considering these passages. First, that they use phenomenal language. That is, they describe simply what the viewer observes and makes no cosmological claims beyond simply description of what one sees. We even use these terms of the sun rising and setting today and we know the earth moves around the sun. Fair enough. The only problem is that the ancient writers were pre-scientific and did not know the earth went around the sun, so when they said the sun was moving from one end of the heavens to the other they believed reality was exactly as they observed it. They had absolutely no reason to believe in a "phenomenal distinction" between their observation and reality.[12]

The second objection is that some of the language is obvious metaphor. David painted the sun as a bridegroom coming out of his chamber or of being summoned by God and responding like a human. This is called anthropomorphism and is obviously poetic. But the problem here is that the metaphors still reinforce the sun doing all the moving around a stationary immobile earth.

1Chr. 16:30
Tremble before him, all the earth;
yes, the world is established; it shall never be moved.

Psa. 93:1
Yes, the world is established; it shall never be moved.

Psa. 96:10
Yes, the world is established; it shall never be moved."

Understandably, these texts have been thought to indicate that the Bible is explicitly saying the earth does not move. But the case is not so strong for these examples because the Hebrew word used in these passages for "the world" is not the word for *earth* (*erets*), but the word that is sometimes used for the inhabited world (*tebel*). So it is possible that these verses are talking about the "world order" as does the poetry of 2Sam. 22:16.

---

[12] "The Firmament And The Water Above: Part I: The Meaning Of Raqia In Gen 1:6-8," Paul H. Seely, *The Westminster Theological Journal* 53 (1991) 227-40.

But the problem that then arises is that the broader chapter context of these verses describe the earth's physical aspects such as oceans, trees, and in the case of 1Chron. 16:30, even the "earth" (*erets*) in redundant context with the "world" (*tebel*), which would seem to indicate that "world" may refer to the physical earth.

Lastly, *world* can be interchangeable with *earth* as it is in 1Sam. 2:8, "For the pillars of the earth are the LORD'S, And He set the world on them."

And this adds a new element to the conversation of a stationary earth: *A foundation of pillars.*

## Pillars of the Earth

The notion of an immovable earth is not a mere description of observational experience by earth dwellers; it is based upon another cosmographical notion that the earth is on a foundation of pillars that hold it firmly in place.

> Psa. 104:5
> He set the earth on its foundations, so that it should never be moved.

> Job 38:4
> "Where were you when I laid the foundation of the earth? Tell Me, if you have understanding, Who set its measurements, since you know? Or who stretched the line on it? "On what were its bases sunk? Or who laid its cornerstone,

2Sam. 22:16
"Then the channels of the sea were seen; <u>the foundations of the world were laid bare.</u>

1Sam. 2:8
For the <u>pillars of the earth</u> are the LORD's, and on them, <u>he has set the world.</u>

Psa. 75:3
"When <u>the earth totters</u>, and all its inhabitants, it is I who keep steady its pillars.

Zech. 12:1
Thus declares the LORD who stretches out the heavens, <u>and founded the earth.</u>

Ancient man such as the Babylonians believed that mountains and important ziggurat temples had foundations that went below the earth into the abyss (*apsu*) or the underworld.[13] But even if one would argue that the notion of foundations and pillars of the earth are only intended to be symbolic, they are still symbolic *of a stationary earth that does not move.*

Some have pointed out the single verse that seems to mitigate this notion of a solid foundation of pillars, Job 26:6-7: "Sheol is naked before God, and Abaddon has no covering. He stretches out the north over the void and <u>hangs the earth on nothing</u>." They suggest that this is a revelation of the earth in space before ancient man even knew about the spatial location of the earth in a galaxy. But the reason I do not believe this is because of the context of the verse.

---

[13] Horowitz, *Mesopotamian Cosmic Geography*, 98, 124, 308-12, 336-37.

Within chapter 26 Job affirms the three-tiered universe of waters of the Abyss below him (v. 5) and under that Sheol (v. 6), with pillars holding up the heavens (v. 11). Later in the same book, God himself speaks about the earth laid on foundations (38:4), sinking its bases and cornerstone like a building (38:5-6). Ancient peoples believed the earth was on top of some other object like the back of a turtle, and that it was too heavy to float on the waters. So in context, Job 26 appears to be saying that the earth is over the waters of the abyss and Sheol, on its foundations, but there is nothing under *those pillars* but God himself holding it all up. This is not the suggestion of a planet hanging in space, but rather the negative claim of an earth that is *not* on top of an ancient object.

## Sheol Below

Before we ascend to the heavens, let's take a look at the Underworld below the earth. The Underworld was a common location of extensive stories about gods and departed souls of men journeying to the depths of the earth through special gates of some kind into a geographic location that might also be accessed through cracks in the earth above.[14] Entire Mesopotamian stories engage the location of the subterranean netherworld in their narrative such as *The Descent of Inanna, The Descent of Ishtar, Nergal and Ereshkigal,* and many others.

Sheol was the Hebrew word for the underworld.[15] Though the Bible does not contain any narratives of experiences in Sheol, it was nevertheless described as the abode of the dead that was below the earth. Though Sheol was sometimes used interchangeably with "Abaddon" as the place of destruction of the body (Prov. 15:11;

---

[14] Horowitz, *Mesopotamian Cosmic Geography*, p 348-362
[15] "Sheol," *DDD*, p 768.

27:20),[16] and "the grave" (*qibrah*) as a reference to the state of being dead and buried in the earth (Psa. 88:11; Isa. 14:9-11), it was also considered to be *physically* located beneath the earth in the same way as other ANE worldviews.

When the sons of Korah are swallowed up by the earth for their rebellion against God, Numbers chapter 16 says that "they went down alive into Sheol, and the earth closed over them, and they perished from the midst of the assembly (v. 33)." People would not "fall alive" into death or the grave and then perish if Sheol was not a location. But they would die after they fall down into a location (Sheol) and the earth closes over them in that order.

The divine being (*elohim*), known as the departed spirit of Samuel, "came up out of the earth" for the witch of Endor's necromancy with Saul (1Sam. 28:13). This was not a reference to a body coming out of a grave, but a spirit of the dead coming from the underworld beneath the earth.

When Isaiah writes about Sheol in Isaiah 14, he combines the notion of the physical location of the dead body in the earth (v. 11) with the location beneath the earth of the spirits of the dead (v. 9). It's really a both/and proposition.

Here is a list of some verses that speak of Sheol geographically as a spiritual underworld in contrast with heaven as a spiritual overworld.

> Amos 9:2
> "If they dig into Sheol, from there shall my hand take them; if they climb up to heaven, from there I will bring them down.

---

[16] "Abaddon," *DDD*, p 1.

Job 11:8

It is <u>higher than heaven</u>—what can you do? <u>Deeper than Sheol</u>—what can you know?

Psa. 16:10

For you will not abandon <u>my soul</u> to Sheol, or let your holy one <u>see corruption</u>.

Psa. 139:8

If I <u>ascend to heaven</u>, you are there! If I make my <u>bed in Sheol</u>, you are there!

Isa. 7:11

"Ask a sign of the LORD your God; let it be <u>deep as Sheol</u> or <u>high as heaven</u>."

These are not mere references to the body in the grave, but to locations of the spiritual soul as well. Sheol is a combined term that describes both the grave for the body and the underworld location of the departed souls of the dead.

In the New Testament, the word *Hades* is used for the underworld, which was the Greek equivalent of Sheol.[17] Jesus himself used the term Hades as the location of damned spirits in contrast with heaven as the location of redeemed spirits when he talked of Capernaum rejecting miracles, "And you, Capernaum, will you be <u>exalted to heaven</u>? You will be <u>brought down to Hades</u>" (Matt. 11:23). Hades was also the location of departed spirits in his parable of Lazarus and the rich man in Hades (Luke 16:19-31).

---

[17] "Hades," *DDD*, p 382.

In Greek mythology, Tartarus was another term for a location beneath the "roots of the earth" and beneath the waters where the warring giants called "Titans" were bound in chains because of their rebellion against the gods.[18] Peter uses a derivative of that very Greek word Tartarus to describe a similar location and scenario of angels being bound during the time of Noah and the warring Titans called "Nephilim."[19]

> 2Pet. 2:4-5
> For if God did not spare <u>angels</u> when they sinned, but <u>cast them into hell [*tartaroo*] and committed them to chains</u> of gloomy darkness to be kept until the judgment; if he did not spare the ancient world, but preserved Noah.

## The Watery Abyss

In Mesopotamian cosmography, the Abyss (*Apsu* in Akkadian) was a cosmic subterranean lake or body of water that was between the earth and the underworld (Sheol), and was the source of the waters above such as oceans, rivers, and springs or fountains.[20] In *The Epic of Gilgamesh*, Utnapishtim, the Babylonian Noah, tells his fellow citizens that he is building his boat and will abandon the earth of Enlil

---

[18] "They then conducted them [the Titans] under the highways of the earth as far below the ground as the ground is below the sky, and tied them with cruel chains. So far down below the ground is gloomy Tartarus...Tartarus is surrounded by a bronze moat...above which the roots of earth and barren sea are planted. In that gloomy underground region the Titans were imprisoned by the decree of Zeus." Norman Brown, Trans. *Theogony: Hesiod*. New York: Bobbs-Merrill Co., 1953, p 73-4.

[19] 1.25 ταρταρόω [*tartaroo*] Louw, Johannes P., and Eugene Albert Nida. *Greek-English Lexicon of the New Testament : Based on Semantic Domains*. electronic ed. of the 2nd edition. New York: United Bible societies, 1996. Bauckham, Richard J. Vol. 50, *Word Biblical Commentary : 2 Peter, Jude*. Word Biblical Commentary. Dallas: Word, Incorporated, 2002, p 248-249.

[20] Horowitz, *Mesopotamian Cosmic Geography*, p 334-348.

to join Ea in the waters of the Abyss that would soon fill the land.[21] Even bitumen pools used to make pitch were thought to rise up from the "underground waters," or the Abyss.[22]

Similarly, in the Bible the earth also rests on the seas or "the deep" (*tehom*) that produces the springs and waters from its subterranean waters below the earth.

Psa. 24:1-2
The world, and those who dwell therein, for he has founded it upon the seas, and established it upon the rivers.

Psa. 136:6
To him who spread out the earth above the waters.

Gen. 49: 25
The Almighty who will bless you with blessings of heaven above, Blessings of the deep that crouches beneath.

Ex. 20:4
You shall not make for yourself a carved image, or any likeness of anything that is in heaven above, or that is in the earth beneath, or that is in the water under the earth.

---

[21] *The Epic of Gilgamesh* XI:40-44. *The Ancient Near East an Anthology of Texts and Pictures.* Edited by James Bennett Pritchard. Princeton: Princeton University Press, 1958, p 93.
[22] Horowitz, *Mesopotamian Cosmic Geography*, p 337.

Leviathan is even said to dwell in the Abyss in Job 41:24 (LXX)[23]. When God brings the flood, part of the waters are from "the fountains of the great deep" bursting open (Gen. 7:11; 8:2).

**The Firmament**

If we move upward in the registers of cosmography, we find another ancient paradigm of the heavens covering the earth like a solid dome or vault with the sun, moon, and stars embedded in the firmament yet still somehow able to go around the earth. Reformed scholar Paul Seely has done key research on this notion.[24]

> Gen. 1:6-8
>
> And God said, "Let there be an <u>expanse</u> [firmament] in the midst of the waters, and let it separate the waters from the waters." And God made the <u>expanse</u> [firmament] and separated the waters that were under the <u>expanse</u> [firmament] from the waters that were above the <u>expanse</u> [firmament]. And it was so. And God called the <u>expanse</u> [firmament] Heaven.

I used to think, what is that all about? Waters below separated from waters above by the sky? Some try to explain those waters above as a water canopy above the earth that came down at Noah's flood. But that doesn't make sense Biblically because birds are said to "fly over the <u>face</u> of the firmament" (Gen. 1:20) with the same Hebrew

---

[23] "[Leviathan] regards the netherworld [Tartauros] of the deep [Abyss] like a prisoner. He regards the deep [Abyss] as a walk." Job 41:34, Tan, Randall, David A. deSilva, and Logos Bible Software. *The Lexham Greek-English Interlinear Septuagint.* Logos Bible Software, 2009.

[24] "The Firmament And The Water Above: Part I: The Meaning Of Raqia In Gen 1:6-8," Paul H. Seely, *The Westminster Theological Journal* 53 (1991) 227-40.
http://faculty.gordon.edu/hu/bi/ted_hildebrandt/OTeSources/01-Genesis/Text/Articles-Books/Seely-Firmament-WTJ.pdf

grammar as God's Spirit hovering "over the <u>face</u> of the waters" (Gen. 1:2). But the firmament cannot be the "water canopy" because the firmament is not the waters, *but the object that is separating and holding back the waters*. If the firmament is an "expanse" or the sky itself, then the birds would be flying *within* the firmament, not *over the face of* the firmament as the text states. So the firmament cannot be a water canopy and it cannot be the sky itself.

The T.K.O. of the canopy theory is the fact that according to the Bible those "waters above" and the firmament that holds them back were still considered in place during the time of King David long after the flood:

> Psa. 104:2-3
> Stretching out the heavens like a tent. He lays the beams of his chambers on the waters;

> Psa. 148:4
> Praise him, you highest heavens, and you waters above the heavens!

Seely shows how the modern scientific bias has guided the translators to render the word for "firmament" (*raqia*) as "expanse." *Raqia* in the Bible consistently means a solid material such as a metal that is hammered out by a craftsman (Ex. 39:3; Isa. 40:19). And when *raqia* is used elsewhere in the Bible for the heavens, it clearly refers to a solid material, sometimes even metal!

> Job 37:18
> Can you, like him, <u>spread out</u> [*raqia*] the skies, <u>hard as a cast metal mirror</u>?

Ex. 24:10
And they saw the God of Israel. There was under his feet as it were a <u>pavement [*raqia*] of sapphire stone, like the very heaven</u> for clearness.

Ezek. 1:22-23
Over the heads of the living creatures there was the likeness of an <u>expanse [*raqia*], shining like awe-inspiring crystal, spread out above</u> their heads. And <u>under the expanse [*raqia*]</u> their wings were stretched out straight.

Prov. 8:27-28
When he established the heavens… when he made firm the skies above.

Job 22:14
He walks on the vault of heaven.

Amos 9:6
[God] builds his upper chambers in the heavens and founds his vault upon the earth.

Not only did the ancient translators of the Septuagint (LXX) translate *raqia* into the Latin equivalent for a hard firm solid surface (*firmamentum*), but also the Jews of the Second Temple period consistently understood the word *raqia* to mean a solid surface that covered the earth like a dome.

3Bar. 3:6-8

And the Lord appeared to them and confused their speech, when they had built the tower... And they took a gimlet, and sought to <u>pierce the heaven</u>, saying, <u>Let us see (whether) the heaven is made of clay, or of brass, or of iron.</u>

2Apoc. Bar. 21:4

'O you that have made the earth, hear me, that have <u>fixed the firmament</u> by the word, and have <u>made firm the height of the heaven.</u>

Josephus, *Antiquities* 1:30 (1.1.1.30)

On the second day, he placed the heaven over the whole world... He also placed <u>a crystalline [firmament] round it.</u>

The Talmud describes rabbis debating over which remains fixed and which revolves, the constellations or the solid sky (Pesachim 94b),[25] as well as how to calculate the thickness of the firmament scientifically (Pesab. 49a) and Biblically (Genesis Rabbah 4.5.2).[26] While the Talmud is not the definitive interpretation of the Bible, it certainly illustrates how ancient Jews of that time period understood the term, which can be helpful in learning the Hebrew cultural context.

When the Scriptures talk poetically of this vault of heaven it uses the same terminology of stretching out the solid surface of the heavens over the earth *as it does of stretching out an ANE desert tent over the*

---

[25] Quoted in *The Science in Torah: the Scientific Knowledge of the Talmudic* Sages By Leo Levi, page 90-91.
[26] Seely, "The Firmament," p 236.

*flat ground* (Isa. 54:2; Jer. 10:20)—not like an expanding Einsteinian time-space atmosphere.

Psa. 19:4
He has set a tent for the sun.

Psa. 104:2
Stretching out the heavens like a tent.

Isa. 45:12
It was my hands that stretched out the heavens,

Isa. 51:13
The LORD... who stretched out the heavens and laid the foundations of the earth.

Jer. 10:12
It is he who established the world by his wisdom, and by his understanding stretched out the heavens.

Jer. 51:15
"It is he who established the world by his wisdom, and by his understanding stretched out the heavens.

Keeping this tent-like vault over the earth in mind, when God prophesies about the physical destruction he will bring upon a nation, he uses the symbolism of rolling up that firmament like the tent he originally stretched out (or a scroll), along with the shaking of the pillars of the earth and the pillars of heaven which results in the stars falling from the heavens because they were embedded within it.

Isa. 34:4
All the host of heaven shall rot away, and the skies roll up like a scroll. All their host shall fall, as leaves fall from the vine.

Rev. 6:13-14
[An earthquake occurs] and the stars of the sky fell to the earth as the fig tree sheds its winter fruit when shaken by a gale. The sky vanished like a scroll that is being rolled up, and every mountain and island was removed from its place.

Matt. 24:29
"The stars will fall from heaven, and the powers of the heavens will be shaken."

Job 26:11
"The pillars of heaven tremble, and are astounded at His rebuke.

2Sam. 22:8
Then the earth reeled and rocked; the foundations of the heavens trembled and quaked.

Is. 13:13
Therefore I shall make the heavens tremble, and the earth will be shaken out of its place at the wrath of the LORD of hosts.

Joel 2:10
The earth quakes before them, the heavens tremble.

## Waters Above the Heavens

Now on to the highest point of the Mesopotamian cosmography, the "highest heavens," or "heaven of heavens," where God has established his temple and throne (Deut. 26:15; Psa. 11:4; 33:13; 103:19). But God's throne also happens to be in the midst of a sea of waters that reside there. These are the waters that are above the firmament, that the firmament holds back from falling to earth (Gen. 1:6-8).

> Psa. 148:4
>
> Praise him, you highest heavens, and you waters above the heavens!

> Psa. 104:2-3
>
> Stretching out the heavens like a tent. He lays the beams of his chambers on the waters.

> Psa. 29:3, 10
>
> The voice of the <u>LORD is over the waters</u>... the LORD, <u>over many waters</u>... The LORD sits <u>enthroned over the flood</u> [not a reference to the flood of Noah, but to these waters above the heavens][27] the LORD sits enthroned as king forever.

---

[27] Robert G. Bratcher, and William David Reyburn. *A Translator's Handbook on the Book of Psalms*. Helps for translators. New York: United Bible Societies, 1991, p 280. Psalm 29 takes place in heaven amidst God's heavenly host around his throne.

Jer. 10:13

When he utters his voice, there is a tumult of <u>waters in the heavens,</u>

Ezek. 28:2

"I sit in the seat of the gods, in the heart of the seas."

The solid firmament that holds back the heavenly waters has "windows of the heavens" ("floodgates" in the NASB) that let the water through to rain upon the earth.

Gen. 7:11

All the fountains of the great deep burst forth, and the <u>windows of the heavens</u> were opened.

Gen. 8:2

The fountains of the deep and the <u>windows of the heavens</u> were closed, and the rain from the heavens was restrained.

Isa. 24:18

For the <u>windows of heaven</u> are opened, and the foundations of the earth tremble.

## So, What's Wrong With the Bible?

The sheer volume of passages throughout both Testaments illustrating the parallels with Mesopotamian cosmography seem to prove a deeply rooted ancient pre-scientific worldview that permeates the Scriptures, and that worldview consists of a three-tiered universe with God on a heavenly throne above a heavenly sea, underneath which is a solid vaulted dome with the sun, moon, and stars connected to it, covering the flat disc earth, founded immovably firm on pillars, surrounded by a circular sea, on top of a watery abyss, beneath which is the underworld of Sheol.

Some well-intentioned Evangelicals seek to maintain their particular definition of Biblical inerrancy by denying that the Bible contains this ancient Near Eastern cosmography. They try to explain it away as phenomenal language or poetic license. Phenomenal language is the act of describing what one sees subjectively from one's perspective without further claiming objective reality. So when the writer says the sun stood still, or that the sun rises and sets within the solid dome of heaven, he is only describing his observation, not cosmic reality. The claim of observation from a personal frame of reference is certainly true as far as it goes. Of course the observer describes what they are observing. But the distinction between appearance and reality is an imposition of our alien modern understanding onto theirs. As Seely explains,

> It is precisely because ancient peoples were scientifically naive that they did not distinguish between the appearance of the sky and their scientific concept of the sky. They had no reason to doubt what their eyes told them was true, namely, that the stars above them were fixed in a solid dome and that the sky literally touched the earth at the horizon. So, they equated appearance with reality and concluded that the sky must be a solid physical part of the universe just as much as the earth itself.[28]

---

[28] Seely, "The Firmament," p 228.

If the ancients did not know the earth was a sphere in space, they could not know that their observations of appearances were anything other than reality. It would be easy enough to relegate one or two examples of Scripture to the notion of phenomenal language, but when dozens of those phenomenal descriptions reflect the same complex integrated picture of the universe that Israel's neighbors shared, and when that picture included many elements that were *not* phenomenally observable, such as the Abyss, Sheol, or the pillars of earth and heaven, it strains credulity to suggest these were merely phenomenal descriptions intentionally unrelated to reality. If it walks like a Mesopotamian duck and talks like a Mesopotamian duck, then chances are they thought it was a Mesopotamian duck, not just the "appearance" of one having no reality.

It would be a mistake to claim that there is a single monolithic Mesopotamian cosmography.[29] There are varieties of stories with overlapping imagery, and some contradictory notions. But there are certainly enough commonalities to affirm a generic yet mysterious picture of the universe. And that picture in Scripture undeniably includes poetic language. The Hebrew culture was imaginative. They integrated poetry into everything, including their observational descriptions of nature. Thus a hymn of creation such as Psalm 19 tells of the heavens declaring God's glory as if using speech, and then describes the operations of the sun in terms of a bridegroom in his chamber or a man running a race. Metaphor is inescapable and ubiquitous.

And herein lies a potential solution for the dilemma of the scientific inaccuracy of the Mesopotamian cosmic geography in Scripture: *The Israelite culture, being pre-scientific, thought more in terms of function and purpose than material structure.* Even if their

---

[29] Horowitz, *Mesopotamian Cosmic Geography*.

picture of the heavens and earth as a three-tiered geocentric cosmology, was scientifically "false" from our modern perspective, it nevertheless still accurately describes the teleological purpose and meaning of creation that they were intending to communicate.

Othmar Keel, one of the leading scholars on Ancient Near Eastern art has argued that even though modern depictions of the ancient worldview like the illustration of the three-tiered universe above are helpful, they are fundamentally flawed because they depict a "profane, lifeless, virtually closed mechanical system," which reflects our own modern bias. To the ancient Near East "rather, the world was an entity open at every side. The powers which determine the world are of more interest to the ancient Near East than the structure of the cosmic system. A wide variety of diverse, uncoordinated notions regarding the cosmic structure were advanced from various points of departure."[30]

John Walton has written recently of this ANE concern with powers over structure in direct relation to the creation story of Genesis. He argues that in the ancient world existence was understood more in terms of function within a god-created *purposeful order* than in terms of material status within a natural physical structure.[31] This is not to say that the physical world was denied or ignored, but rather that the priority and interests were different from our own. We should therefore be careful in judging their purpose-driven cosmography too strictly in light of our own material-driven cosmography. And in this sense, modern material descriptions of reality are just as "false" as the ancient pictures because they do not include the immaterial aspect of reality: Meaning and purpose.

---

[30] Othmar Keel, *The Symbolism of the Biblical World*, Winona Lake; IN: Eisenbrauns, 1972, 1997, 56-57.

[31] John H. Walton, *The Lost World of Genesis One: Ancient Cosmology and the Origins Debate* (Downers Grove: IL, InterVarsity Press, 2009), 23-36.

Biblical writers did not *teach* their cosmography as scientific doctrine revealed by God about the way the physical universe was materially structured, they *assumed* the popular cosmography to teach their doctrine about God's purposes and intent. To critique the cosmic model carrying the message is to miss the meaning altogether, which is the message. God's throne may not be physically above us in waters held back by a solid firmament, but he truly does rule "over" us and is king and sustainer of creation in whatever model man uses to depict that creation. The phrase "every created thing which is in heaven and on the earth and under the earth" (Rev. 5:13) is equivalent in meaning to the modern concept of every particle and wave in every dimension of the Big Bang space-time continuum, as well as every person dead or alive in heaven or hell.

The geocentric picture in Scripture is a depiction through man's ancient perspective of God's purpose and humankind's significance. For a modern heliocentrist to attack that picture as falsifying the theology would be cultural imperialism. Reducing significance to physical location is simply a prejudice of material priority over spiritual purpose. One of the humorous ironies of this debate is that if the history of science is any judge, a thousand years from now, scientists will no doubt consider our current paradigm with which we judge the ancients to be itself fatally flawed. This is not to reduce reality to relativism, but rather to illustrate that all claims of empirical knowledge contain an inescapable element of human fallibility and finitude. A proper response should be a bit more humility and a bit less hubris regarding the use of our own scientific models as standards in judging theological meaning or purpose.

For additional Biblical, historical and mythical research related to this novel, go to http://www.ChroniclesoftheNephilim.com under the menu listing, "Scholarly Research" or *Click Here*.

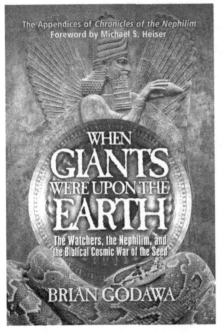

# GREAT OFFERS BY BRIAN GODAWA

## Get More
## Biblical Imagination

### Sign up Online For
### The Godawa Chronicles

## www.Godawa.com

Updates and Freebies
of the Books of Brian Godawa
Special Discounts,
Weird Bible Facts!

## Nephilim Giants, Watchers, Cosmic War. All in the Bible.

## www.Godawa.com

# CHRONICLES OF THE APOCALYPSE

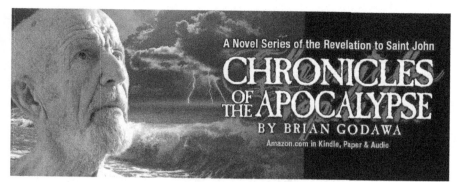

A Novel Series of the Revelation to Saint John

# CHRONICLES
## OF
## THE APOCALYPSE
### BY BRIAN GODAWA

Amazon.com in Kindle, Paper & Audio

## A Novel Series About
## the Book of Revelation & the End Times.
## A Fresh Biblical View.

### www.Godawa.com

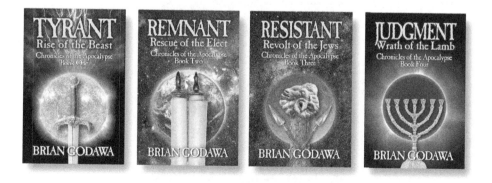

CHRONICLES OF THE WATCHERS

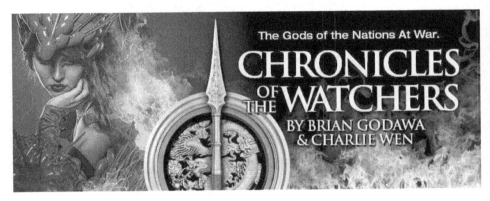

# A Series About the Watchers in History.
# Action, Romance, Gods, Monsters & Men.
The first novel is *Jezebel: Harlot Queen of Israel*

## www.Godawa.com

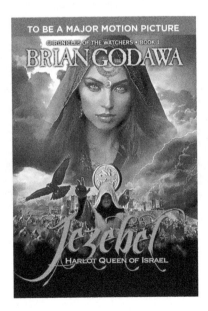

# VIDEO LECTURES

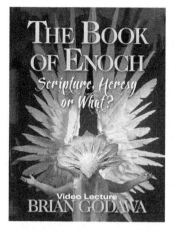

### The Book of Enoch: Scripture, Heresy or What?

This lecture by Brian Godawa will be an introduction to the ancient book of 1Enoch, its content, its history, its affirmation in the New Testament, and its acceptance and rejection by the Christian Church. What is the Book of Enoch? Where did it come from? Why isn't it in the Bible? How does the Book of Enoch compare with the Bible?

Available on video.

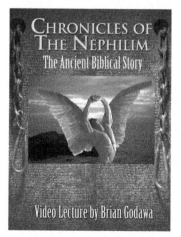

### Chronicles of the Nephilim: The Ancient Biblical Story

Watchers, Nephilim, and the Divine Council of the Sons of God. In this dvd video lecture, Brian Godawa explores the Scriptures behind this transformative storyline that inspired his best-selling Biblical novel series Chronicles of the Nephilim.

Available on video.

**To download these lectures and other books and products by Brian Godawa, just go to the STORE at:**

# www.Godawa.com

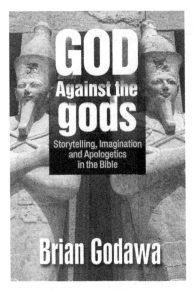

## How God Captures the Imagination

This book was previously titled *Myth Became Fact: Storytelling, Imagination & Apologetics in the Bible.*

Brian Godawa, Hollywood screenwriter and best-selling novelist, explores the nature of imagination in the Bible. You will learn how God subverts pagan religions by appropriating their imagery and creativity, and redeeming them within a Biblical worldview. Improve your imagination in your approach to glorifying God and defending the faith.

**Demonizing the Pagan Gods**

God verbally attacked his opponents, pagans and their gods, using sarcasm, mockery, name-calling.

**Old Testament Storytelling Apologetics**

Israel shared creative images with their pagan neighbors: The sea dragon of chaos and the storm god. The Bible invests them with new meaning.

**Biblical Creation and Storytelling**

Creation stories in the ancient Near East and the Bible both express a primeval battle of deity to create order out of chaos. But how do they differ?

**The Universe in Ancient Imagination**

A detailed comparison and contrast of the Biblical picture of the universe with the ancient pagan one. What's the difference?

**New Testament Storytelling Apologetics**

Paul's sermon to the pagans on Mars Hill is an example of subversion: Communicating the Gospel in terms of a pagan narrative with a view toward replacing their worldview.

**Imagination in Prophecy & Apocalypse**

God uses imaginative descriptions of future events to deliberately obscure his message while simultaneously showing the true meaning and purpose behind history.

**An Apologetic of Biblical Horror**

Learn how God uses horror in the Bible as a tool to communicate spiritual, moral and social truth in the context of repentance from sin and redemptive victory over evil.

## For More Info
## www.Godawa.com

# THE IMAGINATION OF GOD

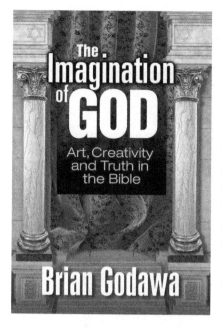

## Art, Creativity and Truth in the Bible

In his refreshing and challenging book, Godawa helps you break free from the spiritual suffocation of heady faith. Without negating the importance of reason and doctrine, Godawa challenges you to move from understanding the Bible "literally" to "literarily" by exploring the poetry, parables and metaphors found in God's Word. Weaving historical insight, pop culture and personal narrative throughout, Godawa reveals the importance God places on imagination and creativity in the Scriptures, and provides a Biblical foundation for Christians to pursue imagination, beauty, wonder and mystery in their faith.

This book was previously released with the title, *Word Pictures: Knowing God Through Story and Imagination.*

## Endorsements:

"Brian Godawa is that rare breed—a philosopher/artist—who opens our eyes to the aesthetic dimension of spirituality. Cogently argued and fun to read, Godawa shows convincingly that God interacts with us as whole persons, not only through didactic teaching but also through metaphor, symbol, and sacrament."

— Nancy R. Pearcey,
Author, *Total Truth: Liberating Christianity from its Cultural Captivity*

"A spirited and balanced defense of the imagination as a potential conveyer of truth. There is a lot of good literary theory in the book, as well as an autobiographical story line. The thoroughness of research makes the book a triumph of scholarship as well."

— Leland Ryken, Clyde S. Kilby Professor of English, Wheaton College, Illinois
Author, *The Christian Imagination: The Practice of Faith in Literature & Writing.*

## For More Info
## www.Godawa.com

# ABOUT THE AUTHOR

Brian Godawa is the screenwriter for the award-winning feature film, *To End All Wars,* starring Kiefer Sutherland. It was awarded the Commander in Chief Medal of Service, Honor and Pride by the Veterans of Foreign Wars, won the first Heartland Film Festival by storm, and showcased the Cannes Film Festival Cinema for Peace.

He also co-wrote *Alleged,* starring Brian Dennehy as Clarence Darrow and Fred Thompson as William Jennings Bryan. He previously adapted to film the best-selling supernatural thriller novel *The Visitation* by author Frank Peretti for Ralph Winter (*X-Men, Wolverine*), and wrote and directed *Wall of Separation,* a PBS documentary, and *Lines That Divide*, a documentary on stem cell research.

Mr. Godawa's scripts have won multiple awards in respected screenplay competitions, and his articles on movies and philosophy have been published around the world. He has traveled around the United States teaching on movies, worldviews, and culture to colleges, churches and community groups.

His popular book, *Hollywood Worldviews: Watching Films with Wisdom and Discernment* (InterVarsity Press) is used as a textbook in schools around the country. His novel series, the saga *Chronicles of the Nephilim* is in the Top 10 of Biblical Fiction on Amazon and is an imaginative retelling of Biblical stories of the Nephilim giants, the secret plan of the fallen Watchers, and the War of the Seed of the Serpent with the Seed of Eve. The sequel series, *Chronicles of the Apocalypse* tells the story of the Apostle John's book of Revelation, and *Chronicles of the Watchers* recounts true history through the Watcher paradigm.

Find out more about his other books, lecture tapes and dvds for sale at his website www.godawa.com.

# BLANK PAGE

BLANK PAGE

# BLANK PAGE

# BLANK PAGE

# BLANK PAGE

# BLANK PAGE

BLANK PAGE

BLANK PAGE

Made in the USA
Monee, IL
30 August 2021